MAGPIE

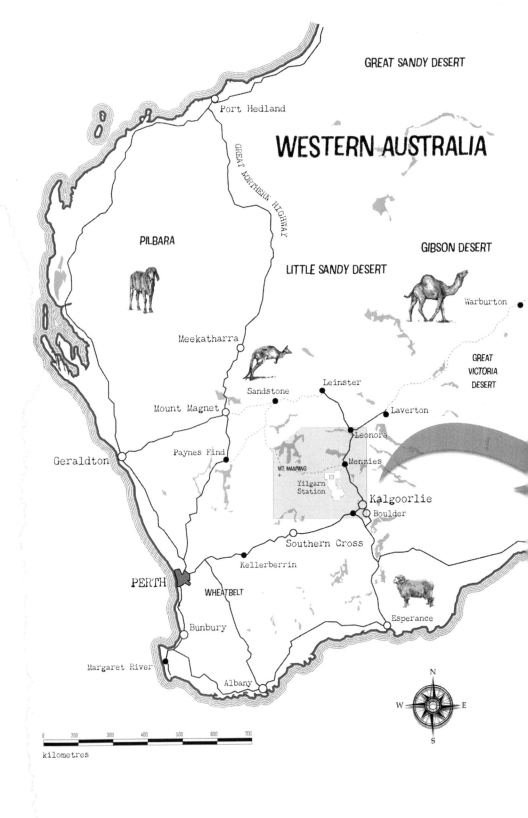

GREAT SANDY DESERT

WESTERN AUSTRALIA

Port Hedland

GREAT NORTHERN HIGHWAY

PILBARA

GIBSON DESERT

LITTLE SANDY DESERT

Warburton

Meekatharra

GREAT
VICTORIA
DESERT

Sandstone

Leinster

Laverton

Mount Magnet

Leonora

Geraldton

Paynes Find

MT. MANNING

Menzies

Yilgarn
Station

Kalgoorlie

Boulder

Southern Cross

Kellerberrin

PERTH

WHEATBELT

Esperance

Bunbury

Margaret River

Albany

N

W   E

S

0   200   300   400   500   600   700

kilometres

ALAN RYAN

MAGPIE

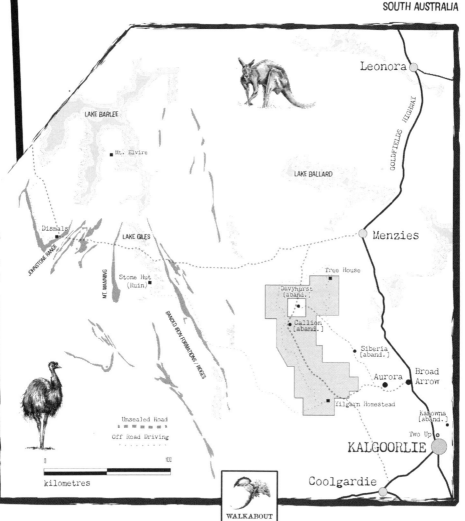

Docker River

Yulara

ULURU

NORTHERN TERRITORY

SOUTH AUSTRALIA

Leonora

LAKE BARLEE

Mt. Elvire

LAKE BALLARD

GOLDFIELDS HIGHWAY

Menzies

Dismals

LAKE GILES

Tree House

Davyhurst
[aband.]

JOHNSTONE RANGE

MT. MANNING

Stone Hut
(Ruin)

Callion
[aband.]

BANDED IRON FORMATIONS / RIDGES

Siberia
[aband.]

Aurora

Broad
Arrow

Yilgarn Homestead

Kanowna
[aband.]

Unsealed Road

Two Up

Off Road Driving

KALGOORLIE

0   100

Coolgardie

kilometres

WALKABOUT

Published 2021 Gone Walkabout Books

alanryanauthor.com
Follow Magpie on Facebook.

Print ISBN: 978 0 9548529 4 8
eBook ISBN: 978 0 9548529 5 5

Cover, map and typesetting by Alan Ryan.

FOR MY PARENTS,
MY WIFE AND CHILDREN.

WE ARE ALL IN THE GUTTER, BUT SOME
OF US ARE LOOKING AT THE STARS.

    —WILDE, *LADY WINDERMERE'S FAN*

ACKNOWLEDGMENTS

Magpie is a work of fiction that draws from my experiences living and working in Australia at different times over the last thirty years.

In 1989, I spent a few months working on Credo sheep station in the West Australian Goldfields. I must acknowledge and thank, Tim and Megan, my employers at Credo. I may not have been much use but they still put up with me. When the job finished, I went walkabout in the area for a while. Tim and Megan loaned me the equipment to make that possible. Every time I parked Tim's old Ford truck below my tree house after a day's mooching around the bush and climbed the ladder to watch the sunset from my balcony, I felt like a king. Occasionally, I would travel to the remote Ora Banda Inn for supplies. The tragic story of The Ora Banda Inn has inspired some of what happens in *Magpie*, although the details and characters in *Magpie* are entirely fictional.

My time at Credo was wonderful and without it I would never have written this story. Time has moved on and things have changed at Credo but I suspect the spirit of the place remains with everyone who has passed through there.

I returned to Australia as a qualified geologist in the mid nineties and again in the noughties, to work in the gold and iron ore industries. Thank you to all those who toiled around the drill rigs with me and gathered later around the campfires. I am grateful to you for your company and geological knowledge.

To all the Skerries gang in Sydney, we had some fun and made great memories. It has been an emotional journey opening the memory box from that time over thirty years ago. It is funny how recalling one small incident unlocks so many more. I have only just been reminded of a job interview that happened on a building site next to the Opera House. Who would have thought that commuting on the London Underground in no way qualified you for a job digging the Sydney Harbour tunnel?

Australia is a long way from home. There were times after landing in the country, before finding my feet, or times between jobs, when I relied on the kindness and generosity of others. Many of these people came into my life only briefly but left an indelible mark. They may still be out there somewhere. I could not let the opportunity pass without thanking you all. You are too many to name.

Thanks also to Garvan, Ann, Phil and Siobhán who along with Eimear and my parents have waded through the many early drafts of *Magpie* and offered suggestions.

Thanks to Jonathan Curzon of Daniel Goldsmith Associates, Victoria Woodside of proofreaderni.com who both advised on the structure of earlier drafts. Thanks also to my editor Stephanie Campion, who fastidiously worked through the manuscript with a fine-tooth comb. Thanks for the trojan work.

Writing doesn't come easy to me. It's a slog. Admittedly, an enjoyable slog that excited me every time I sat down to the computer. This book has taken a long time to complete and taken me away from my family more than I thought it would when I started. My wife Eimear never complained (except maybe about the grass) and has let me indulge myself, while often having to fill both parent roles – all while making a wonderful home for the rest of us. My two young children, Emily and Luke have been unwavering with their encouragement and regularly checked in to see how it was going. They were always ready with 'brilliant' ideas for me to include in the story and credit to Luke who suggested I animate the fly. When the two of you are old enough to read *Magpie*, I hope you enjoy it and understand why I spent so much time sitting at my desk when we could have been out bouncing on the trampoline. You have both grown up so much since the day I opened the laptop on a whim and started this. The same day you both decided Max Collins was to be a baddie. I am very proud of you. I've been told we are getting a dog. I am in no position to argue.

PROLOGUE

OVER A CENTURY had passed since the dry blowers first came to the area. They brought with them their overloaded wheelbarrows and high hopes. They came in their thousands. With little or no water, they laboured, in the dust and heat of the Goldfields. Once the surface gold had been picked clean, they followed it underground. Crawling on empty bellies, with pickaxe and shovel, they chipped away at the white quartz reefs that led them deep into the Earth. They toiled in the dark labyrinth of their coffin-like tunnels. People got rich. People lost everything. Dispersed populations and mining camps coalesced into townships. Manners were put on the miners. Indigenous communities were destroyed.

In time, they took away all the gold their technologies could reach. They took away their towns. They left behind the scars of mining and their dead.

CHAPTER 1

A WHOLE WORLD AWAY

SOMETHING IN HER SIMPLE binary brain told her it was time to move on, time to leave her brood behind. A caring mother, she had wrapped the eggs in silk before placing the neat bundle under the pink bark of the salmon gum. For three weeks, she stood guard – willing to die for her progeny. She went without food. Behind her, the embryos grew. When the time came, she tore the silk and eased their passage into a brutal, arid world. Two hundred and two hatchlings scampered free. Ever vigilant, she stayed with them, while they shed their first delicate skins. They were hardy now, tiny yet perfect copies of their mother. It was time to eat again. Time to find a mate. Time to start over.

A little after sunset, the huntsman crawled out from behind the shedding bark and onto the corrugated iron roof. Under a waxing, gibbous moon, she scurried crablike across the undulating metal towards a gap missed by the slipshod builder. Her full coat of hair-like setae detected the warmth and movement inside. She does not set a web, preferring to hunt and ambush. A bite of potent venom will paralyse and partly liquefy tissue, before her powerful mouthparts tear it apart. Passing easily through the narrow opening, the giant spider dropped onto the bed.

HAPPY TO SHARE its territory with the newcomer, the magpie busied itself, working through debris from the carnage of the night before. There were easy pickings to be had underneath the gas lamp and around the embers of a smouldering fire. The bird's carolling woke the young man, who lay quietly enjoying its confident song. As ever, the dawn reveille reminded Jim just how far from Skerries he had come.

Soon the sun would climb above Bungarra Rock and the warming air force him from his bed. And of course, the flies would be about the place. Rolling onto his side, Jim extended a lazy arm and fumbled for his luminous red, made in Hong Kong, Donald Duck watch – a bargain picked up at the Nullarbor Roadhouse on the way across. His fingers explored down the side of the bed, but came up empty. More blind rummaging and he retrieved the watch from under a discarded pair of shorts.

Of minimal horological value and dubious taste, surprisingly Donald kept good time. That said, accurate time mattered little to Jim. These days, the approximate position of the sun in an endless blue sky, and the temperature, governed his activities. Nevertheless, first thing every morning, he would cast a quick eye over Donald's hands. Once he did the sum in his head, and subtracted the eight hours, he could picture what everyone back home would be up to at that very moment – yesterday. At the other end of the day, alone by the fire, he might do a similar calculation and imagine how things were in Copenhagen.

Jim reached to remove a balled-up woolly sock that had found its way onto his pillow. The sock shuffled closer to his face. That's odd …

socks don't crawl, his sleepy brain pondered. A warning sounded in Jim's head. His body jerked backwards.

'Jesus Christ!'

Set out in two rows of four, eight blank, 8-ball eyes stared back at him. Jim's own wide eyes did not blink. The giant spider's could not. The Irishman and the huntsman considered each other – neither moved.

Trawling through the many images of venomous spiders collected in his head, Jim scrambled to identify this monstrous beauty. Until recently, he might well have panicked at such an intimate encounter, but six months of living and working in the Australian bush had knocked the edge off Jim's small town, Irish sensibilities.

Huntsman! Yeah, deffo a huntsman, he convinced himself, and remembered what he knew of them. Not deadly, rarely bite, localised swelling, minor pain.

Reasonably confident he would live, Jim tried to will the spider away. But, not blessed with the capacity to read minds, she stayed put. Jim had no desire to share his pillow with the huntsman and all those stubbly legs. Neither was he about to allow such a close encounter unearth any dormant arachnophobia he might be suppressing. That would not do. Not out here.

Jim's bedroom was small, tiny in fact. A low-sloping corrugated roof provided shelter and enough height to allow him to sit comfortably. The walls were sheets of canvas, the floor a wooden panel door he came across on one of his many scavenging trips through the bush. A fly-wire mesh screen and crude wooden frame formed a window looking out from the foot of the bed to the tidy camp below. Filling all available floor space and more, the bed, an old feather eiderdown of incalculable depth, swallowed its occupant whole.

At night, before retiring, Jim would shake out the eiderdown and his sleeping bag to remove daytime visitors. Obviously, it did nothing to help with the night-time crawlers and, try as he might, he was always obliged to share his bed with the resident ants. Mercifully, and peculiar for Australian fauna, they did not bite. The ants merely tickled his legs, while they marched defiantly in formation through the bedding. Still, the bed was comfortable. It gifted Jim a good night's sleep and many great dreams.

Exiting the bedroom involved a small climb that finished with a tight shimmy through a hessian flap, up onto a 'balcony' higher in the salmon gum. Today's unwelcome guest complicated this manoeuvre. The huntsman appeared unfazed when, summoning the courage and without taking his eyes off her, the naked man slowly untangled himself from the bed. She watched Jim's toes seek out and open the flap to the outside. Then, walking backwards on his hands over her, he disappeared feet-first, through the opening and beached himself inelegantly on the balcony.

The spider's demeanour did change when the man returned bearing arms. Hanging headfirst through the flap, Jim went after his uninvited bedfellow with a long stick. Following some remarkable shows of speed and reflexes from both parties, the giant huntsman sought refuge in an empty powdered milk tin that Jim had placed across her path.

Jim released his prisoner on a nearby tree and then stoked the fire for breakfast.

WHISTLING STEAM POPPED the lid to one side. Seething water hissed and spat over the rim, vaporising in puffs of dust on the coals. Hooking the loose wire handle with his stick, Jim fished the blackened billy from the fire and set it down at his feet. Using a baggy cotton hat to protect his fingers, he removed the lid and lifted the billy by the rim to pour. Why a billycan can't be made with a proper handle puzzled him. It would have been easier to boil the water in a saucepan, but in the Australian bush, it has to be the billycan. The world is full of amusing instances, where culture and tradition prevail over practicality. A billion Chinese know of the knife and fork, but persist with chopsticks. Jim never got the hang of chopsticks, but he liked his awkward and well-used billy.

The water surged up the hot metal sides and boiled again, bubbling violently, before it landed on the generous mix of instant coffee and powdered milk he spooned into a battered enamel mug. With the back of the spoon, Jim made a token effort to squash the bobbing doughy lumps of powder against the side of the mug, but quickly admitted defeat. The coffee tasted fine. Mixing the milk in advance with cold water is always preferable, but unfortunately, yesterday's batch already stank. The homemade Coolgardie fridge was not up to the job at all really. It needed work. The sour milk and rancid smell inside the fridge box this morning brought him right back to his wet summer at sea, trawling for prawns and preparing meals in the fetid galley deep within the bilge of the fifty-footer. Too recent to be happy memories, but his fishing days were not far off becoming fond ones.

Breakfast was the last of the damper baked in the camp oven the previous night. The tiny, twinned-black spots drew Jim's attention to the maggots. Experience taught him to be meticulous about replacing lids, but the blowies had found their way into the butter again and laid their eggs. Casually, Jim picked out the offending maggots and flicked them to the ground for the magpie, or any of the small lizards that occasionally cleaned around the camp, to enjoy. Then, not looking too closely, he scooped up a healthy portion of runny butter with a knife and spread it over the two thick wedges of damper. Neither the maggots nor the soot on the crusts spoiled breakfast. It tasted good.

Sitting by the fire, sipping his coffee, Jim listened to the sounds of the morning. He enjoyed a strong coffee to get him moving, but when the day got hot, and in the Western Australian Goldfields it got hot, his preference would change to tea. To his surprise, he found hot tea more refreshing and far better at quenching a thirst than any amount of the tepid well water he kept in drums under the balcony.

Already, he could smell the heat coming into the day. It carried the wonderful scents of the plants and the earth with it. He watched a tiny maggot contort and wriggle at his foot. It covered itself in the red dust. For the second time that morning, he contemplated how he had adapted to life in this strange and beautiful land. There were things to do.

Jim got up and knocked back the last of his drink. As he did, his gaze fell on the prominent salmon gum off to the right of the Ford. The tight, almost polished, brassy bark flowed beautifully along the trunk and over every seductive curve. About a metre from the ground, the single trunk divided and two elegant parting 'legs' continued skyward. He noticed it some weeks ago and, once seen, the female form began to appear in trees everywhere. But this one had a name. Sometimes, he gazed on it and felt shame, other times happier emotions would flush through his thoughts. Jim raised his empty mug to the nubile tree.

'Morning, Ellen.' Having put time and a whole world between them, he could still not let her go.

* * *

THERE WAS A Heath Robinson look about it that appealed. For nearly seventy years the elements, not to mention the bugs, had ravaged and eaten away at the magnificent wood and steel structure. Yet the bones of it endured. It still imposed itself on the surrounding landscape. Jim pictured the great arms of the machine crushing enormous quantities of rock and releasing the tiny grains of gold hidden within. What came out of the Waihi Battery would have either made the dreams of those who laboured here, or shattered them.

A trickle of water gathered pace and picked up some dusty red earth on its way down. It meandered around the fold of the eye and joined with another droplet of sweat above the nostril. The sudden change in volume accelerated its passage to the tip of the nose, where it hung momentarily, before dropping with a splash onto the open pad of watercolour paper. The sweat lifted a circle of pigment from the carefully worked foreground. The white of the paper showed through. With a controlled swipe of a round sable, Jim blended in the additional water. The dust, he decided, added an authenticity to his work. He took off his wide-brimmed hat and wiped his face with it. A fresh streak of red ochre came off onto the hat. Everything he owned, including he himself, had turned a deep, earthy red.

Sitting on the tray of the Ford F250, and hunched over as he worked, Jim had been lost in his painting all morning. The splash broke his concentration. It must be lunchtime, he decided. He put the brush in a mug of murky water and propped the watercolour pad against the spare wheel. Bracing himself with both hands, he threw his numb legs forward and jumped to the ground. On landing, a grey, humming cloud of flies rose up off his back. They circled his head fleetingly, before returning to their roost.

Jim stepped back a few metres and studied his work. He took great care to sketch it out, before highlighting the preferred pencil lines with Indian ink. Then, hoping the colours would bleed into each other, he had washed over the ink with dilute paint. Jim tipped his head to the left, back to the right, then squinted.

'Not bad,' he whispered, almost as if saying it out loud might be considered immodest. The perspective looked fine. The scale and decay of the old battery seemed to be there. However, the washes were not behaving as he wanted. The early afternoon heat dried the paper and paint too quickly. He would finish it later on the balcony with a drink in his hand, the sun setting, and no flies.

Jim opened a tin of peaches and flicked on his transistor radio to enjoy the company of another human voice over lunch.

I wish to put it plainly that the Government has taken a firm decision to release Mr Mandela unconditionally.

It had been a few days since President FW de Klerk's Friday speech to the Parliament of South Africa, but it still occupied the media's attention. Jim listened intently to the discussion around de Klerk's historic words, while forking peaches from the tin into his mouth. He waited to hear if Mandela was out. It seemed not. Disappointed, Jim switched off his transistor to save the batteries and poured himself a milky tea from a flask.

After lunch, he left the truck at the battery and went off to explore the area on foot. Rusty, contorted scrap metal, bricks and rotten timbers told some of the story of long-departed miners. Old mine shafts were crudely boarded up to prevent Jim and others from getting too curious for their own good. Resembling giant anthills, mullock heaps of spoil dotted the old workings. When diesel replaced sweat and sinew, many of the smaller mines were consolidated into huge opencast pits. These, too, now lay abandoned, their treasures carted away. Jim marvelled at the scale of the magnificent terraced scars left on the face of the earth – man-made canyons, monuments to human endeavour. For those who knew about such things, the story of the rocks exposed in the walls presented a window into the beginnings of the history of the planet itself.

Beside the canyons, sterile grey monoliths of crushed slag left over from modern mining rose as significant hills and cast their bleak shadows across the area. With hard, angular edges, scarred by rainwater-washed gullies, they had none of the aesthetic of the pits from which they were dug, or the charm of the quaint anthills of waste thrown up by the old boys.

Jim continued on to the old townsite of Davyhurst, one of many settlements to spring up around the mines. Today, a small hand-painted wooden sign marked the site. He found himself in a dusty clearing, where all around, patches of bluebush and spinifex grass were reclaiming the ground for the bush. A few lonely gum trees grew near the centre. He liked to think they might have once offered shade to a couple of old-timers lamenting the price of a drink. A brick chimney stump and piles of rubble remained where a more substantial building had stood. Broken glass bottles and the ubiquitous rusty tin can were more evidence that people made homes here.

The town existed now only in a few hazy memories, sepia photographs and old map drawers. Jim walked over the area, trying occasionally to kick up a bit of history with his boot. He wondered how this happened, how a town just disappeared. Big mining still operated nearby, much of it over the same ground the pioneers worked. He could see the major Cons. Ex. Gold operation beyond the far trees. The gold never ran out.

He remembered a faded map in Old Bill's study. It showed ten wide streets or more, laid out in an ordered grid pattern. Cassidy, Kenny and Eileen streets were three that Jim recalled. Oasis and Siberia, two others that teased his imagination. Old Bill owned a fascinating collection of photographs and postcards from the pioneering days at Davyhurst. In its heyday, the town boasted hotels, shops, schools and other less family-friendly, but nonetheless, popular comforts.

Jim turned slowly, taking in the emptiness around him. He imagined a busy street, the hotel filled with revellers. Someone sold newspapers on a corner. In a high-chair out front of a barber's tent, a young fellow rubbed his newly razored chin in approval. Shave finished, he pulled his braces back over his shoulders, while the barber assisted with the fiddly collar studs on the shirt. Children ran home from school, their white smocks gleaming in the bright light. A dapper gentleman lifted a pocket watch by the gold chain from a waistcoat and confirmed the time. A bicycle leaned against a post outside Kurth's General Store. The smell of fresh bread baking percolated through the noxious sulphurous odour hanging in the air.

Jim imagined the noise from the constant pounding of the battery heads out of town, crushing ore. He saw a line of water tanks cooking over wood fires. These were condensers that transformed brine pumped from underground into a passable facsimile of potable water

– harder to stomach and more expensive to buy than beer and spirits, if Old Bill was to be believed.

The Woodline Railway came through and offloaded a mountain of fresh-cut timber. In times gone by, the Goldfields had an insatiable appetite for wood. Some they used to build homes, but much of it went underground to support drives and shafts. The rest they burned. According to Old Bill, the Woodline harvested fifteen hundred tons of timber every day, as it snaked through the region collecting and delivering the vital resource to the mines and towns. Jim pictured the billowing smoke rising from the fires, the smelter furnaces and condensers. It mingled with clouds of rock dust-blasted from the pits.

The flies buzzed in Jim's ears. A spiral of wind blew a wave of dust off the vanished street.

Mining is a dirty, noisy business, he thought. Davyhurst may well have been a lively little town, but it had to be a dirty, noisy place to live.

The brilliant white, and probably well-starched, clothing preferred by the inhabitants of Old Bill's photographs always intrigued Jim. Given the environment they lived in, he wondered how the townsfolk looked so clean and, to a certain extent, why. Surely, it would have required considerable effort. Perhaps the cooling benefits of white outweighed the extra laundering. Perhaps the 'Sunday best' came out for the novelty of having your image immortalised. Plausible for the more formal studio portraits, but many of Old Bill's photographs were of residents going about their business. Maybe the photographer staged those scenes. Maybe the pristine whites were partly an artefact of early photographic techniques. Whatever it was, keeping things clean in those conditions must have been bloody hard.

With ever decreasing returns, Jim struggled to keep his own clothes presentable with modern detergents and the wash cycle of a sealed bucket bouncing around on the back of the Ford. He would freely admit he was made of lesser stuff than the early pioneers and had all but given up, opting instead to wear less as time went on.

There were not too many smiling faces captured in Old Bill's photographs, the occasion of having your photograph taken seeming far too serious a business for such frivolity. Old Bill mentioned how the long exposures required at the time would have tested even the most jovial character's ability to hold a smile. Posing for an imaginary photograph, Jim stood straight, with his shoulders back and smiled. His cheeks soon tired. A fly entered an ear. He flicked at it. A photographer popped out from under the dark cloth and scolded him for moving and wasting a plate. Jim sensed his imagination begin to run away on him again, the images in his head too real - always a sign he should get in out of the sun and drink.

Despite the challenges of living in this place, the ghosts of Old Bill's photographs were a content, proud people. Folk back then, Jim figured, were prepared to endure great hardship and get on with living the best they could, cheerful in the certainty a fortune would be found with the next blow of the pickaxe. For a few, it was.

Jim returned to the truck and drove the short distance south to the town cemetery.

ARRANGED BY THE diligent gravediggers, like trapdoors to the afterlife, for the majority of Davyhurst's dead, a neat rectangle of white quartz pebbles was all that marked their final resting place. Picked out by streams of sunlight falling through the stands of salmon gums, the pebbles shone bright against the dark purple ground. Even the smallest stone rectangles, of which there were many, were bare. Jim wondered how a town could bury its children in unmarked plots. He supposed the people had their reasons, but still, he thought it unforgiveable. Perhaps time had removed any simple wood or iron markings.

'Ernest Kurth, beloved husband of Emma Kurth,' read the inscription on the most elaborate and tallest grave in the cemetery. An ornate, cast-iron surround protected a lopsided, polished-marble cross with lillies carved in relief. Jim remembered Kurth's General Store from Old

Bill's photographs. It struck him as odd that the most prominent grave in a town of gold miners belonged to the storekeeper. Then maybe, it wasn't odd at all.

Moving on, he stopped by a group of three tiny graves. Two infant graves were unmarked, but behind the modest wrought-iron railing of the third, a pointed-arch marble headstone told a tragic tale and it broke Jim's heart.

IN SAD AND LOVING MEMORY
OF OUR DEAR CHILDREN
HARRY ROWE
AGED 7 YEARS.
AND ROBERT
AGED 5 YEARS.
WHO WERE ACCIDENTLY KILLED
AT DAVYHURST 2ND SEPTEMBER 1911
DEEPLY MOURNED
WHY SHOULD WE WEEP; THEY'RE SAFELY O'ER
WAITING FOR US ON THE GOLDEN SHORE.
ERECTED BY
THEIR SORROWING PARENTS.

One afternoon, while mending a fence near Davyhurst with Helen, she told him the story of the two brothers. The children had snuck off on a Jules Verne inspired adventure to the centre of the Earth. They imagined an old mine shaft as one of Verne's lava tubes and climbed into the blackness. One of the boys lit a match to light the way and set off explosives stored at the base of the shaft. It was easy to picture the horror of the incident and the trauma of a small community.

Great sadness unquestionably hid behind many of the proud faces in Old Bill's drawer of photographs. Jim wanted to leave something, but could see nothing that resembled a flower in the parched cemetery.

Part hidden under a pile of leaf litter blown up against the base of the railing, two venomous eyes assessed the threat. The snake sniffed the air with whips of its forked tongue. Silently, it watched the lone figure sit and take a notebook from a shirt pocket. Jim began to draw. Squeezing its trunk muscles, the snake pulled hundreds of paired ribs tight along an almost endless spine. It lifted a scaly head clear of the leaves. Cocked, the colourful serpent waited for instinct to decide between a strike and a stealthy retreat.

Jim drew a small bear, elbow deep in a honey jar and a curious looking pig distracted by the swarm of bees above the bear's head – or perhaps they were flies. When finished, he placed the sketch under a stone on Robert and Harry's grave and stepped back. His attention now turned to the two tiny, unmarked graves. Two brief lives, who should have had names to be remembered and stories to tell. The infants got their own character from *The Hundred Acre Wood*.

Sitting again, Jim thought of home. He grew up in a noisy, happy house by the sea, a house full of children. His youngest brother was not much older than Harry. Jim missed home. He wiped his eyes, got to his feet and left the babies to rest in peace. Unseen, the snake too moved away – a meandering furrow trailing behind.

On his way out of the cemetery, Jim spotted a small bronze plaque fixed to a simple undressed headstone.

'Jesus!' he whispered, after stooping to read the inscription.

IN MEMORY

- OF -

JAMES MICHAEL MACKEN

AGE 23

ACCIDENTLY KILLED

- ON THE -

GOLDEN POLE G.M.

18TH FEBRUARY 1910.

ERECTED

- BY -

HIS COMRADES.

Jim stood a moment, head bowed, hands clasped as if in silent prayer, and contemplated the life and death of the stranger with whom he shared a name and age.

'I hope you found your gold, Jim,' he said, as if his namesake stood next to him, 'and that nobody back home grew old and died waiting for a letter that never came.'

Out of the sun, in the shade of the cab, Jim wondered if any women were buried back there. The few marked graves he found were all male. Surely, some of the children and babies must have been girls. Did women have no 'comrades' in turn of-the-century Davyhurst? He took a swig of warm water. It did little to satisfy his thirst. A giant ore truck rumbled by, pulling a cloud of dust behind it. Holding his breath until the worst blew over, Jim saluted the driver.

CHAPTER 2

A TIME WITHOUT FLIES

V APOURS FROM THE sandalwood and eucalyptus oils mixed with twists of smoke to produce a sweet, familiar smell. Working quickly to build the fire, Jim laid a delicate lattice of twigs over the burning tinder. He continued with a more robust tepee of larger branches angled to catch the emerging flames. Quickly, fire rose high from the circular pit, where a ring of stones defined a boundary that hot coals were never to cross. Atop four hinged legs, a steel grill plate edged into the flames. Jim remembered when the plate last fried a steak. It had been too long. It rankled that he had not exploited Australia's mad-cow disease free status nearly enough since landing Down Under. Rations were low. It would soon be time to make amends, and the long trip to Aurora for supplies.

Marauding beasts never bothered Jim at night. Flaming torches were not needed to keep nature at bay. Even so, Jim could not settle into the evening until he lit the fire. Fire sterilised his water. It cooked his food and provided light. However, it was more than that. Without the fire, the camp just seemed bleak, austere and unwelcoming. Fire provided companionship to the lonely soul. Over the many dark nights, Jim could sit for hours watching the flames, reassured by their sounds, the pop and the crackle, while remembering his past and imagining a future. Occasionally, in the privacy of his isolation, he danced around his fire. Fire is energy. It breathes, moves and grows. It can reproduce and it can kill. By many definitions, fire is alive.

Jim came to appreciate the ritual of the campfire as something primal, something interwoven over millennia into the coils of his DNA. He imagined how, after the business of surviving the day was done, language, story and music evolved around the fires of his distant ancestors. Over the cold winter months, no matter how healthy the blaze, he remembered how his dad would always check and poke the fire on entering the sitting room. Keeping the fire alight is important work.

A solitary beetle made its way towards the flames. Why was it, he wondered, that nocturnal insects so mesmerised by fire, sacrificed themselves to it? If they craved the light or the heat so much, why did they not get up during the day? Daylight brought its own dangers, but surely nothing more terminal than crawling into a fire! Jim imagined, millions of deluded moths, attracted by the light on a cloudless night, attempting the impossible journey to the moon? With a big-toed flick, he rescued the beetle from a fiery end. But there's no shortage of the little buggers out here, so who was he to question their lifestyle choices?

Jim built his camp along the northern boundary of Yilgarn sheep station. Here, the magnificent single-trunk gum trees that dominated the Goldfields woodlands gave way to the open mulga scrub and sandplains of the interior. He chose this place for its seclusion and for its accessibility to a freshwater well to the east, at the foot of Bungarra Rock. The location proved an ideal base from which to explore the old mining works of the greenstone belts to the south and east, and the empty granite country beyond the Yilgarn boundary fence. Farther north, huge salt lakes, yet to be visited and painted, awaited him.

With the fire established, Jim climbed the five rungs of his home-made ladder up to the balcony. He sat with his legs dangling and peeled a few potatoes while watching the sun go down over the Gold-fields. His favourite time of the day, when the light was magical and the sunsets always spectacular, a time when the breeze dropped and the dust settled. The flies and the oppressive heat would go, leaving a serene half hour or so, before the beetles and moths took over. The high balcony commanded wonderful views of the stunning landscape. From his lofty vantage point, he could watch mobs of kangaroos and emus, who kept to the shade during the day, forage in the cooling air. One evening, he observed the bizarre sight of two camels moseying by.

When the vehicle turned on the sandy track, the sweep of the headlight beams peeked above the trees, grabbing Jim's attention. There were no working mines nearby, no obvious reason for anyone to be on that track at this hour – or any hour. Except for Ray the roo shooter, nobody passed this way in all of Jim's time at the treehouse. Even then, he only ever encountered Ray once, when out for a jog over to Bungarra Rock.

Anticipating he would recover on the downhill, Jim had been pushing hard on the last few strides up to the ridge, when he heard the grumble of an engine below. Startled, he stopped and turned to see a beat-up old Jeep emerge from the trees. Luckily, pale Irish skin is difficult to mistake for the furry hide of a kangaroo. A curious, wild-looking bushwhacker of a man brought his Jeep to a stop along-side the scrawny, almost naked Irishman, who happened to be out for a run in the middle of nowhere, in the middle of the day. Concerned for Jim's mental wellbeing, and keen to confirm the actual existence of a camp, the roo shooter insisted on driving Jim home. Impressed with the treehouse, he stayed for a chat and a billy of tea.

No sooner had Ray left, and much to Jim's horror, the man returned with a large kangaroo dangling off the Jeep's roll bar. Blood still dripped from the bullet hole in the animal's head.

'Here! Reckoned you wouldn't turn your nose at some fresh meat, mate. You look like you could do with it,' Jim's new friend said, before releasing the kangaroo from its restraint. It flopped to the ground with a thump and a bounce, immediately attracting the attention of the flies. Ray drove off again, leaving Jim touched by the gesture, but a little unsure what to do with the beast.

Back at Yilgarn, he had watched Old Bill slaughter a sheep. Hardened by a lifetime in the bush, Old Bill remained detached and clinical in the execution. In fairness to the man, the end came quickly for the ewe. Jim wanted to look away, but as he had chosen that particular sheep from the pen and brought it inside to seal its fate, he felt it cowardly not to witness the full consequences of something he was party to. What disturbed him most about the gruesome deed were the sounds. It was nothing like working on the boats, where fish don't scream and death is silent. He remembered the sad bleats of the petrified animal, who may have anticipated her fate from the smell that haunted the abattoir shed, and then the scraping of hooves on the ground in useless protest, as Old Bill pressed the blade into the jugular. Unlike his boss, Jim knew he could never get comfortable with what he just witnessed. Old Bill expertly butchered the carcass in minutes and, as much as Jim could remember, it seemed like a straightforward business.

Out of respect for the roo, and an ingrained abhorrence for wasting food, Jim resolved to butcher the animal. It could not be very different from the old ewe or, at a stretch, the many fish he gutted on the trawler. They were all vertebrates, after all. He fetched the saw and a penknife from the toolbox on the Ford and started into his gruesome task with no enthusiasm.

The process of removing the head turned Jim green. It bobbed and wobbled, when he hacked his way through the neck. Skippy's sad eyes stared back. Its little tongue, drooping limply from the side of the mouth, did nothing to ease Jim's conscience or settle his stomach. The internal organs were horrific, but interesting, as they first oozed, then flowed to the ground. Decapitated, gutted and drained of blood, the animal now resembled something that hung from the line of hooks above the dead wasps in the window of the Skerries butchers.

From that point on, Jim surprised himself and took some satisfaction in finishing. The skin and fur came away easily from the warm flesh as he ran his hand over the bones of the ribcage. He found the sensation oddly pleasant. Not knowing the proper cuts, he removed the tail and then a muscular rear leg for stewing.

The tail he cooked the traditional way in the embers of the fire, as Old Bill described, and ate it like you would a giant corn on the cob. Each gnaw revealed more of its fascinating architecture of intricate, interlocking bones, with their faceted joints and elaborate arrangement of tendons. Considering its size, the amount of meat disappointed, but what there was of it, he thought reasonable. The taste reminded him of ham. Over the next few days, Jim worked his way through a large pot of kangaroo stew and then got sick of the stuff.

He worried about the viability of the remaining meat left on the carcass hanging in a tree. Having rubbed it in salt and stuffed the chest cavity with eucalyptus leaves to ward off flies, as recommended by Ray, Jim was frustrated to discover the roo shooter's advice proved useless. The carcass became a magnet for every fly in the Goldfields and began to smell. And to be honest, he suspected it created a bad impression in the unlikely event that another visitor should happen by. The sensible thing to do was just bury the remains of the poor animal out the back of the treehouse and before it could poison him half to death.

The lights kept coming down the track. 'Christ, if that's you, Ray, I hope you haven't brought another roo!' Jim muttered. He dropped a peeled but grubby red potato into the pot for washing.

Set back about one hundred metres from the track, an unobservant traveller might easily miss the camp in daylight. But at night, with the fire blazing, Jim knew whoever was coming would stop. He left his pot of potatoes behind and climbed down to greet the visitor.

Spotting the fire, the driver of the white Toyota Land Cruiser turned off the track and bounced the truck across the uneven ground. It came to an abrupt stop next to the Ford. The driver's door swung open. A large black and white border collie shot out and bounded over to Jim. Stopping suddenly in the dust, the dog's hindquarters overtook its head and it tumbled then skidded past Jim's feet. A quick correction followed and it began to circle, yelping.

'Hiyah, Dudley,' Jim said, bending to stroke the delighted animal.

Old Bill Mitchell got out of the cab behind Dudley, but with a bit more dignity.

'How's it going, Irishman?' he said in a cheery, booming voice, landing two firm slaps on Jim's shoulder. 'Good to see you're still alive.'

Old Bill was a large, distinguished-looking man of indeterminate age. Jim guessed he must be around sixty, but never asked. He had the frame of someone used to hard 'yakka' and his skin showed signs of having spent a life under the Australian sun. The picture of a stockman, dressed in his Akubra hat, permanently pressed sky-blue safari shirt, navy knee-length shorts and tan Blundstone boots, Old Bill always presented impeccably. Much to his wife's relief, he did not go in for the high, white woollen socks popular with his bush contemporaries. An unkempt moustache growing wild under his nose rebelled against his otherwise tidy appearance. He spoke in a thunderous, sometimes intimidating, voice developed from years of shouting after sheep and dogs. But Old Bill was a gentle old soul.

'Jaysus, Bill. Good to see you!' Jim said, delighted with the visit from his former boss. 'What you doing up here?'

'Helen's been worrying about you. I told her you'd be fine.'

'So she sent you, anyway.'

'Nah, mate. Was in the area. Been talking to those Cons. Ex. blokes near Davyhurst about grading the roads for them. Thought I might as well look you up.'

'Ah, right. Yeah, sure. How'd you find me?'

Old Bill made his way around to the far side of the Toyota. Jim turned his attention back to entertaining Dudley.

'You've been spotted,' Old Bill said, while untying an army-green tarpaulin. 'The bush telegraph's been busy.'

Reaching in over the sidewall, he lifted out a large blue plastic cool box and carried it across to the solid wooden table Jim used for preparing food.

'What's for dinner?' he asked.

Old Bill set the cool box down reverently, lifted the lid and produced two ice-cold cans of Emu Gold.

'Helen thinks this is a leg of lamb,' he said, tapping the side of his nose, before passing a can to Jim. 'Though looking at you, Jim, I'm wondering do you even eat dinner these days?'

'Ah, the good stuff! You can stay, Bill. Spuds with a couple of tins of braised steak and onion stew. Nothing fancy.'

'That'll do just fine.'

Jim lifted the ring on his beer to break the seal. A sharp fizz emanated as the pressure in the can equalised with the outside world. Pale foam bubbled out. Eager not to waste a drop, he slurped it up. His anticipation for the liquid inside heightened. He bent the ring more and the small triangular flap of aluminium pushed down with an echoing click. Open, Jim put the can to his mouth and took a large gulp of his first properly cold drink in weeks. It went down well. The sparkling fluid danced over the dry, shrivelled pieces of leather that passed for tongue and lips. His body refused to wait for the peristaltic movement of the throat to bring the cold beer to his stomach. Instead the amber liquid dropped, gravity assisted, straight in. A refreshing wave of pleasure rippled out to his extremities before turning back and making for the brain.

Jim liked the odd drink, but never considered himself a big drinker. His constitution and his wallet would not allow it. That said, in the bush nothing came close to a cold beer. He hoped there were many more Emu Golds buried under the ice in Old Bill's esky.

In honour of his guests, Jim lit the gas lamp as the last faint glow of sunlight dipped below the silhouette of eucalyptus canopy. Once the thorium-coated mantle became hot enough in the flame to incandesce, an explosion of brilliant white light fell across the camp.

Old Bill took his drink with him and strolled around the base of the treehouse, inspecting the workmanship. He could see the young lad had done a decent job. Old Bill tugged at a few of the joints and smiled when they refused to budge. Next, stopping under the balcony, he flicked through the books on the shelf. Dudley ran off into some thick acacia scrub behind the camp.

Jim peeled a few more potatoes and threw them, along with a drop of cooking oil, into the cast-iron camp oven, first making sure to fish out any moths that took a detour on their way into the light. He placed the camp oven into a small pit he had dug in the hot coals at the edge of the fire, before shovelling more red-glowing embers over the heavy lid. Getting the temperature right took experience. Too generous with the coals and the spuds would turn to ash. Once cooked, he would pour the tinned stew over the potatoes and simmer for a minute before serving. If Old Bill brought enough beer, dinner might just be palatable.

'What d'you reckon?' Jim asked, nodding towards the treehouse.

'Not bad.' Old Bill put a book back on the shelf. 'Not bad at all. Some nice twitching going on there.'

'You won't find a nail in it.'

'I've taught you well.'

'At first, I swagged it out under the stars, but things evolved, when I kept finding great stuff out yonder.' Jim indicated the general direction with an expansive wave of an unopened tin of stew. 'No harm making yourself comfortable.'

'Indeed,' Old Bill said, as he unfolded the second of Jim's two camp chairs, and set it down beside the fire. After a firm push on the backrest to settle the legs in the dust, the elderly man dropped into the low chair, removed his hat, stretched his legs and took a sip of beer. 'Corrugated iron, wood, canvas and the Cob & Co hitch. That's what built the Goldfields. You're continuing a long tradition here, son. Find any gold yet?'

Jim reached up to the shelf, took down a large zip-up black ring-binder and handed it to his visitor. Old Bill opened the zip and saw the folder contained about twenty watercolour paintings and sketches, each one protected within its own transparent plastic envelope. Without saying a word, Old Bill sat with the folder on his lap, flicking through the images. Jim waited, eager for a reaction and considered prompting one, when Old Bill looked up.

'Jesus, Jim!' A man, not given much to cursing, Old Bill seemed impressed. 'I knew you said you painted now and again, but mate, these really are something. I mean, I know nothing about art, but this is stunning.' He showed Jim a picture of a dusty mob of sheep. A lone motorbike drove the sheep along a dry riverbed. Copper salmon gum trees lined a sandy bank. Shafts of sunlight streamed through the gaps. He flicked back a page to a second muster scene set in an open paddock of bluebush and spinifex. 'They're gorgeous, Jim. You've really caught it. That's my Yilgarn, mate.'

Jim sensed a tinge of emotion in Old Bill's voice. Not something often heard.

'How come you never did any at the homestead?' Old Bill asked.

'Ah, you know, too many people around, they'd be watching.'

'Bloody oath. You have to do something with these. Helen knows art. Knows people in Perth.'

'That wouldn't surprise me. What does surprise me is how such an elegant, cultured woman ended up marrying you!'

Old Bill grunted, then had to laugh. 'Can't argue with you there ...

But she has to see these, Jim.'

'Yeah, I'm pleased with them. This place sure does inspire me. Suppose you could say I've hit a rich vein, but no gold.'

'Ha! You saw one of these?' He held up Jim's study of a curious-looking insect. 'A trilobite beetle. Well I'll be! They're very rare.'

Old Bill's endorsement of his work pleased Jim. 'Listen. Take out those two pictures of the sheep and give them to Helen for me, will you? Call it a belated Christmas pressie.'

Jim was keen to show his appreciation for everything his old boss had done for him, but knew Old Bill would make a scene if he tried to give him the paintings directly.

'Helen'll be stoked with these. She'll make sure they're framed nicely too. She'll like that.' Old Bill carefully unclipped the pictures from the folder and got up to put them in the cab of the Toyota. Dudley came back, wondering if they were leaving already.

'Not yet, Dudley,' Old Bill said, returning to his seat. The dog came and sat beside him but was gone again in a flash. 'Something over there's got his attention. Looks like he's been digging. How's the driving going? That old Ford giving you any trouble?'

'It's been great. Starts every time.'

'Hit anything else?'

'Nope. Getting the hang of it now. Even took it into Kalgoorlie last month for supplies—'

'What! You drove to Kal with no doors or windows? Not forgetting the small matter of no licence or insurance!'

'Yeah … I needed paint. It can't be got in Menzies.'

'Kal's a big place, Jim, and let's be honest. You're not the best driver.'

'It's bigger than I was led to believe, all right. And more cosmopolitan.' Jim busied himself rummaging for the tin opener. He knew the anticipation of food always distracted Old Bill. 'I thought the place would be crawling with bangers. The shearers made Kal sound like the Wild West.'

Old Bill scratched his head. 'Had you ever driven on a street with traffic lights or even road markings?'

'Er, no. I did get a bit of abuse from other drivers a few times.'

'If the coppers caught you … you could've got yourself deported. And my poor old Ford seized.'

Jim looked sheepish.

'Look, mate. Promise me you won't take her in again … and that goes for the bike, too!' Old Bill poked the fire with a stick, flicking some charred branches into the flames. 'Ah. That's better … Listen. Helen can always get you art supplies or anything else when she's in town. Just call in and let her know.'

'Thanks, I promise. No farther than Aurora from now on.' Jim changed the subject. 'Did you find many more stragglers? I've seen no woolly sheep around here at all.'

As soon as Jim mentioned sheep, Old Bill's demeanour changed. Without replying, he sat forward in the chair and stroked his moustache with an open hand. He took a long drink of beer. Then, gripping the tin in both hands he stared deep into the fire. Sensing something was up, Jim stopped what he was doing at the table and turned to look at his friend.

'I got another half-bale of wool, Jim. That's all.'

Shit! That's not good, Jim thought. He knew Old Bill and Helen were counting on cobbling together a few more bales from sheep that evaded the muster and other escapees repatriated from Balfour Downs, a neighboring station to the south.

Jim remembered Helen telling him how, on the last day of their honeymoon, she and Bill signed the lease on Yilgarn. Every day since, they grew a little older and worked together to improve their property. They knew boom years and hard times. Such is the nature of growing wool. But in the main, Yilgarn had been good to them and they were good for Yilgarn. The couple had made every effort to ease grazing pressure on the land. Old Bill coveted a smaller but more valuable flock. He reduced numbers and rolled out endless kilometres of new wire fences to implement a more sophisticated stock rotation system. They sank many new wells. Their tenure oversaw the largest phase of rainwater dam construction and rehabilitation since the giant sheep station was created back at the turn of the century. Outside of prolonged periods of drought, all paddocks should now have access to year-round fresh water. The couple hoped the odds were tipping in their favour and, for a while, it seemed they were. However, in recent years something had changed.

'Only one measly half-bale. That's it!' Old Bill repeated himself, still staring into the fire. He took another sip of beer. 'You'd think with the new dams, more sheep would have made it through the year. It's just too dry,' he said, shaking his head. 'Honestly, I think the climate has shifted up here.'

After good rains, the dams were an oasis in the desert and well capable of sustaining the flock throughout the summer. Analogous to ancient earthwork defences, these massive structures reminded Jim of something only an army of slaves could have built in times before machines. Such were their size, a truck driving along the retaining walls would not have to worry about slipping over an edge. On his second day at Yilgarn, they put Jim to work helping with the construction of a new dam. Much like in opencast mining, explosives were first used to shatter the leached, concrete-like soil, before the earthmover came in to dig it out and shape the sides.

Jim would freely admit that, in the beginning, despite his eagerness, he was not much use on the station. He couldn't even drive. His already fragile confidence took a knock after the incident with the tractor. He got a ribbing too from the other hands, because he didn't know what the explosive ANFO was, especially coming from Ireland. The gag irritated him. But it was having no useful skills outside of wielding a shovel or pickaxe that annoyed him most. Both were redundant anyway in the face of the awesome destructive power of the Komatsu's blade and ripper. Only after Helen schooled the young Irishman in using ammonium nitrate and the art of bomb-making, did he become a little more useful to have around.

In his second week at Yilgarn, however, Jim discovered an aptitude for fencing. Blessed with the ability to walk in the heat for hours without flagging or moaning, he could hang more aluminium spacers on the many kilometres of tensioned new-wire fence than anyone else in a day. It became his thing, earning him a little kudos from the others and it helped Jim settle.

The winter rains were insufficient last year. The summer rains never came. Dams, new and old, never filled. The yabbies retreated into the mud, when the already low water levels continued to drop in the summer heat. From its inception, the station's viability had always been marginal. Now, Old Bill feared, all their efforts may have been in vain. Yilgarn was still very much at the mercy of its geography, El Niño and global warming. It was just too far into the parched interior to graze sheep for profit anymore.

'The science may be out on this "greenhouse effect", Jim, but I see it in our records. You know, they used to run well over ten thousand sheep here in the old days and it paid. I've been killing myself trying to breed a smaller flock for near thirty years and now it's costing me money. This last drought has just about wiped us out. Wasting me bloody time and Helen's.'

Old Bill turned the can slowly in his fingers, squeezing the sides until it kinked. 'The crazy thing is … even with the drought, the wool price is on the floor. There are warehouses on Melbourne docks packed to the rafters with mountains of it. Nobody is buying the stuff anymore. It's all cheap, man-made fibres nowadays and even cheaper clothes from Asian sweatshops.' He took another drink. 'I've decided to sell the rams.'

The rams were magnificent creatures, in as much as a sheep could ever be a magnificent creature. Even Jim who, before arriving at Yilgarn had never been up close and personal to a ram or a ewe, or a wether or hogget for that matter, could tell the rams had breeding. They were a class apart. Their fleeces were finer and felt softer than all the thousands of other sheep that had recently passed through his hands. On Yilgarn, Old Bill's rams were kings. They got the best paddock and the best feed. When their services were not required, they spent much of the year down south by the coast on Helen's family property, basking in the sea breeze.

Jim knew all Old Bill had ever wanted was to breed a valuable flock of high-quality, fine, low-micron wool. It was in the man's blood. Old Bill bragged about how his ancestors introduced the merino sheep to Western Australia. It was something he told anyone who would listen, and many who would not. Selling his prized rams would break his heart. Jim stopped what he was doing and sat by the fire to give Old Bill his undivided attention.

'Going to run wethers. Sell into the live meat market. Helen wants me to try cattle. They're hardier than sheep, for sure.' He poked the fire again with the stick. Sparks flew into the night. They glowed for a few seconds, then faded. 'I'm a sheep man, Jim. Always been a sheep man. What do I know about cattle?'

'You never know. You might take to them. Might be easier.' It annoyed Jim that he couldn't think of anything more reassuring to say.

'Nah, it's fucked, Jim. All fucked. Sorry. Still, God knows, we've had it rough before and we always got through.'

The couple had known tragedy in the past. Old Bill never spoke of it and Jim never brought it up, but Helen told him of their beautiful little four-year-old girl who died from meningitis. There were no other children. Where it may have torn them apart, tragedy and adversity brought them closer together. They seldom fought. They were mad about each other. Every time he watched them together, Jim could see that.

A happy welcoming place, Yilgarn's isolation did not prevent a regular stream of visitors from dropping by the homestead. End of muster and shearing celebrations at Yilgarn were legendary among the wider Goldfields community. This season, despite the disappointment of the poor harvest and the financial pressure Old Bill and Helen were under, they maintained the tradition of the big party. It was important for the couple to show their gratitude and appreciation to everyone who helped with the shearing, from the lowly Irish jackaroo to their wide circle of friends.

Old Bill had a fondness for home brew, something he indulged in on a grand scale. This season, he brought forth a batch of stout for the shearing and was delighted to have an Irishman to test it on. Jim knew nothing of stout, but gave an approving nod at the official tasting. It tasted bloody awful.

From the first night Jim landed at their door, the couple made him feel welcome. When the work finished, it was Old Bill who encouraged Jim to head off and experience something of the bush in his own time. He saw how the place and the stories of gold had captivated the young Irishman. Old Bill gave him the equipment he needed to make his bush adventure possible. Jim now worried for his friends and knew he could do little to help.

'Ah, look. I'm not going to wind myself up about it now. Things'll be fine. I have work grading the roads for the mines. That'll give me time to think it over.'

'I don't know, Bill. I suspect a Stetson might just suit you,' Jim joked, trying to lighten the sombre mood. 'You already have the cowboy moustache … and I know you're a closet Country and Western fan.'

Old Bill snorted and threw an empty Emu Gold, hitting Jim on the shoulder.

'Strewth! Go fetch two more Emus from that esky, and hurry with the tucker. Listen, before I forget, your parents were on. They've got a phone. Here's the number.' He handed Jim a note from his breast pocket.

'Wow! After twenty years, they've only finally gone and done it. I won't have to ring the next-door neighbours anymore.'

'With eight children I don't blame them. Think of the bills!'

'You know, you can't just go and buy a phone in Ireland. You have to rent it from the State and it's months before Posts and Telegraphs get around to installing it for you – unless you know someone, that is.'

'Isn't it the same everywhere?'

'Nah, we're a feckin backward little country, really. Geldof was right.'

'The Live Aid bloke?'

'Yeah. Before his beatification, he had a few digs at Ireland. Did you tell the folks what I'm up to?'

'I kind of mentioned something about it, but assured them you were safe. Said you would call soon. Make sure you do now! Don't make a liar of me. OK?'

'Will do.'

'Your father wanted you to know the economy and employment are picking up back home.'

'Believe it when I see it.' Jim stood up. 'Ah, Christ! I bet Dudley's been digging up the remains of that roo I buried over there. Would he eat a tin of Spam if I opened one?' Jim started rummaging through a box of tinned food.

'He would.'

Old Bill gave a shrill whistle. Dudley appeared from the shadows and returned to his master's side.

'When the wind blows from over that way, the smell is feckin awful. I should have buried it deeper. I just can't bring myself to go near it again.'

'You didn't run over it, did you?' Old Bill chuckled. He already knew how Jim came by his kangaroo.

The braised steak went down well. Dudley had his Spam. Jim need not have worried about the beer supplies. Old Bill's esky arrived full.

They talked of cricket and Merv Hughes' moustache, the sorry state of northern hemisphere rugby, fossicking for gold, the Irish history of Western Australia and the changing face of Europe. Jim enjoyed the opportunity to chat. He knew there were tough times ahead for his friends and he felt for them. Dudley lay at Old Bill's feet, but the carcass of the roo was never far from his mind.

A LITTLE AFTER sunrise, Old Bill rolled his swag and threw it into the back of the Toyota. He whistled for Dudley to come. Jim heard them moving around and climbed down to see his visitors off. Old Bill stuck his head out the window and, looking back over his elbow, called to Jim.

'There's a leg of lamb in your pot. Look after it!' and then he drove off.

Jim raised a hand in acknowledgement, while shielding his eyes and his delicate head from the morning glare.

'Thanks! Ye big softy, ye,' Jim shouted after him.

The Toyota turned onto the track and away.

CHAPTER 3

AURORA

K ELLY PORCINI POSITIONED herself underneath the large revolving ceiling fan above the bar. Over the main doorway, an air conditioner rattled along on full power. The spirited little machine fought gallantly and lowered the temperature around the entrance a degree or two. Just enough to fool a hesitant punter into thinking sanctuary away from the blistering heat of the midday sun awaited inside. Staring out the window, Kelly watched every ore truck pass and wondered if she would not be better off getting into the next one that stopped.

At least the pub's quiet, she thought, and the early lunchtime air was still free of smoke and the stink of thirsty miners coming off shift. Except for the young Irishman, who took his lunch away from the dining area, and the two old boys nursing stubbies at the bar, the place was empty. Kelly liked when Pete and Ron were in. They had elevated themselves to regulars in recent weeks and were always eager to chat.

The Aurora Inn was a solid, single-storey structure, built of cut red sandstone blocks. The fine-pitched cross-laminations visible within the blocks told a story of deep geological time, when water flowed more freely through an ancient landscape. There was a look of permanence to the inn, unusual for Goldfields buildings of its age. The red brick quoins on the corners and around the windows and doors added a dash of flair. A double-hipped corrugated roof sloped down to meet a broad verandah apron that wrapped the building on all sides in shade. There was nothing brash about The Aurora Inn. It sported none of the ornate filigree and ostentatious facades of the big, Federation-style public houses common to large country towns. It stood almost alone, but proudly, at the junction of two wide dirt roads.

'You finished? Will I take your plate?' Kelly asked, passing by Jim's table.

'Yes, thanks.'

'Everything OK?'

'Lovely. Actually, I was—'

'Statistician!'

Jim looked perplexed.

'Statistician.' Kelly gestured towards the television. 'Burgo's looking for an occupation that gathers, and analyses data.'

'Oh, right. Very good ...' He glanced at the screen. 'God, it's a dreadful quiz. Still if it's on, you kinda have to watch it. There's some head on that Burgess chap.'

Now Kelly looked confused. 'Can I get you anything else?'

'Actually, how's about another steak.'

'Another twenty-ounce steak?'

'You might as well give me the chips and coleslaw too.'

'OK. Medium rare, mushroom sauce?'

'No, wait. Pepper sauce. To be honest, the mushrooms tasted a bit mouldy. Tinned, I presume?'

'That's what they are, aren't they ... mould?'

Jim smiled and nodded.

'Hard to get fresh veg out this far,' Kelly added, in defence of the cook. 'So, medium rare, pepper sauce it is. Won't be long.' She cleared the table in front of Jim and started to walk away, before looking back. 'Free coffee, if you eat it all!'

On the television, the *Wheel of Fortune* clicked to a stop and a lady named Sue won enough money to buy a *Fowlers Vacola* preserve-making kit. Behind his moustache, the host, John Burgess, prattled with delight and complemented Sue on her 'lovely yellow dress.'

Jim got up to have a quick look around and walk off lunch, before his second serving arrived. The front bar was a drab rectangular room with a high ceiling. On one long wall, at the end of a line of four tall windows, a sturdy pair of double doors swung open out onto the verandah and the main road. A few low tables were placed randomly below the windows. The dark, polished hardwood floorboards answered back when walked on and bore the scars of generations of miners' work boots. The floor contrasted with the pale yellow smoke stained walls. A solid varnished-wood and brass-edged counter ran almost the length of the far wall. A line of simple metal stools was set out in front, ready for business. Behind the bar, a bank of well-stocked, glass-fronted fridges hummed.

Above the fridges, a shelf of assorted empty glass bottles caught Jim's eye. Discarded by the early diggers, many were of significant age, their colours dulled by years in the sun and the work of wind-blown sands. Rare varieties fetched a decent price these days and were something Jim always kept an eye out for on his travels. So far, he had amassed a fragmented collection of bottlenecks and punts. He couldn't say why he kept them. Perhaps he liked their connection with the past. He had a vague idea to use them as part of a still life. Maybe he just liked how they shone in the evening light on the balcony.

At one end of the room, a large, ornate wrought-iron fireplace dominated a small annex. Jim wondered if they ever lit the fire. Red-

and-white chequered oilcloth covered the tables here, differentiating the restaurant from the rest of the bar. He couldn't help thinking the fancy covers were out of place in an isolated outback miners and pastoralists watering hole.

A second door beside the bar led to a corridor that opened to a shaded beer garden and the accommodation block out back. Next to the main entrance, a collection of old black and white framed photographs recalled various gold rushes and, along with two television screens at opposite ends of the room, added visual interest to the otherwise bare walls. Jim paused at a recent photograph of the West Australian businessman, Alan Bond, and some other gentlemen standing proudly in front of a magnificent yacht moored in Freemantle Harbour.

'That's the America's Cup, mate, the year we lost it,' one of the old boys at the bar volunteered, looking out over his beer.

'Yeah? I remember watching it on telly back home. *Kookaburra III*. It was big news, even in Ireland.'

'That's the owner of this place next to Bondy. Max Collins.'

'Ah, yeah. I see him now. He's certainly well connected.'

Jim moved along and parked himself in the door frame and under the air conditioner. He looked out past the verandah, across the dusty, unsealed road to the clearing in the scrub beyond.

Aurora knew good times before The Great War, but after the young men went off to fight, the gold mines shut down and the town ceased to be. When the fighting stopped, the mines returned to production, but Aurora never recovered. Now The Aurora Inn sat almost alone in the shadow of big mining. The greenstones deep below the abandoned streets still ran rich with microscopic grains of the precious metal. Valuable near-surface nuggets of the stuff, missed by the old boys and found by metal detectors, were occasionally passed around the bar. However, the bright lights of Kalgoorlie, just over ninety kilometres down an ever-improving road, were too big an attraction for anyone to call Aurora home. BHP supplied mine-site accommodation in the area, but it was too transient and too far out of town to be included in any official census. Aurora claimed a semi-permanent population of four.

A little embarrassed by the state of his Ford, Jim had parked the F250 a short distance downhill from the pub and in front of two wrecked, possibly 1960s, single-decker coaches. Having never seen Aurora in daylight and looking around him now, he realised his battered Ford did not look at all out of place among the wonderful decay. Unlike Davyhurst, a few of the original buildings continued to defy the ravages of time and survived in various stages of dilapidation. Up the road, another old battery loomed high over the townsite and, perhaps with some love, this one looked as if it could be put to work again. Across from the inn, the shells of two vintage automobiles, old enough to have rolled off one of Henry Ford's first assembly lines, were being absorbed back into the earth. Jim imagined they might have belonged to two miners who never came home from the war. He did not know enough about cars to say which war. Everywhere, rusting fragments of obsolete mining equipment encroached from the margins.

If it were not for the angry contractions of an overactive stomach, he would have found a shady spot and taken the sketchbook out as soon as he arrived. Instead, after a peek through the fence at the battery, he had made a direct line for the pub and its lunch menu. The sketching would wait.

A blast of hot air encouraged Jim back under the air conditioner. Wiping the sweat from his forehead, he cursed the heat. Considering the day that was in it, maybe the sensible thing to do would be to just take some quick photos of this curious place. Jim owned a decent camera, a Minolta Dynax 7000i. It looked impressive with its fancy lens. He liked the idea of the camera, but he was no photographer, much preferring to paint *en plein air* or from sketches. Under pressure to capture movement or a passing moment of light, he tended to panic, struggled with the mechanics of the machine and often missed the shot. He rarely got around to developing his films and seldom had the money to do so anyway. When he did, the results always disappointed. Somewhere back home in Skerries, among his most treasured possessions, although he couldn't bring himself to look at them anymore, was an arty collection of photos. In many of the shots, his blurred fingertips partly obscured the well-framed composition of a pretty blonde girl in front of various London landmarks.

Ellen gave him the Minolta for his twenty-first and encouraged him to enrol in a night course in photography – his one brief effort to better himself since leaving school. After the first class, he never went back. Getting there required two tube changes. It was too much hassle and 'anyway, full of student types'. Instead, he bought a book on photography and a few glossy photographic magazines. He remembered them fondly. Ah, the glamour, he thought, but was then reminded of how his attitude and behaviour had disappointed Ellen. At the time, though, he couldn't see the problem.

Since coming to Australia, Jim had only shot two rolls of twenty-four exposure film, both of which were now stashed in a box back at the camp. They would probably have to wait until he returned home to Ireland, before seeing the light again. Still, it was just too hot to sketch today, he decided.

KELLY WATCHED THE Irishman attack his second steak with the same gusto he had the first. She remembered him from one of her first nights at Aurora. Hadn't he come in with the shearers from Old Bill's place? He was of similar age to her, early to mid-twenties, she guessed. His near shoulder-length black hair hung loosely tied back from a tanned, handsome and well-proportioned face. A few short, wavy strands having escaped the tight bobbin, now curled out in front of his ears. She thought he could do with a shave.

He had been quieter than the company he kept that night. He had a nice laugh, genuine, not forced, and appeared to listen carefully when others spoke. His replies were measured. She noticed he did not engage in their lewd banter either. There was no arrogance about him. Neither did he make a fuss ordering beer nor when she forgot his change. He did get a little drunk, however, and chuckled to himself as the night went on. His conversation became more animated, but he remained good natured and polite to her. The others seemed to defer to him on matters of fact. It surprised her how much she remembered. Perhaps it was the soft Irish accent. She liked his gentle green eyes.

Jim walked over and placed the empty plate on the bar. She didn't remember him being quite so skinny though.

'A white coffee, please.'

'I'm impressed. Old Bill not been feeding you, then?'

'No … Yes.' He wasn't sure what the correct reply should be. 'I finished with Bill a while ago.'

She wondered if he had joined the mines, but with the double pluggers on his feet, long board shorts and faded red vest, he didn't dress like someone working for the mining companies. If the miners were not wearing their company-issue branded clothes and regulation safety glasses, which they almost always did, they still tended to be better dressed than this shabby Irishman. His cheap sunnies, she suspected, offered little protection from any wayward rock chip. She wondered if perhaps he was now a driller, but they travel in packs and never allow themselves to get that hungry.

'So what have you been up to, then?'

'Gone walkabout, I suppose.'

That would explain the state of him, she thought. 'Prospecting, then. Find anything?' she asked.

'Nah, not really. Just having a look around.'

'When did you finish up with Old Bill?'

'After shearing.'

'That's about the time I started here. So you've just been looking around for two months!'

'Yep … It's a big place.'

Kelly suspected there must be more to his story, but he wasn't giving much away. 'Hey, boys!' she called to the two battlers down the bar. 'This Irishman says he's been walkabout for two months. What d'you reckon?'

'Find any gold?' Ron, the larger of the two old men asked.

'No, not really looking.'

'You got a detector?'

'No.'

'Wastin' your time without a detector, mate.'

'Ah, yeah. Just looking around. Came in for some supplies.'

'That's all I got from him, too,' said Kelly, 'but can't help feeling there's something more. What d'you think, boys?'

'You running away from the law, son?'

Jim laughed. 'No.'

'Ah, Ron. Does he look like a crim to you?'

'I was working out at Yilgarn. Just thought I'd have a look around, when I finished up. The old mining history around here is very interesting. Plenty of Irish stories.'

The second gentleman shifted on his stool, looked out from under his peaked cap and added his voice to the conversation. 'Sure were a lot of Paddies in these parts in the day. Hannan started it all in Kal and O'Connor brought us the water.'

'Yeah, but the Italians brought wine, Pete,' Kelly said proudly, while pouring boiling water into a mug of instant coffee.

'You the bloke living in the treehouse, who does the paintings?' Pete asked. 'Old Bill says you're bloody good, mate.'

'Nice of him to say so. Yeah, I do a bit.'

'Jim, the Irish artist! One complimentary coffee. You've earned it. Are you staying around for the fight?'

'If you're expecting trouble, I might just skip town,' Jim said, surprised but pleased Kelly knew his name.

'Nah, mate. Kelly is talking about Tyson. Max is showing it on delayed satellite link from Tokyo. Should be a big crowd in,' Ron said, rubbing his hands together in anticipation of a good afternoon ahead. 'Say nothing if you already know the result.'

'Yeah, I saw the sign outside. No haven't heard a thing. I wasn't planning on staying, but sure, maybe I will.' It was nice to be asked.

* * *

'JESUS, JIM! HEY, Mary, quick, it's Jim. He's on the phone. Get the kids up.'

Jim could hear urgent shouting going on upstairs and out the back. 'Good to hear your voice, Dad. Sorry about the time. How's everything?' Jim loaded the green armour-plated CT3, or Telecom's Coin-Operated Telephone Three to give it its full title, with dollar coins. Another stack of the thick brassy coins balanced on top of the phone, ready to go when the red warning lamp came on.

'Good to hear you too, Jim. Where are you?'

'Hi, Jim! Hi, Jim! Hiyah!' A chorus of muffled, sleepy greetings came at him, each voice farther away from the handset than the last. His mother had gathered the clan.

'How are you, Jim? Everything OK?' she called out, when everyone had settled into their allocated positions – the smaller children peering down over the banister.

'Your boss said something about you finishing with him and you were gone looking for gold,' his father added.

'Things are great here. I'm still in the Goldfields.' Clunk. Another dollar dropped into the strongbox. 'Haven't really been prospecting.'

Jim turned and looked around. Nobody waited to use the phone after him. 'But I have found some, a few nuggets. Don't think they'd be worth much. Pure luck.'

'Are you serious?'

'Yeah, Dad. Maybe a few hundred bucks. It won't make me rich.'

'He's struck gold!' His father relayed the message back.

'That's nice. Are you eating? Where are you ringing from?' His mother spoke again.

'The same pub as before. Called in for some supplies and a feed. Can't believe you got a phone. Bet the Murphys are relieved. No more disturbing them in the middle of the night.'

'They're good, and asking for you,' she said, taking the handset from her husband. 'You know, the economy is picking up here, Jim. There will be jobs.'

'Great. What's happening in Skerries? Everyone well?'

Clunk went another coin down the chute.

'This must be costing you a fortune, Jim.' His precarious finances were always of concern to his mother, and with good reason.

'Tell him about the letter from Denmark,' a sister shouted. 'I'll read it for him, if he wants.'

'Don't let her near it, Mum. Send it on to the Mitchells. I think I'll be here a bit longer.'

'What about snakes and spiders?' another sister asked.

'Loads! But I promise, Mum. I keep my distance.'

'Yuck,' said the sister.

'Deadly! Would they go near ye?' his youngest brother asked, now very interested.

'Now you be careful,' added his alarmed mother. 'I know what you're like!'

Things were good in Skerries. Jim enjoyed catching up on the gossip. After talking about it for years, his Mum had joined a choir and was back singing. It only took her twenty-five years to get around to doing something for herself. She loved it. Sean, the eldest, was off to France for the summer to work on a Masters in Architectural History, through French. Another brother had formed a band and the youngest just mastered the skateboard. One sister had started a job in the bank and the three others were facing exams, from secondary school to college finals. An excellent time to be out of the house, Jim thought. God help his parents.

As it happened, the family were to be herded out later that morning for the unveiling of a bronze plaque Jim's father had sculpted for the church. Incorporating the relief of a goat's head, the plaque was to be set into an exterior wall, below a beautiful, understated Portland stone figure of St Patrick by the renowned sculptor, Albert Power.

'No pressure, Dad!' Jim teased, knowing his father, an English teacher and not a sculptor, would be nervous about how his work would stand up against that of the master craftsman.

The parish priest commissioned the bronze after seeing a Pollyfilla relief of a goat's head his father made many years previously, his only other three-dimensional work to date. It still hung on the wall above the local rugby club bar. Jim remembered watching fascinated, his father shape the goat's head from the wet, lead-grey Pollyfilla. With the touch of the alchemist, he then painted it a beautiful metallic gold. Jim always liked it, but never understood how, at some time over subsequent years, the head had not slid off its blue, gloss-painted, chipboard mount. As his father could turn his hand to most things, Jim knew he need not worry. The bronze goat would sit well at the feet of the saint.

He remembered his father telling them the legend of St Patrick's goat, when they moved to the new house on the seafront. The four islands off Skerries were visible from the stunning view framed in the sitting-room window. Prominent among these was St Patrick's Island. Shortly after arriving in Ireland in 432 AD, St Patrick, or plain old 'Patrick' at the time, along with his goat, took up residence on said eponymous island. The ruins of his church survive there to this day.

Never a man to stand still, on one infamous occasion, when away possibly banishing the snakes, the hungry folk of Skerries ate his goat.

On his return, the good bishop, less than pleased and not above the odd curse, declared that 'from henceforth, all the women of Skerries shall suffer problem chin hair, lest they forget the fate of my beloved goat.' The menfolk apparently were spared any direct curse, their punishment more nuanced. The new plaque was by way of a rather belated apology and a symbolic returning of the goat.

Jim's remark that he hoped, for the sake of two of his sisters, the offering would mollify the saint, who might then reconsider the curse, caused much slagging down the line. The house was as noisy and happy as ever. The family were managing just fine without him. And what was Ellen writing to him about? Already a sense of nervous anticipation began to build. It would be a long week or two before he would find out.

On his way back to the bar, the talk of St Patrick got Jim to thinking of the poor goats out at Yilgarn and how they usually ended up on the receiving end of a bullet. Donkeys and feral cats and dogs were a problem too. They all met with a similar fate. In fact, whenever anything feral crossed Old Bill's path, the rifle came out. Jim disapproved. He knew there was no place for these animals in the bush, but could not help but wonder if Old Bill might just be a little trigger-happy.

Only once did Jim ever handle the rifle himself. He took the gun down from its mount above the windscreen inside Old Bill's Land Cruiser to observe a wedge-tailed eagle through the telescopic sight. He watched the bird in intimate detail feed its chick high in the crown of a gum tree. The very act of pointing a gun at such a magnificent creature, even without malice, bothered him.

* * *

MAX COLLINS SAT on his usual stool next to the hatch at the end of the bar. From here, he kept a watchful eye on his customers and his staff. Dressed in a charcoal-grey suit and always a loose necktie over his white shirt, even on the hottest of days, the man cut a striking figure. In a place where work boots and thongs were the footwear of choice, Max's expensive Italian leather shoes that never wanted for a high polish, stood apart. It took no little effort to avoid being mistaken for just another Aussie battler. Contrary to the demographic of the clientele and the pub's isolation, things seldom ever got out of hand at The Aurora Inn. Max Collins' reputation as a hard man preceded him.

Born into Coolgardie gold mining stock, Max declined to follow in the family business, preferring instead to join the Western Australia Police Department. He enjoyed a glittering career and rose to the elevated rank of Head of Criminal Investigative Branch. However, a little over two years before this stifling afternoon, and somewhat prematurely, Max retired.

In between the occasional bite of a steak and beetroot sandwich, the proprietor worked his way through a copy of Friday's *West Australian*. He took great care to analyse every article and opinion piece in the paper, as an experienced detective might.

Although she refused to comment, it appeared likely that Carmen Lawrence would become Australia's first female state premier on Monday. That news did not sit well with Max. Neither it seemed, did the sandwich. His mood darkened as hydrochloric acid etched the lining of his stomach and he delved deeper into the paper.

Lawrence was a vocal opponent of former premier, Brian Bourke, and his hard-right faction of the Labour party. For the guts of a decade, Bourke rode shotgun over the state's affairs, either directly or through his cronies in the West Australian Development Corporation. The not unrelated sorry saga of the demise of Rothwells Merchant Bank featured prominently in the pages, compounding Max's worsening mood. He ran an exasperated hand through his head of well-combed, quartz-white hair, before consciously patting any disarranged tresses back into place.

Not taken with golf, Max bought the almost derelict Aurora Inn to restore and run as a hobby in his anticipated long retirement. He saw it as a place where he could continue to play the big man, the local boy done well, somewhere to command respect and still wield a little power. He would divide his time between the outback and the city, where he shared a fine home in the affluent suburb of Cottesloe with his wife. Not caring much for the flies and dust, she chose to spend her days in Perth, happy to let Max pander to his ego in the Goldfields.

Max's grand plan involved engaging the services of a full-time manager to run the business. But Max was broke. Having sunk considerable monies into the Aurora, he needed the place to work. The police pension came nowhere near servicing his loans. Now unable to afford a manager, Max seemed to spend all of his time at the inn. He grew to despise the Aurora and the people who frequented it. The Goldfields no longer held any romantic allure for him. In his youth, he was only too happy to leave for the city. It annoyed him that, at the time he bought the Aurora, he had forgotten this.

Noticing Max study the paper, the BHP shift manager felt obliged to offer an opinion. 'Bet you Lawrence will call a Royal Commission, Max. It's all going to come out now. Mark my words. Bourke and his cronies will do time.'

Max needed the man's business, so he tempered his reply. 'More than likely.'

'Bet you're glad to be out of it. Might get messy.'

'Your implication being?'

'Nothing, Max. Just … you know, the extra workload.'

The manager left it at that and retreated. Max took another reluctant bite of the now cold sandwich and his eye caught the photo on the wall, of himself next to Alan Bond.

Everything changed, changed utterly since the crash of October '87. Black Tuesday hit Max hard. Fabricated on property speculation and lies, the whole house of cards that was West Australia Inc. collapsed spectacularly. Even the great captains of wealth generation,

Bondy and Connell, were in trouble. Despite the best and mostly illegal efforts of the State Government to prop it up, Laurie Connell's Rothwells Merchant Bank went under and took Max's plans for a comfortable retirement down with it. Max had invested in Rothwells much of the not insubstantial sums of money he had acquired through private means over the years.

It was all gone now. Blinded by forceful personalities and the high-octane glamour of it all, he had gambled his future on Rothwells, a menswear outlet from Queensland that came to masquerade as a merchant bank in Western Australia. He let his judgement be impaired by America's Cup photo shoots, airship trips over Sydney Harbour and his own vanity. Bondy was his mate too, not just Canberra's. But when it all fell apart, everyone rushed to cover their own arses and, no longer useful, they tossed Max aside. That said, for some reason he could not bring himself to take down the photo.

Max returned to his paper. He did indeed worry about what any future Royal Commission might dig up. More immediately, he worried about not paying the bills. Most of all, he worried about losing face. But he knew where the bodies were buried. Some people might do well to reconsider their positions.

SPOTTING OLD BILL enter the bar, Jim raised a stubby in salute. 'Hey, Bill! What can I get yah?'

Old Bill glanced over. Neither Jim nor the offer of a drink registered. Old Bill's expression did not change. His mind was elsewhere. Stepping around the groups of chatting men, he made his way across to the end of the bar and to Max.

'Bill looks bothered,' Ron muttered.

Jim and Pete copped it too. With a gesture of the head, Old Bill invited Max to join him at an empty corner table, where a whispered discussion ensued. Curious, Jim discreetly observed the animated but inaudible conversation, until Ron distracted him.

'You know, the Aurora's only been open about three years, Jim. It was derelict before that. Collins spent a fortune renovating the place. It's opened and closed many times since it was first built. All depends on the price of gold and the number of thirsty miners roaming the bush.'

'Same with the Broad Arrow Tavern,' Pete added.

'Where's that?' asked Jim.

'On the way to Kal. Not too far from our claim.'

'You've a claim?'

'Yep, Mulgarrie, across the road from Broad Arrow. We reprocess old spoil heaps. With modern gear, we can recover a lot of the fine gold from the waste that the old boys couldn't get at. Small scale, but pays the bills.'

'Just the two of you?'

'Yup, we either camp there or commute from Kal. Depends on the mood of this fella's old lady.' Pete put a friendly arm around the shoulder of his companion.

Ron shuddered. 'Yeah, it was a handy number until his nibs here fell out with the owner at the Broad Arrow.'

'Prick!' muttered Pete. 'This is a nicer pub anyways, and besides, we wouldn't have met Kelly otherwise, eh? That right, Kel?'

'The pleasure's all mine, boys.'

Things were getting busy for Kelly. Thankfully, the afternoon help was due in soon.

'See this bar here?' Pete said, slapping the counter hard with an open palm. Max looked over from the corner table.

'Easy there, Pete!' said Kelly, eyeing her boss.

'Sorry, Kel. Jarrah, Jim. Good solid Aussie hardwood. It's only a few years old this bar. But that gutter there.' He pointed down to the patinated metal trough that ran the length of the counter. 'Original!'

'Is that not a footrest or something?' Jim asked.

'Nah, mate.'

'Spittoon?'

'Close … If you go down that end you will see where the tap was, and over there …' Pete pointed to the far end of the bar, '… is a drain.'

He stood as if to begin a speech. 'In more enlightened times, when sheilas were not permitted to enter public bars, that … my friend … was a *pissoir*. Freed of not having to worry about upsetting the fairer sex, gentlemen in the need of a call of nature, could whip it out and relieve themselves without having to go outside and run the risk of their seat being taken. It would have been almost considered rude not to avail of such a convenience.'

Jim feared they were in for a practical demonstration, but mercifully, Pete took off to find the gentlemen's room, muttering something about the bloody Dark Ages as he went.

'I've been working with that fella for twenty years, Jim. He's a good mate, but by Christ, he's a lazy bastard.'

Old Bill finished whatever business he had with Max and came over to Jim and Ron. 'Boys, a word of advice, keep the heads down tonight. Don't hang about too late after the fight. There's a bad element rolling into town. Things might get rowdy later. Jim, you're hardly driving home?'

'I'll be grand, Bill. Just going to put the swag down somewhere quiet. You know me. I'll probably be asleep before Douglas comes to.'

'No worries. We'll look after him, Bill. He can stay with us and we'll drop him back here in the morning.'

'Fine by me. I'll swing by tomorrow, Bill, and say hello to Helen, promise. You not staying?'

'Make sure you do, Jim. Anyway, I'm off. I've to go home and mend a fence, so to speak. Be careful, gentlemen.' And with that, Old Bill left.

PETE RETURNED TO the bar whistling to himself. Before taking his seat, he looked down and did a final check. Finding everything in order, he eased himself onto his stool and took one of the three fresh beers Kelly placed in front of them.

'Hey, Max!' Pete shouted up the bar. 'I see we have some undesirables setting up a camp at the oval.'

'How many?'

'I'd say about thirteen, if you count the mamas.'

'Fuck, that's all I need,' Max said, abandoning any idea of getting back into his newspaper. He pushed it aside. 'Kelly, how's about a Bundy for the boss.'

Max watched her pour his drink, while she took an order from one customer and shared a joke with another. She's the only good thing about this place, he thought. Great behind the bar and a nice piece of ass. And the bitch knows it.

Kelly sensed Max staring at her. Without looking up, she pushed the Bundy his way. It was not the first time he made her feel uncomfortable. If he did not owe her three weeks' wages, she would have walked. Instead, she leaned across the bar and flirted with two drillers. It made their day.

CHAPTER 4

READY TO RUMBLE

TWO YOUNG WOMEN in from Balfour Downs Station now helped behind the bar. In the short time it took Jim to have 'a gander' outside
at the bikes, the Aurora had filled. Ron and Pete kept guard over Jim's
barstool. Having invested a few hours settling in ahead of the big fight,
the three men had no intention of surrendering their prime positions
to any latecomers.

'Come on, Irish. It's about to start.' An arm went up, directing Jim
through the crowd and back to his seat.

'Lots of shiny chrome out there. Some nice-looking bikes, all right.
All Harleys, I'm guessing.'

'Did you get a close look?' Pete asked.

'Not bloody likely.'

'Quiet, knuckleheads! They're being introduced.' Done admonish-
ing his companions, Ron adjusted the angle of his stool for the best
view. Next, he removed his hat and placed it on the counter beside his
beer to define his space. He made sure to secure enough room for at

least one elbow. Jim smiled when he noticed the old digger rehearse reaching for the stubby while looking directly up at the screen.

'Everything in order there, Ron?'

'Bloody oath, Irish. Let's be having it.'

The glass bottles clinked when Kelly put three full stubbies on the bar next to Ron's hat. Jim handed over a ten-dollar note to pay for the round. Something about the way their fingers touched, and how she lingered over the exchange, got Jim's attention. He lifted his head and met her beautiful dark eyes looking directly at him, their tapered edges narrowed into an enchanting smile. Jim panicked, but overcame the impulse to look away.

'Thanks,' he said, before doing a Groucho Marx with his eyebrows.

Ah, Christ! What the hell was that? Idiot! Jim scolded himself. Come on. Say something intelligent, fool. If that's not possible, something nice would suffice. Why haven't Ron or Pete piped in and filled the silence?

A customer came to Jim's rescue and shouted for a drink. Kelly turned away. Glancing back in Jim's direction, she drifted along the bar through the smoky air to take the order.

Was that a moment? Jim wondered. Perhaps it was. He twisted the cap off his beer and chugged the liquid down to quell the flutter that had arrived in his stomach. You and your bloody imagination. Don't be daft. Why would she make eyes at you? Jim turned his attention to the television.

The camera focused on Tyson pacing the ring – two hundred and twenty and a half pounds of menace, his gaze fixed on the floor, his expression blank.

'He looks in good shape.'

'Indeed, Ron. Single life must agree with him, but I bet it suits the ex-wife better,' Jim said.

The two heavyweights' statistics scrolled across the screen.

'You know, Tyson is two days younger than me,' Jim added, 'but he's packed a hell of a lot more into his twenty-three years.'

Ron chuckled. 'And possibly been lifting a few more weights than you, too.'

'Brick shithouse,' Pete added. 'Can't say Douglas looks scared, though. He oughta be.'

'Douglas has a twelve-inch reach advantage. That's gotta help,' Jim suggested. Though no student of pugilism, he went on. 'Simple mechanics, height, levers, mass, that kind of stuff.'

'Nah, hasn't a hope,' said Pete, dismissing the notion out of hand. Jim omitted to factor in the intangible force of nature that was Iron Mike Tyson.

'Thirty-seven wins, Jim. Thirty-three by knockout. It wouldn't matter if Douglas were Stretch Armstrong.' Pete had settled it.

It was unlikely anyone in the bar had any real boxing experience. However, as is the nature of a room full mostly with men and a lot of beer, expert opinion proliferated. Regardless of his size, weight advantage and the lack of fear in his eyes, nobody gave James 'Buster' Douglas the slightest chance in hell. The big money saw it lasting a round, maybe two, and then the normal business of the bar would resume. Everyone would settle into the usual pleasant, warm Sunday afternoon into evening at the Aurora. Some in the bar might already have heard the result, but knew better than to say a word.

The ring cleared of dignitaries. The two fighters acknowledged each other before returning to their respective corners to wait the bell.

The television voice of HBO analyst, Larry Merchant, who was in agreement with the Aurora clientele, broke through the excited background chatter in the bar,

... Douglas insists that he is going to shock the world in this fight, and if he should upset Mike Tyson, it would make the shocks in Eastern Europe seem like local ward politics. He would shock most of the world if he could make it into the later rounds.

At the bell, silence fell over the Aurora. Nobody wanted to miss the one punch that would finish it before it started. Tyson tore across the ring and threw out a jab. It landed. The two fighters wrapped each other up and clinched. Tyson hit on the break and got a warning from the Mexican referee, Octavio Meyran. Unfazed, Douglas diligently went about his business. Sugar Ray Leonard, brought in by HBO for his expert insight, noticed how well a slimmer Douglas moved. Anchorman Jim Lampley and Leonard spoke in complimentary terms of Douglas' left jab. There would be no first-round knockout today. By the second round, Tyson was looking puzzled. This was not in his script.

'We're going to get a fight here!' Pete said, peppering with excitement, his movements synchronised to the punches onscreen.

The unexpected start to the fight introduced the faint possibility its result might not be a foregone conclusion. No longer a Tyson exhibition match, people had to decide for the first time who to shout for, who they wanted to win. The volume in the bar rose. En masse, the crowd audibly shifted across to supporting the underdog.

Jim was in two minds. Tyson, with his perfect professional record, was a once in a generation fighter. If not, even more than that. He may not be the nicest of individuals, but he teetered on the cusp of becoming perhaps the greatest heavyweight boxer of all time. That would be something to see. But who doesn't enjoy a great sporting fairy tale, when against all the odds, the underdog triumphs?

One of the many benefits of being Irish was the nation's perennial tag of underdog. Conferred with good reason, it made the rare victory on the international stage all the more special. For the first time in the country's history, the Republic of Ireland had reached the finals of soccer's World Cup. The achievement provoked an enormous groundswell of national pride, and for Jim, some memorable nights out at Sydney's Bondi Junction.

Qualification for Italia 90 meant everything to the Irish. Should they bow out early in the tournament, it didn't really matter. Except of course, Ireland faced England in the first match. Jim feared a thrashing and dreamed of some sort of moral victory. He knew that, short of an exhumation of the brothers Grimm to pen one last fairy tale, nothing would get Ireland past the Saxon foe or the Dutch with their dread-locked assassins who waited in the long grass. All going well, Jim planned to be home in June to enjoy the occasion and firmly embed himself within the green army. Who would want to be West German or Brazilian? Where was the fun in that?

Jim's thoughts turned back to the fight. Impressive as Buster's en-couraging start was, Jim knew the Brothers Grimm would not arise from their graves and add their own ending to today's predictable tale. Before the bell rang for the fourth round, Tyson buried his head into the shoulder of his second, Aaron Snowell. The second hugged him and whispered private words of encouragement in his ear. It became a ritual, a tender moment they shared between rounds and contrasted with the brutality of all the other moments. Douglas landed a big right that caught Tyson square on the chin.

'Ohhh!' A sharp intake of breath sounded around the room.

At first, nobody noticed Clayton Marshall and his sergeant at arms, Big Red, enter. Both formidable men, they strode through the crowd. On seeing them, patrons stepped aside and an unimpeded path to the bar opened up. Marshall rested a large, black, steel-toed work boot on the trough right next to Jim, and supporting himself with his elbows, leaned in on the counter. He glanced along the bar searching for a familiar face. Big Red, a man wider than he was tall, stood to Marshall's right. Two more bikers entered. Marshall's underdressed Old Lady made her way across the floor. She wrapped herself and her long peroxide blond hair around her husband in an over-the-top display of affection. A surly looking young prospect, who Marshall named Pigeon, because of how his head bobbed when he walked, was last in and took up a position at the back of the group.

'Well, if it isn't The Village fucking People,' Max Collins announced to almost the entire room without removing his gaze from the television. The background chatter in the pub stopped.

'Ah! There you are, Max. Good to see you, too. Enjoying your retirement?' Marshall turned to Jim, who had been trying to look inconspicuous and, at the same time, wondering if he should hand over his barstool.

'How's the fight going, citizen?'

Shit, what's the etiquette here? Jim wondered. Do I look him in the eye or keep staring at the TV? Play it cool, mumble a response and follow that up with a spit in the trough? Would he prefer a simple smile, a harmless comment on the nice weather we're having? Perhaps I should regale him with anecdotes of my recent Honda XR 200 troubles.

Leaning a shoulder in slightly, Jim turned his head towards his neighbour. He saw the massive tattooed forearms. Jim's own insignificant arms were folded across a chest so small he could almost shake hands with himself around the back.

'Good, yeah. Douglas is putting it up to him.' Jim didn't chance any eye contact and took a sip of beer to signal he was finished talking.

Round five kicked off with Douglas dominating again. Ray Leonard's voice could be heard over the noise of the Tokyo crowd,

... *Buster definitely seems inspired because of the trauma and the passing of his mother* ...

'Enjoy your holiday in Freo, Clay?' Max shouted over. 'Nothing to do with that riot, I hope.'

'Very pleasant, Max. A nice break. Sea air, plenty of exercise. Can't you tell I've been working out?'

'Could you get our friends a few beers, Kelly? They won't be staying long.'

'Not sure I'd agree with you there, Max. You know how much I enjoy a good fight.'

Jim felt a gentle prod in the ribs. He looked around to see Pete's grinning face.

'Nicely played, Irish.'

The bikies accepted the offer of a beer. Smirking, Marshall raised a tinnie and signalled his appreciation down to the end of the bar. The room relaxed and went back to their drinks and the fight – except for Max. Max pulled out the newspaper again and flicked through it far too quickly to be reading it at all.

Roars of encouragement went up for the underdog once more.

… Another right hand and now Tyson seems to be wobbled …

Every time Jim reached for his beer or, occasionally, when he would switch his gaze to the far television, he would steal a glance at the biker woman. Her behaviour fascinated him, almost as much as her fashion sense. Underneath an open sleeveless jacket, she wore a bra-type thing and a gold chain with a simple cross. Black knee-high boots and the tightest, most immodest shorts completed the ensemble. It would have turned many heads, but for the company she kept. The woman appeared restless, giddy and most probably high on something other than alcohol. She constantly demanded attention from Marshall, who tired of her antics and passed her on to Big Red and Pigeon, neither of whom looked too comfortable with the arrangement.

In large, yellow block-lettering sewn into the back of her jacket were the words: PROPERTY OF PUPPET MASTER CLAY. Jim wondered … was it a charming declaration of her love for her man or something altogether more sinister? If what Nigel, one of the shearers, told him was true, Clay owned her. Nigel seemed knowledgeable on all matters bikie and claimed to be saving for a Harley. He loaned Jim a few dog-eared editions of *Easyriders* magazine as proof of his bona fides. Jim was inclined to believe him and his nauseating assertion that women were the property of the bikie gangs. It always amused Jim that Australians used the endearing term 'bikie' for the vicious outlaw motorcycle gangs that roamed the streets and endless empty highways of Australia.

What might have started out as a great rebellious adventure for an attractive young girl had over the years, it seemed to Jim, turned sour. He pitied her and hoped his first impressions were wrong. The woman spied Jim watching her. Fearful she might take his head off, he looked away. She blew him a kiss and then, laughing, bumped against Big Red, spilling his drink. Although none too pleased, Big Red forced a smile, when the woman tried to dab him dry with a beer mat.

Tyson came out for the sixth with a swelling over his left eye.

'Jim, here … I've been meaning to give you this.' Ron reached into a shirt pocket and produced his emergency spare stubby holder. He popped it into shape and placed it on the bar. Printed across the small neoprene cylinder, the word 'Ozdrill' overlaid a stylised map of Australia. 'For God's sake, you gotta keep your beer cold, mate. Can't be drinking warm piss like them Poms!'

'Brilliant. Ta. It's still bloody hot in here, all right.'

'How do you manage at the treehouse?'

'I don't. Can't stomach lukewarm beer. Even warm minerals and water don't go down easy. The water is only cold when it's straight from the well. Hot tea is my usual tipple. Actually, I've tried to make a Coolgardie fridge, but it doesn't work.'

Ron wasn't sure what Jim meant by 'minerals', but let it pass. 'Ah, you're mucking around, mate. Too complicated. Have you tried a sock?'

'What?'

'Put a can in a wet sock and hang it in a tree. Come back in half an hour and bonzer!'

'Fair dinkum?' An expression Jim liked, but only ever met one real-life Australian who used it. 'No way. Too easy.'

'Yep, make sure you try it,' Ron said, prodding Jim with an index finger to the shoulder. He was imparting important information, important bushcraft, and wanted to be sure Jim understood that. Ron took a sip of his beer and nodded towards the screen. 'Two of the best haircuts in the business there in the front row.'

When the camera came in close to the fighters, the television audience could see the serious-looking suits in the expensive seats behind the ropes.

'Huh?'

'King and Trump there beside each other, in the front.'

'Ah, the two Donalds.'

'Duck!' Pete shouted, as Tyson attempted to unleash a big left.

The seventh round ended and the teams busied themselves, encouraging their men, cooling them down.

The jab's the shot, Baby, said Douglas's second, while smearing his fighter's head with a thick layer of grease. *Tyson's running scared.*

'Hey, Max! I need a few slabs of beer for the camp.' Marshall worked his way over to the end of the bar.

'The bottle shop is closed. You know it's illegal for me to sell take-out now.'

Marshall sat on a stool that had promptly become available beside Max and adopted the posture of a good mate in jovial conversation.

'You're the man around here, Max. When did the law ever stop you doing anything?' A smug grin formed across his wind-burned face. 'Anyway, I wasn't planning on paying for it.'

Max grunted something incomprehensible, while drawing on a cigarette. However, a look of disdain made it perfectly clear what he thought of the bikie's legal loophole.

'Ah look, Maximilian. Best give us the beer. Otherwise, you'll have ten more thirsty and unruly brothers in here upsetting your nice customers. Believe me. You're better off if they stay outside.'

Marshall's request seemed reasonable to anyone within earshot.

'Because it's you, Clay ... to celebrate your recent release from incarceration ... Sure, why not? Consider it a gift.' Extravagantly, Max instructed Kelly to open the bottle shop and 'grab five crates of anything cold for our friends here'.

Eager for a break from the stifling heat behind the bar, Kelly did not hang about and ducked under the counter hatch and out the side door. Jim wondered if she would appreciate some help. For a few diffident seconds, he debated the merits of the idea and, after downing a fortifying swig of beer, he slipped off his barstool. One step later, he overheard Big Red order Pigeon after Kelly. Disappointed, though slightly relieved, Jim casually stretched his back and shoulders before remounting the stool.

'And ice!' Marshall shouted to Pigeon and sent his Old Lady out to help – glad to be shot of her for a while.

Before returning to Big Red, Marshall moved in closer and eye-balled Max. Barely an inch separated the two men's faces. 'I want to talk to you in the morning, mate. Make sure you're still here.' Then louder, so those around could hear. 'Thanks, brother. When we run out, my man Pigeon may be back for more.'

The atmosphere in the bar had changed again. Almost everyone, except probably Pete, kept one nervous eye on the exchange and the other on the fight, but as soon as Pigeon went to collect the crates from Kelly, the air of palpable tension eased.

'What's up with that fella's head?' Pete asked indiscreetly when Pigeon bobbed past. 'Never seen anything like that nod before.'

'They call him Pigeon,' Jim said, with more consideration as to how his voice might carry.

'Ah! He's a flaming galah, if you ask me!'

Onscreen, Jim Lampley got very excited.

We're in the eighth round, folks. A heavyweight champion, regarded as completely invincible in these circumstances, is in big trouble … Could you imagine Buster Douglas as undisputed heavyweight champion of the world? It boggles the mind.

'Woooh!' Above the background chatter, the snap of a glove connecting with a chin resonated. A dejected sigh ran through the bar. Douglas lay on the canvas. Normality returned. It looked like the fall of the Berlin Wall would remain the big story.

As soon as Douglas' shoulders hit the canvas, the official ringside timekeeper put a white-gloved index finger in the air and started the count. Douglas rolled onto his right elbow, took a breath and punched the floor with his left glove in dazed disgust. Meyran, the referee, got down on one knee beside him and bellowed his own count into the face of the stricken fighter. There was a two-second difference between the timekeeper's count and Meyran's. The referee looked to both corners when he got to six. Douglas stayed down to gather himself. On Meyran's seven, Douglas made it onto his knees. By nine, he was just about vertical.

He got a little over-confident. He got a little loosey goosey …

The official timekeeper counted him out, but referee Meyran had Douglas up at ten and deemed him well enough to continue. The referee clapped, 'OK!' and signalled to Tyson to come back in from the neutral corner. Tyson came forward, eager to end it. The bell sounded. Douglas, shaking his head, staggered back to his corner. He would need all sixty seconds to recover.

Tyson came out for the ninth, ready to put an end to this impertinence. Douglas met him with a left jab. He was not finished yet. Tyson kept coming forward, kept attacking. Douglas moved well, considering his legs had gone from under him not much more than a minute before. They stood toe-to-toe and exchanged big punches, both fighters too exhausted to move out of the way. Tyson's swollen left eye much worse now.

With one minute remaining on the clock, Douglas found a reserve of energy from somewhere and got off a brutal combination of punches. Hurt, Tyson grabbed the ropes. Sensing something was about to happen, hordes of press photographers leaned in across the base of the ring, their lenses focused on the faltering fighter. Tyson hung on, waiting for the bell. 'Ding!' It came to the rescue.

Jim Lampley summed up the ninth on the television.

The most action-filled, heavy-punching exchange round of Mike Tyson's career.

The crowd at the Tokyo venue remained silent. The commentators put it down to Japanese reserve. But the boisterous miners of the Aurora were quiet, too. Nobody believed what they just witnessed. Douglas had come back from the canvas at the end of the eighth and, in the next round, nearly put Tyson down for the first time in his professional career.

Jim leaned across to Pete and elbowed him to get his attention. 'Jaysus! I've not seen anything like that since Apollo Creed beat Balboa on a split decision in '76!'

Pete laughed. The two bikers who overheard Jim did too, and far too loudly for Jim's liking. He prayed his comment would not instigate another exchange.

All Tyson's corner could do now was hold an ice-filled rubber glove to their man's closed left eye and hope. Despite the heightened excitement, Max still showed no interest in the fight. Giving up on the paper again, he sat on his barstool chain-smoking and stared blankly at the tiny flame of his lighter as he flicked it on and off.

The bell sounded for the tenth. Tyson shuffled out to face his foe. Douglas looked fresh. Larry Merchant observed from his vantage point ringside,

It appears that Tyson is virtually a one-eyed fighter at this point.

His colleague added,

A desperate one-eyed fighter …

Douglas landed five straight jabs. Tyson offered no defence. Douglas dipped his right shoulder and, in one brutal movement, released everything behind a right uppercut. It sent Tyson's head violently back. The champion's legs went from under him. He was going down. Tyson was still falling, when a powerful left hook changed the trajectory of his fall, driving him backwards. Douglas kept attacking. He landed a long right. Tyson fell quicker now, his torpid frame almost horizontal, when a final left sent him crashing to the canvas.

He landed on his back in Douglas's corner, his head out of the ropes. The referee got down on one knee again. He looked straight into Tyson's eyes assessing the fighter's condition and began the count. On three seconds, Tyson moved. He rolled onto his right elbow. By the count of five, he got clumsily to his knees. He groped for his mouth guard with his right glove and shoved it back sideways into his mouth on seven. If he had his wits about him, he would have left it for Meyran to pick up and thereby steal precious extra seconds. Still operating on instinct, Tyson tried to drink in oxygen from the stale Tokyo morning air and regain his senses. His vacant expression told a story. At nine, he put weight on his left leg and tried to stand. He stumbled. Octavio Meyran, with both arms outstretched, signalled it was over. He wrapped Tyson in an embrace to hold him up and to comfort him. Meyran rocked the broken hulk of a man from side to side. Both were thankful it had ended. Mayhem ensued around them.

After a moment of shocked silence, the Aurora erupted in cheers. Jim was no longer torn. Nobody, not even Don King, could begrudge James Buster Douglas his extraordinary victory. Douglas had achieved the unimaginable. He stood with his arms aloft, the new Undisputed Heavyweight Champion of the World. The new champion had done it for his recently deceased mother and his God.

Letting his guard down a little, Jim thumped the air in delight and to the amusement of those within earshot, he uttered what could only have been interpreted as a battle cry.

'Bring on the English!'

* * *

THE COIN DROPPED. 'Hey, Dad. Did you see the fight? Tyson lost! Can't believe it!'

'Yeah, heard the result. Couldn't get it on the telly here. Was it a good fight?'

'Ah, yeah. Brilliant. Vicious though.'

'You're still at the pub, then? Hope you're not driving anywhere now.'

'Nah! No, no. I'm going to stay the night. I've fallen into bad company, I'm afraid. Hey! What about Mandela? That's something else. It's just been on the news here.'

'Yes. I almost didn't recognise him. He's a frail old man now.'

'Yeah, nothing like that photo they always use. Did you notice the first hand he shook when he came out was a white man's?'

'I did indeed, showed class. I think he will do all right.'

'Steve Biko would have been pleased … if the bastards hadn't killed him. How'd the unveiling go?'

A BEAUTIFUL EVENING fell over the Goldfields. Low on the horizon, a thin speckled band of iridescent purple, pink and orange cloud picked out the last of the sun's rays like the scales of a colourful serpent. Jim was in great form. It had been a good day. On his way back from the payphone, he did a lap of the Aurora verandah to enjoy more of the sunset and the warm, fresh air. The good news and the beer had him singing to himself.

As usual, the words eluded him. It was more of a hum and interspersed sporadically with 'Free Nelson Mandela'. How, he asked, could the whole bar watch two black boxers go at each other for ten rounds without anyone commenting once on skin colour or race? Yet as soon as the news came on of Mandela's release, there were snide comments thrown about, mainly by the bikers. Big Red's suggestion that the 'fucking coon should have been left to rot in his cell' was extraordinary and, for a fraction of a second, Jim considered challenging him on it. Thankfully, the bikers had now fucked off back to their camp. 'Free … Nelson Mandela.' It annoyed Jim that he couldn't remember the words, but it did not stop him humming the tune.

A muffled cry came from the bottle shop – a grandiose description for the pokey storeroom around the back, next to the slightly bigger storeroom that was the Aurora Grocery & Supply Store. Jim paused outside. He heard a crash. Sticking his head around the open door, he saw Kelly pinned against a stack of beer cartons. Someone he recognised as Pigeon stood in front of her. Pigeon had one hand inside Kelly's top and the other over her mouth.

'Oops, sorry!' Jim assumed he had interrupted an intimate moment and started to back out. Then it struck him – Kelly was trying to push Pigeon away. He saw her kick the biker's shins. Unperturbed, Pigeon stepped forward and buried his head into Kelly's neck.

'Oi! What the fuck are ye doing?'

The biker flashed Jim a piercing cold stare. Pigeon was not a big man, but he was bigger than Jim and not at all happy about being challenged.

'Do yourself a favour, boy, and fuck off outta here!'

'No! Leave her alone!' With trembling legs, but full of Dutch courage from an afternoon in the bar, Jim just about stood his ground. He hoped his shorts were long enough to conceal his fear.

Fighting to pull the bikie's hand from her mouth, Kelly shook her head from side to side. Her animated eyes implored Jim to leave. Now there was a witness, she believed the assault would end – no need for anyone else to get hurt.

Jim felt himself take a step forward. 'Come on, Kelly. Let's go back to the bar.'

Pigeon lunged and landed a heavy right hand into the Irishman's chest. It knocked the air from Jim's lungs. He stumbled backwards and collapsed.

'Fuck you!' Jim wheezed, while trying to catch a breath and get to his feet. 'Kelly, let's go. Come on!'

'You're beginning to piss me off, Irishman.'

Pigeon threw a stubbie of beer at Jim's head. Jim dodged it and charged low at his attacker, knocking him into the same stack of beer Pigeon had pinned Kelly against moments earlier. The two men fell. Cans spilled across the floor. Arcs of spray shot from one as it catherine-wheeled out the door. Pigeon got to his feet first and planted a tirade of heavy kicks into Jim's back. Then, grabbing an antique-green wine bottle by the neck, he smashed the base against the edge of the brick door frame. Shards of glass and wine sprayed over the wall. Streams poured down, colouring the floor crimson.

'I'm going to cut you open, boy.'

The bikie bent over and grabbed the prostrate young man by the hair. He dragged Jim's head back, lifting it about a foot off the floor. In the movement, Jim caught a glimpse of Kelly holding a crate of beer above her head. He braced for when it would come crashing down and the chance to pull free. Pigeon swung a leg over Jim's shoulders and stood bent, as if to shear a sheep. Trapping Jim's head tight against the inside of his thigh, he then made to fillet the side of Jim's face with the shark-toothed edge of the broken wine bottle. Jim could smell the oily filth of the man. The glare from the room's bare light bulb danced across Jim's eyes, leaving comet tails in its wake. Everything went blurred. He had no idea what was to come or why Kelly had not followed through.

Then, before drawing blood, Pigeon stopped. Something cold pressed hard against his temple.

'Don't fucking move, son.'

Max had his .38 standard issue, Smith and Wesson Model 10 revolver in his outstretched hand and a mad look in his eyes that said he wanted to use it.

* * *

HAVING ANNOUNCED HE was closing the bar early, Max again manned his post at the end of the counter. People were drifting off when Jim, now cleaned up, returned from the ablution block. He went straight over to Max.

'Thanks again. Thanks for that, mate.'

'Look, no worries. Anyway, that scumbag deserves more than a good scare. You staying here tonight?'

'Nah, I'm planning to sleep out under the stars.'

'Ah look, son! Do you want a room? We have dongas out the back. Kelly, get a key for your knight in shining armour friend here. I suppose the least we can do is give him a soft mattress for the night.'

'OK. Great, thanks. That's very decent of you.'

'C'mon, Jim. I'll get you sorted,' Kelly said, pleased Jim took Max up on the offer.

'One second.' Jim went over to Pete and Ron, who were already up to speed on all the excitement. 'Lads, it's been a pleasure. Thanks for the company. I think I need to go lie down.'

The three men shook hands. Ron extended an open invitation for Jim to call to their camp and promised to give him the guided tour. The two old diggers were keen to see his paintings.

'Yeah, I'd like that,' Jim said. 'Perhaps the two of you might sit and have your portraits done. I'd enjoy the challenge.'

Jim got a key from Kelly and headed out to grab his gear from behind the seat of the Ford.

'KELLY, WHO HAVE we in tonight?' Max asked once they were alone.

'No one, except for Jim. I think the bikies scared them all away. Even Chef has gone into Hay Street for the night.'

'Randy git. Off with yourself. I'll do the tills and lock up. Unless you fancy staying for a drink?'

'I'll pass, Max. It's been a long day.'

'OK. See you in the morning.'

* * *

OUTSIDE THE PERSPEX window, a few hardy miners passed by on their long walk back to the mine-site accommodation. The last of the Land

Cruisers that were parked out front of the inn moved off. Jim swayed slightly while waiting. Unlike earlier, the ringtone sounded far away. Then the operator spoke.

'Would you accept a collect call from a Jim Macken in Australia?'

'Yes, of course.'

'Go ahead, Sir.'

'Me again, Dad. I'm off to bed now. I need a good kip. Ye know, I think I've had enough.'

'Beer?'

'No. Yeah, maybe that too. I'm a little unsteady on the feet all right. God, I'd love a cup of tea. No, what I mean ... I've had enough of this place. I think I'll come home.'

'You all right? You sound a bit down?'

'Nah, I'm grand. Just tired.'

'You know there is always a room here.'

'Ah, yeah. Think I'll look into college when I'm back. Are there any special arrangements for mature students who can't spell? Would I qualify for a grant? Am I even mature? Probably not. Might do something with the art, maybe even rocks, geology ... if it's done anywhere in Ireland. I'll sleep on it, Dad.'

'Yeah, worth looking into son and you know we would help, but best go to bed now.'

'That was great about Mandela. Tell everyone I love them.'

Jim hung up abruptly and shouldered open the phone box door. The glow from the biker's campfire lit up the night sky behind the inn. The noise from someone over that way trying to burn out a tyre on the dirt disturbed the peace.

'Wasters!' Jim mumbled. 'With any luck, you fuckers'll be gone by morning.'

Max had reassured him there would be no more trouble from Pigeon. Kelly seemed to be pretty much over her ordeal, too. Jim suspected she was made of tougher stuff than him. On a different night, and with much less beer on board, he might have stayed to talk to her, or at least tried. But he needed sleep and she didn't need another drunken idiot annoying her. Careful with his faltering steps, he wandered down the unlit road, hoping he could muster the nerve to talk to her in the morning and that she would be kind enough to tolerate his awkward attempts at conversation.

He may have forgotten about the free bed or did not fancy the walk back up the hill. Whatever the reason, when Jim finally reached the Ford, he climbed inside and stretched out across the single seat. With his head hanging below the steering wheel and feet protruding from the gap where a passenger door once belonged, he closed his eyes. As comfortable as only someone who had drunk quite an amount of beer and with a possible cracked rib or two could be, he fell asleep. Jim was out for the count.

* * *

MAX COLLINS SAT in the darkened pub alone with his thoughts and a near empty glass of Bundaberg in his hand. On the counter in front of him was a packet of Winfield Blue cigarettes, a calico bag with the night's takings and his gun. Outside, the bikes roared up and down the dirt road. The sins of the past were catching up with Max.

Just who the hell does that greasy gimp of a bikie think he is, coming here to my business and trying to intimidate me? Marshall's sneering, taunting face occupied the dark corners of Max's mind. If Marshall and his mates had to be the fall guys for a deal that went bad, so be it. The scumbag should have manned up and accepted it. If he had a grievance, there were channels he could have gone through.

'Not this way,' Max whispered, before downing his rum.

And Kelly, she in her own subtle way tormented Max, too. It was time to put his affairs in order. If that meant going back into the swamp, so be it. It would be on his own terms.

CHAPTER 5

FIRE AND MOONLIGHT

T HE BONFIRE CRACKLED and spat as the sap in the wood boiled in the heat of the flames. Several small trees went into its making. The blaze cast a dancing play of dandelion orange and yellow light over the figures gathered around. Warm highlights set against the black of the shadows evoked a Caravaggio painting. The raucousness of earlier had died down. The engines were shut off and the drag racing along the road stopped. The bikers chatted, drank, smoked, did lines and had sex. Two women danced naked to the sound of Michael Hutchence and his 'Devil Inside' on a portable radio. Pigeon was charged with the task of keeping the fire fuelled and a fresh beer within easy reach of the full-patched members.

The President of the Puppet Masters 1%er Motorcycle Club, Clayton Marshall, had enjoyed winding Collins up and looked forward to progressing matters in the morning. Collins owed him, owed him big. It was time to collect. Pleased with himself, Marshall shuffled closer to the fire. After rotting away in that dingy cell, it was great to be out and on the open road with the bike again.

'You all right there, Pigeon?' Marshall asked, when Pigeon dropped another large branch on the flames, releasing thousands of ephemeral orange stars into the sky. 'You've gone quiet, brother. Hey Red! Does Pigeon look shook to you?'

Pigeon replied before Big Red could get a word in. 'Nah, just going about my business, Clay, making sure you don't get cold or go dry.'

'First time having a shooter pulled on you, mate?' Big Red asked.

'He'll get used to it. It's only a problem when they pull the trigger.'

'That's easy for you to say, Clay. You've been to war!'

Pigeon knew Marshall liked it when people acknowledged his service. It was often enough to steer the conversation away from anything else.

In '65, barely twenty years old, the Federal Government conscripted Marshall into the army. The following year, while going 'All the way with LBJ', Prime Minister Harold Holt shipped him off to Southeast Asia. At the Battle of Long Tan, Marshall watched eighteen of his compatriots die. Demobbed, he found himself in Western Australia working as a boilermaker in the mines of Kalgoorlie and got into motorbikes.

The belief of many Australians that the Vietnam veterans did not fight a 'real war' disappointed Marshall. That many World War II old-timers felt the same particularly hurt. Marshall turned his back on conventional society, moved to East Perth and founded The Puppet Masters. Years of living by the strict, self-imposed culture of low standards fostered in the outlaw motorcycle community had hardened him to a life outside the law. The bikies organised themselves by a rank-and-file structure similar to the one that served many of them well in the forces. With The Puppet Masters, Marshall recreated a band of brothers, who would kill and die for each other.

'Eh, Red. He's doing all right, isn't he? Showed class there today. Anyone who can upset Max Collins that much has earned his patches in my book. Can't be long now, Pigeon, before you get voted in.'

'Won't have to take any more of our shit, then!' Big Red added. 'Well, not so much.'

Pigeon forced a laugh and bobbed off for more firewood.

* * *

BEHIND THE ACCOMMODATION block, hidden by scrub, a patch of open ground rose a little higher than the surrounding area. It might well have been a spoil heap left from the dry blower days. Some time ago, Kelly found an old car seat and dragged it against a tree stump at the edge of the clearing. If ever she needed to get away or just wanted to look at the stars, it was here she would come. The best thing about working in outback Western Australia is the stars. To be honest, the only good thing, she believed. One magical night, Kelly had sat for hours enjoying a rare display of the Southern Lights at this latitude. For her alone, the sky glowed and danced a beautiful emerald green.

Unable to sleep, Kelly took the short walk out past the accommodation block to her secret seat beside the stump. The moon shone bright, but the stars were still spectacular. Looking up, her tears glistened in the moonlight. The trauma of the assault affected her more than she cared to admit. Back in her claustrophobic room, it all came out. Kelly knew rough times in her young life and always resolved to bounce back from them stronger. However, she was not as tough as she liked to put out there. Despite Max's assurances, Kelly still worried. Bikies, she suspected, do not take kindly to having a gun pointed at them.

Max unsettled her too. She didn't like how there were no other staff staying tonight. She asked Cook to hang around, but he refused.

Kelly didn't like being owed money and, seeing how the takings were so good today, she cursed herself for not bringing the matter up with Max when she had the chance. In fairness, after what happened, she just wanted out of there.

Some weeks ago, a slick and persistent young shot-firer from the mine, unaware of the inn owner's reputation, slipped a small bag of grass and a packet of rolling papers into Kelly's hand. Not wanting to make a scene across the bar, she took the package. Kelly might have appreciated the gift back in Melbourne, but not now. She didn't bother with that kind of thing anymore. Hidden in the bottom drawer of her bedside locker, the grass remained untouched and forgotten until tonight. Maybe a smoke would help. She didn't like that she knew it wouldn't.

She liked Jim though, and considered knocking on his door when passing. Kelly wanted to pour her soul out to someone and he struck her as a good listener. Hell, she would have just liked to lie beside him and have him put an arm around her. But he was well on by the end of the night. Chances were, she may not have been able to wake him. She didn't like that she didn't try. Kelly reached into the back pocket of her cut-off jeans for the grass. Then someone called her name.

'Kelly! Kelly, are you awake? We need to talk.'

Loud bangs on a door followed.

Jesus. It's Max! He's actually come looking for me. Her donga was not visible from the old car seat, but Kelly knew that voice well. It got louder.

'Come on, Kelly! Open the door, for fuck sake! I just want to talk.'

Max calling to her room at night didn't frighten her. It probably should have, but it did make her skin crawl. She could take his leery stares and inappropriate comments, but not this. Shit! That's it. I'm leaving in the morning, she told herself. And if that dickhead has left anything in the till, I'm taking it with me.

All went quiet down at the accommodation block. Max must have gone, she thought. Kelly relaxed, made tentative plans, curled up in the seat and closed her eyes.

* * *

THE DARKLY DRESSED figure lingered a moment at the back of the small stone bungalow next to the inn and tipped his face to the sky. He felt no breeze on his cheeks – that would help, he knew. In one hand, he carried a brown leather sports holdall. A grey rifle case hung over a shoulder. Pulling on a black baseball cap to hide a crop of white hair from the moonlight, Max walked on.

At the Land Cruiser parked behind the fence, he put the holdall on the passenger seat and, with the stock end to the floor, propped the rifle case against the inside of the passenger door. Walking around to the driver's side, he tapped the water tank bolted under the Toyota's tray. It sounded full. Max then levered himself silently into the driver's seat and clicked the door shut. The engine started. With its headlights off, the vehicle meandered a well-used narrow trail from the back of the bungalow out onto one of the mine access roads. Max knew that, come morning, every ore truck that lumbered this way would cover all tracks made in the night.

Not far out of town, Max brought the vehicle to a stop on the side of the road. Stepping out, he slung the rifle case over his shoulder again and, sticking to the tyre tracks, walked back the way he came. He felt his heart beat fast – too fast. He needed it to slow down. The rum should have calmed him. It had not, but it did help him see things clearly.

Arriving in town, Max stepped off the road onto a patch of rocky calcrete. Careful not to leave footprints, he stayed to the hard ground and hurried across to the battery. Passing tourists, indifferent to the fence, had left their many footprints in the dust around the entrance. Not concerned about adding to these, he slipped through the loosely chained gate. Avoiding the twisted sheets of corrugated iron lying about, he mounted the metal steps into the bowels of the machine. Max made his way by torchlight over to a tall ladder and nimbly climbed to the top floor. He pushed the rifle bag through an upper-storey window and lowered it onto a broad exterior ledge. He then clambered out after it.

On a dead calm and clear night, Max admired the sweeping panorama before him. The moon, a day past full, shone brightly, casting strong shadows. Had it been yesterday, he would have to deal with a total lunar eclipse, probably making his task impossible. Some way off, there were lights on over at the BHP operation. The inn and the few old prospector huts scattered through the bush were shadows, except for the silver moonlight reflecting off the roofs. The bikies' fire, however, glowed bright, illuminating the scene at the oval. Clearly visible, people sat around the fire. He calculated they were about three hundred metres away. Unzipping the bag, Max went about his business.

* * *

SOMEWHERE AROUND THE back of the throat close to the tonsils, something, probably a gland, on receiving a message from below, adds a chemical signal to the saliva. Once released, this modified saliva trickles over the base of the tongue and alerts the sleeping, or perhaps inebriated, brain to what is coming next. Jim woke to the realisation that his early warning system had kicked in. Unfortunately, the volume of beer consumed earlier slowed the brains response to the signal.

Luckily, his head, much like when Tyson hit the canvas, already hung out over the side of the Ford. For the first time he appreciated the lack of doors. His eyes opened about halfway, his woozy head lifted and his slack jaw dropped. The muscles in his stomach twisted into involuntary spasm. Steak and beer sprayed from his mouth, splashing onto the ground with such ferocity the mixture blasted a depression into the soil. Jim's ribs hurt more with every retch. Eventually there was nothing left.

Unable to move, Jim remained face down across the seat, feeling sorry for himself. A feeble whimper emanated from his lips. He heard his mother's voice chastise him. 'You only have yourself to blame!' The light from the moon reflected off the pond he had created below the door frame. No way was he going to spend the rest of the night looking down on that! The smell alone would initiate the production of more.

With his left hand, Jim groped for the handbrake and pushed it down. The Ford rolled forward. Old Bill always recommended parking on a hill if possible. When not in use on the station, all his knockabout Land Cruisers and the Ford, lived up on 'Battery Hill' behind the homestead. A shrill tearing sound preceded a reverberating clatter. The side of the Ford had ripped a rusty panel off one of the derelict coaches. Buckled, the panel fell over the Ford's tray. The noise barely registered with the occupant of the cab. Having wedged itself between the two coaches, the truck stopped. Jim pulled the handbrake and he soon slept again, to dream of mugs of milky tea, gold and biker women.

* * *

EVERYTHING FELT STABLE. He lay prone behind the British-made Parker-Hale M82. The muzzle of the 28-inch chrome molybdenum steel barrel stuck out a few inches over the edge of the building. A bipod attached to the sling stud supported the front of the rifle. The butt of the beautifully shaped and polished walnut stock nestled into Max's shoulder. He rested his right cheek on top of the stock, while his left arm, folded underneath, provided a firm, accommodating base.

Max acquired the gun years before during a raid and was delighted with his good fortune at the time. Later, he added the expensive 'good glass' German scope with its large ocular lens and illuminated reticule.

The rifle had served him well on the range and on many adventures in the bush. His peers considered him a good shot, as did he.

With the moon and firelight in play, the shot was just about achievable. Max knew in this light he was pushing the limits of the scope and his ability as a marksman. He positioned his right eye in line and two centimetres back from the eyepiece. He paused to brush a stray eyebrow hair out of the way and reset.

The distant shadows drew nearer. Just off to the right of the fire, he recognised the distinctive bald head of Marshall. Clearly visible in the scope, the sneering skull of the puppet logo on the back of Marshall's 'cut' taunted Max. To Marshall's left, he made out the unmistakable bulk of Big Red and his greying mop of faded red hair. Max's gloved right hand comfortably held the curved pistol grip of the stock. His index finger wrapped gently around the underslung trigger. He did the maths. He adjusted. He listened to his breathing. His heartbeat slowed. He inhaled, then released a gentle, alcohol-fuelled breath.

He waited. Inhaled again. He blinked one last time, then focused on the reticule. Another beat of the heart. When the slack between beats aligned with the pause in breath, Max increased pressure on the trigger. The gun fired. There was a slight recoil. He continued to pull through the trigger. There were no sudden movements on his part.

Something happened with the target at the moment of release, but he knew he scored a hit. There was spray. With a flick of his index finger, he lifted the bolt handle. The bolt slipped back to his thumb, dropping the spent 7.62 NATO cartridge onto the ledge. Max picked it up and packed the rifle away. He then left through the window and retraced his steps.

* * *

MARSHALL WAVED AN empty can in the air. Pigeon collected two cool ones from the ice and brought them over. Pigeon sat down beside his president and, leaning forward, placed the tins in front of them. Their shoulders touched. Marshall moved.

Pigeon felt pressure in the back of his head, followed for a split second by an oozing, popping sensation between his ears. And then oblivion. The bullet had smashed through the skull and shattered numerous teeth along with the lower jawbone as it exited. Pigeon's body began to shut down and descend back into the infinity of nothing. The same nothing from which his beautiful unborn son would soon emerge. The many hours they were to have spent together restoring old bangers would never happen. His long, contented retirement fishing out of Kalbarri never got the chance to become a dream.

* * *

WAS THAT A scream? No, surely not. Kelly put it down to a dream. But there it was again, a lingering, high-pitched wail off in the distance. It sent shivers through her bones. She knew that sound. The memory never leaves you. She tried to dismiss it as rekindled hijinks over at the bikie camp, but her conscience would not allow it. Something terrible had happened. Stay away! Don't get involved! It's none of your business, she told herself.

However, almost immediately, and against her better judgement, Kelly got out of the chair and made her way down past the dongas. Sneaking into the beer garden, she tiptoed around the verandah to the front of the pub. A little way off at the bikie camp on the oval, dark figures dashed for their bikes in the dim light of the dampened fire. Motors revved. Thankfully, the screaming had stopped. Keeping to the shadows and hurrying between breaks in vegetation, Kelly crept closer to the oval and a better view.

All but one motorbike had moved off the open ground. They now stood abandoned at the far tree line. Except for a lone figure kneeling by the dying fire, none of the bikies were visible. Then without warning, a

Harley carrying a pillion passenger, burst through the trees and roared past her. A startled sharp breath drew the engine's exhaust fumes into her lungs. Kelly backed deeper into a bush allowing its thick branches to envelop her. The bike raced off in the direction of the BHP mine. Whatever had happened obviously agitated, indeed scared, the bikies into breaking camp.

The faint sound of angry voices drifted out from the trees. Kelly watched on with mounting apprehension. Eventually, and without its passenger, the bike returned from the mine. A white Land Cruiser troop carrier followed behind. The troopie stopped by the fire, where the driver and the kneeling figure lifted what appeared to be a body into the back and laid it flat on the floor.

The vehicle left with its grim cargo and headed for the trees and the bikes. Someone removed a jerry can from the front passenger seat. Behind the cover of the troop carrier, individuals emerged and remounted their bikes. Engines revved. The noise level escalated. Before Kelly could comprehend what was happening, nine Harleys, some with passengers, streamed out from behind the troopie and rolled full-throttle across the oval towards the inn. The troopie sped off along the tree line and onto the Kalgoorlie road.

Breaking formation, the bikes moved in wide random arcs, picked out by the headlamp beams, sweeping into each other's dust trails. Kelly stepped farther back into the scrub. Realising this night of violence was not over, she knew she had to warn Jim.

Kelly started to run. Off to her right, between the trees, she saw the bikies lay siege to the inn and to Max's house. Thankfully, they had yet to show interest in the dongas out back. Cutting through a thick patch of scrub, she made a direct line for the accommodation block. The sharp spinifex grass and low branches tore at her skin, drawing blood, but she felt nothing.

* * *

Max took one last drag of his cigarette and flicked the butt onto the pile of clothes in the shallow pit. The clothes failed to ignite. He lit a book of matches. It flared, briefly illuminating the scene, before he dropped the burning book in after the cigarette. The fuel-soaked fabric went up immediately. He added dry branches to help things along. Naked, Max stood watching the fire. When everything turned to ash, he back-filled the pit with a short-handle shovel, placing dead wood and strips of bark over the disturbed soil.

Crouching beside the water tank at the side panel of the Land Cruiser, he opened the tap and scrubbed himself clean with a bar of fragrant soap. The water, still warm after yesterday's sun, evaporated off his skin, raising goose pimples and making him shiver. Max spent an inordinate amount of time soaping and rinsing his hands, before getting dressed into the clothes he wore in the bar.

On the ten-kilometre drive back to town, he reached for an orange from the glove compartment. Max always kept a few to clear his throat of dust on a long drive. Holding the steering wheel with his knees, he peeled and ate the orange. From a long way out, he could see the fires.

* * *

It came as no surprise Collins was gone. The house burned and Marshall turned his attention to the main building. The bikies forced an entry and scoured the place for the proprietor. On the verandah, another bikie filled old beer bottles with petrol from a jerry can and stuffed fuel-soaked rags into the bottlenecks. He lit the rags and handed the cocktails out to passing riders.

* * *

Outside the donga, Kelly fumbled with a set of keys, while whispering Jim's name into the door. She feared raising her voice to a level he might hear would attract attention from other quarters. She knew it was pointless, but kept trying. Eventually, the correct key turned in the lock. She opened the door to an empty room and a made-up bed, exactly as she left it that morning. Biting down hard on the fingertips of one hand to choke back any sounds, Kelly stood for a few seconds in the door, staring at the empty bed. Her thoughts turned dark.

She closed the door and then ran to her own donga, where she grabbed a small bag of clothes and the few cherished personal items she owned. Kelly always suspected she might have to leave in a hurry. With remote bar work, it kind of went with the territory, but she could never have imagined her departure would be this dramatic.

She ran back to the hill behind the accommodation block. Looking behind her, an orange glow flickered in the windows of the main building. The pub was burning. Passing the old car seat, she continued on into thick scrub on the far side of the hill. Her head spun. What had they done to Jim? Could that have been him in the troop carrier? What if the bush goes up? Kelly's world had collapsed again. When the trees closed in, she sat down. She wrapped her arms around her bloodied legs and lowered her face onto her knees.

Please, God. Let it pass over me, she prayed.

* * *

Gas cylinders exploding in the heat blew out the kitchen windows. The boom rolled down the hill and inserted itself into the bizarre biker tea party going on in Jim's head. A female guest suggested the explosion had no place in the narrative and it would be best if he woke up. The growl of a passing Harley confirmed her suspicions and Jim opened his eyes. Peeking low through the Ford's narrow back window, it took a moment for his brain to grasp the gravity of what he saw up the hill. The Puppet Masters circled on their bikes, raining fire down on the pub and outbuildings. He watched the phone box deflate and melt into the blackened soil.

Jim recalled news footage from a generation of riots up North. The reports always finished with images of burnt-out buses and cars. He was not breaking cover, but he was not happy about being sandwiched between the two old coaches either. Was this retribution for the incident in the storeroom? Were they looking for him? Then, before utter panic set in, they left. The bikes thundered past in unison and vanished into the dark.

* * *

THE SUN HAD not yet crossed the horizon, but the glow that preceded it pushed over the trees to the east. Searching for some decent music to suit his mood, Max sat in the Land Cruiser and fiddled with the radio, while below at the base of the tailings dump, his town burned. Nothing but Country filled the pre-morning airwaves, prompting Max to turn it off. He held a pair of binoculars to his eyes and watched the bikies ride away. Before turning the key in the ignition, he checked the rifle was well concealed under the flotsam behind the seats. Now he needed to play the victim and tie up the loose ends.

* * *

EXCEPT FOR THE violent sounds of the raging fires, a sort of calm fell over Aurora once more. There were no engines, no voices, no shouts, no cries for help. Smoke hung in the air. Luckily for Jim, the derelict coaches and, by association the Ford, proved beyond combustion. Jim crawled out from between the wrecks, dazed. If not so distracted by what just happened, he would have noticed the pain in his back and a pounding headache. With some dread, he ran towards the pub. On his way up the hill, he saw the dongas ablaze. If anyone had been in there, he could do nothing for them now.

The heat and smoke prevented Jim from getting anywhere close to the inn. The posts supporting the verandah roof looked as if they were about to give. Skirting around the building, he made his way into the beer garden and found a surreal oasis bound on two sides by a wall of flame. Up until now, the lack of breeze had confined the inferno to the buildings, but he feared at any moment a wayward spark could yet ignite the hedging and engulf the garden. He knew not to stay long.

'Hello! Can anyone hear me? Is anyone here?' Jim yelled. And then he saw Max.

'Jesus, Max. Thank God you're all right. Where's Kelly? Is she OK? Was anyone left in there?'

Shoulders hunched, Max sat slumped on a rustic metal bench with a bulky calico bag across his lap. He stared at the ground, his world burning around him. Jim thought he looked smaller, older, even frail. A broken man. A remarkable change in the space of a few hours. Max didn't reply. Jim tried again.

'Max, have you seen Kelly? Was anyone else staying here? Is Kelly OK?'

'Ah look, mate, I'm sorry. I haven't seen her. For all I know, she's in there. I thought she might be with you. You know what she's like!'

'What?'

Max put his hands on his head, took a deep breath and sat up straight. Taking his time, he ran his palms down over his face, while weighing up his options. He appeared to be getting himself together. 'That's your Ford down the hill? You're a backpacker, right?'

'Yeah.' Jim began to lose patience. Understandably, the man was upset, but there was no urgency about Max and what the bloody hell has being a backpacker got to do with anything? 'OK, Max. I'm going to have a look about, see if I can find her. Was anybody else staying here last night?'

'No … No, just Kelly and you. Wait! Here eat this. It'll help with the smoke.' He produced an orange from his jacket pocket and threw it to Jim.

'I'll take it with me.' Jim turned to walk away.

'No, you will peel it now and eat it.'

There was a coldness to the man's voice. Jim looked back. Max stood with a pistol in his hand.

'Eat the fucking orange!'

'Jesus Christ, Max. Take it easy.' He's fucking lost it, Jim thought. Max didn't seem in any way concerned about the missing girl. 'Is this about Kelly? I wasn't with her, I swear. And I'm sorry if what the bikers did to this place was in any way related to my actions last night. You got to believe me and we need to look for Kelly.'

'I told you to eat the fucking orange.'

'OK. OK. I'll eat it.' Jim's hands shook. He peeled and ate the orange. It tasted sweet, but the juice stung his mouth. The stomach acid of earlier and the dry, smoky air had opened small lesions in his throat. He gagged and thought he might be sick again. But nothing came up.

The jigsaw pieces were falling into place in Max's mind. 'It appears someone shot a bikie here last night and I figure it must have been you. I bet you were pissed about what went on in the bottle shop. Yeah, and you didn't like being humiliated in front of the girl. Wouldn't be surprised if the two of you even concocted the plan together, or maybe you did it just to impress her. Isn't that the truth, mate?'

'What! That's bullshit. I was asleep in my truck all night.'

'Can anyone confirm that? I think not!'

'I don't have a gun.'

'If you have shot no one, why corrupt a residue test with the orange? That will look a tad suspicious, won't it? Ah, look. The no gun thing can be sorted. I'll make sure of it. My mates might find something in that wreck of a truck of yours. You see, I'm the law around here and if I say it happened like that, then that's the way it went down.'

Max paused and took a deep breath. 'Look, mate. You wouldn't be the first backpacker to go on a rampage in WA. The papers will love it. You Irish make good copy. Who knows? The bikies might even buy into it.'

Jim realised Max didn't know the final version of the story yet. It could change in the next few minutes. He contemplated the various alternate realities that Max might settle on. For the first time in his life, Jim understood the true meaning of fear. If someone got shot here last night, Jim knew Max would be more than capable of murder.

Max went to sit down again, when off to the right of Jim, he noticed Kelly standing in the shadows. 'Ah, Kelly. There you are. Good girl. Nice to see you're still in the land of the living. That's a relief I must say. Come here and join us. I was just explaining to our backpacker friend here how he shouldn't go about shooting bikies in the night to avenge a girl's honour. Even yours, my dear.'

Jim turned and saw Kelly step into the glow cast by the fires. Her face sparkled with sweat, but her expression conveyed only anger.

'I think the bikies might have other ideas about who did it. Look around,' she replied coldly.

'Maybe, but you're going to sow the seed of doubt in their minds for me. When my old mates in Kal interview you, you're not to spare them any of the gory details about our crazy night of passion. We were at it so hard, we didn't even hear the fatal shot. Isn't that right? And don't forget to mention the scar over my right hip either!'

'You're a mad, sick bastard.'

'Mad? I'm fucking livid, missy!' Max turned to Jim and laughed. 'Look what you and this tart have brought down upon me.' Max waved his gun in a wide arc, pointing out the destruction in front of them.

'And if I don't go along with your story?' Kelly asked.

Max pointed the gun at Jim's head and pretended to shoot him, like a child playing cops and robbers. 'Bang! Bang! For lucky Jim's sake here, and perhaps your own, let's hope you do … OK kids, move! It's time the three of us took a trip into town. Don't worry, Kelly. I'll work out the finer details on the road.' He shoved Kelly into Jim. 'Hold his vest and start walking.'

Max swung the calico bag over his shoulder and with impatient flicks of the gun, the group moved off. Their route took them close to the burning verandah, towards a gap in the smouldering hedge and Max's Land Cruiser parked out front. Hunched over, the three gagged and coughed as they shuffled along. Jim felt the fierce heat from the fire to his left and shielded his face with a hand. Palls of thick smoke obscured his view to the hedge. His pace slowed. Irritated, Max prodded the gun into Jim's back to hurry him along.

The group reached the verandah, when the last of the supporting posts on the corner of the building gave way. Buckled metal sheets, atop glowing timber beams separated from the sandstone wall. There was no warning, no time to react. A post brushed past Jim's hand and struck him on the shoulder, knocking him back into the beer garden. For a brief second, he thought Max had actually gone and shot him. But no, this was something else. Down, disorientated and gasping for air, Jim started to count.

'One … two …' He heard metal twist and fall. He heard Kelly curse in what seemed to be the far off distance.

'Three … four …' He scrambled onto all fours and tried to fill his lungs with the cleaner air close to the ground. On his knees, below the worst of the smoke, he looked about. He could not see the others anywhere, but Kelly still cursed.

'Five … six … seven …' Jim struggled to stand. Kelly stopped cursing.

'Eight … nine …' He got up. 'Kelly, are you OK?' he shouted, gasping and panting for air.

An indistinct acknowledgement came from under a corrugated

metal sheet beside him. He lifted it off her. With his help, she got to her feet.

'I'm OK. I'm OK,' she said between coughs. 'Where's Max?'

They both scanned the wreckage around them. Jim saw him first, part buried under a heavy timber beam. Max lay motionless on his back and appeared to have received a significant blow to the head. Blood streamed out of a cut above his ear. His white hair ran red.

'Is he dead?'

Jim bent down and grabbed the gun that had fallen from Max's hand. He leaned over the body to check for signs of life.

'He's still breathing.'

'Come on, Jim. We've got to get out, now!'

'We can't leave him like this.'

'Christ, Jim. That ratbag was probably going to kill us. He might still do it, if we don't get the hell out of here!' She pulled at Jim's arm.

Still groggy, they left their would-be captor behind and started for the gap in the hedge. Kelly stopped. Handing her bag to Jim, she went back to her boss and prised the calico bag from his fingers. The bag's weight surprised her. It really was a good night.

'You owe me this!'

Max opened his eyes. He tried to sit up, but the smouldering timbers held him down.

CHAPTER 6

GOLD

'SHIT, HE HAS the key,' Jim said, rifling through the contents of the glove compartment. 'We'll take mine.'

'OK, but shoot his tyres out first.'

'What! No way am I doing that. This could be a murder weapon. I'm ditching it as soon as we're outta here.'

'You do understand if he gets up, he's coming after us!' Kelly pulled the sun visors down in search of a key.

'Yeah I know, but what can he do? We have his gun.' Jim skipped around to a front wheel, got down on his hunkers and pushed the sharp corner of a stone into the tyre valve. Air hissed out.

'Don't assume he only has the one,' Kelly said, throwing the floor mats out the driver's door. She found nothing but dirt underneath and admitted defeat.

Jim looked up at her. 'I'm parked between the two old coaches. Get down there and I'll be right behind you, once I've disabled this thing.

Go on! I'll only be a minute ... And just in case you're wondering. Yes, it will start!' He tried to sound calm and composed, as if matters were in hand.

'OK, but don't hang about!'

She had gone before Jim finished the second tyre.

'No ... THAT CAN'T be it!' A quick scan of the area confirmed Kelly's fears. 'Christ!'

She threw her two bags into the cab, climbed onto the back of the Ford and began to free the sorry-looking vehicle from its mangled metal sandwich.

WITH A ROCK stolen from a barren flowerbed, Jim smashed a small pipe that looked integral to the smooth running of the engine. Next, he ripped out any tubes or cables within reach. Once satisfied Max's Land Cruiser was immobilised, he took the gun from the waistband of his shorts and ran.

Sprinting is never easy in flip-flops and it is almost impossible to keep them attached to feet unless the chord between the big toe and its neighbour is pulled tight. This is best achieved by curling all toes inward, which makes for an awkward gait. Although hampered by the severe pain in his back and his loose footwear, Jim managed to cover the ground quickly – very pleased to have paid the extra premium for the more robust double-pluggers. He doubted his last pair of cheap, single-plugged flip-flops would have survived the sprint. Funny what pops into your head in a crisis, he thought.

The tight squeeze on the driver's side forced him in over the back of the Ford. Kelly watched, relieved to see Jim drop in beside her.

'Nice truck!' she said, when he landed.

'Does the job,' he replied, placing the gun on the seat between them and taking a key from his pocket. He turned the key halfway in the ignition and paused. Using the thumb of his other hand, he pressed the glow plug on the dashboard. Kelly watched intently, waiting to hear the rumble of an engine spring to life. Nothing.

'Come on! Come on! He'll be after us!' She twisted her neck to check the rear window. A figure appeared up on the hill and still no reassuring noise from the engine.

'Shit, Jim! He's here! Come *on*!' The springs protested as she bounced on the seat to shake the truck and the driver into action. 'What's the problem?'

Silently, Jim looked straight ahead, stock-still, except for the rapid pulse beating across his temple. Lifting his thumb from the glow plug, he turned the key to full. The engine started first go and roared when he tested the accelerator.

'Bloody diesels,' he muttered and muscled the Ford into reverse. The truck shuddered and scraped its way back out from between the scrap metal. Now free, Jim wrestled the long awkward gear lever again and stood on the clutch for a few seconds before eventually forcing the Ford into first gear. It moved forward and down the track. It picked up speed and Kelly stopped looking back. Clouds of grey-black smoke rose high in the sky behind them, delaying the Monday morning Aurora sunrise by a few minutes.

MAX WATCHED THEM go. He considered getting the rifle, but that risked blowing his story apart. With the bikies gone, there were now signs of movement over at the mine. Max still believed he could fix this.

* * *

'DON'T THINK I'LL be drinking there again anytime soon!'

'You're barred,' Kelly replied softly.

Nothing further was said for a while. Both used the time to calm down and try to make sense of what had happened. Eventually Kelly broke the silence.

'I thought you were dead. I saw a body. I thought they'd killed you. Your room was empty. I did try and warn you.'

'Thanks ... I mean, sorry. I just lay across here last night and fell asleep.'

'Nice parking by the way.'

Jim didn't bother to defend his driving skills. For the first time in a while, he surprised himself and laughed.

Kelly smiled. 'Seriously, Jim. I was sure they'd killed you.'

'Same here. I thought you were dead. When I saw Max there alone, I was afraid you hadn't got out. Your boss is a fuckin' psychopath, by the way. The bastard didn't care whose lives he destroyed, just to settle an old score with the bikers. Anyway, he's lost everything now and we're all right, thank God.'

'Yeah, he'll be pissed. But he won't give up. He still has to pin it on us. If he doesn't, the bikies will finish him.'

'Yeah, and if he succeeds, they'll come for us! Sorry to be so pessimistic.'

'What now, Jim? Any ideas?'

'I don't know, but we need to keep our heads down until the police get involved. They'll see through his bullshit quick enough.'

'Do you know who Max is?'

'He's a retired cop, isn't he?'

'He was the boss! Just about as high as you can get in the WA Police Department. The Big Don ... and, yeah, he's a retired cop, a bent bastard of a cop. They're all bloody bent. We're in the shit, Jim.'

'Nah, they can't all be crooked, and besides, he's out of it now.'

'I don't know. I worked at a bar in Kal. Turns out it was owned by this crim, except he had a silent partner in the business, who was a bent fucking Kal detective. They're all crooked to some extent. If Max wants us framed for a bikie he shot, we're fucked. He knows too much about everyone. He's very well connected. Don't expect the papers or TV to be on our side either. The owners are all his mates. Max used to organise security for their business and went to all their parties. The things he's boasted to me about would make you sick. We have to get out of WA! Simple as.'

'Ah, Jesus! We're not living in Ceausescu's Romania. Justice will prevail.'

'Don't be so naive. Who cares if a backpacker gets locked away for something he didn't do? Nobody around these parts does, that's for sure. I've no family here either. We're on our own.'

Jim let that hang there for a while before speaking again. The Ford clattered over a sheep grid and bounced on corrugations in the dirt. The road had not been graded for some time. He increased the speed to try to smooth out the ride.

'First, we have to get rid of that gun.'

'We might need it, Jim.'

'For what? We're not going to shoot the cops. If they think we're armed, they'll shoot first and ask questions later. Whatever happens, we can't give them any excuse to start. You might think they're all corrupt, but they're not all murderers. If it comes to it, I'd rather take my chance in court, no matter how stacked, than go down in a gunfight.' Jim shook his head. Had he really just said that? 'Fuckin' hell, Kelly. This is mad.'

'OK, fair enough, I suppose.'

'Here, just chuck it out the door.'

'What door?'

'Better give it a wipe first.'

Kelly lifted the gun, as if it were someone else's dirty underwear and wrapped the barrel in a ten-dollar note pulled from Max's calico bag of loot. Gripping the covered end and mindful to point it away from them, she wiped the handle clean of fingerprints with the bottom of her soot-stained T-shirt. The Ford hit a bump in the road.

'Jesus, be careful!'

'Sorry about that,' Jim said. 'Didn't see it coming.'

Swapping the gun into her other hand, Kelly flung it hard out the absent door. The note uncoiled and fluttered in the turbulent air, while the gun spun in an arc some way farther, before landing in a puff of red dust at the side of the road.

'Thanks. If someone finds it, they'll figure out we're not armed,' Jim said, relieved to be rid of it. 'Was it loaded?'

'How would I know? We really have to get out of WA, Jim. Get to a different jurisdiction and put our story to the cops there.'

'I appreciate that, but we're in no position to do anything yet. Soon, every road out of the Goldfields will be blocked. I think the best thing for now is to go to my place and lie low. Only a few people know where it is. It's difficult to find and I have to get my stuff, anyway. In a day or two, we'll head over to Old Bill at the homestead. He'll have a better idea what to do. Bill will vouch for us. If we decide to make a run for it, he'll have what we need.'

'Why not go now?'

'That's more than likely the first place they'll look for me. I barely know anyone else this side of Sydney. We can sneak into Yilgarn at night after the cops have been there.'

Kelly agreed it made sense. They had no other options. Jim looked a mess, covered from head to toe in soot, scratches and bruises. She knew she must be in a similar dishevelled state. Alarm bells would go off in every town or roadhouse, as soon as they rolled up in this heap of junk, looking as they did. They were in no condition, and in no way prepared, to make any journey across country.

Kelly tried to get comfortable, but without a door to lean against and with the constant rattling from the corrugated road it wasn't easy. Turning sideways to face Jim, she folded her arms and hauled her dirty, bloodstained legs onto the seat.

'That's better,' she said and rested her head and right shoulder against the soft seat back. Quietly, she studied the Irishman's filthy face in profile, as he drove them to safety. Jim was a picture of concentration. Outwardly, he appeared to be holding it together. That relaxed her. Her first impressions that night two months ago it seemed were correct. He's a good bloke, someone she might allow herself to trust.

'I lied to you yesterday,' she said out of the blue.

'Yeah? That's all right. I forgive you.'

'Italians didn't introduce wine to WA. Just made it up. Couldn't have you Paddies claiming everything.'

'Ha-ha!' Jim guffawed. 'That's all right. We Irish do it all the time. Promise me you won't tell a sinner this but ...' He looked over to Kelly and whispered, 'St Patrick was English.' Jim turned his attention back to the road. 'Yep, the chap who saved us from the snakes was from the land of our mortal enemy!'

After a few seconds of silent deliberation, Jim continued. 'While we're at it, I suppose I'd better come clean myself. Have a shufti under the seat.' He lifted a hand from the wheel and patted the space on the seat between them. 'Under there. You'll find something interesting I hope, pushed in between the springs.'

Intrigued, Kelly leaned forward and curled her arm around the edge of the seat. Her fingers touched a hard, cloth-bound object hidden within the foam cushioning. Prizing it out, she placed the heavy parcel on the seat between her legs. Tentatively she unwrapped it. Inside she found gold. It could be nothing else.

'Jesus. I knew it! Gone walkabout, my arse!'

Two small nuggets, each about the size of a wine cork, lay alongside something altogether more significant. Kelly picked up the third nugget, a tablet-shaped lump that filled her hand. Cold and weighty, the gold shone a brilliant metallic yellow.

At some time during its billion-year journey, the nugget found itself on a riverbed, where the abrasive load of sand and gravel carried within the flowing water removed the hard corners and polished its surface smooth. Kelly ran a finger along one edge, where a string of pearly-white beads of quartz appeared to be set into the gold. The beads were all that remained of the quartz vein in which the metal precipitated many kilometres down in the Earth's fiery depths.

'It's beautiful, Jim. Why didn't you say anything yesterday?' Kelly gave him a friendly thump on the shoulder. 'You're a cagey bugger.'

'Ouch! That hurt.'

'Sorry. Can't believe you didn't say a thing to Ron and Pete. Or did you?'

'No, it was killing me. I would have cracked if all this hadn't gone down. The thing is, I only found it a couple of days ago. Don't know if I can legally keep it. It's possible I was on someone's claim. I need to talk to Bill before saying anything.'

'So you weren't looking for gold then. Yeah, right.'

'No, I swear. I haven't even got a prospecting licence. It's embarrassing really, I stopped to do a sketch, reversed in under a tree for shade, hit the tree and knocked it over. That lot came up in the roots.'

'Seriously?'

Jim looked sheepish and nodded.

'Occasionally, blokes passed nuggets around the bar. Nothing ever looked like this. This has to be worth serious money.' Kelly bounced it with a little effort in her palm. 'This is special. Should be in a museum.'

'Soccer.'

'What?'

'You Italians. You brought soccer to Australia.'

'Yes, I suppose we did,' and with that, Kelly thought she might just be falling for this quiet Irishman.

'Tell me I can trust you, Jim, and we're going to be all right.'

'Of course you can trust me. We'll be OK.' He wasn't so sure about the second part.

'HEY, KELLY. WAKE up!'

They were on the road for nearly an hour and had not seen another vehicle. A large ore truck now bore down on them, a tempestuous dust cloud in tow. Kelly opened her eyes.

'Truck coming. You might need to hold your breath for a minute.'

Keeping the Ford well over to the left, Jim slowed to a crawl. The ore truck's horn sounded a greeting and the cab of the Ford filled with dust. Jim squinted to see through the clearing air. Once sure it was safe ahead, he accelerated and the dust dispersed.

'You can breathe now. Sorry about that. I thought we'd be long past here before they started. Unfortunately, it means we've been seen. But not to worry, I'll be turning off soon and there shouldn't be another soul around. How're you feeling?'

'Tired, anxious, but I'll be OK, thanks. You?'

'Sore. My back is killing me. I need a wash and I'm starving. Otherwise, OK too. Been doing some thinking, trying to work things out in my head. Sorry, I haven't come up with anything yet. I'm new to all this criminal stuff.'

'Haven't much experience myself. Tell me about your camp.'

Jim explained about working at Yilgarn and how Old Bill encouraged him to go explore the area when everything finished up. How he felt compelled to paint what was around him and that he knew nothing about prospecting for gold.

They left the main dirt road and followed a series of ever-diminishing trails, many of which tested Jim's limited driving skills and the truck's four-wheel drive. But he knew the country well, its landmarks and its dangers. When the track disappeared, the Ford headed for a distinctive line of distant trees across some beautiful, open bluebush country, before joining the small, seldom-used trail to Bungarra Rock. Jim brought Kelly through some stunning, quiet Goldfields scenery, away from all the slag heaps and the mines. In different circumstances, she would have enjoyed the trip and more, particularly the company.

And then, when the Ford turned off the track and lumbered

across the by now well churned-up, dusty approach, Kelly saw Jim's treehouse.

'Wow! It's gorgeous … in an outback Tarzan, Lord of the Jungle sort of way.'

With a broad grin on her face she got out and stood beside the Ford. She seemed to forget her troubles for a moment.

'Sorry. I'd have tidied up, but I wasn't expecting visitors.'

'It's beautiful. It's perfect.' Kelly shook her head in disbelief. She had no idea what to expect. If the truck was anything to go by, she had to admit to being apprehensive. For all she knew, he may have gone feral and be living in a pigsty. But there was artistry and order here. The building displayed a certain architectural integrity that sat well in its surroundings. She liked the quaint campfire with its neat stone border and that his pots were clean, stacked and in their correct place. He had a washing line, always a good sign, and a shelf with books under a ledge.

The magpie called out to welcome Jim and his guest home.

'I'm going to have a look around,' Kelly said, still smiling.

'Feel free. It shouldn't take long.'

Curious to see how her companion lived, Kelly dashed off, not the least bit coy about rummaging through his possessions. Pleased with her reaction, Jim watched her climb the ladder to the balcony. He worried she might have thought him a nutter.

'Aghhhhh!' Standing high above the camp with her arms aloft and facing the morning sun, Kelly let out an almighty roar. Turning to the four points of the compass she pumped her fists, acknowledging each horizon with another roar. 'Hey Jim, Pigeon didn't get us. Max didn't get us. We escaped the fire. We're still alive. That's something worth celebrating.'

'That's right, Rocky. Now come on down. We need to get organised.'

'Show me your paintings.'

Jim retrieved the black folder from his secret space between the balcony and a branch of the supporting tree. He passed it up to Kelly, who sat on the rudimentary bench and unzipped the folder on her lap. Jim began sorting through his belongings.

He decided to take only what he could carry in his rucksack. Jim was a hoarder. It pained him to leave anything behind. Everything had sentimental value or might be of use. Hard decisions needed to be made. Gone was his well-thumbed handbook, *Monothremes, Marsupials & Australian Reptiles*, his large volume on WA History and *The Fatal Shore*.

Choosing what clothes to bring was easier. He didn't have much. Kelly needed something to cover her arms. He grabbed his denim jacket. Then there was the heavy woollen jumper Ellen had knitted him. It travelled with him to London and the lads laughed when he packed it for Australia. Of course, Jim never thought he would need to wear it. He glanced over at the forked salmon gum. He couldn't bring himself to leave the jumper behind. He needed happy memories. It made the cut.

The sound of a quiet sniff slipped down through the gaps between the boards of the balcony. Jim lifted his head and saw Kelly sitting with her arms clutched tight around his paintings. She stared out over the trees and Jim could tell she had been crying. He climbed the ladder and, after a moment's hesitation, he sat down and put a nervous arm on her shoulder. Pleased she did not rebuff him, Jim hugged her rather awkwardly.

'It's going to be all right. We'll show them,' he said.

'Your pictures are beautiful. It's so unfair. What have you done to deserve any of this? You're a kind, considerate, talented person, who wouldn't harm anyone. It's just not fair.' She rested her head on his chest and sobbed. 'If you hadn't tried to help me, you'd be sitting on the back of your truck somewhere right now, painting.'

He squeezed her hard, even though it hurt his ribs. 'I'd more likely be looking at Pete and Ron's ugly mugs over breakfast, regretting I ever offered to sketch them. You don't deserve this any more than me.

And listen … I'm not sorry I tried to help you. I'm only sorry I didn't hit the prick harder. Next time, I won't hold back.' Jim wiped the tears from her filthy face. They formed pale streaks streaming from the corners of her eyes, turning to follow her delicate jawline.

Anyone who met Kelly could not help but be struck by her beautiful Italian looks and her confident, sassy manner. On his two trips to Aurora, Jim enjoyed watching her go about her work. He could have eaten his lunch in the dining area yesterday, but under the pretence of looking at the television, he brought his meal into the bar. In a room already lit by the early desert sun, her presence somehow brightened the place even more.

Except for ordering food and drink, he would never have mustered the courage to talk to her. Of course, the beer helped, as did having Pete and Ron there. But it was always Kelly who initiated their brief conversations. Jim found it much easier to be part of a group, chiming in occasionally with some well-rehearsed witticism, as opposed to having a one-to-one, grown-up conversation with a girl.

He was uncomfortable in the company of women, and although unwise to admit it, he became particularly tongue-tied around beautiful women. Having spent most of his years since school working menial jobs, lazing on couches, sitting on barstools drinking with his mates and generally doing nothing, he was sure women found him boring. There wasn't much about him to impress any potential suitor and, if honest, he even bored himself stupid in recent years. Particularly since Ellen left.

Staring down on Kelly now, even with the dirt and the bit of snot, she looked beautiful. He rocked her gently, like Meyran had rocked Tyson, and then combed her messy, long, chestnut-brown hair with his fingers. He brushed it off her face, tucked a few curls behind an ear and remembered how she touched his hand yesterday.

'Sorry for getting upset. Your paintings set me off.' She sniffed, before continuing, 'Old Bill's right. You have a special talent!'

'Come on now. I'll get a small fire going. We'll get cleaned up and there may be a bite to eat.' Jim encouraged Kelly to her feet. 'First, I want to show you something.'

They climbed down the ladder and Kelly watched in astonishment as Jim, in obvious discomfort, leapt around on the ground trying to catch a grasshopper under his thong.

'What are you doing?'

'Wait!' He held up an index finger, seeking her patience.

Eventually he snared something. Taking Kelly by the elbow, he guided her in under the treehouse to the base of the trunk, where a few old bricks were stacked next to his water barrels. Kneeling down, he presented the grasshopper and tapped on the bricks with a finger. Moments later, a tiny triangular head peeked out. Its serious eyes swivelled around and spied the ill-fated insect between Jim's fingers. It scurried to accept the offering. Kelly watched amused as the lizard sat, with the twitching legs of its meal protruding from both sides of its mouth, and allowed Jim to stroke its back and tail.

'Hello, fella,' she said smiling. 'But could you not have found a dead one?'

'Sorry. Here. Have a go yourself.' Jim beckoned Kelly closer.

THE TOILET FACILITIES were far from salubrious. Kelly wasn't sure if Jim had been serious when he gave her a shovel and suggested she go pick her spot. But at least the washing setup was better. Hidden in a dense clump of acacia trees next to the treehouse, Jim had 'installed' a shower. Not for reasons of modesty, the curtain of trees functioned to dampen the wind chill. Irrespective of ambient air or water temperature, showering outside in the bush was always a bracing experience. A simple arrangement of a rope, a high branch and a bucket with holes, worked well for the shower head. An old wooden pallet kept clean feet off the muddy ground. A shampoo bottle hung from a wire hook on the trunk. The bucket was large enough and the holes small enough to provide a decent flow of water for about two minutes.

Kelly only needed one refill to feel transformed. The water washed her tears and the dirt down into the earth. It cleansed her wounds. It made her feel strong. Leaving her work clothes in a pile on the ground, and before making her way out, she put on a clean pair of knee-length shorts, a pink T-shirt and sturdy sandals.

When she returned, Jim handed her a mug of tea and showed her to one of the two chairs beside the fire. No smoke came off the few glowing embers, but there was enough fire to work with. Kelly sat on the chair next to his packed rucksack and smiled when she noticed a bundle of paint brushes sticking out the top of the bag.

'You look much better … I mean, not that you ever looked bad … You know what I mean,' he said.

'Thanks.' She smiled again.

'I'll miss this place.' Jim looked around at what had been a good home to him. 'I wonder if I'll ever be back. Should really take a few snaps before we go.'

'You *will* be back and you'll make sure to invite me along, too. I want a proper tour of the area.'

He felt himself blush. 'Listen, as soon as I've cleaned up, I think we should leave. Best not spend the night here, just in case. I know a few places nearby where we can hide the Ford under cover and hang out for the day, before making a run for Yilgarn.'

'Why the change of plan?'

'I've made a lot of tracks around here and they all converge on this spot. The camp has quite a footprint from the air. I'm a bit nervous about it, I guess.' Jim leaned across and poured Kelly a bowl of mushroom soup from a pot simmering on the grill plate. 'It's tinned, I'm afraid!' he said, passing her a spoon.

'Thanks. Tinned, eh? Hard to get fresh mushrooms out this far, I believe.'

'Bill won't say a word, but the roo shooter may have spoken about this place. If he mentioned Bungarra Rock to anyone, they'll find us sooner than later. The bush telegraph will be working overtime right now. Best we head off after I've showered.'

She noticed Jim struggle and wince getting out of his chair. 'Here, let me see your back.'

Jim tried to remove his top, but laboured to get his arms above shoulder height. Kelly got up and helped him out of the vest. Sucking air through her lips, she made a sound that suggested it looked bad. Resembling the result of some paper chromatography experiment, dying blood cells formed dirty red, yellow, purple and black concentric circles on his back. Each circle centred on a site where the steel tip of the bikie's boot landed. Similar variegated patterns covered his left shoulder and swept down his side.

'The bastard may have cracked a rib or two,' Kelly said. Reaching out, she ran a soft hand over his injuries.

With no medical or first aid training, she hoped, in some holistic way, her tender touch might bring comfort – as his hug did for her. She stepped around him and her fingertips traced the prominent outline of his left collarbone. It felt smooth and unbroken – not that she could tell for sure or be able to do anything about it.

Jim stared over her shoulder into the distance. It had been a long time since anyone touched him that way. He reached out, put his hand on her upper arm and looked directly into her eyes. Christ, you are beautiful, he thought. Should I tell her? After a moment's silence, some stuttering words came out of his mouth.

'Thanks ... now, eh, keep an eye out for anything while I shower. Emm ... I won't be long. There're a few biscuits on the table ... That's all I have, I'm afraid.'

Kelly smiled, 'That's OK. Hey! Did you pack your gold?'

'Jesus, no. Stick it in my bag will you – in case we need to ditch the Ford in a hurry.' He grabbed clean clothes and turned towards the trees.

Kelly ate the soup and biscuits, while she listened amused to Jim cursing under the cold shower. She retrieved his gold, then stuffed all of the Aurora takings uncounted into her own leather shoulder bag. To make room for the money, a cherished pair of shoes were left behind. Some other bits and pieces she snuck into Jim's rucksack. At least they weren't going to be stuck for money, should they ever get the opportunity to spend any of it. She noticed Jim had packed a book. A novel, with an emerald green cover and an old black and white photo of a gunman on the front. *Reprisal*, by Hugh Fitzgerald Ryan. It appeared to be the only book he took off the shelf. The handwritten inscription inside the cover suggested the author was a relative.

Kelly threw some soil onto the remnants of the fire and took Jim's book up to the balcony to flick through, while keeping watch. She smiled at his collection of broken glass and colourful rocks arranged neatly around the edge of the wooden platform. Jim emerged from the shower and she thought he looked almost smart in his change of clothes.

'You're a bit of a magpie, aren't you, Jim Macken?' Kelly quipped, as he sat below, tying the laces of his work boots.

He smiled up at her. She had a point.

The shower had revived Jim, but its beneficial effect soon wore off. As he gathered some of Old Bill's gear, the bright light of the hot sun shimmered in his peripheral vision, just like when he would bail on a boozy mid-summer session with his mates to walk home in daylight. His thoughts and movements were slow. His body craved a snooze. A few minutes, that's all it needed. But he wouldn't let himself give in to the urge. Already, they had hung around the camp longer than intended. But he figured he might as well return Bill's stuff when they got to the homestead. To leave it behind would play on his conscience.

Skimming the early pages of Jim's book, Kelly had to some extent escaped into a different world. Occasionally, she would move to lash out at the flies obsessed with the cuts on her legs or stand to scan the horizon for signs of company. She had lost track of time, but the position of the sun suggested it must be around midday.

'Jim! I can see dust.' She shouted, pointing in the direction of an insipid pillar rising above the trees.

Jim threw the eiderdown onto the back of the Ford and made a dash for the ladder.

'Might just be a willie willie ... one of those dusty whirlwinds,' he said, almost vaulting the rungs to join Kelly on the balcony. 'Fuck! Get your bag and head for those trees!' He gestured off to his right with a nod of the head. 'I've a bike hidden out there. We've only got minutes.'

CHAPTER 7

SHAME AND A ROO RUN

WITH THEIR BAGS on their backs, they ran ducking and weaving through the thick scrub. A car horn sounded a friendly warning. Jim stopped and signalled to Kelly to keep low and quiet. The horn beeped again.

'Why would anyone tell us they were coming? Wait here. I'll see if I can get a look.'

Before Kelly had a chance to object, he sprinted off towards the trail. Between the trees, Jim saw Old Bill's Land Cruiser pass, and pull up beside the Ford. Jim turned to go back for Kelly, but she was already behind him.

'It's OK. It's Bill!' Jim put a reassuring hand on her shoulder.

She brushed his hand away. 'Don't you ever leave me on my own out here again!'

'I'm sorry. It's OK. It's Bill. It's Old Bill!'

ALL THREE WERE gathered around the driver's side door of the Land Cruiser. Old Bill stood stooped, with one boot on the running board and a forearm resting on the open window frame.

'I told Collins the last I heard, you were working the ground for nuggets up by Siberia and you'd made camp over that way. He's gone off to check. He said he wanted to find you before the bikies did – for your own safety. I knew the bastard was lying. He had a crazy look in his eyes, not to mention he was covered in blood.'

As he spoke, Old Bill repeatedly swiped at a stubborn fly hell bent on getting through the brambles of his moustache and into a nostril. 'It's all over the radio. That bikie bloke died. They're saying you two are wanted for questioning.'

Old Bill got back into the driver's seat, gripped the steering wheel with both hands and took a couple of deep breaths before continuing. 'Collins is a desperate man. He's broke. Believe me, he'll do anything to get himself out of this mess.'

Old Bill had his own story to tell. 'I'm ashamed to admit this, but … I'd planned to burn down the Aurora …' Old Bill hesitated, before continuing. When he did, he spoke softer than Jim ever remembered. 'I was going to do it, too—'

'Fuckin' hell, Bill! Why?' Jim was gobsmacked. Kelly looked equally surprised.

'He's after the insurance. Collins knows of my circumstances and promised to pay me well if I did it for him. Last night I told him I was out.'

Unable to look Jim or Kelly in the eye, Old Bill stared through the front windscreen and locked his gaze on the distant stone cairn high on the ridge of Bungarra Rock. The flies were now free to feed off his face and lay their eggs. Old Bill no longer cared.

'Helen realised something was up. She has her ways of getting things out of me. You know what she's like, Jim.'

'I do. She's a tenacious woman, all right.'

Tears mixed with shame in the eyes of his old boss. 'She said she'd leave me if I went through with it. She'd rather we surrendered the lease on this place. Yilgarn means more to her than anything. You know that, son.' He stopped again and wiped his forehead with a handkerchief. 'We had a hell of a blue. After all our years of marriage, she wondered did she really know me at all. That hurt. I was only doing it for her, Jim. You must understand that.'

'I do, Bill, but I'm glad she made you see sense.'

'She's right. I was a fool. It'll take a while, but we'll be OK.'

'Seems Max has got what he wanted anyway,' Kelly added.

'Maybe so. Maybe not, if I let it be known what he was up to. Listen, we need to get you two somewhere safe until this gets sorted. Come to the homestead tonight. The best way is along the fence line we put in near Callion and then in by Boggy Corner Dam. You remember that one, Jim?'

'Yeah.'

'You won't be seen if you go that way. Just be careful crossing Callion airstrip and park the Ford behind the water tower. I'll come and get you when it's safe.'

The wind shifted direction and blew the faint rumble of an engine across the camp.

'Did you hear that?' Jim asked.

'What?' Kelly looked around. She heard nothing.

'There it is again.'

Kelly heard it this time. 'Please, no!'

'Shit! They'll be round that bend any second. It's too late!'

'No, Jim. It isn't. I'll stall them.' Old Bill jumped out of the seat and ushered the two away. 'I'll tell whoever it is I missed you. You were long gone. Go for the bike. Hurry!'

Jim ran off to pick up their bags again. Kelly started after him. Old Bill stopped her with a gentle hand on her shoulder.

'He's a good bloke. Look after him for us.'

'I know, Bill. I will … and thanks. We'll see you later.' She gave him a kiss on the cheek and ran to Jim, who waited below the treehouse. The two men saluted each other.

THEY HEARD A vehicle pull up and a door slam. Behind the fleeing couple, a cloud of bulldust detached from the parked truck and drifted away, falling slowly as it went. Jim stopped running. He grabbed Kelly's arm and drew her close to him. They had made it as far as the first broken line of trees beyond the camp clearing.

'We can't get to the bike now,' he whispered into her ear. 'It's too late to cross the open ground.'

Kelly's eyes widened in alarm, but already onto their next move, Jim pulled her in a different direction.

'This way.'

He guided her around the back of the treehouse to a patch of thick acacia surrounded by high tussocks of spinifex. It provided good cover, but seemed alarmingly close to camp. Then the smell of the roo hit.

Kelly gagged. 'Jesus Christ! What's that?'

Jim motioned her to keep low, to stay still. She crouched beside him and pulled the top of her T-shirt over her mouth and nose. The smell, combined with fear, made it difficult to breathe. The sound of a heated argument blew in. Max's voice registered immediately.

'It's him,' Kelly whispered, from behind the T-shirt.

Jim palmed a few leaves aside, opening a small peephole in the foliage. He saw two blurred figures face each other at the trucks. They were a little far off for his tired eyes to make out clearly. Squinting did nothing to sharpen the image. Frustrated, he rubbed his eyes. Kelly noticed and gestured to the camera lens jutting from a side pocket of his rucksack. Nodding, Jim slid the bag off his good shoulder and removed the camera.

After wrapping the camera body in Ellen's knitted jumper to muffle the motor noise, he trained the long lens on the camp. For once, he managed to find the on–off button at the first attempt. The thick wool did its job when the electronics pinged to life. But the image would not focus. In frustration, Jim tapped the shutter release button repeatedly, as if sending a coded telegram. Still nothing. He shook the camera, tried again. The camera motor whined in protest and the image stayed blurred.

'Shit!' he whispered, when he realised what might be causing the problem. The tightly bound jumper prevented the autofocus ring on the lens from spinning. He fumbled with the camera, nearly dropping it before flicking to manual focus. A green light came on in the view-finder. The image improved. It was Max all right, who now wore a large bloodied bandage around his head. The logo on the door of the last truck, in a row of three, suggested Max borrowed a BHP vehicle from the mine at Aurora. It appeared to Jim he had come alone.

Jim watched Max pace and gesticulate wildly. In marked contrast, Old Bill stood calmly by the side of his Land Cruiser, his folded arms resting on the bonnet. Max kicked at the ash in the fire pit, pointed to the wisp of smoke that came off and then began another tirade. The small LCD screen showed seventeen exposures left on the film. Jim nervously pressed the shutter release button. The click of the shutter and whirr of the next frame winding into place were almost silent under the jumper.

Old Bill waved a dismissive hand back at Max. He had heard enough. Reaching into the cab, Old Bill unclipped the handset from the two-way radio. Stretching the coiled cable to its limit, he pulled the handset out through the open window and put it to his mouth. Jim pressed the button again and got a photo of Max grabbing something from the passenger seat of the BHP truck. The camera lens followed Max as he turned and scurried low around the open door. The shutter clicked again as Max placed a rifle on the bonnet. He took aim and fired. A hard explosive report rang out.

Jim flinched. Crouched next to him, Kelly recoiled, edging farther into the cover. She stared at Jim, wanting an explanation, but the camera hid his face. She noticed his hands shaking, and quietly, so did she. A magpie watching from a high branch took flight. For a second, Jim's brain refused to register what had happened. He panned the camera along and stopped on the sight of Old Bill lying face down in the bulldust. Click!

Maybe it was the stress of the last sixteen hours, or perhaps tiredness had dulled his emotions, but when the magnitude of what had happened struck home, Jim barely reacted. Deep inside, of course, his heart broke. Terror, shock and anger began to rage. His subconscious took over. It told him that, if they were to survive and maybe even get justice for his friend, he must park all emotion. Now was no time for reckless decisions, no time for overt panic. He checked the camera was in point and shoot mode. He didn't trust himself to adjust for exposure or aperture.

He steadied his hands, making sure his fingers were not impinging on the lens, and tracked Max walk with the rifle in hand over to Old Bill. He got the shot, and another, when Max pushed the body with his foot to check Old Bill was dead. All the time, Max kept the rifle pointed at the old man's head. Jim believed he got every shot, in frame and in focus. He reached to his side and put a hand on Kelly's back to reassure her. He felt her tremble. Neither said a word.

Max appeared to decide no execution or *coup de grace* was necessary and turned his attention to the treehouse. A few well-placed strikes with the rifle butt knocked out the window frame and its mesh screen. Except for a large spider, the room lay empty. On being disturbed, the spider retreated into a small crack. Balancing the rifle in the bend of an elbow, Max put two hands to his mouth and yelled out to the trees.

'Come on out, backpacker! ... Ah, look. I'll find you anyway! You can't hide from me. Might as well get it over with, son. Hey, Porcini. I want my money back, you bitch!'

He walked the perimeter of the clearing, repeating his words and letting off the occasional gunshot, always picking up the spent cartridge with a gloved hand as he went. At one point, he took aim at a startled kangaroo and missed.

THEY HEARD THE snap of twigs breaking under foot beside them. Kelly, her eyes tight shut, retreated into the depths of her mind, while physically making herself as small as possible. The flies were eating at her cuts.

Another twig broke only inches from her head. She opened her eyes to face her demon. Max was close enough now, that if his expensive Italian shoes had not lost their shine, she might have seen her own face reflected in them.

Jim held her hand. Kelly pressed her fingernails deep into his palm. He thought of home, his family and the sea. He jumped into the cool, choppy waters of the Captain's bathing spot and sank deep down between the rocks to the dark and the crabs on the bottom. He held his breath, waiting for his father to reach down and pull him to safety, like all those years before.

From somewhere a voice told him, 'Man up. Your father is not coming. You have to do this yourself. End it now. Charge him. Take his gun and it's over. Old Bill's rifle is clamped above the windscreen inside the Land Cruiser. Run for that!' A shadow moved behind the leaves. It was now or never. Jim hesitated.

THE STENCH OF the roo carcass hung in the air. 'Jesus wept!' Max stepped away when the first lungful mugged his senses. Spinning on his feet, he strode back to the camp, where he took rest in a chair to catch his breath and consider his options. He decided Mitchell must have been telling the truth. It did appear they were gone. Max began to untie his shoelaces. All this time, Old Bill lay alone in the bulldust, his life drained from the wound in his neck.

Spooked by a distant sound, Max sat bolt upright, his hand moved for the rifle trigger. Craning his neck, he glanced around and, satisfied it was nothing, crouched over again and slid his bony, opaline toes under the straps of Jim's thongs.

'HE'S TAKEN HIS shoes off!' Jim trained his camera on Max again.

Getting out of the chair, Max took the billycan from the hot-plate beside the fire and hung it from a large gum tree at the edge of the clearing. Next, as if seeding a lawn, Max calmly scattered the spent cartridges from his pockets onto the ground in front of the treehouse. With his lawn set, he dropped to a knee and fired off a rap-id volley of shots at the gum tree. Several holes punched through the billy before he deliberately missed with the last few rounds, striking the bark for effect.

Target practice over, Max untied a jerry can from the back of the mines truck and doused Old Bill's Land Cruiser and the Ford with fuel. With the burning pages of a sun-bleached newspaper he had found on Old Bill's dashboard, Max torched the two trucks. The diesel-soaked upholstery resisted for a few seconds, but soon two new fires raged in the Goldfields. The camera shutter clicked once more.

Jim accepted Old Bill's rifle was now gone. A part of him was re-lieved. Their only option now was to wait. They had the photos and proof. Then, without warning, the camera's automatic rewind kicked in. A different noise from the others, the motor kept on whirring, changing pitch and growing louder as the film reversed off the spindle. Panicking, he shoved the camera into the rucksack and wrapped him-self around it. Cocooned under the many layers, it fell silent.

Still blissfully unaware of his audience, the poker-faced killer stared down at the muddy red halo behind the head of his victim. Max lifted a foot and pressed Jim's thong into the bloodied bulldust. Mud oozed out from under the sole, sticking in part to the rubber edges. He made a point of stepping over the body twice, before returning Jim's thongs to where he had found them. Once back in his own footwear, Max continued about his grisly business.

Old Bill's body left a macabre trail in the dust, where Max dragged it backwards by the armpits across to the BHP truck. It had slipped twice from Max's grasp, before he managed to shove the dead weight into the cab. After hiding the rifle behind the seat, he clambered in breathless and sweaty, and drove off. The ammunition in Old Bill's Land Cruiser began to pop in the flames. A little over twenty minutes had passed since Max Collins had tracked Old Bill to the treehouse. For the two figures cowering in the bush, it seemed a lifetime.

Jim wondered if he had really gone. Could Collins be planning to double back on foot, take cover, and wait to see if anyone emerged from the trees? If that is what he intended, Jim realised they needed to move fast.

'Quick, let's go!' He manhandled a recalcitrant Kelly across the open ground and into the trees. When they put some distance between themselves and the camp, Kelly broke free of Jim's arm and stopped. She lowered herself to the red earth and, on her hands and knees, threw up. Jim stroked her back for a moment, then thinking it might be inappropriate, stopped.

'Sorry. Here, take this.' He splashed water over a T-shirt pulled from the bag and handed it to her. 'For your face.'

Kelly got up and tended to herself. Watching her clean her face, Jim saw the shock behind her distant stare. He tried to say something comforting or reassuring, but no words came to mind. He just looked at her, sad. When finished, Kelly nodded and handed back the T-shirt.

'What's the point? Old Bill's dead. We'll be next.'

'No. No, we won't. Come on, Kelly. You're stronger than Collins. We can't let that fucker win. We have evidence now that proves we're innocent.'

* * *

THE DIAL WAS set on 5360 kHz, the Royal Flying Doctor's frequency in the Goldfields. Max put down his binoculars and lifted the microphone from its mount to the left of the steering wheel. He reached across in front of his passenger and pressed the red emergency call button on the Codan 7727 HF radio transceiver. He knew to keep the button pressed for twenty seconds before the Royal Flying Doctor Service automated systems recognised it as a genuine emergency call. A continuous tone signal transmitted out from the robust whip antenna bolted to the front roo bar. By some wizardry of physics, the radio waves bounced along a layer in the high atmosphere, taking them many thousands of miles over the horizon and around the curve of the Earth. The Kalgoorlie base, a mere one hundred and twenty kilometres away, answered Max's call. A friendly female voice came through on the speaker.

'VJQ Kalgoorlie responding to emergency call. Can you confirm identity and nature of your emergency? Over.'

With a swipe of his finger, Max cleaned the dust off a piece of tape stuck to the front of the radio and revealed a code written in pencil by some BHP technician years previously. Max read out the code.

'VJQ. This is VMS211 calling. I have a male gunshot-wound victim seeking immediate medical assistance. Over.'

'VMS211, can you state your position? Over.'

'I am in an isolated area approximately ninety miles northwest of Kalgoorlie. I am en route, in a four-wheel drive to the abandoned Callion mine airstrip. I spell Charlie, Alfa, Lima, Lima, India, Oscar, November. Situated north of Yilgarn homestead on the Coolgardie North Road. My expected ETA at airstrip is four zero minutes. Over.'

'Can you describe the nature of the injuries? Over.'

'Recent gunshot wound to the neck. Victim is male, aged approximately six zero. Victim is unconscious, I repeat, unconscious, and breathing with difficulty. Has lost a considerable amount of blood. I have tried to maintain an airway and put pressure on the wound. Respectfully request a rendezvous with aircraft for emergency evacuation from Callion. Over.'

The clarity and calmness in the voice coming out of the operator's speaker impressed her.

'Is the victim in receipt of medical attention? Over.'

'No. I'm a police officer ... retired and alone with victim. Over.'

'OK, Sir. Stand by for further instructions. Over.'

'Standing by.'

There followed about thirty seconds of static hiss.

'OK, VMS211. I will dispatch a plane to Callion airstrip, ETA four zero minutes. Please leave radio on for updates. If possible, could you complete a roo run of the airstrip on arrival?'

'Roger, VJQ. Over.'

'Good luck, VMS211. VJQ out.'

Off in the distance, two pillars of dirty black smoke rose into the blue sky as rubber, plastic and hydrocarbons burned. Max reversed back from the stone cairn on the ridge of Bungarra Rock. Nothing moved below. There were no dust trails, no flashes of sunlight off a mirror or windscreen. Neither did anybody sneak out from under the trees down at the camp, but he couldn't be sure. The matter was in the hands of his former subordinates at the Police Department now. They'll find them soon enough.

Max looked across at the body slumped in the seat, the seatbelt being all that kept the old man from sliding to the floor. His face was a cold mix of deep blue and red. His head hung down. It didn't matter that his airway was blocked. He was long dead.

'Look at what you've gone and done, mate! You shouldn't have threatened me or reneged on our little arrangement.' Max folded a handkerchief he took from his jacket pocket and placed it under Old Bill's neck. Then drumming the top of the steering wheel, he took a purposeful breath. 'Right—' He began to cough. His chest hurt. When the discomfort eased, he started again. 'Right. Before we get you seen to, I'd better lose this rifle. Pity. It's a bloody good one. But you know that already, don't you?'

He drove down the potholed, rocky slope, avoiding the loose granite sheets that had onion-skinned off the surface. Once back on the trail, Max picked up speed, keen to arrive before the plane. He wanted to get there in time to make the roo run and ensure the landing strip was safe and clear of wildlife.

CHAPTER 8

THE HOMESTEAD

T HE MERCURY ROSE on a beautiful afternoon at Yilgarn, but not to the uncomfortable highs of Sunday. A flock of pink and grey galahs swooped and landed on the tiny patch of green grass outside the homestead kitchen door. Back from feeding her girls, Helen Mitchell carried a cup of tea and Jim's two paintings from the kitchen out to her favourite seat on the verandah. The fly-wire door snapped shut behind her, startling the foraging parrots, who took flight again.

Helen would not allow anyone else feed the chooks or collect the eggs. That was her job, her time. She would sit and talk to the birds for a few minutes every day. She knew them all by name and took great pride in not having lost any to the feral cats or dingoes for years now – although some eggs did occasionally go the way of the snakes and lizards.

Today, to get away from the constant crackle of the two-way radio, Helen spent longer in the coop than usual. The news of Aurora upset her and she worried for Jim. The airways were alive with chatter and idle speculation about what happened last night. For the first time in years, she turned the radio off.

Max Collins' arrival at her door earlier in the day only compounded her anxiety. She did not want that man anywhere near her home. She did not let on she knew anything of what he and her husband were planning and even treated his wounds for him. Of course, Collins had everything to do with the fire and the idea that Jim started it ... ludicrous.

All kinds of everyone passed through Yilgarn over the years. Come muster and shearing, the homestead would transform itself into a moderate-sized prospector village. Tents and swags competed for precious ground under every shady tree. At other times, gold exploration teams, working on prospects in the area, were often billeted in the shearers' quarters. In the main, they were all good people and all left having experienced the Mitchell's renowned hospitality. Helen loved the busy times and the extra company. However, there was something different about Jim. She had yet to meet anyone quite so relaxed. Despite never having set foot in the bush before, he adapted quickly to the rhythm of Yilgarn life.

Coming from a small town in Ireland immediately set him apart from the other station hands. For some inexplicable reason, from that first night when his waif-like figure landed at their door, they both took to Jim straightaway. Even after he crashed the tractor the following morning, it wasn't a big deal once they established 'he was grand'. Bill and Jim still argued over who to blame. He was a good worker, not the fastest, mind, everything done deliberately and unhurried, but right. The first to rise every morning and the heat never seemed to bother him. In her time, Helen saw many hardy bushies wilt on the hot days out fencing. But the young Irishman just ploughed on through and kept smiling.

She enjoyed watching Jim and her husband together. They could sit and talk for hours about all sorts of rubbish, or not say a word for just as long, and eat – often to the detriment of the job in hand. For such a small bloke, he could eat. In Jim, Bill had a captive audience and a keen student. Having grown up close to an Aboriginal community, Bill had an intimate knowledge of the old stories, the bush and the Dreamtime creatures that roamed it. Jim appreciated hearing them all.

Of course, the often harsh reality of growing wool in a desert was not always to Jim's liking. The beautiful bucolic image he brought from Ireland, of lambs helped into the world by a doting farmer and living out their short but idyllic life in green meadows, had no place here. On Yilgarn, the lambs made their own way into a very different, world. A world where they soon found themselves on their backs spread-eagled on Bill's homemade 'operating carousel', to be docked, crutched and the males castrated. An ugly, harrowing business for both the lambs and the new station hand. Sympathetic to Jim's reservations, Bill excused him any direct involvement in surgical procedures.

She smiled at the memory of Jim's face, when Bill explained how he normally castrated his lambs by biting off the poor creature's testicles. Convinced he was having his leg pulled, Jim refused to believe her husband. But just in case, he declined the offer of a demonstration. Helen began to chuckle.

'Thanks be to Jaysus!' She tried an Irish accent.

That's what Jim said, when he heard Bill was trialling a new method of castration this season. It involved wrapping tight rubber bands around the lambs' testicles and tails. The idea being that the band cut off the blood supply to the relevant extremity and, in time, the bits simply withered and dropped off – rendering her husband's aging teeth redundant. Bill was still to be convinced, however. He suspected the long drawn-out discomfort to the poor animal would be far worse than the short, sharp shock of a bite. Of course, Jim never accepted that they needed to be castrated at all. Live and let live and love was his mantra.

She remembered how quiet Jim became when he watched her

crutching some lambs and how he tried to nurse them after. Crutching removed wool and skin from around the base of the tail and anus, an area prone to the build-up of faecal matter and potential infection. Any hint of an infection to the daggy end of the sheep and the blow flies were in laying their eggs. The hatching maggots would eat the flesh down to the bone. Helen hated crutching her lambs, but the sight of a half-eaten, fly-blown sheep hobbling in the paddock, unable to get to water, was the saddest bloody thing.

Like any young lad, there was always the fantasy of the treasure hunt and finding gold out here. With Jim, there was some of that. However, the big reward came from simply living in the bush. Being so different from back home, everything about the place was new and exciting. He marvelled at the space, the wildlife, the dust and the heat. From early on, he made a tenuous peace with the flies. Jim kept talking about the light and the colours. Helen didn't really understand what he meant until she saw his paintings. It was as if he put a mirror up to her home and forced her to see it just a little differently after all these years. She loved him for that.

Helen took a sip of tea and looked again at the two paintings. This is not the work of someone who would go off on a drink, drug and sex-fuelled murder rampage with a barmaid, as the bush telegraph gossip would have it. She refused to believe it.

Helen knew Kelly from the bar. She seemed like a nice girl. All the boys liked her. Too worldly wise for Jim, Helen would have thought. Besides, had he not spent his time in Yilgarn pining for that Danish girl who left him in London? He once admitted to Helen that he still couldn't look at anyone else. Apparently, he had not quite given up on Ellen – wasn't that her name? Helen remembered one of the pretty wool classers making overtures to Jim at the homebrew uncorking and him respectfully declining her advances. Helen smiled again at the memory. Drunken, drug and sex-fuelled murder rampages were just not his style.

She accepted that Collins was allowed to be angry over the shooting and the night's takings stolen – if that's what happened. But he didn't look to be in any mood for letting the legal system take its course. She did not know what went on last night, but until everything was resolved, she wanted Jim back here and safe. Bill will get to them soon and bring the two youngsters home, she said to herself. Calm heads will prevail.

How Bill ever believed getting involved with Collins was a good idea baffled Helen. Regardless of her total disbelief at what he almost did, she still loved that big, stupid, kind, hard-working man of hers. Contrary to that nonsensical nickname of his, until recently she always thought he looked and acted appreciably younger than his years. But lately, Helen noticed subtle changes in her husband. Still physically sound of body and mind, she sensed he had lost some of the fight in him. He seemed more cautious, more conservative. She was aware they were both getting old and, with age, came change. A younger Bill Mitchell would give cattle a go and be bloody good with them.

But she kept returning to what her husband and Collins were planning. How could he allow that man to jeopardise everything she and Bill believed in and worked for? It hurt deeply. Bill was obviously more troubled than she realised. How did she not see it coming, or did she choose not to recognise the signs?

No matter how desperate things appeared, going in with Collins was never the answer. She accepted there is only so much fight in someone before time wears them down and problems seem insurmountable. Was it selfish on her part wanting so much to stay on Yilgarn? Had her unwavering ambition to not give up on this place pushed her husband to despair? She consoled herself in the knowledge there was plenty of fight left in her, and whatever challenges lay ahead, she and Bill would face them together.

The twin-engine, turboprop aircraft came up from the south and flew low over the homestead. Lost in her thoughts, the noise startled

Helen. Dudley barked in the shed. She looked up and saw the distinctive red underbelly of the Royal Flying Doctor Service aircraft. Her
heart stopped. The mug of tea fell from her hands.

* * *

IT SEEMED TO Kelly they trekked quite some distance from the camp
to get to the bike. He had it hidden well, far from any beaten track.
How he found it again, she did not know. Everything around here
looked the same to her. If the Ford was anything to go by, she knew
not to expect much from Jim's bike. It did not disappoint – this was
no Harley. Two hundred CC's of battered, ten-year-old Japanese
trail-bike engineering, with the recent addition of an Australian fleece
bound crudely to a frayed seat, did not look up to much, let alone the
job.

After a few unresponsive kicks, the engine turned over. Taking a
firm hold of the handlebars and ensuring both his feet were planted on
the ground, Jim twisted gingerly around and beckoned Kelly to climb
on behind him. 'The important thing to remember,' he said, before
they got going, 'is to look over my left shoulder when we turn left
and the other one turning right.' The motorbike then set off northeast
towards Menzies.

OK, easy enough, she thought, except for the lack of road ahead
and no warning before he changed direction. Jim had strapped Kelly's
smaller bag to his waist, resting it on the fuel tank, while Kelly bore the
heavier rucksack on her back. She realised with the first acceleration,
that if she forgot to lean forward and cling on, she would be straight
off the back. Not long after starting out, they experienced one close
call, when the rear wheel fishtailed on an unseen patch of loose
sand. However, it had been plain sailing after that. After about three
kilometres, while traversing rocky ground, they turned west and began
to make their way circuitously to Yilgarn homestead.

The bike chugged along, straining at times under the weight, but it never missed a beat. Kelly, to her surprise, found the ride comfortable. The sound and feel of the engine knocking out every stroke, working hard on their behalf, soothed her. The warm scent of outback and fragrant soap that came off Jim's back had a similar effect. Unlike cowering helpless in the bushes, their fate lay in their own hands again. She reminded herself over and over to the rhythm of the engine, they were still alive, they were still moving.

With every bump, or when he jostled the bike over an obstacle, she felt him wince. Jim neither complained nor uttered a sound. He concentrated only on staying upright and getting the two of them to Yilgarn. That was until the emu jumped out.

Alarmed by the oncoming putt-putt of the Honda, the magnificent long-necked ball of chaotic feathers sprung from behind a clump of trees and loped into the cleared ground that ran along the fence line.

Emus can move. They top out at close to fifty kilometres an hour. With vestigial wings and a short tail hidden under shaggy plumage, it would have been incorrect to say the bird running ahead of the motorbike was in a flap. Despite the busyness of its body and long neck, the emu's head remained perfectly still. It never looked back. Similar to the habit of its cousin, the ostrich, there was a metaphorical burying of its head in the sand. The bird seemed in denial about the speed of the approaching motorbike. Perhaps it believed it could outpace the angry monster or, more likely, it was too frightened to compute the simple way out and run back to the cover of the trees. The emu continued to follow the four-strand, high-tensile wire fence that stretched, not quite as straight as it should have, all the way to the horizon.

Many times before, Jim had driven behind mobs of emus and he always enjoyed their antics. Gangly legs bending all the wrong ways, their rear ends shaking like a cheerleader's pompom, they never failed to raise a smile. Few sights in the Australian outback rivalled a running emu for its pure Benny Hill slapstick. Happy to slow every time,

Jim would wait for the birds to figure out what they needed to do. Today, Jim did not ease off on the throttle. He did not care if the bird fighting to stay ahead was suffering.

Eventually, in utter desperation, the hapless animal threw itself at the fence. Hitting the wires in an explosion of feathers, the emu bounced back onto the track. The motorbike kept coming. Obviously, in shock and panicking, the emu tried a second time. It hit as hard as before. Another shower of feathers fell to the ground. Then, with a feat of escapology to rival the best Vegas act, this time the giant bird somehow scrambled through between the middle two narrowly spaced wires and disappeared. Miraculously it did not break its neck or leave Looney Tunes slices of itself behind. A drip of blood hung below a clump of down on the bottom wire. The hum of the vibrating tensioned steel travelled along the fence and away across the paddock.

'WHY DIDN'T I slow?' Jim asked despondently. Standing by the fence, he stared at the scattering of feathers left behind by the emu. 'I should have slowed.' Hunkering down, he wiped the wire clean of feathers and blood, before scooping a fistful of sand. Scrubbing his hands with the sand, he continued to talk, although never directly to Kelly, who had stayed by the bike. 'I should have kept the gun. Bill would be alive if I kept the gun. This would all be over.' Jim shook his head. 'I was wrong.'

Kelly came over and knelt beside him. She picked up one of the larger feathers and ran it slowly through her fingers. 'There's nothing you could have done,' she said. 'It was just an argument and Collins flipped.' She could see tears stream out from behind Jim's sunnies.

'I'm a coward. I could have taken him in the bushes. I should have. I let my friend down. I've blood on my hands.'

'That's crazy talk! Collins was holding a fucking gun. He's a trained marksman and a killer. You'd be dead and, most probably, me too. Even if by some miracle you disarmed him, what could we do –

hand him over to his mates? And the film? You said it yourself.' Kelly got to her feet. 'We need to stay alive and get the photos to the right people. Come on, you're no coward. Let's go and make this right.' She offered him her hand.

THE REST OF the journey passed without incident. Approaching Callion airstrip, they watched the Royal Flying Doctor aircraft take off in the distance. For a moment Jim imagined Old Bill might still be alive, but knew after seeing how Max behaved at the camp, calling in the plane was simply more of Max's efforts to fabricate a truth.

Before crossing the airstrip, they stopped in the shade and waited a reasonable amount of time to allow Max, or whoever would drive the mine truck back, to leave. While waiting, they shared the last few biscuits and drank from Jim's green army canteen. The warm water was not particularly palatable, but much needed. After Callion, Jim kept to the fence line as Old Bill advised, stopping briefly again to rest his back and shoulder. The rough terrain took its toll. However, the bike performed exceptionally, a testament to the mechanical skills of its now deceased owner. By the time they chugged over the top of Boggy Corner Dam, the sunset filled the western sky. Lollipop shadows stretched out from the base of the trees. Jim pulled the bike in behind the homestead water tower and killed the engine.

Tucked away in a distant hut, they heard the generator's persistent background rumble being carried in on the warm evening air. Jim's heart sank when he realised Bill would not be out tonight to turn it off. For over thirty years, armed only with a few rusty spanners and the occasional new filter, Old Bill somehow kept an uninterrupted supply of electricity to the homestead. Every night, when the old man decided it was time, he would take his torch, walk out to the genny and bring the day to its official close. The sound of it starting back up in the morning was the call to work.

The couple continued their journey on foot as the lights from the main house began to cast a welcoming glow out into the dusk. The imposing dark form of the old shearing shed loomed over the scene, quiet and forgotten now, not the great centre of boisterous activity and fun that Jim remembered. A ghostly ewe bleated a sorry song in a pen below the shed. Jim guessed Bill must have brought her in for treatment … or maybe dinner.

Creeping in the shadows, while staying close to the outbuildings, they gave the chicken coop a wide berth. The dimly lit garden fence of the main house came into view as they approached the side of Old Bill's large, open-fronted workshop.

'Stop!' Jim whispered and raised a hand in warning. He pointed through the gloom to the two cars parked at the front gate, a police saloon and Max's BHP truck.

The fugitives were about to turn back towards the water tower, when they heard a loud click. The creak of a winding, heavy-metal spring that followed and the snap of the fly-screen door slamming shut, suggested someone may have come out of the house. Hurrying into the workshop to hide, Jim almost fell over a sleeping Dudley. Delighted to be disturbed, the dog sprang to his feet, yelped, then darted between his old friend's legs, wrapping his chain around Jim's ankles in the process. After a long, boring day chained up with just his bowl of water and a mutton bone to chew on, Dudley wanted to play. A whole day without Bill and, apart from the giant noisy bird, not even a rat happened by for entertainment. Jim freed himself from the chain and the three retreated behind a pallet of sheep drench into the darkest corner of the workshop.

'DUDLEY! I AM not leaving without Dudley.' Hearing the dog, a distraught Helen pulled away from the female police officer accompanying her. 'I'm going to get my husband's dog.'

'That's OK, Mrs Mitchell. You can bring him,' the male officer said. 'I'll get him for you.'

'No! He won't come with you. Wait here. I'll go.'

'It's OK, Helen. You go and get your dog,' a weary Collins interrupted to hurry things along.

The female officer raised her eyebrows and looked to her colleague for confirmation. He gave a nod.

Helen did not wait for permission and had already set off along her modest garden fence. Rounding the corner, she crossed a barren patch of dusty ground and made her way over to the workshop.

Dudley came running out to tell her about Jim, before doubling back again to check for sure.

'Dudley. Come here, boy!' The dog was not on its lead. Helen suspected she had more visitors.

'Jim, is that you?' she whispered.

Jim knew from Helen's tone, she was alone. He eased himself out from behind the pallets.

'I am so, *so* sorry, Helen! We could do nothing. I couldn't save him.'

'I know that, Jim.'

'You have to believe me. I didn't do it. We did none of this.'

Helen walked over to him and put a hand on his cheek. She saw he had been through hell in recent hours. He hurt, just like her. 'My dear boy, I know you didn't kill Bill, or that other man at Aurora.'

Keeping her distance, Kelly stepped into view. The two women acknowledged each other, but said nothing.

Jim sniffed and dried his eyes with a sleeve. 'Helen, we have proof. All we need is time to get it to the right people and there will at least be justice for Bill.' He did not want to say he had photos of her husband being shot. Neither did he want to say who pulled the trigger. He suspected she knew. Very possibly, she could be seated next to her husband's murderer on the journey to Kal. For sure, Collins will at some point orchestrate the opportunity to grill her about what Bill may have said, if the bastard has not done so already. Jim did not dare imagine what might happen if Collins suspected she knew something.

'It pains me that I can't tell you more.' Jim took Helen's hands and held them. 'Don't let on to anyone you know anything, not even what Bill told you about the pub. It's safer that way for now. Trust me, I swear I'll make sure the person who did this gets what he deserves.'

'OK, Jim. I have my suspicions and you have your reasons. Just be careful, you two.' She hugged him.

'And you, Helen. I'll be in touch when this is over.'

'You know, Bill always enjoyed having you around.' Helen stepped back and put a hand on his shoulder. 'Take anything you need, anything at all … and Jim, you need to eat.'

'Thank you, Helen. I'll miss him terribly. He was a good man and a good friend. You better go.'

MAX'S IMPATIENCE GREW. He went to go after Helen, but then she appeared around the corner of the house.

'Everything all right?' he asked politely. 'We have to get going. Where's the dog?'

Helen put two fingers to her lips and whistled. Dudley bounced out of the dark to her side. Without so much as a glance to Max, she got into the backseat of the car beside the female officer. Dudley settled at their feet. The two vehicles left together down the long track. They passed the sombre, shadowy outline of the empty shearing shed and moved out onto the main road.

* * *

THE ORANGE GLOW from an outside street lamp peered around the edge of the roller blind. On his mattress by the door, the Bubbles lay on his back, naked, gazing into the near total blackness. He had already kicked the bed sheet off, but sleep continued to elude him. It was a warm night in Sydney's Bondi. A mozzie buzzed an ear earlier, but the

Bubbles had heard nothing from God's most contemptible creature for a while now. He wondered if perhaps, having stolen its fill of blood from Cyril instead, it then buggered off. Surely Cyril's tasted better at the moment, less adulterated.

Not yet over a hard weekend up at the Junction, a weekend that continued well into Monday, the Bubbles craved sleep. If he wanted to keep the coveted flagman duty, he needed to be on site early in the morning. Being the only person on the job big enough to challenge the Maoris for that handy number, he felt obliged to volunteer himself. He didn't mind sharing it around, but not in this weather. Sitting in the shade, directing deliveries and traffic down a narrow lane, beat hauling bricks up a ladder any day.

It must have been well after one, he reckoned, when the commotion kicked off outside. Across the street from their third-storey unit, a camp of squabbling flying foxes hung out in a giant fig tree. High on sugar from the ripening fruit, they made a hell of a racket. The Bubbles struggled to tune out the antics of the gorging bats. He tried distracting himself with memories of fishing boats, the Irish Sea and a cooling spray splashing across the deck while he 'tailed his yans'. But for the life of him, he could not get to sleep.

The uproar outside woke cousin Cyril, who until now enjoyed a grand slumber on the opposite side of the room. Given to bouts of late-night leg cramps, Cyril started to thrash and kick out under his bed sheet. Like a grasshopper calling a mate, he rubbed his feet together in the hope that friction might ease his discomfort. It didn't, but it did add to the cacophony of sound passing across the room. He let out a loud, frustrated sigh, rolled onto his side and began to massage his lower limbs in an intensified effort to alleviate the cramping.

Over by the door and still awake, the Bubbles knew if he passed a remark, the two cousins would no doubt slag each other off and end any chance of either of them drifting away in the medium term. He kept his counsel. Eventually, when he all but gave up, the Bubbles

heard himself emit a long reverberating snore and his thoughts of fishing boats became the vivid, living pictures of his dreams.

With the noise outside and his legs still at him, Cyril's simmering
agitation boiled over. He sat up, spun himself off the mattress and
stood in the dark. Reaching out, he pulled the cord on the roller blind
and released the mechanism. Mindful of not disturbing the sleeping
giant in the opposite corner, he held onto the end of the chord to
prevent the blind crashing to a sudden stop against the lintel. Bright
orange light from the high-pressure sodium streetlamp flooded the
room. Carefully, Cyril clicked the latch on the single-glazed aluminium frame and opened the window. Pushing a full head and shoulders
out, he inhaled the warm Sydney night air deep into his lungs.

And then he bellowed, 'Will you ever ... shut... the fuuuck up!'
with emphasis firmly on the expletive.

The strong Dublin accent bounced off the walls of the apartment
blocks, down over the water and out across the bay. Again, not wish-
ing to disturb the Bubbles, and feeling much better about things, Cyril
withdrew from the window and eased it closed. Quietly, he lowered
the blind and crept back into bed.

'Ah Jaysus, Cyriler!'

'Eh sorry, Bubbles, sorry about that. Didn't mean to wake you!'

'Feck it!' The Bubbles got up to visit the loo and get a cold drink.

USELESS UNDER HIS bulk, the springs, offered no resistance. The
Bubbles sank deep into the lime-green couch. He lowered the pint of
water in three gulps. The glass looked small in his hands. Shortly after
arriving in Australia, he decided, if they were going to force him to
drink out of those ridiculous schooner glasses in the pub, he would
at least make sure they had a decent selection of proper 'drinking
receptacles' in the flat. It was an added bonus that, having purchased
his pint glasses from The Irish Shop in Darling Harbour, they were all
branded with the Guinness logo.

Sitting alone, the Bubbles again replayed summers back home in his head. He did it a lot on these strange balmy nights in Australia. Summers spent steaming past the Rockabill Lighthouse and heading for the harbour with a hold crammed full of freshly tailed and iced prawns. The seagulls would follow the boat in from The Rock after the gannets bade them farewell. Once ashore, and always with a few crabs wrapped in newspaper tucked under an arm, he made for home, routinely stopping off at Joe May's on the harbour road for a quick pint and catch-up on the town gossip. Truth be told, most of the time, they seldom caught more than two or three fish boxes of prawns on a trip. Truth be told again, the crabs normally made it home well before the Bubbles. As soon as his father got wind that the boats were in, he got impatient waiting at home and came looking for his crabs. Invariably, he had them cooked to perfection and eaten long before the Bubbles' giant form darkened the door.

A bloke in the pub was only telling him at the weekend that there are jobs back in Ireland these days. The Bubbles wondered if he should chance going home. The phone on the armrest next to him rang, deferring any decision for now. At this hour, it could only be Skerries.

'G'day, this is Sydney, the Bubbles speaking. How may I be of assistance?'

'Bubbles!'

'Hey, Jimbo. That you?'

'Yeah—'

'Ah, howaryah? We got your card. Outback still treating you well? What the feck are you ringing for at this—?'

'Listen...' Jim's reply was blunt. 'Listen, Bubbles, I need your help. Everything here is fucked, really fucked. I'm in big trouble.'

'Wha?' The Bubbles did not quite grasp the anxiety in Jim's voice. 'Hey, I saw something on the news tonight about a biker war over there, burning pubs, and an Irish backpacker apparently kicked it all off. You're near Kalgoorlie, aren't yah?'

'It's all bollox. It's not true.'

'Christ. What are you saying? That was you? Fuck off!'

'Yeah, believe it or not, but it's all bullshit. Bubbles, listen very fuckin' carefully. I haven't much time. I really, really need your help. I'm in serious trouble over here. Me and this girl are being framed. It's a long story, but we haven't done anything.

'I need you to get in touch with the media – radio, TV, the press, even your man Hinch. Tell them you know me. Tell them everything you can about home and our time over here. Tell them the truth. They might ask for my photo. Give them one of Chris.'

'He's gone home.'

'Yeah, I know, but he's got black hair and is about the same size as me. With any luck it'll cause some confusion, buy me time. I bet one of the girls has a photo of Chris. I need it done quickly, like to-morrow.

'Tell them I rang you from Kalgoorlie. If the cops get onto you, let slip I was looking for an address in Perth.'

'We don't know anyone in Perth.'

'Didn't Cyril's mate, Healy, live there a couple of years ago? Cyril might still have an address. The two of them came out here around the same time. Bubbles, I just need something to send the police looking the wrong way.'

'Yeah. Got yah.'

'And one other thing. Well two, and this is very important and really why I rang. You must stress this. Tell all the media, I want it known that if we are caught … that's me and Kelly … if we are caught, arrested, whatever happens, both of us have no intention whatsoever of taking our lives in a prison cell. Jesus, you must stress that. Whatever happens, we will not commit suicide in detention! Got it?'

'Yeah, I got you loud and clear. Phoning from Kalgoorlie, no intention of doing away with yourselves in custody. Christ!'

'Same goes for Kelly. Bubbles, I can't overemphasise just how fucked things are here. Oh, and the other thing, we're not armed and we're both innocent.'

'Fuck! They think you have a gun? No worries, Jimbo. I'll pull a sickie tomorrow and do that.'

'Try the papers now!'

'Yeah, good idea.'

'Thanks. I'll be in touch. I may send a package in a few days if I can. I'll explain everything in that, but I'll leave it for now. OK?'

'Jesus, Jimbo. Look after yourself.'

'Thanks, I'll try me best.'

The Bubbles hung up. 'Oi! Cyriler, come 'ere!'

* * *

KELLY HEARD THE pick-up and then the handset must have been dropped. After some scratching noise and a muffled curse, a familiar adenoidal breath panted down the line.

'Troy, are you there?'

'Fack sake, Kel. Is that you? Where's me fackin car? What did ya do with me car?'

'Forget about the car. The car's gone.'

'I want my car back, bitch.'

'Listen, I supported you and you cheated on me. I sold the fucking car and what I got for it barely covered what you owed me.'

'Fack sake, Kelly. It was a V8. It was mint. It was worth a fackin fortune.'

'Oh, grow up, Troy. You're too old to be a hoon. You got a job yet?'

'I'm in business for myself now, doing very well too, by the way.'

'Listen, you moron. I need somewhere for me and a mate to lie low for a while. I'm in a bit of strife. I'll pay you. Two hundred bucks if we can crash at your place for a day or two.'

'Is she cute?'

'Who?'

'Your mate?'

'Yeah, she's very cute. Too cute for you.'

'Yeah, we'll see about that … So what's the problem?'

'Police are looking for me. I got mixed up in some crap in Aurora.'

'No shit! Why does that not surprise me? All right, you can stay, only if she's cute and only a couple of days. And I still want compo for the V8.'

'OK, we're in Kal now and planning to follow the water pipeline track to Perth. So, it'll probably be late tomorrow night before we get there, or Wednesday morning. You can have the bike we're coming in on. It's worth something.'

'Interesting. What is it?'

'I don't fucking know. It's just a bike. Listen carefully, if you're not there and don't leave a key out, I promise, Troy, I'll fucking kill ya.'

'Yeah, no worries. Is she a skimpy?'

'Prick! Tomorrow night, remember!' Kelly slammed down the phone and looked at Jim. 'You've probably guessed, not one of the best choices I ever made.'

'Mmm.' Jim removed a pen from his mouth. 'A rough diamond, perhaps?'

'Nah. But I know him well. He won't be able to keep his big gob shut.'

Writing didn't come easy to Jim. He had sat for quite a while agonising over what to say to Helen, but after a few false starts, he managed to finish a letter, signing off just as Kelly hung up.

'Here, have a gander at this. Is it OK?' Jim slid the folded sheet of watercolour paper across the table. Before opening it, Kelly took a quick bite from a sandwich and then a sip of coffee. 'What can you say?' Jim added, with a shrug. Kelly began to read:

Dear Helen,

Again, I would like to say just how heartbroken and horified I am about Bill's murder. I know it is of no real comfort, but I am certin he was not aware of what happened. I am confident he felt no pain and did not suffer. At the time he was trying to help us and if it wasn't for him, we might not be alive either. For that myself and Kelly are eternaly grateful.

The person who did this to him is known to all of us and is a cold-blooded killer, with a certin amount of political infulence. Please don't confront anyone who you suspect just yet. I believe the killer is mentally unstable and is obviously capable of anything. As I said earlier, I have evidence that will see him put away, but I can't risk him or his acquintances getting their hands on it. In time that wont be a problem. Apologies for being vague, but I want to be careful, just in case somone else may see this note before you.

I'm afraid we need to take some of your supplies and camping gear. As much as I would prefer not to, we will also need to take the Hilux. It's with a heavy heart that I do this and I promise, I will in time reimburs you for everything. I hope the enclosed will go some way to covering the costs.

I know anything I say is inadequite at this terrible time, but I feel I must still thank you and Bill for all you have done for me. Up until the horific events of yesterday I have had the time of my life at Yilgarn and will miss you both terribly. I'll never forget Bill and I know I'm a better person for having met the to of you.

Take care. I hope your with family right now. I'm so sorry,

Jim

'That reads fine, Jim.' He had an elegant hand for a southpaw, she thought, but his spelling was surprisingly poor. She didn't mention it. 'How much do you suppose we leave Helen? We'll need cash for ourselves.'

'I wasn't planning on leaving her money. I doubt she'd accept it or want anything that belonged to Max.'

'Belonged to me! He owed me for three weeks and let's not forget he wanted to kill us. I reckon that entitles us to anything over and above my wages.'

'Yeah, but you know what I mean. Anyway, I'll leave her the nugget. Who knows, it might cover the rent of the Hilux.'

'The big nugget?' Kelly asked. 'You can't just leave that here. This place will be crawling with coppers before Helen ever gets back.'

'Yeah, probably, so we can't hang about too long either.'

'Where you going to leave it then?'

'The chicken coop.'

'Right, OK! The obvious place.'

'There's a hidden ledge inside the coop, where Helen hides a packet of smokes. You wouldn't know it was there. She'd sneak a fag every morning. I caught her once and was sworn to secrecy.'

Jim got up from the kitchen table and left the room. He came back with an armful of maps taken from Old Bill's study and laid them out on the table. 'Bill hates ...' He checked himself, '... hated cigarettes. He knew, and she knew he knew, but it was an unspoken understanding they had.'

'That's marriage for you. So where are we going?'

'Ever been to Alice Springs?'

AFTER SCOURING THE sheds for field equipment and camping gear, Jim loaded anything and everything he thought useful onto the Hilux. Two swags, two chairs, a gas bottle and stove, an empty water barrel, shovels, two spare tyres, tyre levers, patches, a compressor and a roo-jack, were all tied down neatly and securely. Jim hoped to create the impression they were a couple of well-prepared tourists on an outback adventure.

The Mitchells had only owned the Hilux a few months and used it mostly for trips into Kalgoorlie or rare excursions south to Esperance on the coast. It would be many years before the Hilux earned its place on Battery Hill. This was to be the shiny new vehicle's first proper off-road experience.

Packed, it looked the part, but Jim worried the tyres were no good. He hoped Old Bill had put a decent set of all terrains on it, on the off chance he might sometimes need the Hilux for a more demanding job. Jim reckoned Old Bill would do that. To Jim's untrained eye, the tread appeared right. If he was wrong, every broken twig or loose piece of wire could punch through the sidewalls. Even with the two spares, they wouldn't get far. He knew how to fix a puncture, but that took time, which they didn't have. Apparently, you can stuff a tyre with spinifex grass and you might just limp home on it. With almost half a continent to cross, they were not going home and could ill afford to limp.

While looking for more spare tubes and patches in the shed, Jim remembered the old Arnotts biscuit tin on an upper shelf and Helen's Luger inside. The Mitchells never kept guns in the house. But it shocked Jim just how casual they were about storing them elsewhere. Helen used the gun to protect her chooks from feral cats, and not just to scare them off. She despised cats as 'the scourge of the outback'.

Should he take the Luger? His impotence at the camp haunted him. He thought again of Old Bill lying in the dirt and him cowering in the scrub. Old Bill's death had changed everything. With some difficulty and in pain, Jim stretched his arms above his head and took down the tin. The loose bullets inside rumbled and rolled to one side. He sat on a low stool with the tin on his knees and agonised over the right thing to do. They might need to defend themselves or at least convey that impression to anyone who got in their way. Would bringing the gun put Kelly in more or less danger? He felt responsible for her. She placed her trust in him and accepted his plan to try for Alice Springs. Now he must deliver. How would their story stack up if they were detained and found to be in possession of a gun? Of course, stacking up becomes irrelevant if they are dead. His mind kept going back to the image of Old Bill face down in the dust.

Beneath the years of dirt and mottled rust, Jim noticed the faded image of a teddy bear on the lid and the words, 'Arnotts Teddy Bear Biscuits'. He remembered the boys' grave at Davyhurst and the sketches he drew. He remembered James Macken's headstone with a depressing sense of foreboding. It then occurred to him why Helen might have had the old biscuit tin and why she kept it. He hoped that somewhere in the universe, Old Bill had been reunited with his baby daughter. Jim wiped a tear away and, without opening it, put the tin back.

Life is too precious and too short to even consider taking the gun, he decided. It could bring no good. It was the right decision at Aurora and it was still the right thing to do. Jim continued his search for the extra tubes.

KELLY RAIDED THE Mitchell's sizeable larder. She filled a cooler and a second container with non-perishable food and then returned the kitchen to the immaculate state they found it. On her way out, she saw the two paintings Jim gave Helen and came close to tears again.

JIM DROVE THE Hilux over to the fuel depot and enjoyed his first ever experience behind the wheel of a proper vehicle, with its full complement of doors and windows. One he did not have to wrestle into gear or that shuddered when moving off. He stalled the engine a few times trying to start it and hoped Kelly did not hear from inside the house. But soon, he got the hang of things and discovered the Hilux was a pleasure to drive.

In a moment of panic in the dark, having already started to wind the handle on the drum pump, Jim realised he had not checked the pump was screwed into a diesel drum.

Christ Jim, think! Keep your wits about you, he rebuked himself. Their situation demanded absolute and constant attention to detail – something that might be at odds with his normal disposition.

This time he got lucky. He filled the six empty jerry cans he had found among the clutter of the various sheds and secured them on the back of the Hilux. He filled the water barrel. Now they were almost ready to go. Yilgarn would soon be swarming with activity. He wanted to leave before it got bright.

Driving back to the homestead to collect Kelly, Jim let the old ewe out of the pen below the shearing shed and turned off the generator.

KELLY WATCHED ON while Jim walked among the chooks in the run, his way lit by the headlights. She saw him put his arm around the door of the coop and produce a packet of Winfield Red 25s. Holding the packet up, he waved to her, grinning. Opening its top, Jim pushed the silver foil back to reveal an almost full complement of cigarettes. If he ever wanted an excuse to start smoking again, now would be a good one. After all the grief and tension, just the one would be nice and perfectly understandable.

'Feck it! Don't need it,' he muttered, and wrapped the packet in with his gold nugget. Jim then placed the bundle on the ledge behind the door frame and smiled to himself. I may have added a few years to my life expectancy, he thought, but I won't be counting any chickens yet.

'OK, back down to Boggy Corner Dam and first left for the Never Never,' Jim said, climbing into the driver's seat.

Kelly offered him her hand. 'Kelly Porcini,' she said, 'It's a pleasure to meet you.'

Jim accepted and they shook. 'Jim Macken, likewise.' He smiled at her formality.

She pulled him towards her and gently kissed his lips. 'Now we can go!' Kelly said and waved him on.

CHAPTER 9

A GOOD BLOKE

'IT APPEARS TO be a shallow grave,' said Senior Constable Laurie Holt to the Detective Sergeant from the Major Crime Squad.

The stench assaulted the detective's delicate olfactory system. He took a step back and covered his nose with a handkerchief. 'OK, Laurie. Thank you. We'll have the Doc look at it when forensics arrive. How was your night? Any activity to report?'

'All quiet, Stan. Our friends in the media haven't shown their faces here yet.'

'Sweet. They're bloody all over Aurora,' the detective said. 'We'll need them soon enough.' Turning his back on the disturbed ground, Detective Sergeant Stan Sidoli lowered his handkerchief and gazed over at the two burnt-out trucks. 'Christ, what a mess!' he sighed. 'Don't go too far, Laurie. We'll need your local knowledge. All this bloody scrub looks the same to me.'

Ducking under the cordon tape, the detective issued his final instruction to the constable. 'And don't forget to run your boots by forensics,' he said, before striding off.

Sidoli's parting words rankled with the Senior Constable. Stan didn't have to say that, Holt thought, and Stan knew it. The man hasn't changed ... except, he's carrying more weight these days and aged beyond his years. Since their paths last crossed, it seemed a crow had gone walkabout over Stan Sidoli's puffy grey face and left its mark. Holt put it down to Sidoli's fondness for the good life.

SENIOR CONSTABLE LAURIE Holt worked out of the two-man rural police station at Menzies, a small town one hundred and thirty kilometres on sealed road north of Kalgoorlie. Like all towns in that part of the world, Menzies established itself around a gold find and the dream of making it rich. Over the next century, the town diced with ghostliness, its population tied in with fluctuations in the gold price. Today's good spot of AUD553 an ounce was enough to sustain a standing population of sixty hopeful residents.

Along with keeping a watchful eye over the sleepy town, the station was directly responsible for policing 145,000 square kilometres of empty scrubland, pastoral lease and far-flung native communities. A challenge Holt had enjoyed now for five years at Menzies.

Late the previous afternoon, Holt and his colleague were manning a roadblock just south of town, when word came through of a second and possibly related shooting near Bungarra Rock. As the crow flies, they were the closest available officers to the crime scene. Holt, who knew the back country well, was ordered to proceed to the area, secure the scene and await the arrival of the Major Crime Squad. Having flown in that morning from Perth, the Squad was still fully occupied at Aurora.

Holt drove out along the dirt road west from Menzies. Had he wished, he could have continued on the same track for almost four hundred kilometres, following it around the western shore of the enormous expanse of Lake Barlee and on north to the small town of Sandstone. Instead, after seventy kilometres, and just before the sun descended low in the sky, making driving difficult, Holt turned south.

He crossed onto Yilgarn Station to negotiate a seldom-used lumpy trail that passed near Bungarra Rock. The last of the smoke hanging in the air over the Irishman's camp, guided him to the exact location. In his many years of service to the Department, Holt had been the first officer to arrive on a crime scene more times than he cared to remember. He parked well away and undertook a quick reconnaissance of the area before taping off a large perimeter cordon.

In the bloodied ground near the burnt-out vehicles, he saw drag marks left behind, where the victim was moved. Picked out beautifully by the low sun, trailing fingers had ploughed lines of tiny furrows in the bulldust on either side of the main drag mark. Holt deduced the casualty was held under the armpits and dragged backwards unconscious, or dead, before being put into an off-road vehicle with some difficulty and driven away.

As an ambitious young recruit, Holt showed great promise. He entertained aspirations of moving into a plain clothes role, or taking a job in one of the more prestigious specialist squads. In the early days, he applied for all suitable transfers or promotions that came up. Management repeatedly turned him down. He knew why, but refused to compromise his integrity or look the other way in his work. It did not make him popular with some colleagues and a certain clique in management. Officially, the records would show Senior Constable Laurie Holt's career had stalled. He would serve out his time floundering in several far-flung country postings as a community police officer. At first he challenged it, but eventually lost the hunger for the fight and stopped putting himself forward. He was not proud of that.

But there was something of a release, when he put it all behind him. It allowed Holt to reconsider the path they had forced him to take. Community policing, it turned out, brought fulfilment. He enjoyed dealing with the public and was good at it. He could read people as well as he could any crime scene. He earned a deserved reputation for honesty and compassion. He felt he made a difference, no matter how small. More than anything, he valued his time working with the indigenous communities. Holt spent many evenings around their campfires, listening to the Dreamtime stories of ancestral times, when spirits and great beasts rose from the earth or came down from the sky to create the landscape and all living things.

At times, he witnessed terrible suffering too. Often, life was tough in their world. In recent years, the scourge of alcohol and petrol sniffing had all but decimated a generation. The elders did their best to address the ongoing problem by prohibiting the consumption of alcohol in many remote townships. It had limited success. Holt understood as much as any outsider the complexities of Aboriginal society and culture, its beauty and its harshness. Two hundred and two years of European settlement, he believed, had treated them and their Dreamtime landscape criminally. He saw how Australian law still did not always sit well with Aboriginal traditions. It was a complex and sensitive hand Holt had to play, while acting in the best interests of all under his watch, and he did it better than most in the Department.

How much of a role he speculated, did alcohol play in this incident? Holt examined the scene around him. He spotted a small, clear-plastic packet of what he recognised to be marijuana beside Kelly's discarded shorts. And drugs. It's always about drugs in the Goldfields these days, he lamented.

Holt saw the cartridge casings scattered in the dust. Target practice, he guessed. Approximately sixty metres from the camp, he had found what looked like a shallow grave. Judging from the smell, he knew it must have been there a while. Holt kept well back. Fragments of charcoal around the grave hinted at a failed attempt to incinerate whatever was buried in the ground.

The officer observed at least three sets of recent shoe prints nearby. He strung plastic tape on the bushes, marking off a separate area from the main cordon. As far as Holt could determine, there were no other casualties in the immediate vicinity and nobody else about.

He was taken by the care the builder put into the construction of the treehouse and the ordered layout of the camp. There were items strewn around, suggesting a hurried departure, but much of what they left behind spoke of a more peaceful time, before the horrors that were to befall the place earlier in the day. On a shelf, he saw a few books on history, a handbook on native animals and a beginner's guide to the blues harmonica. Two grey-paint stained jam jars, with well-used artist's brushes fanning out from the jars' necks, were tucked away behind the books. Despite the brutality of the scene in front of him, the burnt-out vehicles and blood-soaked ground, Holt imagined the campsite as a serene retreat for the Irishman.

He met him once, Jim Macken, sketching on the back of the now blackened old Ford. They had a pleasant conversation, while Macken drew the Menzies Town Hall. The young fella had talent. Nothing about him would have foreshadowed the bloodbath of recent hours. That troubled Holt. What did he miss that day? But then, isn't it always the polite, quiet ones? Living out here, Macken certainly did keep to himself.

Confident Macken and the girl were long gone, Holt still spent a nervous night watching over the crime scene, his firearm never far from his hand. Twice, the police aircraft circled overhead and reported zero sightings of a campfire or headlights fleeing the area.

Holt occupied his time imagining what might have happened and trying to figure out why. If the Aurora killing was over a girl, why this second one? He listened to the police reports in his cab and was saddened when they confirmed the identity of the victim. He knew Old Bill well. Macken had mentioned working for him. It was the only reason Holt did not draw attention to the understated roadworthiness of the Ford. It made no sense. Then, Josef Schwab, the German tourist, who murdered five strangers in a shooting rampage across the Top End three years ago, made little sense either.

* * *

FOR FORTY MINUTES, Old Bill's new Hilux bounced along a series of well-used narrow tracks west from the homestead over to Emu Dam and the western boundary of Yilgarn Station. A route Jim knew well, although it was two months since he last passed this way and never before in the dark. A mob of kangaroos and a few sheep shared the last of the winter rains, now only a muddy puddle in the bottom of the giant dam. The animals scattered on hearing the vehicle approach. The pitch of the engine did not change when the Hilux easily climbed the earthen bank and followed the track along the rim to the boundary gate on the far side. A magpie sang nearby and the top of the sun broke the horizon, when they drove west through the station gate and out into the vast emptiness of Crown land beyond.

Dragging the gate shut after them, Jim noticed, low to the east, the flashing lights of a plane heading north against the brightening sky.

Back inside the Hilux, he kept what he saw to himself and switched on the cab light. 'Right, you're driving from here. I'm navigating.'

Reaching behind to the back seat, he grabbed a bunch of maps and withdrew a large folded sheet titled, *The Southern Region of Western Australia*. After wrestling with the creases to isolate the relevant area, he placed the map on the dash and patted it flat.

'We're here, Yilgarn Station.' Jim pointed to a tiny black dot. 'That's the homestead.' Sliding his finger west through an empty expanse of yellow, he stopped at a small, insignificant patch of contoured shading in the middle of nowhere. 'We'll try to get to these hills by tonight. That should give us loads of time. They're only about a hundred kilometres away, but I can't promise the going won't be rough.

Tomorrow, we'll shadow the hills northwest, until we hit this main track here.'

His finger traced the proposed route. 'That's the Menzies–Sandstone road. I know it's in good nick near Menzies, where I've driven it. Should be grand everywhere else too. It doesn't see much traffic, only a few cattle stations use it, I'm guessing. Once we're on it, we can make a quick dash for Dismals Station … here.' He pointed to a black dot at the point where the road turned north to Sandstone. 'I know the owner. He's a good old bloke, someone we can trust. I'm hoping he'll let us stay, until we work out the best way to cross to Alice.'

'You're sure? What if he's heard the news? He could dob us in.'

'He won't. He was a good mate of Bill's. A true blue Aussie and a champion of the little man. So what if he knows, he'll still hear us out. It's the middle of nowhere. He'll have no choice.'

'OK, fair enough.' That part of the plan seemed reasonable to Kelly. 'But what about… umm…' She tapped the big blank area on the map. 'There is nothing out there and you want to find a small hill somewhere in front of us, by tonight? Can we do it? I mean, you hear stories all the time! We're not going to get lost and die, are we?'

'Not at all. I promise. Look.' Jim produced Old Bill's set of striking, multi-coloured geological maps. 'These are great. They're a better scale than the road map, much more detail.' He placed one on top of the big map. 'Don't worry about all the funny colours and diagrams. I've no idea what they mean, but if you look closely, you can see what I'm sure are old tracks marked on it too.'

Jim stuck his nose into the 1:250,000 Kalgoorlie Geology Sheet. His eyes darted back and forth across the map.

'There's been feck all, if any, gold mining in this area. The geology is wrong for gold. Old Bill told me the rocks here are mainly granite. But there are still a few old tracks. Probably put in by the early prospectors or sandalwood-cutters. Who knows?'

He pointed to a tiny dashed black line, hiding among all the elaborate coloured shapes on the geological map. 'Ah! Here we are, a little to left of the homestead.'

Nudging Jim out of the way, Kelly crouched over the map.

'Do you see it?' Jim asked.

'I think I do, if you mean that wavy thing that stops and starts.'

'Follow it west. See how it comes up on the blue and indigo bands of colour? I think they're the hills.'

Jim suspected the colour change meant the hills were made of a different rock type and therefore a different colour on the map from everything else. 'Yeah, if those shapes are hills, I'll give it to you. On this scale, they do look easier to find. And if those dotted lines are old tracks, it's doable – I suppose.'

Kelly felt a little reassured.

'I don't expect the track will always be easy to follow on the ground,' Jim continued. 'Parts are bound to be overgrown. When that happens, I'll walk ahead and pick out the way for you. Even if we have to bush-bash, we can work off the compass until we find a trail again.'

Jim opened a second geological map, the adjoining Barlee Sheet, and placed it on top of the previous one. In the southeast corner, the purple and blue of the hills continued through from the Kalgoorlie Sheet.

'Can you see? The track carries on here. There are more going up to the Menzies–Sandstone road too. It's about seventy kilometres to Arthur's place from the road.'

He looked over at Kelly, who continued to silently study the map, a tight fold of skin forming between her eyebrows.

'Look,' Jim added. 'We've got plenty of supplies, spares, power steering, all our doors, tinted windows and even feckin air-conditioning! Don't worry, we're laughing. I promise.'

For hundreds of millions of years, no shifting tectonic plates had raised high mountains here, from which great torrents could flow and carve jagged features into the land. No sheets of ice passed this way, to scrape and pile rock and soil into valleys and hills. No seas transgressed, to lay down thick sequences of fossil-rich sedimentary rocks. For much of the age of the Earth, this part of the world had known only the unhurried but indomitable action of weathering and erosion. Two unheralded forces of nature, working forever in tandem to level the landscape. Occasional low hills formed, where more weathering-resistant rock stood proud over the endless bush around them.

Kelly turned the key in the ignition. With some trepidation, she released the handbrake and moved off into the lifting blackness.

* * *

AT FIRST LIGHT, the Major Crime Squad descended on the treehouse. Shortly after, the forensic expert took over all police activity inside Holt's cordon. Forensics established a baseline and mapped the crime scene in minute detail. They photographed every bloodstained inch of dust, every footprint, spent cartridge case and discarded item of clothing. Positions were marked with plastic-numbered pegs in the ground and recorded, relative to the baseline on the map. Outside the perimeter, officers conducted line searches. They followed a fresh trail of footprints that led into the scrub. Some way in, the footprints stopped and motorbike tracks continued. Lots of tracks. The police couldn't be sure which tyre marks were the most recent.

Perth's Major Crime Squad Detective Sergeant Stan Sidoli coordinated the operation and kept in constant communication with units in Perth, Kalgoorlie and Aurora. A systematic air search of the area was underway. Earlier, a police helicopter broke off from its investigation of the surrounding bush to compile an aerial photographic record of the entire crime scene. The Goldfields road network was shut down.

Senior Constable Holt heard talk that the Tactical Response Unit was on standby at Kalgoorlie airport, should there be any reported sighting of the suspects. With their combat fatigues, field radios, weaponry and training, the TRU was more military than police. Once called into a theatre of operation, it spelt curtains for anyone who resisted arrest or was deemed a danger. Holt knew those boys meant business. Their swift and decisive ending to Top End murderer Schwab's killing spree was proof enough. Holt prayed it would not come to that.

* * *

BEHIND THE SKY-BLUE cubicle curtain, Max lay flat on his back, staring at a fluorescent strip light on the ceiling. A nurse leaned over, blocking his view. She adjusted the nasal cannula that discharged a gentle stream of fresh oxygen into both nostrils. The oxygen went some way to easing the discomfort caused to his chest by the smoke. The nurse lifted the control that hung from the side rail on the cantilevered bed and pressed the Up button. The motor hummed. Max's perspective changed as he ascended to a seated position. He could now see his visitor. A short, unassuming, uniformed police officer, with a small and what Max considered ridiculous moustache, stood in front of the curtain, shifting his weight from foot to foot.

The nurse finished adjusting the pillows behind Max's shoulders, then moved the IV stand to the far side of the bedside table and out of the way. Happy her patient was comfortable, she left the cubicle, pulling the curtain closed after her. The two men were alone.

'That's a nasty looking wound you have there, Max,' his old mate, Detective Superintendent Barry 'Baz' Harper of the Major Crime Squad observed.

Harper had been brought in to oversee the now multi-department investigation into the Aurora and Yilgarn Station killings. His instructions were to handle the situation delicately and resolve it expeditiously. The involvement of a retired and controversial former police chief made many people back in Perth uneasy. And of course, it would be preferable if Harper could wrap everything up without starting another cycle of bikie violence.

After years of shootings and bombings, Western Australia now enjoyed a tentative peace between rival bikie organisations. A year ago, the four Western Australian outlaw motorcycle gangs formed an unholy alliance to repel the Mongrel Mob, a New Zealand gang, who unsuccessfully attempted to establish a chapter in Perth. Since their violent expulsion, the fragile truce between the victors appeared to be holding.

Considerable pressure weighed heavy on Detective Superintendent Harper's narrow shoulders. He realised he needed to tread carefully with the irascible Collins. In readiness for the inevitable media briefings, he wore his best clean and decorated uniform. It looked smart and intimidating, but Harper knew Collins wasn't one to be intimidated.

'Twelve stitches they tell me, Baz. Hardly warrants a night in hospital, but they were insistent.'

'Ah, best be cautious. It was quite a knock and you're not getting any younger.'

Max picked up the copy of *The Kalgoorlie Miner* that Harper had left for him on the bedside table. He stared briefly at the large front-cover, black and white photo of the charred remnants of his pub, then threw the paper back down. 'I trust this is not just a well-intentioned courtesy call, to check on the health of your old boss.'

'When you're ready, Max, we'll need a detailed statement.' Harper looked furtively around. Satisfied they were still alone and, with his head cocked to one side, eyebrows raised, he lowered his voice and continued. 'Is that going to be a problem?'

With a subtle movement of his fingers, Max beckoned Harper closer. The police officer obliged and stepped towards the bed.

'Listen, mate!' Max whispered, 'I've got a safety deposit box in an out-of-state bank. In it are detailed records, accounts, diary entries … everything. Even photos of every dodgy deal, every kickback and more, that went down over the last thirty years. There will be no fucking problem with my statement. Understand!'

Outside the small, four-bed public ward, it was a busy Tuesday morning at Kalgoorlie Regional Hospital. A uniformed officer sat by the door, observing all the comings and goings.

* * *

SUDDENLY, JIM WAS gone. He had skipped ahead to identify a way through and the bush closed in around them. At first, the bladed leaves on the wattles' supple outer branches caressed the sides of the Hilux. A few metres farther on and the harder wood caught and pulled the wing mirrors out of alignment. The track disappeared and then the scraping, banging and snapping started in earnest.

Twenty thousand years before Western Australia turned to scrub and desert, before the climate last changed and humans began to manage the landscape, slow-moving rivers flowed through a greener, wetter land. When the temperatures rose, rivers vanished and their channels filled with sediments. Lakes turned to salt.

Fresh water can still be found underground, along the base of the channel fills. In times of drought, deep roots tap into these reserves. Broad, bifurcating ribbons of healthy vegetation and tall trees now straggle the landscape, picking out the paths of ancient drainage systems.

Away from the buried rivers, the drought of recent months had killed off large swathes of scrub. The scorched earth exposed the almost fossilised ruts made by wheels in bygone times. Following these old tracks on open ground proved easy enough. However, when a track disappeared into a line of trees, it was a different matter entirely.

Inside the cab, the volume and tension rose with every snapping branch. Kelly worried about damaging the bodywork and the pristine paint. She concentrated on moving forward. Passing over rough ground, the Hilux pitched and fell, throwing her about. But she grew in confidence and became more familiar with the capabilities of the four-wheel drive. She learned to use the heavy steel plate of the roo bar out front to fight back and trample a path through. The Hilux rolled on, swallowing small trees and bushes. Some sprang back up, like a roly-poly toy. Others, uprooted or snapped at the base, stayed down. She made slow, stuttering progress in pursuit of open ground.

Farther in, the vegetation grew too thick, the trees too large. With a jolt, everything stopped. No way forward, no way back. The engine cut out. The bush held her in a vice, trapped. Her shoulder and neck muscles contracted. She tightened her grip on the wheel and perspired in the cool air-conditioned cab.

ALL NOISE STOPPED. Jim scanned about. Not certain which way was behind anymore, he stood still to get his bearings and listen. The needle on the compass contradicted his sense of direction. His watch and the sun agreed with the compass, but establishing north did nothing to help Jim find his way back to the Hilux. With his pulse rate rising, he searched for his footprints in the thick undergrowth. The last few warm drops from the water bottle were not enough to dampen his thirst.

'Kelly!' Jim shouted, but nothing came back.

His first instinct was to run, cover the ground faster and find the Hilux sooner. But he remembered Old Bill's advice, 'Stay calm and never, ever run.' Then he heard a long blast of the horn.

ANXIETY BECAME PANIC. Was this how it would end? Kelly blasted the horn again.

Suddenly, out front, Jim appeared, waving and shouting. 'Come left, hard left.'

Although relieved to see him, all she could think to do was shout angrily back. 'What kept you?'

The lack of an immediate response annoyed her more. Kelly re-started the engine, spun the steering wheel anticlockwise and, with eyes shut, launched the Hilux at a dense wall of mulga. It parted and she was free, back in open country. In the distance, another line of large trees loomed, only this time, and for no obvious reason, a good track cut right through.

* * *

AROUND MIDDAY, A second helicopter came in over Bungarra Rock and dropped down towards the busy crime scene. The pilot brought the craft to a steady hover some way off. With six kilograms of television camera balanced on one shoulder and his two legs dangling from the open cabin door, the news cameraman recorded what he saw on the ground. He decided they needed to get nearer.

Responding to a signal from his cameraman, the pilot took the aircraft in close, too close. The downdraught from the rotors kicked up a thick cloud of dust, sending Detective Sergeant Sidoli below on the ground apoplectic with rage. The swirling dust would destroy his evidence. Air traffic control at Kalgoorlie was quickly on the radio, ordering the helicopter away. The hand gestures from some officers left the cameraman in no doubt of their disapproval. The pilot's voice came on the headphones.

'You'll probably need to edit that last bit, Les!' The pilot chuckled before finishing. 'We'd better get out of here!'

Les gave him the thumbs up.

* * *

CROSSING A LOW granite crag, Jim stopped the Hilux to check out what looked suspiciously like a gnamma hole. He had never seen one before, but Old Bill had described what to look for and spoke of gnammas in almost masonic tones.

When the rains come, run-off can collect in cavities below rocky outcrops. If the geomorphology is favourable, fresh water may still be found at these places in high summer – if you know where to look. Knowledge of their whereabouts made it possible for people to move freely through the otherwise arid land. The Aborigines treasured and managed the gnammas, often placing a slab of rock over the openings of the smaller ones to slow evaporation and keep wildlife and live-stock away.

Having brought sufficient supplies with them for several days, the young outlaws did not need extra water. Jim was just curious. Finding a secret water source in the bush was in many ways like finding gold. In some ways, better.

After doing battle with a spectacular giant black and orange potter wasp, Jim persuaded the beautiful, self-appointed guardian of the entrance to move aside. Pushing back the granite slab, Jim found, as he suspected, a deep pool of fresh, clear water underneath. Dipping his hands in, he stirred the cold, soothing liquid, while pondering when the pool last quenched a traveller's thirst. It saddened him to think it may have been long ago in a different time. He splashed a few drops on his face, but drank none. He felt it was not his to drink. Kelly came across to check out his discovery for herself.

'Kneel down here and put your hands in. It's good.'

She did. And it was nice. 'Listen to the quiet, Jim.'

A hot breeze played a delicate sound, easy on the leaves. Flies buzzed nearby. Other than that, nothing, just silence. She took a hand-ful of water and dribbled it over Jim's head and then put a cold, soft hand on his cheek. He let the water trickle down and smiled. She smiled back at him, but could see he looked tired.

'We're still here, Irishman.'

Her smile convinced him they were doing the right thing. He left the gnamma hole as he found it, with its sentinel once again guarding the entrance. In the near distance, they could see the irregular ridge of dark-blue hills.

Apart from a few more tight squeezes, the journey passed without incident. Kelly got lumbered with most of the driving. She enjoyed the cool air inside the Hilux and the refuge from the flies. Jim popped in and out. He busied himself checking maps, tapping his compass and scouting ahead through the thicker bush. Sometimes, he doubled back to a point and then set off again on a slightly different bearing. Whenever they encountered a steep gully or dry riverbank, Jim flagged the best route across in advance. Having navigated their way over the empty yellow space on the big map, they were in the hills by lunchtime – well ahead of schedule. So much ahead, that Jim became concerned and began to wonder if he had missed something.

For lunch, they each enjoyed a tin of pineapple in syrup, eaten and drunk on the move, while following the hills northwest. Their progress slowed when the ground broke up and the track became rockier. The geology had definitely changed. On his return from a comfort stop, Jim picked up a loose, cobble-sized lump of the striking red and dark metallic, grey-striped rock that dominated the slopes. The key in the margin of the geological map indicated most of the hills were formed from something called 'banded iron formation'. The opaque, glassy bands in his piece reminded Jim of the flint he collected on the beach as a youngster.

Many times in his childhood, Jim knocked flints together hoping to make fire, but never managed to set anything alight. He had better luck fashioning crude arrowheads from the flint and passed them off in school as the genuine Stone Age article. This Australian flint that the map called 'chert', was a deep Indian red. Not the creamy brown of his arrowheads. Interlayered within it were beautiful, straight, metallic-grey bands of mineral. This must be the iron, he guessed. He told Kelly of his school art teacher's decree that 'there are no straight lines in nature.'

'Well, she was wrong. Here's the proof!'

Jim licked a flat surface of the rock and took a closer look. Hundreds of paper-thin layers of grey and vibrant red appeared. The thin layers bunched into thicker bands, all perfect and all parallel. At one corner of the rock, a section appeared to have exploded apart into many small blocks of different sizes that were then randomly stuck back together.

'That'll make a nice paperweight,' Jim suggested, aware he might well provoke a response from the driver.

'Who collects rock samples, when they're on the run from the law? Come on, tell me! Who does that?'

'Yeah, fair enough.'

Jim put the rock on the floor. He believed he might just slip it into his bag when she was not looking. They continued northwest for another twenty kilometres up the east side of the hills. Then the Hilux turned west through a wide valley cut by a long-disappeared river and onto the now sunnier western slopes.

THE MOVEMENT HIGHER on the slope caught her eye before the vivid colour registered. A Day-Glo pink ribbon, tied to the top of a tall, square wooden stake, flapped in a lazy breeze. Assuming it was there for a reason, Kelly turned off the rocky track and drove up to investigate.

'Hey, sleepyhead. What's this?' she said, poking Jim with the end of the stake to wake him.

Written in black texta, two numbers ran down one side. Jim recognised these as map coordinates and the stake, a surveyor's mark. Probably one of a line or grid of evenly spaced, similar marks put in by an exploration company.

'They're used to show potential drill sites or tenement boundaries,' Jim explained. He reached for his geological map.

Farther east in the greenstone belts, where most of the mining is concentrated, he had come across generations of these stakes littering the bush. This one looked new, a recent addition and the first they saw since leaving Yilgarn. He plotted the coordinates as best he could onto the map.

'If I'm reading this right, we're pretty much where we should be, maybe a little farther north.' He checked again and arrived at the same point. 'Yep.'

'So we're not lost then? That's nice to know.'

'Nope,' he said, chewing the end of a pencil.

In the privacy of his own imagination, Jim celebrated wildly. In there, his T-shirt now covered his head while he ran in circles, pumping his fists and shouting happy obscenities at nobody in particular. There was every possibility the stake could have exposed him as the spoofer his conscience kept telling him he was.

There was every possibility they were nowhere near where he thought they were. He really had been making it up as they went along – while trying to appear calm and decisive. He had agonised over every twist and turn on the way. Old Bill warned of the 'mulga trap'. How everything looked the same out here. How heat impairs judgement and creates disorientation, panic and bad choices. How you can get lost just yards from your truck and never be seen again.

When handing over the keys to the Ford, Old Bill strongly advised against leaving the familiar ground of Yilgarn or the main tracks. The risks were much too great. But so far, they had feckin pulled it off and, depending on their next move, the worst of it could well be behind them.

'You know, we're closer to the Sandstone road than I thought. We have a decision to make. We could chance going onto that track in the morning and beetling the seventy kilometres over to Dismals. With any luck, the police are concentrating their effort east of here and towards Perth.'

'Or?'

'We keep heading west for another day and try coming into Dismals from the south. That way we stay off the road, but there are a few hills, possibly mountains, to negotiate.' Jim looked up from the map and over at Kelly. 'Less chance of being spotted, but rough terrain, or maybe not, I can't be sure.' He shrugged. 'What do you think? Should we chance the road?'

'About an hour by road you say?'

Jim nodded.

'Presume I'm driving?'

Jim nodded again.

* * *

THROWING THE REMOTE down beside him on the couch, Troy grabbed a beer and swung his feet onto the coffee table. The television in the corner whooshed. A thin strip of light jumped out to fill the screen. He looked forward to catching up with his old girlfriend.

He sort of missed Kelly, and the money she promised would come in handy. Not to mention what the bike might fetch – 'seed money for the hydro'. Troy smirked and complimented himself on the pun. With any luck, she's hot. Curious to meet whoever Kelly was bringing, he lit the first of a few joints planned for the evening and considered keeping one for his mystery guest. Perfect to help her relax – should she care to indulge. His mind wandered into the realms of fantasy.

'Sweet! Kell'd be spewing,' he said to the empty room and enjoyed another deep, smug drag that brought on a cough. Troy knew he was a charmer. Still, she owed him. That V8 was mint!

The grand intro to the Nightly News came on the television. Galloping strings, followed by a fanfare of trumpets, then back to whimsical, airy strings took the viewer on the wings of Pegasus around the globe, to be educated in all the great news stories of the day. The female news anchor cut in over the opening music.

Tonight! Murder in the Goldfields. Police name the two individuals they are seeking to question in relation to the recent fatal shootings in the Kalgoorlie area.

Her male co-host delivered his headline.

As WA's historic first female Premier, Carmen Lawrence, settles into her new role, she insists stamping out corruption in WA is a top priority.

The female presenter came back in with the last headline.

And in boxing ... Down but not out. Mike Tyson's manager, Don King, blames referee error for Tyson's loss in Sunday's big title fight in Tokyo.

The camera came in for a tight close up on the female presenter.

Good evening and welcome. Tonight in the Goldfields, the police name the suspects they are seeking in connection with two separate Goldfields killings and appeal to the public for information.

Troy chuckled away while half-following the news through a haze of smoke and the haze of a few misfiring neurons. He swayed along with some shaky aerial footage of a camp in the outback, straining to keep his eyes parallel to the unsteady horizon onscreen.

Two portrait photos were overlain onto an image of the burnt-out shell of a building. One, a young man in glasses, the other Troy recognised instantly. It was Kelly's driver's licence picture. He sat up, leaned towards the set and tried to concentrate on what was being said. The camera cut to a senior police officer with a lot of brass on his shoulders. The words began to filter through.

Wanted ... two killings ... bikies ... arson ... robbery ... believed to be armed and dangerous.

'Armed and fackin dangerous! Shit!' Troy spat the words back at the television, the remnant of his joint dangling from his lower lip.

Members of the public are warned not to approach the pair. Instead, they should ring the number onscreen or contact their local police station.

'Fack! What's she done to me?' He got off the couch and did laps of the room. He continued to talk to himself, his dreams of skimpy sex shattered. 'Fack! Asking me to hide a double murderer, some nut job with a gun, in my flat? Is she fackin mad? What if the filth find out? ... Or worse, the bikies!

'That bitch is not bringing her shit storm down on me. No fackin way! Not having it. They can fack off and stay somewhere else! Christ, what if she told him about me cheating on her? Fack!' Did the TV say anything about a reward? It's worth a try. Troy didn't think twice and reached for the phone.

On the television, footage played from Sydney of a large gentleman claiming to be a friend of the Irish backpacker. He informed the reporter of how the suspect rang him on Monday night from Kalgoorlie, protesting his innocence and wanted it to be known that, should he or the girl be caught, neither of them had any intention of committing suicide in custody.

* * *

SITTING AT THE bar of the Menzies Hotel on Shenton Street, Senior Constable Holt polished off a magnificent lamb shank dinner. He pushed the prongs of his fork into the last oily piece of meat left on the bone. Circling the plate with the skewered flesh, Holt wiped up the remaining gravy.

'Everything OK, Laurie?' enquired the stout, middle-aged landlady.

Laurie bobbed his head approvingly, until the final mouthful reached his well-sated belly. 'Sweet as, Sheila. Thanks.'

'That was terrible news about poor Old Bill. Have you got anyone for it yet?'

'Nope, nobody. Word is the two we're after might be in Perth already, or on the way there at least.'

'People are saying it's that young Irish lad that did it. He was around here painting. Ate lunch where you're sitting now. Seemed like a nice, polite young fella.' She folded her arms across an ample chest, then added, 'Drugs and drink, heaven forbid!' It was as much a comment on the state of the younger generation as it was on what drove the Irishman over the edge.

Holt wondered why she hadn't included sex, something she would happily discuss with a few select punters at any opportunity. On a few lonely nights over the years, he had occasion to discuss it with her too.

'So it appears. But you know, Sheila, I can't see it. It's been bothering me. Why the hell would you want to start a war with a bikie gang and then shoot a good mate? I mean, he would have made his point, if he just ran over a Harley in his ute and hot-tailed it into the bush.'

The police had been tipped off that the two suspects may be travelling the 530-kilometre Kalgoorlie pipeline to Perth. This started a flurry of activity within the Major Crime Squad ranks. The focus of the main search moved south to Kalgoorlie and beyond to Perth. Holt did not believe it would come to anything. Just getting from the treehouse to Kalgoorlie unnoticed would have been bloody difficult – getting to Perth on a motorbike unseen, near impossible. They would have to refuel along the way too. Holt suspected the couple were still in the area. He decided to head back out on the Menzies track in the morning, overnight in Sandstone and return the following day. The track passed relatively close to Bungarra Rock. Maybe the few pastoralists on the way up to Sandstone noticed something.

Ray the roo shooter swaggered into the bar, like big John Wayne, all barrel chest. His sharpshooter eyes swept the saloon, alert to any sudden movement. He spotted Laurie finishing a beer. The roo shooter moved in.

'G'day, Ray. Behaving yourself, I hope?' Laurie said, noticing the big man's approach.

'Course, mate. Bagged me a few boomers this arvo. Think I might wet the old pipes to celebrate another honest day's hard yakka.'

'Good man. Keep it up.'

'Let me get you a cold one, Laurie?'

'Early start, Ray. Just heading off. Thanks all the same. You didn't happen to come across anything or anyone suspicious on your travels out bush over the last few days? Maybe even heard a bike in the distance?'

'Nah. Sorry, mate. All quiet out where I was. No sign of Old Bill's killers then?'

Holt shook his head, stood up and put money on the counter.

'I met that Irish fella a while back. He brewed me a billy at his camp. Great little place he had, too. Good bloke.'

'Yeah, so everybody keeps saying.' Holt started to leave and saluted the landlady, who busied herself collecting empties at the far end of the bar. 'Cheers, Sheila.'

Sheila gave him the slow wave and wide-eyed look that suggested a few late drinks were available, if he fancied them.

'Shot a roo for him, I did. He sure looked as if he needed to eat—'

'You what, Ray?'

'Yeah, got the feeling he hadn't much tucker. Still, he insisted I ate a sanger with me tea. So I comes back and dropped him off a roo I shot on his track. You know, one good deed, mate—'

'He didn't shoot it, then?'

'Na, mate. It's not that easy. He wasn't a big fan of guns anyway. Told me as much.'

'Jesus. They were claiming him to be an expert marksman.'

'Yeah, it was a good shot by me. So he didn't eat it, then?'

'Seems he skinned it. The tail and a leg were missing. He made a fair stab at eating it, I'd reckon. And you can't brew a tea with a billy full of holes now, can you?'

CHAPTER 10

IN PLAIN SIGHT

S CRATCHED INTO A rusty barrel, the graffiti read 'R. Dimer 1957' and told of a previous visitor to this abandoned spot. Only a few feet of crumbling rough-cut, granite-block wall remained of the stone hut. If someone once made a home here, it must have been well before R. Dimer happened by. The eight-hundred-year-old remnants of St Patrick's church, marooned on its own stormy island off Skerries, were in better nick.

All the same, even if the ruins had a roof, neither he nor Kelly would have contemplated spending the night under it, what with the spiders and the snakes. But finding the stone hut, as it appeared on the map, pinpointed their exact location and removed any niggling doubts in Jim's mind. From the hut, the map indicated a trail north for about fifteen kilometres that hugged open ground along the shores of a number of small salt lakes, before it joined the Menzies–Sandstone road. Pleased with themselves for making it this far and without a single puncture, they parked for the night, hidden under a thick cover of trees next to the vertical face of a rocky breakaway. Tomorrow morning, they would make the run for Dismals homestead.

Kelly sat on the back of the Hilux swinging her legs. Beside her, a saucepan of water boiled on a single-ring gas stove. For an evening meal, Jim had dished up what the label on the tins claimed to be Irish stew and served it with slices of bread and runny, maggot-free butter. Although she ate almost a full tin of the 'gruel', Kelly remained to be convinced about Irish stew and gave Jim something of a hard time about his use of the term 'Irish cuisine'. In his defence, he had argued that whatever it was in the tins, except for the name, bore no resemblance to the stews his mother put in front of the eight kids back home.

'Bacon and cabbage, then!' Kelly offered as another example of the oxymoron that was Irish cuisine.

'Simple fare, I'll grant you,' Jim replied indignantly, climbing into the cab, 'but tasty. Anyway, you're in no position to be slagging off Irish food. Need I remind you of the Chico Roll?'

'Ha!' Kelly laughed, 'Not fair. That's a roadhouse snack, not a meal.'

'Doesn't matter. Has anyone other than the manufacturer any idea what's in it? The problem is, you think you're buying some sort of battered spring roll, but you're not. There're no delicate spiced bean sprouts or crispy veg inside. The Chico Roll doesn't even have chicken in it, for God sake!'

Reluctantly, Kelly conceded on the Chico Roll, but would not give him 'the Burger with the Lot.' Some things are sacred. She shut the debate down with mention of her Italian roots, spag bol and lasagne, before returning to a more pressing matter.

'Tell me, Jim Macken, I know you're not the loner or the drifter they said you were on the radio. Why did you really go off alone into the bush? Were you trying to find yourself or running away, or what?'

'Perhaps,' Jim replied, from the backseat, while pulling all the gear from his rucksack. He found Ron's stubby holder flattened at the bottom of the bag. 'You beauty!' he said, popping the neoprene cylinder back into shape.

Kelly thought his enthusiasm for finding the stubby holder a little odd, but said nothing. Next she knew, he was on the back of the Hilux dragging everything asunder. A dislodged swag rolled dangerously close to the burning stove.

'Oi! Be careful.' She pushed the swag away. 'So, what were you trying to achieve, running off alone into the bush?' she probed again.

He didn't respond. She watched him drag a metal box to the side and heard the distinctive sound of tools knocking together.

'Good man, Bill!' Jim seemed pleased.

'What is it, then?' She asked, a little irritated.

'Insulation tape.'

Kelly neither knew nor cared why he seemed so excited by insulation tape and passed no comment. Instead, she stirred powdered milk into two freshly poured mugs of coffee and handed one up to him.

'Thanks!' Jim said, putting the spoils of his rummaging down. 'Do you really want to know? It's not very interesting. Nothing juicy, I'm afraid.'

'Go on. I'm not particularly busy at the moment.'

'Apathy! I was running away from apathy, I suppose … if anything.'

'Explain.'

Jim, mug in hand, eased himself down next to Kelly. 'Nothing interested me. I didn't care. I always took the path of least hassle. It goes back to when I lived in London with some mates from Ireland. We all had crap jobs, if we even bothered to turn up. No qualifications. No drive. No intentions of going to uni or anything …

'We lay about drinking and smoking for days on end, sneering at anyone who dared think about trying to better themselves. Waiting for the world to do us a favour. Ah, Christ! There was more life in a feckin amoeba than in the lot of us.'

Swinging his legs in time with hers, he looked at the ground. 'And my childhood sweetheart, a beautiful, sensible Danish girl by the name of Ellen, gave me the elbow around about then too. That's great coffee, by the way. No lumps.'

'Was she living with you in London?'

'Ah, not really. She moved in with us for a while. That was a bad idea from the start.'

Jim shook his head and grimaced at some of his private memories of that time and then went farther back to the happier ones. 'I met her when she was visiting relatives in Skerries. We were only sixteen. Most of our relationship we conducted by correspondence. Her English was perfect, and sure, I couldn't put two words together on paper. It was kind of one-way traffic, really.'

'Yeah, I noticed your dodgy spelling in Helen's letter.'

'Funny how it doesn't bother me anymore. But you can imagine how a self-conscious, awkward teenager might feel trying to write love letters to this exotic, sophisticated creature from the continent. But, to be fair, we were mad about each other and, after leaving school, we got together more and more. She deferred her uni studies in Copenhagen and moved over to London. But ...' He shook his head and frowned. 'I was still the same useless twat, lying around on the couch all day. She packed me in pretty quickly.'

Jim paused and took a sip of coffee. His face hardened again. 'She was right. It was completely my fault and I've kicked myself ever since ... So, to mend my broken heart, I came to Australia and put the world between the two of us. I also wanted to leave that London version of me far behind.'

'Did it work?'

'Old habits die hard. Soon enough I was living on a couch in Sydney and settled into the same safe, easy routine. Only with better weather outside the window ...

'One morning, about seven months ago, I finally decided I needed to give myself a good kick in the arse and make some big changes. I stopped smoking. Started jogging. I convinced my mate, the Bubbles, who owned a car, we needed to get out of Sydney and see Oz. We eventually ended up in Perth, where he sold the car, got the bus back to Sydney and I got the job at Yilgarn. Away from the couch and the TV, my eyes were opened again. That's the gist of it. The rest you know.'

'Yeah, but what about the broken heart and Ellen?'

'She met someone else. Actually, she used to write to me every time she had a fight with her boyfriend. She never mentioned their arguments, but I could tell. Her parents divorced and she's an only child, so I'm glad she wasn't alone. Funny thing is … I still loved hearing from her. Then the letters stopped. Maybe the fights stopped too.'

'So have you found yourself … out here? I mean, before all this shit happened?'

'Oh, yeah … for sure. I got off the couch and moved on. I'm curious about stuff again – like when I was a kid. And I went back to painting. Turns out I'm not too bad.

Jim slid himself off the back and walked around to the driver's door. He stood staring at the door for a moment. In a decisive movement, he finished off the coffee with a substantial gulp, shook any grit out of the bottom of the mug and placed it on the bonnet. Wiping the door with his hand, he removed an arc of dust and ran his fingertips over the clean paint underneath.

'What was it like, not seeing another person for days out there? Were you not lonely?' Kelly asked.

'To be honest, I didn't particularly notice. It's not that I don't enjoy company. I was too busy experiencing new things and making the camp work.'

Then, realising he'd been talking too much about himself, he ventured, 'What about you? Aurora is no metropolis? How'd you end up there? Running away yourself?'

'Ah, that's simple. I found out Troy cheated on me, so I took his car to Kalgoorlie. Sold it cheap to a backpacker and got a job in a bar. A bent copper mate of Max's owned the bar. I met Max there and he offered me a job at his place. The bastard promised me a management position. That didn't quite work out, did it?'

Something about her brief matter-of-fact delivery suggested to Jim she had glossed over a lot of detail.

'What about Melbourne? What was life like there?' He walked back over to her and picked up the stubby holder again, examining it closely.

'I left Melbourne when I was young.' That was all she wanted to say on the subject. 'Anyway, what are you doing?'

He didn't push her. Another time, perhaps. First, Jim figured he'd better run his idea past her. 'Hide in plain sight, that's what we'll do. At least, I hope so.'

'What are you on about?'

'OK! You're driving around the Goldfields. Apart from all the nature stuff and the road trains, what are you most likely to meet on your travels?'

'Road kill?'

'OK, though that could be classified as nature stuff. What about exploration and mining industry traffic?' Jim handed her the stubby holder. 'Ozdrill. They must have the biggest fleet of anyone in WA, right?'

'Yeah, that's true. Their trucks and rigs are everywhere.'

'Precisely! If we were driving an Ozdrill vehicle, nobody would give us a second glance.' Jim pointed to the image on the stubby holder. 'It's a simple logo, just three colours, a yellow and green stylised map of Australia and the name overlaid in black. I think I can paint it on the sides of the Hilux. It's worth a try.'

Jim returned to rummaging in the cab and found his box of acrylic paint tubes.

KELLY KNELT ON the back seat. Her denim-clad elbows hung over the open window, her chin rested comfortably on her interlocking fingers. She watched Jim work. Neither spoke much, but there was nothing awkward about their silence. She asked him idle questions about his life in Ireland, if he'd ever been to Denmark, how he spent his days at the treehouse.

'Most of my time there was fairly mundane, really. Hours could be spent pulling water from the well, or making damper and trying to keep the flies away from it.'

She loved how his face was as animated talking about the house-keeping, as it was when telling her again about finding the gold. She complimented his art, just to watch him blush and change the subject.

'What would you do if you won the Lotto?' Jim asked, after one of their long silences. He thought if he explored her dreams, it might help him unravel her past.

'That's easy. I'd buy a vineyard on the Margaret River and make wine.'

'You know about wines?'

'No, nothing more than what I learned in the pub trade. I have this romantic idea of nurturing vines and sending my wine to market.'

'House of Porcini. You don't have to win the Lotto to get a start in the business.'

'No, indeed not. I'd been thinking of taking a trip down sometime and talking to people there. I just couldn't get out of Aurora. Labouring in the vineyards would be OK to start with, but it'd be nice to study wine-making too. Maybe even do some sort of apprenticeship.'

'Right! When this is over, first thing you'll do is take the Hilux to Margaret River.'

'I hear the light is great for painting there.'

Jim smiled.

Getting the proportions correct and of similar size on both doors proved difficult and the cause of some colourful language. Kelly came to the rescue with a ruler she fashioned from an almost straight branch. By pressing the open face of a spoon into the soft wood, she created a standard interval. Twenty spoons equalled one branch. It worked perfectly. Jim took at least an hour to sketch the logos on the cab's front doors. He used the insulation tape to define the edges of the lettering and to mask out the emblematic Ozdrill pinstripes that ran below the windows of its entire fleet.

She watched him apply a coat of yellow paint to the map he had drawn of Australia. He looked awkward working the brush with his left hand, but his brushstrokes were smooth and precise. From her vantage point, the logos were coming along nicely. The paint covered the white enamel well and he seemed to get a good clean edge to the lettering. She thought he must be uncomfortable crouched over on the camp chair, and hoped his injuries were not hurting him.

Kelly fell asleep. Jim had not noticed until he stood to light the lamp. The side of her head still rested in her folded arms on top of the window frame. A small dribble of saliva trickled down from her open mouth to between her delicate fingers. He thought he should encourage her to lie across the back seat. Would it be inappropriate to lift her? She would sleep better lying down. It was a clear night with no cover of cloud to trap the warm air on the ground. It could get cold. Perhaps she needed a blanket over her.

Gently, Jim helped Kelly off the window, all the time talking her through his manoeuvres, in case she misunderstood his intentions. He got a few mumbled OKs and a thank you. Then she curled up on the back seat. Jim placed an old sleeping bag over her and retreated. Looking in from the opposite door at the peaceful sleeping figure, he wondered should he kiss her good night. God she's beautiful, he thought. OK, so she kissed you earlier, he reminded himself, but that may have just been a friendly gesture, a show of compassion, tenderness amid all the madness. Best not, he decided and regretted his decision almost immediately. By then it was too late.

Without the need for a performance, Jim had seen a different side to the feisty barmaid who knew his name. He liked this Kelly Porcini. In fact, he liked both Kelly Porcinis a lot. But if it wasn't for circumstance throwing them together, would she even have given him a second glance? Considering where they found themselves, was it right to be thinking of her this way? Perhaps, when things were less fraught, and they were safe, then he might tell her of how much he wanted to kiss her that night.

He worked on through the early morning hours, fighting tiredness, the paint, the pains in his back and the many moths and beetles that came by to check him out before climbing into the fire of the lamp. For the first time in over a year, when left to himself, his mind did not turn to Denmark and Ellen. Instead, the girl now sleeping only three feet away inhabited all his thoughts and that startled him.

Dawn was breaking on Wednesday morning, when Jim peeled off the tape and applied a few delicate strokes of touch-up paint. He stood back as far as the confining trees allowed, to admire his work. A lot depended on him getting the Ozdrill logos right.

'That'll do, Jim,' he whispered, pleased with his efforts.

BY THE TIME JIM unrolled the swag on the ground and laid his exhausted, damaged body down, Laurie Holt had finished packing the last of his provisions into the back of the police wagon. Holt was about to begin his long journey from Menzies to Sandstone.

'WHO'S A CLEVER boy, then,' Kelly said, waking Jim with an offer of coffee and toast. 'Those logos are brilliant!'

'You think so?' Jim sat up and eagerly took his breakfast from the vision before him.

'Yeah, superb!'

'They'd be better with some dirt on them. But we have to be careful. The paint scratches off easily. What time is it?' he asked, enjoying her cheery face and not wanting to look away to check his watch.

'Technically, it's still morning. Eat that quickly, because I'm going to cut your hair.'

'What ...?'

Puzzled, but also secretly delighted, Jim finished his toast. He watched Kelly collect the chair from where he had left it, and carry it over. She looked refreshed after her first real sleep for some time. He noticed her change of clothes and how fine she looked in her clean white blouse and how her denim shorts matched his denim jacket. It never looked like that on him, he thought.

Kelly gestured for him to take a seat. 'I found some scissors. They look sharp, so you're getting a short one. No arguing now.'

Jim did as he was told and moved over to the chair. She stood behind him and removed the bob at the back of his head, letting his mop of dusty black hair fall loose. Gathering tufts between her fingers, she began to snip. Curly, dark locks fell from his shoulders to the ground. He had not seen that amount of hair come off since he said goodbye to the seventies. Kelly appeared to know what she was doing.

'You've done this before.'

'Maybe.'

There she goes with the obfuscation again, he thought. 'You're not to give me a mullet, OK?'

'No chance. I want you to look like a smart Ozdrill manager about town, out checking on a rig somewhere.'

Jim went quiet. Kelly continued to gather locks and cut. He closed his eyes and enjoyed the sensation of her busy delicate hands on his head. Sometimes, she would gently encourage his head over to a different angle, or she might change her position to work the sides. She leaned forward and tipped his head back against her breasts to cut the front. Jim's mouth went dry. He wanted to swallow, but was afraid it might be obvious. She left his head on her breasts, but turned it to the side with a soft hand and cut neatly around his ear. He felt a nipple through her blouse against his cheek. Oh! She's not wearing a bra.

Kelly blew the cuttings off his neck and from behind his ear. Christ! He sensed his face flush with blood and turn red. He realised it was not the only part of him flushed with blood. He tried to convince himself that any young man off-grid for as long, who had not observed a real woman in weeks, would respond to her touch the same way.

How could you not? You talk to imaginary naked women in trees for God sake ... She might not see it like that, though! Jim snuck a glance down to check his shorts were not betraying him and quickly repositioned his arms.

Kelly turned his head again and cut around the other ear. He was sure she pressed him closer. He listened to her shallow breaths and felt the moist air leaving her mouth against his neck. She ran her fingers through what remained of his hair to check length, then blew more clippings away.

Ah, Jaysus! He screamed in his imagination, over which he had lost all control. You're killing me, Porcini! Fearing the dream might end, Jim refused to open his eyes. You can cut it all off, if it just means you keep going.

Eventually, he would have to say something and he knew that, whatever quip he might come up with would be rubbish. In fact, he was afraid anything he ever said to her again would be rubbish. Kelly stepped back to signal she had finished.

'Ta-daah! There you go and you still have two ears!' Check in the wing mirror, if you don't trust me.'

'Great! Thanks ... Thanks. I'm sure it's perfect.' Jim clapped. Then, as if scrubbing in for surgery, he rubbed his hands vigorously together. 'Right, we'd better be off!'

CHAPTER 11

IRON COUNTRY

I N REALITY, THE Johnstone Range, as appeared on the geological map, was only a strip of low parallel hills. The wide Menzies–Sandstone road followed a path cut by a dry stream across the strike of the narrow range. Banded iron formation again, Jim guessed, having spotted the striped, red and dark grey outcrops. The map confirmed it with a streak of vivid indigo, the same indigo it used for yesterday's hills. Jim had begun to make some sense of the geological map and its complicated jigsaw of coloured shapes.

He now recognised features on the ground and correctly predicted their colour on the map. The descriptions still baffled, though. Anything other than granite, sandstone and chert in the key stumped him.

'More banded iron!'

'Marvellous.' Kelly wasn't quite as excited as Jim by the changing geology around them.

Jim folded the map and grabbed the camera off the back seat. 'Say cheese.'

'Hey! Don't do that. I look terrible.'

'No – far from it.' Jim smiled. 'Don't worry, there's no film.'

Kelly checked her hair in the visor mirror, just in case. Jim aimed the camera at the passing scenery.

'God, I love the light out here. The colours are amazing,' he announced. 'Nothing like back home, where it's all grey – well some green, but mostly grey – and grim.'

'The Emerald Isle can't be grim! Why then have I served so many Irish over the years, who cried into their drinks pining to get home?'

'Those lads seldom, if ever, make it back. Ireland is a miserable, wet theocracy. There's feck all work and crippling tax. It's only family and Irish stew that lures anyone home ... and maybe now the World Cup. I couldn't wait to leave for London.'

Jim took another imaginary photo of Kelly. 'London didn't turn out grim at all, did it?' he said, with a heavy hint of irony. 'Why didn't I take more photos of Yilgarn? I should have learned to use this thing properly.'

'What are you going to do when your visa expires?'

'Don't know, obviously keep painting. Can't go back to London – too many bad memories. I was thinking about studying.'

'London can't be that bad.'

'Ah no, not really. It was my own fault. Ellen leaving for Copenhagen just soured me to the place. She gave me this camera, you know. The funny thing is ... it's possibly saved my life, but it's also sort of responsible for why the two of us broke up.'

'How so?' Kelly asked, not sure if she wanted to get into another conversation about Jim's ex-girlfriend.

'Ahh,' Jim sighed. 'To be honest, I was a tosser. Ellen had confidence and energy to burn. She couldn't understand how I had no plans or ambition.

'The camera was a twenty-first birthday present. She even found a photography course for me. She knew I'd love it.'

'Must have cost a bit.'

'Yeah. I think she borrowed the money from her parents. She also came from a more liberal Scandinavian culture, if you know what I mean.'

'No, sorry. Don't follow,' Kelly said.

'You know, prudish Catholic Ireland and all that.'

'Nah, still don't get you. Tell me more.' Kelly fought hard to stifle a grin.

'I suspect you do…Anyway, it all led to tension in the house after she moved in. I became paranoid. Decided she was flirting with my mates. I even made the stupid mistake of accusing her of it. After that, maybe she did – just to wind me up.

'I remember coming in from my first class and saw her giggling on the couch with one of the lads. They looked far too comfortable. I jacked in the photography course on the spot, just to annoy her. And then she left … Why am I telling you all this?'

Kelly shrugged. 'I don't know. Clear your conscience?'

Jim laughed. 'Yeah, a last confession, perhaps.'

'That's not funny, Jim.'

'I know. I'm sorry.' He put the camera away and, folding his arms, twisted in the seat to face her. 'Out here, I've had a lot of time to think about my behaviour. Maybe I've just grown up. Anyway, Ellen's moved on. At least, we're still friends. Well, I think we are. I found out on Sunday she's written again. Her letter is winging its way from Skerries to Yilgarn as we speak.'

'You must be curious. I know I would be – in fact, I am!'

'Ah, she's just checking in, making sure I haven't lost it completely.'

'You never know. Maybe they've broken up.'

Jim let a moment of quiet pass. He could feel his pulse quicken. He wanted to ask, 'Would it matter?' but talked himself out of it.

Kelly said nothing. Instead, she turned and offered a beguiling smile. Jim smiled back and felt himself blush. He didn't care. The dust probably covered it anyway. There were more giddy, knowing smiles as they drove on.

The graded surface made for easy driving. It wasn't long before they crossed into Dismals land. Unusual for a station property, the public road passed close to the front door, before it swung northwest along Lake Barlee and on up to Sandstone. Nobody passed Dismals in either direction, without attracting the attention of the station owner.

KELLY PARKED THE Hilux beside a rickety old gate that never knew paint. A rusty, corrugated fence encircled a bare patch of ground that might at one time have been a front garden. The main house, a modest structure stood in a similar dilapidated state to the fence. Constructed from weatherboard and roofed in loose corrugated sheets, even in its pomp, the building would never have looked particularly welcoming or comfortable. A few mature trees offered patchy shade, but did nothing to lessen the austere look of the place.

Jim stepped out of the Hilux. A small, dishevelled, behatted man emerged from the front door and refused to acknowledge his visitors. Weighed down by the large axe he carried over his shoulder, he shuffled towards a side building. The knot on his string belt had slipped and the frayed ends of the old man's sagging trouser legs dragged behind the heels of his boots. Kelly remained in the cab. Keeping her eyes on the axe, she checked that the keys were still in the ignition. After a few slow steps, the old man stopped and looked over at Jim, who now stood at the gate.

'Look, mate. I thought I made myself clear. You lot aren't welcome around here.'

'Hey, Arthur. It's me, Jim!'

Arthur removed his sunnies. Kelly watched the small beady eyes struggle to focus. Suddenly, they widened and a broad smile broke out across his time-etched face.

'Well, starve the lizards, if it isn't the little Irish fella. What are you doing over this way, eh?' Arthur pointed to the logo on the Hilux door. 'When did you starts working for that shower of drongos?'

'What? Oh yeah, that. Nah, don't work for them. Hey, it's good to see you, Arthur. Keeping well?'

'As can be expected, eh. You're looking a tad rough yourself, mate.' Then, and not too discreetly, he winked at Jim, while raising his voice. 'I see you got a sheila in there with you. She not coming out?'

'I'm sure she will eventually. I think your axe scared her off.'

Arthur swung the axe off his shoulder and supported himself with the handle. He tipped his Akubra to Kelly and gave her a reassuring wave.

'Ha! It's all right, darling. I was just going to chop wood for me lunch.' He turned back to Jim. 'Did that Old Bill fella send you over to check on me? Is he after some of me cattle, eh? Wasn't Helen only telling me on the radio last week, they was thinking of getting cattle?'

'You haven't heard the news, then?'

'No, nothing mate, eh. I've been out bush, fixing a bastard windmill since Monday arvo. The Tojo's electrics are all on the blink. Couldn't gets anything on the bastard radio. You're lucky to catch me at all, Jim lad. Only back this half hour.'

Kelly noticed a sheet of red scrap metal leaning against the fence. In broad white brushstrokes, Arthur had painted on it, 'G'day, gone bush Monday – back Wednesday arvo. Cheers, Arthur.'

'I'm afraid, I have bad news, Arthur.' Jim blurted it out. 'Bill is dead.'

'Strewth!' The beady eyes opened wide again. He dropped the handle of the axe to the ground. Grabbing the top of the fence with both hands, he stared for a moment up the narrowing road to its vanishing point below the hills. 'That fair dinkum, Jim?'

'Yeah, I'm afraid so.'

'What happened?'

'Max Collins shot him.'

'Jesus! God rest me old cobber's soul. Why?'

'It's complicated.'

'Right. Christ, yeah? Wooh!' Arthur's shoulders sagged, visibly de-flating as he sighed. By now Kelly had alighted from the Hilux. Arthur gathered himself as she approached. 'Look, where's me manners, eh?' He wiped a hand on his manky old shirt and reached across the gate to Kelly.

'Arthur Williamson, station owner, pleased to meet you, young lady.'

'Kelly Porcini, friend of Jim's. Nice to meet you too.'

'That makes two of us, then.' He noticed her firm handshake, a good trait in a woman. 'Come in here, you two young'uns, and I'll cooks us some tucker. I'm starving, eh, and you can fill me in on what happened to me poor old mate. Ah, God,' Arthur sighed again, and took another moment to look out along the road. 'Would you eat a few snags and eggs, eh?' he said quietly, almost to himself.

'Would we what! Would you mind if I put the Hilux in your shed first?'

'No worries, Jim lad. We'll meet you inside and bring some fire-wood will you, eh?' Arthur picked up the axe and passed it over the fence to Jim, who hurried back to the Hilux. Arthur then kicked and pulled the disobedient gate to let Kelly in. 'Something tells me, your-self and Jim have a yarn to tell.'

THE KITCHEN WAS simple and bare. Layers of brown grease, black soot and grey ash coated the tiled wall behind the wood-burning stove. But apart from that one neglected, dusty alcove, the room was clean and tidy. The furniture looked solid, roughly hewn from local woods but not without some craftsmanship. A heavy timber table and four chairs were pushed against a wall. Arthur's modest collection of crockery had its own spacious cupboard. A large chest freezer buzzed away beside an antique upright fridge.

Dotted throughout the room, Kelly noticed small trophies collected from the bush. A simple carved emu egg enjoyed a prominent spot on a shelf. A posy of dried wildflowers hung from a hook, adding a feminine touch. What looked like the moulted skin of a snake wrapped itself around an old green bottle on the table. Wax from the butt of a candle poured, frozen in time, down the neck of the bottle and over the skin.

'That explains the aircraft buzzing about yesterday, and I saw a cop car in the distance earlier, eh. Thought something must be up, all right. Come across from Menzies, I'd say. Heading towards the lake was the car.'

The smell of the frying snags dominated the room. The eggs spat hot grease back at Arthur, when he shook the blackened cast iron pan over the hob. Jim salivated in anticipation of the sausages and briefly forgot his troubles – even Kelly for a moment. 'Wild boar,' Arthur had boasted.

'Here, pull out the table, young fella,' instructed Arthur. 'Won't be long now. You must have just missed the cops, eh. There was tracks here when I got home.' Arthur turned a damper on the stove to calm the fire. 'So, you're planning on heading for the Territory? Isn't going to be easy, that's for sure.' He paused to catch a breath and turn the snags. 'You'll have to go through the middle. You'd have Buckley's if you try for it over the Top End, eh!'

From her seat at the table, Kelly studied the old cattleman. He was one of those old boys whose lips barely moved when he spoke, but his little eyes danced. It might just be the country way, or maybe he was trying to hide the few teeth missing from the front of his mouth. But she suspected he was not a vain man and long ago stopped worrying about his appearance – if he ever had. Jim mentioned never seeing him without his Akubra, tipped backward on his head. Jim chuckled when he recalled spying Arthur climbing out from his swag one morning at Yilgarn, with the hat still on and not much else.

Not like that fella from U2, who always wore the woolly hat, Kelly decided Arthur did not use his Akubra to conceal a bald spot. Jim couldn't be sure if the man even had hair. The hat was a part of him and all he stood for. Arthur was an anachronism, a throwback to a older Australia, a man of the bush, a character in a Banjo Paterson poem, and he dressed the part at all times.

Unknown to anyone, these days, Arthur kept a secret well hidden under his hat. A significant and ugly growth had appeared above his left ear. Like most men of his age, he ignored it at first and now, for no clear reason and based on no medical knowledge at all, he believed it was too late to do anything about it. If he covered the tumour and did not see it, it might not be so bad.

Notwithstanding the tragic and unusual circumstances of their meeting, Kelly could see Arthur enjoyed the company. He lived alone at the station. Always had. According to Jim, there was word of relatives down Southern Cross way, but nobody knew for sure. Every year at muster, Old Bill directed the spotter plane on its way over from Perth to call by Arthur's place and bring him over for his annual few days 'holiday' at Yilgarn Station.

Arthur would follow the muster in a ute and rescue any stragglers, be they sheep or inexperienced Irish jackaroos who fell behind on the bike. It was an opportunity for Helen to check he was taking care of himself and nag him about getting any ailments seen to. This season at Yilgarn, Arthur did not tell Helen about what he hid under his hat. At the time, he thought it might just cure itself.

'Hey, Jim. Did you sees me emu when you were parking the Toyota?'

'No, Arthur. Can't say I did. You still doing your Doctor Dolittle thing, then?'

'Yeah. Brought it in a few weeks ago. Poor critter was in bad shape and no sign of the father, eh.'

'Ha!' Kelly piped in. 'You and Jim both. He introduced me to a gecko that adopted him back at his camp!'

Arthur struggled with the weight of the full pan, while offloading its contents onto the three plates lined up on the table. Jim didn't need to be told to eat and tucked in immediately. Kelly sat politely waiting for Arthur to start, until Jim elbowed her and pointed with a loaded fork to her plate.

'Get it into, you,' he said, before swallowing the half sausage impaled on the end of his fork. 'You'll be waiting a while, if you're expecting an invitation. Arthur doesn't stand on ceremony.'

Jim speared another snag. Kelly frowned at him. Damn! She looks good when annoyed, he thought.

'That's right, Kelly. Just dig in before Jim swipes it all.'

'Thanks. I will,' she said and stuck her tongue out at Jim.

'But it's doing great now. They'll eat anything, emus, eh.' Arthur winked at Kelly, 'Bit like our young Irish friend here. Should be able to put it out in a paddock soon.'

'Why did you mention "the father" before?' Kelly enquired.

'Because the male emu rears the young, eh.'

'I didn't know that!' Jim said, surprised. Is that common with birds? I'm liking the wild boar by the way. These sausages are really something.'

'Yeah, they're good, aren't they? A mate brings me an esky full from Perth when he visits. Hunts the boar and makes them himself.'

'And you're OK with the hunting?' Turning to Kelly, Jim added, 'Arthur is the nearest thing to a green cattle rancher you're ever likely to meet.'

'Ah yeah, mate. Look if it's not native to WA, it's fair game. It's not nice, but it's best for the bush. You could say the same about me cattle, but people gotta eat, don't they, eh?'

'How's the herd?' Jim asked, between another mouthful of sausage and runny, free-range egg.

'I'm destocking, Jim. At me age, I'm getting too old to look after this place on me own. I'll keeps a few head around for company and some meat, eh. It'll probably mean I'll end up on the bones of me arse. Beg your pardon, Kelly, but I don't need much and I have the few savings.' He stopped talking to wipe his plate with a piece of damper. 'I like the idea of easing the grazing pressure on the land, then watching it recover before I go, eh.'

'What's your problem with Ozdrill?'

'You see, Jim, there's iron in the hills here. There's been a few exploration companies nosing around, clearing tracks through me land to get rigs in, making a mess, eh. They leaves gates open. Two of me Brahmin have been hit by trucks since Christmas. There's more traffic about here these days and it's all because of the iron. It's a dirty, dusty business, drilling, and when they hit brine in the groundwater and pump it out, it kills me trees.'

'That's not good,' Jim said, before filling his mouth again.

'Yeah, but it's nothing to what will happen if they find enough iron ore for a mine or two. Have either of you ever been up Pilbara way, out around Newman, where iron ore is big?'

They shook their heads.

'That place is a wasteland. Trucks the size of ships they have, trains that stretch to both horizons, packed full of ore on their way to the coast. They don't just move mountains in the Pilbara, they remove whole bloody ranges and ship them off to the Japs and Koreans, eh.' Arthur stretched out his arms to emphasise the enormous size of things and the distances involved. 'Look, it's going to happen here, too, if we aren't bloody careful. The few hills we have will all end up as new high-rise cities in Asia or as rusty car parts in the dumps of Europe and America. But some bastards will get bloody rich, so that'll make it all OK, eh.

'There are animals and plants that live nowhere else but on those ironstone ridges, things only the blackfellas have seen, and I'm afraid they'll all be gone along with the hills. We won't even know what we've lost. It's bad enough the pollies turn a blind eye to the sandalwood cutting that's clearing the woodlands around here too, eh.' Arthur pushed his chair back. 'Sorry for going off on one, folks, but it's important. Here, I'll make us a brew.' He returned to the stove.

'Doesn't seem right, Arthur,' Jim said. 'Not right at all. It's a shame. It's such a beautiful country. I used to think it was big enough to hide all the mines … that they didn't matter in the grand scheme of things. But I've changed my mind. They're feckin everywhere I go and just keep getting bigger. Then again, this is the country that treats the kangaroo as vermin – your national emblem!'

'Ah look, mate. Roos can be a pest too, eh. Especially when the dams are full, they breeds like flies and upset the balance.'

Kelly was last to finish her food. She brought her plate over to the sink and rinsed it before going outside.

'Christ, she's a corker, Jim! You'd want to snare her, before I start working me old charms.'

'She is nice, isn't she, but the thing is, if I wasn't already so feckin frightened, she'd scare me just a little. What would I do with a girl like that?'

Arthur chortled, while fixing himself straight in the chair. 'Did your parents not explain it to you, eh?'

'Yeah, right. I mean, I've no job and no money to take her out anywhere nice. Not that that's a problem right now, but after this is all over. She's just way out of my league.'

Arthur lifted his hat enough to allow his hand to slide slowly over his head and down the back of his neck. 'Not your decision, mate. That's for her to decide. Must say, she seems smitten on you from what I could see, eh.'

Jim smiled and looked over at the door in anticipation of Kelly's return. There must be something to it if Arthur noticed.

'Tell me, Jim. Did he suffer? Was it quick?'

'Honestly. I can't be sure. It was one shot and he never moved. It'll haunt me forever.'

Arthur leaned across the table and put a hand firmly on Jim's good shoulder. 'You're not to goes blaming yourself now, young man, eh. From what you told me, it's not your fault. Bill's shooting probably had more to do with their plans to burn the pub than your whereabouts, eh!' Arthur shook his head. 'Ah, why didn't he tells me they were in bother, eh. I could have helped ... I hope someone is minding Helen.'

Kelly returned with an unopened four-pack of choc lamingtons. They went down well with the few mugs of tea.

'Look, I'm coming with you,' Arthur said out of the blue, while grabbing the last lamington from under Jim's nose, leaving him to pick at the desiccated coconut left in the plastic tray. 'The coppers will be back down that road at some point. Maybe later this evening or tomorrow, and they'll call in here for sure, eh.'

'Arthur, no,' said Kelly. 'It's very kind of you to offer, but we don't want to put you in danger or get you in trouble with the law.'

Arthur dismissed her objections out of hand, adamant he would take them to Sandstone.

'Ah, look. Bill and Helen were good to me. I have to help, eh.' Arthur dragged his chair closer and leaned in towards the young couple on the opposite side of the table. 'Look, every lunatic God shovelled guts into out here will recognise you and call the coppers. Something to brag about in the pub, eh. If we leave together now, I can brings you to Lake Barlee and on to Sandstone on bush tracks, away from the main road and away from the coppers. I'll fuel Old Bill's Hilux and fill a few jerries in Sandstone, while you two waits out of town, eh.'

As he spoke, he traced out their route with a skinny, calloused finger on the table top. 'Then takes turns at the wheel and heads east across the Warburton, stopping only when you gets to the Territory and Alice, eh. It's one straight dirt track all the ways from Laverton.' He ran out of table and his finger continued plotting their journey in the air. 'You might makes it in two or three days, depending on conditions. I guess about fifteen hundred klicks. But a decent road in the dry, eh.'

'I think he's coming, whether we agree or not, Kelly!'

'Seems so.'

Arthur decided Kelly would travel as his visiting grandniece and, if encountered, he would say they were taking the Ozdrill man in the vehicle behind to an acceptable site for a new driller's camp.

* * *

HELEN PLACED THE last of the eggs into her basket. There was quite a number, three layers, close-packed, speckled brown and white. Each layer separated by a soft cloth. Her Rhode Island Reds and Leghorns did not seem too bothered by the recent high temperatures and had been busy in her absence. She apologised for missing a couple of feeds and told them all the sad news of Bill.

Dipping through the door to leave, Helen remembered her cigarettes. Strange how she hadn't thought of having one since the police knocked on her door. Was it because Bill hated smoking? If she was to be honest, she didn't much like smoking either. She didn't need them. In recent years, seldom would she smoke more than one a day. But she enjoyed the little game with Bill and the time to herself. What's the point now? The last thing she wanted was time to herself. She was done with cigarettes. Helen continued on outside and stood upright in the run. She saw Eloise hanging out manchester on the double clothesline in front of the back grass. Eloise waved to her.

'She's such a good girl,' Helen said to the chooks that followed her outside. 'So like her mother was at that age.'

Helen's brother-in-law and Eloise, had driven up to Kalgoorlie to bring her back to Esperance with them. But all she wanted was to go home, to look after her animals and prepare for Bill's funeral. Eloise offered to stay with her for a few weeks and, with her accountancy background, help sort out Helen's affairs.

Helen knew the family would have to make some tough decisions about the future of the station. An easy going, sensible girl, Helen always enjoyed Eloise's company and already dreaded the day she would leave. For a brief moment, a smile crossed her face. She remembered trying to contrive a meeting between Eloise and Jim. Unfortunately, it never happened. Helen went to close the coop door behind her.

'Maybe I should throw the cigarettes away. Ladies, what do you think? A clean break?' She reached in on top of the door frame.

ELOISE COULD TELL Helen had been crying.

'What day is it, Ellie? I'm confused.'

'Wednesday. I'll start dinner soon.'

'You're very good. Is your father back yet?'

'I was talking to him on the HF. He's on his way. He mentioned he thought someone passed through your western boundary gate in the last day or two, and the dam is empty, I'm afraid.'

'Yes, that's not news. Bill popped down that way a few days ago. He must have been checking the fence. Listen, Ellie, I need a favour. I want you to take me to Kal in the morning. I know we've just come from there, but I have to go back again. Sorry.'

'Sure, of course,' Eloise agreed, but hoped she might talk her aunt out of it later.

'And please, keep off the radio. I don't want everyone knowing any more of our business.'

* * *

'ARTHUR, DO YOU mind me asking? How was it you believed us so readily?'

'Look, I spent a week in Jim's company at Yilgarn. You gets to know people, when you work with a gang of blokes all day and eats with them every night. Tempers can fray, eh. Chasing sheep through the bush can be hard. A person's character comes through, when they're under pressure. Jim had this grin on him all the time I worked with him at Yilgarn. He's a good lad. Good inside, eh.'

'Yeah, I've seen it in him, too. He's kept a cool head over the last few days.'

'I doubt even a beautiful woman such as you could turns him bad. He likes you, by the way. I guess you know that, eh.'

'Ha!' Kelly laughed. 'Maybe. Just not sure how much yet.'

Arthur took them west of Dismals homestead, before turning north along another banded iron ridge. His old red Toyota FJ40 rattled and shook, as it rolled easily over the rocky trails. He pointed out some new access tracks and drill pads put in by the exploration companies. Short PVC pipes emerged at various angles from the ground showing the location and dip of each drill hole. Neat rows of green plastic bags were lined up near the holes. The green bags, Arthur explained, contained rock chips that corresponded to a metre of drilling. At some drill sites, Kelly counted over one hundred bags set out in precise lines of twenty.

'Where's that Irishman gone, now?' Arthur slowed to a stop. Jim found it hard to keep up. A minute or so later, they saw the dust rising and the Hilux rounded the bend. 'Right, we're off again.' Arthur twisted the key. The engine turned over, then stopped. He tried again. The starter motor kicked in, but the engine stayed silent. 'Come on, you little bastard.' Still nothing. 'Bastard ... bastard! Has to be the bastard fuel pumps gone or a hole in the tank, eh.'

EVERY NOW AND again, Jim would be directed to turn the ignition over, while Arthur put his ear against a different part of the motor and listened in anticipation for the sound of petrol flowing. Kelly left the two of them staring into the engine compartment. Keeping the vehicles in sight, she hiked up the side of the hill along a steep drilling access track. She continued past the capped drill hole and the dust-blanketed scrub around it, stopping when she reached the dark purple rock that formed the ridge. Resting on a flat outcrop of the stripey stuff Jim was so taken by, Kelly surveyed all around her.

High out front, a wedge-tailed eagle climbed on a late afternoon thermal. Behind her, Arthur burrowed himself deeper into the engine, while Jim stood back, scoffing something. They did not seem to be making any immediate preparations to get on the road again. Looking west into the sun, a patchwork carpet of atmospheric blue and green eucalyptus stretched out for an eternity, the silence broken only by the laboured sound of Arthur's starter motor and the odd 'bastard' drifting up.

A wave of melancholy came over her. She dwelt on the precariousness of their situation again. It must have been the vehicle refusing to start that brought it on. There were moments when she thought they could pull this off, but now was not one of them.

Overhead, the eagle yelped an agitated warning and, with a languid flap of its powerful wings, abandoned the rising air to float away. The bird's fading cries gave way to the rainy sound of stones pouring downslope. Shielding her eyes from the glare coming off the rock, Kelly scanned for the source of this new noise. Struggling on the loose scree underfoot, a tall figure approached from her right.

'Shit!' she whispered. The thought of running flashed through her mind. What's the bloody point, she told herself. There's nowhere to hide up here.

'Hello there!' a male voice called out.

With a brief raised hand, Kelly acknowledged the stranger. The fact he was not in uniform offered grounds for optimism – though the sleeveless khaki jacket festooned with pockets implied some sort of official livery. High on his elevated head, the wide brim of a maroon cricket hat cast a shadow over his face. A small backpack hung from a shoulder and, ominously, he carried what appeared to be a hammer.

Behind her back, Kelly discreetly curled her hand around the sharp edges of a hefty lump of chert.

'Hello!' the man shouted again, short of breath and a lot closer now. 'Didn't expect to meet another soul up here. You're not searching for a hammer as well, by any chance?' he asked, holding his up by the head in a non-threatening fashion.

With a heavy, blunt head and chisel-like tail, it was a sinister looking implement. Jesus, that could do me some damage, Kelly thought – half expecting him to make a lunge at her. Yet, there was nothing aggressive in his tone and a toothy grin had now emerged from the shadow of his hat. She could not place his accent, yet he sounded vaguely familiar.

'I left my hammer over there last week,' the stranger said, pointing with the handle along the ridgeline. He climbed the last few steep metres and stopped a respectable distance away from Kelly. 'I'm always doing that,' the man chuckled. 'But behold! I've got it back,' he said, putting the hammer down at his feet. The handle rested against the top of his boot. Kelly relaxed her grip on the chert.

'Congratulations. Glad to hear it,' she replied, still with some anxiety in her voice. He's English, Kelly realised.

'Splendid view up here, isn't it?' he said, and hunkered down to undo a zip on his bag.

'Suppose.'

'Good God! Is that you, Charlie? Charlie from The Pump House? Well, I never. Pardon me, of course I meant Kelly, Kelly from The Aurora!'

'Andy, isn't it? Jeff's mate. English Andy. I remember you.'

'Yes indeed, that's me. Are you OK? Do you need a drink? I certainly do.' Andy took out a water bottle and offered Kelly first dibs.

'No, thanks. I'm fine.'

'You do know you're all over the news? There's a lot of people out looking for you, particularly the boys in blue! What the hell happened?'

Kelly shook her head. 'It's all lies.'

'Listen, if it's any comfort, we were talking about it at camp and none of us believe you had any part in it. Jeff won't hear a bad word said about you. As you know, he's a fan. Great to see you're OK, Kelly.'

'Thanks. Yeah, we're still alive … for now, anyway.' Kelly remained seated while she spoke and returned to gazing out at the panorama in front of her. 'Jim didn't do it, either. He's as innocent as I am.'

'I presume the Irishman is one of those two down there,' Andy said, spotting the figures moving around below. 'It sounded like someone was having trouble with their engine, so I came to investigate. Who's that with him?'

'That's Arthur, the station owner. The Hilux is ours. Don't worry. It's not stolen from Ozdrill.'

'I'm in for an ear bashing, if that cranky old so and so sees me.'

'Listen, Andy, we need help.' There was no mistaking the despondency in her voice. 'We really need help. Please tell me you know something about motors?'

'I'm sorry, Charlie—'

'Kelly.'

'Kelly. I'm afraid I don't. I bet Jeff could get it going though. We're not far from here. If you want, I can take you over.'

Kelly perked up, nodding her appreciation. 'That would be great … I'll need to talk to the others first.'

Andy pointed to the men below. 'You have to be completely honest with me. Are there any guns down there? That Irish chap isn't going to go berserk when he sees me coming?'

'Jesus no. It's like I said, we're not armed. We're totally innocent. Jim's a good bloke. Come down and we'll tell you everything.'

'I'm more concerned Arthur might be carrying,' he said with a wink.

'No, but you should see his axe!' Kelly smiled, a disarming smile that could only dispel any worries Andy might have had about following her down.

He offered her a hand-up. 'Listen, you always struck me as a straight-up girl in Kal. Let's see what we can do.'

'You're a geo, aren't you, Andy?'

'For my sins.'

'Jesus. Jim's going to love you!'

The geologist's compassion lifted Kelly's spirits more than he could have known.

'LOOK MATE. SHE needs a new bastard fuel pump, eh! I've an old spare in a shed somewhere. We'll haves to go back for it and try again in the morning.'

'Can't be help—' Jim stopped when he saw Kelly on her way down. She had company. 'Shit! We've been rumbled.'

'Strewth! It's that bloody Pommy geo,' said an already irritated Arthur. 'I was sure they'd moved on to Christmas Creek last week, eh.'

Her hands in her back pockets, Kelly swayed as she walked, sometimes skipping over the broken ground to keep up with the long strides of her companion. She looked relaxed and appeared to be chatting calmly. When she saw Jim had spotted her and Andy, she gave him a cheery wave. Jim's heart rate moderated.

Kelly made the introductions and they told Andy their version of the events that brought them to this spot. He listened, horrified and sympathetic. As it happened, Andy had worked on a gold prospect at Yilgarn Station a few years before and experienced the Mitchells' renowned hospitality himself. Jim glossed over the details of their plans and the exact nature of their evidence. Noticing his reluctance to be specific, Kelly went along with it. Arthur, refusing to get involved in the conversation, busied himself moving things around inside the FJ40.

'COME AND HAVE some grub, at least. Your homestead is a long way back and our camp isn't too far at all. Jeff the driller's a mechanic by trade. I'll have him drive over and look at it for you.'

Arthur looked up from his task. 'Thanks, but it's a bloody fuel pump and I can fix it meself, once I gets the part.' As much as it infuriated him, Arthur knew he was in a corner and the bloody Pom's suggestion made perfect sense. But he had to be seen to object before giving in. Arthur appreciated it was unwise to turn back if it could be avoided.

Andy worked for a small geological consultancy, whose services were engaged by a major iron ore producer to oversee a large exploration programme in a potential new iron ore province around Lake Barlee. Dismals station lands fell within the project area. Ozdrill was the main drilling contractor. Andy had worked with Ozdrill before on projects and he knew Jeff the driller well. He knew Jeff would not object to feeding the fugitives, especially Kelly. He also knew Jeff would grumble a bit before relenting and go look at Arthur's fuel pump. Of course, Jeff would make Andy sign it off as rig moving time on the log sheets.

Jim took Arthur aside to have a word in his ear.

'Come on, Arthur. It's an opportunity to air your concerns over some tucker, break bread with your enemies. Even if only to remind them to close the gates. If you go on a charm offensive, you might wrong-foot them into telling you more than they should about what their plans are. Could be you have nothing to worry about. Would be nice to know, eh?'

'Fairs enough, I'll go. Only because turning back, we risks meeting those coppers. Getting you two and your film to the Territory is more important than anythings else right now, eh.' Arthur frowned behind his sunnies and glanced over at Andy who had his Pommy nose up close to the paint job on the Hilux. 'Let's hope we can trust these blokes.'

Jim tapped Arthur on the shoulder. 'Thanks mate. Kelly says they're fair dinkum and won't dob us in. I trust her judgement, but best keep schtum about the film and the Territory all the same.'

CHAPTER 12

DRILLING

O NE HUNDRED AND thirteen metres down, deep within the guts of the ironstone ridge, the blistered face of the tungsten carbide bit smashed countless times a second into the hard cherty rock at the base of the hole. Compressed air roared down the outer annulus of the drill rods and powered the pneumatic hammer driving the bit millimetres deeper with every strike. The returning air blew the drill face clear of debris and lifted the rock fragments up an inner tube to the surface for analysis. In the industrial pursuit of buried treasures, the reverse circulation drill rig is king.

Standing below the towering red mast and its elaborate array of hydraulic piping, Jeff the driller orchestrated proceedings from his footplate at the back of the Bedford truck-mounted rig. A number on a gauge in front of him read slightly high for his liking. In response, Jeff feathered one of the many levers below the control panel. A temporary shift in the breeze engulfed the driller in the stack of dirty-orange rock dust that came off the nearby cyclone. Jeff pulled the dust mask down from the top of his shaved head and covered his nose and mouth. The extended goatee beard compromised the seal between mask and skin, but the wiry black and greying hairs filtered out some of the dust carried in on his smoky breath.

A rugged, handsome man of generous proportions, he had a liking for tight, almost indecent, denim shorts and body-hugging, preferably sleeveless, Ozdrill shirts. A shrink-wrapped, hard-boiled egg came to Andy's mind when they first met, and someone best avoided down a dark alley. Early in his drilling career, Jeff witnessed what loose clothes caught in a drive shaft could do. The sound of tearing flesh, of snapping bone and screaming, still haunted him. Only outside of work hours, did he relax his clothing policy and let his blood circulate freely. The boss's appearance always amused his offsiders, but they never joked about it to his face. Although typically quiet and of an easy-going nature, beneath the shell, there was a brooding toughness.

The hammer banged away deep below and the ground around the rig vibrated. Jeff's gloved right hand lightly cupped the last rod added to the top of the drill string. The six-metre section of steel pipe rotated anticlockwise, sinking imperceptibly deeper into the hole. The amplitude of the vibrations coming off the pipe into his fingers told Jeff all was working well. The deafening noise of the motor and the violent beat of the compressor struck similar reassuring notes. There are equations a driller can use to determine the optimum rotational speed, air pressure or weight on the drill string for different ground conditions, but Jeff worked primarily on intuition shaped by years of experience.

Taking advantage of the brief lull in activity, he removed the dust mask and headed over to the back of the support truck, where the two offsiders kept a small fire going under a steel plate. A pot of coffee pulled to the edge, simmered away. After taking a swig of cold water from a plastic bottle he grabbed from the cooler by the cab door, Jeff poured himself a mug of strong black coffee. Lighting a smoke, he looked around.

The offsiders silently worked their well-practised routine. Dan fixed an empty green plastic bag to the bottom of the cyclone, ready for the next metre sample to drop into. Garry carried the previous full bag of rock chips the short distance over to the other one hundred and twelve bags of cuttings already arranged in ordered rows.

Away from the rig and upwind of the dust, Hendrik, the young South African geologist, diligently worked off the back of a Land Cruiser. He wore his hard hat with a broad canvas sun visor over the rim and a neck flap hung down in the fashion of a legionnaire. His blonde locks curled out from underneath. Over his beige work boots, Hendrik sported matching gaiters, those sensible elastic covers that prevent dirt and grime from falling into boots. Jeff believed gaiters were dodgy, and why was it only the geos who wore them? Gaiters may well perform a useful function, but to Jeff, they had a look of the 'pixie boot' about them. There was no place for pixie boots in the Australian bush.

Periodically, Hendrik left his Land Cruiser to collect rock chips from the green bags. He would dry-sieve off the fines, before washing the coarser material in buckets of water he kept topped up next to the Land Cruiser. Jeff watched the geologist pour a few wet rock chips onto a thick steel plate on the back of the truck. The geologist then tapped away at the samples with his hammer.

'Those geos are always hammering something,' Jeff grumbled to himself. Seldom would you see a geo without a hammer gripped firmly in hand, ready to bring it down on some unsuspecting piece of rock. Or have one dangling from a hip belt like a gunslinger. Except Andy, of course, who was in the habit of leaving his on an outcrop some-where and walking off.

Jeff noticed the Saffa was under pressure and behind on his logging again. With Jen the fieldie gone to Kal to deliver samples for analysis, the young, inexperienced geologist had struggled on his own to keep pace with the drilling and calling the holes at the correct depth. That didn't bother Jeff, who had no qualms about grabbing a few sneaky metres of easy drilling, when really, he knew the hole should be canned. If only the 'arrogant little tosser' tried to be more pleasant, Jeff maintained he would then happily give Hendrik the heads-up every time the drill-bit punched through the hard chert and into the underlying softer rock. Jeff suspected they were nearing that point now with this hole. Time was against them and he wanted to finish, pull the rods and get set up on the next drill site before knocking off for the day. He decided if Hendrik did not spot the geological boundary, he would let the young South African know – just this once.

The driller finished his coffee and strode back to the rig. He gave Dan an approving nod when their paths crossed at the cyclone. He was pleased with the two brothers. They were hard, honest workers, who had quickly picked up the job. They never said much, except to each other. Probably a good thing. Working and living twenty-four seven in close proximity and under such demanding conditions was hard. It required a thick skin and at least a measure of an easy-going personality. The brothers appeared to have both and were physically tough, which was a bonus.

Working around a drill rig was no place for idle conversation any-way. It's just too damn noisy and too damn dangerous. For the most part, the job demanded absolute attention. There was a rhythm, a strict sequence to how a rig worked. Everyone was expected to know their job and that of their colleagues too. An effective, well-func-tioning team had little need to communicate verbally. Jeff's two new offsiders were shaping up well.

Drillers got paid by the metre, but drilling in banded iron country is slow. Even with the auxiliary booster, the daily metreage in the hard Dismals ground proved to be particularly low. The Dismals project could have been kinder to Jeff's bank balance, but he was not too concerned. The sample return was good and dry. That kept Andy happy. It was important to keep the project geologist onside and have him sign off the drilling logs without too much scrutiny. The next job and they could be drilling through butter. That's just the way it was. There was no point beating yourself up over it.

There were only a few holes left to drill at Dismals anyway. A couple more days and the project would finish. Fond as he was of his work, Jeff looked forward to some time off. Life in camp eventually wears everyone down. After many hot weeks of continuous drilling, he was keen to get his rig to the Ozdrill yard in Sandstone and service it to prepare for its next assignment in the Murchison. With that done, he could then enjoy some R&R back in Perth.

Having qualified as a mechanic, Jeff got his start with a drilling company, aged nineteen. At the tender age of twenty-one, and relatively young in the business, he became a driller with responsibility for his own rig. Over the next twelve years, apart from a brief spell drilling underground at the giant Mount Isa Mine in Queensland, he peppered the state of WA with exploration drill holes.

The money was good. He was effectively his own boss, something he enjoyed. In the limited downtime Jeff allowed himself, he could either be found catching waves off Scarborough Beach, north of Perth, or tinkering in the yard behind his small weatherboard house on the seafront. Here, he worked on his dream of transforming an old single-decker tour bus into a luxurious mobile home. It was a self-build project that rivalled Barcelona's famous *La Sagrada Familia Basílica* in the leisurely pace of the build.

Always frugal, although people who knew him might have called him 'tight', Jeff had squirrelled away a significant amount of money. He invested wisely and got lucky with a small speculative mining venture. It meant, in about another three years, and well before he turned forty, he could retire from drilling.

The grand plan involved selling up and taking his bus on every road and passable track around the infinite Australian coastline, in search of an isolated beach, the perfect wave and contentment. If love happened along the way, that would be nice. The ways of a driller, particularly one who forgoes much of his rostered time off, was not conducive to meeting a life partner. The good ladies of Kal's Hay Street, for the most part, took care of his carnal needs, at least for now. But he could not buy tenderness and he missed that.

Ah, there it is! The penetration rate had shot up. They were through the banded iron. If Hendrik had been watching, he would have seen the dust change from reddish ochre to a dull-grey colour. Jeff ambled over to let the young geo know.

'Here, watch this.' Andy turned to Kelly. 'Soon as he sees us, the hard hat will go on.'

Sure enough, once Jeff copped the two vehicles coming up the access track, he made to look as if he was simply wiping the sweat from his brow and scalp, before pulling his mask back down and grabbing his hard hat from on top of the control panel, where it spent more time than it should.

'I've seen that chap stand in a cloud of dust of his own making, cigarette in mouth, blowing the filters on that rig clean with compressed air. He obsesses about keeping the machinery running sweetly, but has no concern for his own lungs or his head. He needs a woman, methinks.'

The drillers were pulling the last rod from the hole, when Kelly and Andy approached the rig. Andy insisted Kelly wore a hard hat. At first, Jeff didn't recognise her. He looked past the approaching figures to the two that hung back, Arthur and someone from Ozdrill he never met before. Jeff assumed they must be in trouble with that cow cocky again. For what, he hadn't the faintest idea.

'Hi Jeff!' Kelly said timidly, while raising a hand.

* * *

As ANDY PREDICTED, Jeff was happy to help. 'Ah, look! Their story sounds legit. I'm OK with them staying the night and fixing the old boy's Tojo for him. I don't know about the Irish bloke, but I'll vouch for Charlie. She's a good chick.'

The driller, his two offsiders and the two geologists stood at the open cab door of the driller's support truck, discussing what to do about their visitors. Jim took a walk around the rig, while Kelly and Arthur sheltered under a lonely gimlet tree, anxiously awaiting a decision.

Andy backed up Jeff's reasoning, adding that 'Arthur speaks glowingly of Jim, and you know how much of a cantankerous old curmudgeon the cocky is.'

'I don't agree.' Hendrik took issue with allowing them to stay. 'If we're caught harbouring fugitives, you folks might just get a rap on the knuckles. I'd have my visa revoked!' He made his point, finishing in a noticeably higher pitch than he started. 'It's OK for you, Andy. You got citizenship.'

'True, but if what they say is what happened, they're in serious trouble,' Andy insisted. 'They're frightened and desperate. We have to show some humanity. About the risks … I feel it's the right thing to do. If it comes to it, Hennie, I'm happy to say I gave you no choice. It's not as if you can just leave.'

Jeff looked to the brothers. 'What about it, lads?'

'Fine with me,' Dan replied.

Garry agreed. 'It'd be cool having our own skimpy in camp.'

'Right. It's settled. Charlie is staying.' Jeff's tone closed the door on further discussion. 'I know you meant nothing by it, Garry, but treat her with respect, lads. Same as it is with Jen. Keep the skin mags to yourselves.'

Hendrik sighed and muttered under his breath.

'You have something to say there, Hendrik?' Jeff asked, his hackles up.

'Her name is Kelly!' Hendrik replied, churlishly. It wasn't the point he wanted to make, but Jeff's expression cautioned he tread carefully.

'Whatever ... she stays. Got it?'

The impromptu meeting broke up, but Hendrik could not let it go. He cornered Andy, who was on his way over to the group under the gimlet tree.

'I want it on record that I objected and felt pressured into going along with your reckless, criminal behaviour.' Having said his piece, Hendrik turned away and stomped back to his samples.

Andy nodded to the back of the retreating figure. He felt sorry for the young South African and understood his concerns. But he doesn't make it easy for himself, Andy thought. Hopefully he'll learn ... or else someone is going to teach him.

Drilling finished earlier than usual. The rig did not get moved to the next hole. That could wait until morning. After grumbling again for effect, Arthur got into the support truck with Jeff and they headed off to have a look at his Toyota.

Jeff was in good form. He reckoned the mechanical fuel pump on a classic FJ40 would be an easy fix. He looked forward to getting back in time for dinner. Even the earbashing he expected from Arthur on the way over wasn't going to bother him.

Hendrik stayed behind to finish his logging, while the others escaped to camp. Before he left, Jeff instructed the brothers to light the fire and break out the best Ozdrill steaks.

EXCEPT FOR THE desiccated detritus of earlier sandwich-making on the counter, Kelly thought the caravan's small kitchen looked tolerably hygienic. To her surprise, the sink was empty of dirty dishes. She wanted to open the fridge, but erred on the side of good manners. Boxes of unused sample bags and bales of wooden pegs, yet to be numbered, were shoved out of the way above the fridge and under the bed.

The back wall of the caravan appeared to be a framework of cardboard map tubes and charts. Geology books, stacks of academic papers and chip trays were piled high on the bed. An aerial photograph, with the tenement boundary superimposed over it, was taped to a side wall beside two of the geological maps that guided Jim and herself across from Yilgarn Station. Spread out on the table were a number of blueprints, their corners weighted down by rock samples. Kelly smiled when she copped the paperweights. Metal set squares and a packet of coloured pencils obscured the details of the blueprints. A HF radio was plugged in under the window and pushed to the inside edge of the table.

'And this is the exploration office, kitchen and storeroom. It's where I scratch my head and try to figure out what we have here in the ground,' Andy said, finishing his brief tour of the camp with Kelly and Jim.

As ever, the fire was the focal point of camp. Sturdy benches, made from heavy logs and stone supports, enclosed the campfire. On the opposite side of the fire pit, the Ozdrill caravan mirrored the exploration office. A temporary awning of green shade-cloth, supported by two metal poles, cast a cooling protective shadow over a chest freezer outside the driller's door. Both fugitives were pleased to see the dedicated prefab shower and toilet block, a legacy from busier times when three drill rigs worked the project.

Andy expected a low loader on site any day to haul it away. Scattered around the edge of the clearing were several wire-frame camp beds, some with canvas swags rolled out over them, others empty, as they were now surplus to requirements. Set out under another loose shade, racks of drill core were waiting to be logged and had been for a while. The diverse paraphernalia of a drilling project could be seen everywhere, some of it tucked in under trees or tarpaulins.

Spare tyres, oil drums, water barrels, wooden pallets, bulk samples, old discarded drill bits and other junk added character to the place. The soil, churned by months of activity settled as a thick layer of dust over everything, including the swags. A large spotted monitor lizard sniffed the air with its tongue and foraged for scraps between the benches at the fire pit.

Jim pointed to the plans on the table. 'They're cross-sections of the ridge, I suppose?'

'Yep. Three sections in a series of many. I plot on all the drill traces, Hennie's logging info and the assay results, when we get the numbers back from the lab. The aim is to build up a 3D picture of what's happening underground and work out how much iron is there.'

'Sounds interesting. Have you figured it out yet?'

'Whoah! If I told you that, I'd have to shoot you.' Then, realising what he'd said, Andy looked a little embarrassed.

'Ha! No worries, Andy. I'm getting kind of used to people wanting to shoot me.'

'Me, too!' Kelly said from the door.

She stared out across the campsite and watched the lizard rhythmically flicking arcs of sand with its powerful front claws. It had sniffed out some promising buried delicacy. The sun sat low in the sky and transformed the ridge a luminescent Kodachrome purple. The same fleeting purple every tourist waits to capture at an Ayers Rock sunset. Again, as if on cue, the flies disappeared and the breeze abated.

'You know, Tina Turner wouldn't look out of place roaring through here on a quad,' she quipped. 'Yeah ... Mad Max, Mad fucking Max,' she repeated quietly.

ARTHUR AND JEFF were in good spirits and chatting, when they joined the others at the fire.

'Bloody young fella knows his way around an engine, eh,' Arthur said, taking a spot beside Kelly on a bench.

'That's quick. You got her sorted then, Jeff?' Andy had not expected to see them back so soon.

'Straightforward, once you have the tools. She's good for another fifty thousand K.'

'Hey, boss. The veg is done,' Garry said. 'Our steaks are on. Yours are under the lid over there.' Garry enjoyed cooking and naturally fell into the role of camp chef.

'Good on ya, mate. Arthur, how d'you like your steak?' Jeff asked, as he slid two significant lumps of meat onto the sizzling hot plate.

'Sane and bloody rare. I hope those are not any of mine, eh?'

'Strewth no, mate. Yours are way too skinny!'

That brief exchange relaxed the group and set the mood. Garry handed out substantial plates of vegetables and rice. On Jeff's insistence, Dan passed around some welcome tins of chilled Emu Bitter.

Jeff proved an avuncular host. Normally, he made himself scarce during the preparation, serving and tidying after a meal, it being below his station. Knowing this, the brothers smirked at how he fussed over Kelly, making sure he and not Garry served her, and her steak was done exactly how she liked it. Kelly slipped half of it to Jim. The fire worked its magic on the group. The atmosphere was good and the conversation easy.

'Listen folks. I really don't know how to thank you,' Jim said, after scoffing second helpings. 'Your kindness and generosity is much appreciated. It means a lot to us. And the tucker was delicious, Garry. Thanks.'

'No worries. Nice change to get some appreciation around here for my cooking. It's normally abuse I get.'

'Ah, it was lovely,' Kelly added, ruffling Garry's hair. 'Don't mind them.' Garry look pleased. 'Yeah, like Jim said,' Kelly continued, 'Thanks, everyone. It's … it's been a scary few days for both of us. The nightmare is not over yet, but right now, because of you blokes, I feel kinda normal again.'

Jeff looked pensively into the fire, then poked it with a stick before speaking.

'Jim, most of us already know Charlie, and if she says you're a good bloke, that's good enough for me. Arthur told me earlier you and Old Bill were close. Myself and Andy worked a prospect on Yilgarn a few years back. Old Bill and Helen are good people. If, as you say, you have proof that can bring his killer to justice, you can stay here as long as you need. No worries.'

'Here, here! Sounds like a plan,' Andy agreed wholeheartedly, while opening another beer.

'That's very decent of you both but—'

Andy cut Jim off, before he could protest. 'Listen, the freezers are struggling in this hot spell. Everything needs to be eaten quickly. I get the impression you might just be able to help us with that.'

Jim laughed.

Andy took a sip from his tinnie, before continuing. 'We have two legs of lamb that won't freeze. I'd hate to have to throw them out. Isn't that right, Hennie?'

Halfway through chewing his last piece of steak the requisite number of times, Hendrik grunted something incomprehensible, and without looking up from his plate, went straight back to his mastication.

Andy, with a subtle shake of the head and a downturn of his mouth, suggested the guests pay no heed to Hendrik. 'Look, this project is winding up soon.' Jeff's idea made perfect sense to Andy. 'We're all going to be travelling to Sandstone to store our gear in the Ozdrill yard until the next job … You might as well stay the few days and travel up in convoy with us. Your Hilux will blend right in and there'll be safety in numbers.'

Hendrik got up quietly and left for the exploration caravan with his empty plate.

'Might as well,' Jeff agreed. 'Nobody else is using the yard at the moment. It'd be a good place to rest and plan your next move.'

The guttural hum of the water pump from inside the caravan spluttered to life. The clash of roughly handled crockery at the sink raised eyebrows around the fire.

'He'll be all right. He'll come round,' Andy assured them.

'Ah, lads. Listen. You're all too kind. What do you think, Kelly? Should we stay?'

Kelly detected a slight tremble in Jim's voice.

Arthur added his opinion. 'Bloody oath you two! Accept the offer, eh. It's a rippa. And if anyone asks, I'll tells 'em you didn't pass this way, eh!'

Kelly smiled. She was among friends. And that was it. She agreed. They were staying until the project finished and then travelling as part of an exploration team to the Ozdrill yard in Sandstone. There, they would restock supplies before heading east on the long journey to Alice Springs.

As the night went on, they chatted and laughed around the fire. Hendrik returned, but even the few tins of beer did nothing to lift his mood or loosen his tongue. Kelly took out Jim's paintings and proudly passed them about. Jim wondered if he could tag along in the morning and sketch the drillers at work. He had never been up close to an operating rig before.

Jeff remained in good form. He continued to fuss over Kelly, all the while trying to figure out if there was anything between her and Jim. Obviously, the two got on well, but apart from her giving Jim some of her steak, there was no physical contact between them. Had circumstance or destiny thrown them together? Jeff couldn't tell.

'You sure you'll be all right? Why won't you stay the night?'

'Not at all. I'll be fine, mate. I'll take it slowly, eh.' Arthur sat at the wheel ready for the late drive home.

'OK, listen. Thanks for your help. Someday, I'll repay you.'

'You just keeps yourself and that girl safe. Don't do anything stupid, eh. Get to Alice and get that bastard Collins behind bars. That'll be good enough for me, eh.'

'I will. I promise. Hey! You and Jeff seemed to get along.'

'Ah, look. He's a good bloke. By the way, I gave him the rest of those snags for fixing me Tojo. Sorry about that.'

Jim snorted. 'Feck you, anyway.'

Leaning a little farther out the window, Arthur looked past Jim, his beady eyes studying the shadows. Nobody appeared to be within earshot. 'There is nothing bloody here, mate,' he whispered. 'The driller told me so. Well, there's some, but it's the wrong type of iron, eh. The smelters won't takes it. Jeff says maybe in twenty, thirty years they might, but only if they find a bloody lot more and the price of iron shoots ways up, eh. It would takes the likes of the Chinese to get up off their commie arses and create a huge demand for that to happen. And they'd have to build the bastard infrastructure to process it too, eh.'

Arthur shook his head ruefully. 'After Tiananmen Square, Jim, that isn't going to happen is it, eh?' He patted the top of his hat to secure it for the journey. 'Plenty can change in thirty years, mate. Who knows? This place might be a national park by then.'

With the hat secure, he was free to nod his head. 'Yeah, I'm feeling better about things. Thanks, Jim lad. You were right about me talking to them miner blokes, instead of burying me old head in the sand, eh.'

Kelly came over to see Arthur off.

'Couldn't get him to stay the night. Stubborn old git,' Jim said, while they both watched the frail old man reverse his Toyota back from the neat line of vehicles. Arthur saluted through the windscreen and turned away.

'I slipped a few dollars into the glove compartment for fuel,' Kelly said, as she waved.

'How much?'

'A lot of fuel.'

'Good.'

'You OK? You seemed a little quiet back there after dinner.'

Jim watched the lights of the FJ40 flicker behind the trees and then disappear. He took a while before answering. 'I'm just tired. I should put the head down.'

Don't say it, don't say a word, Jim warned himself. It really is none of your business. But he was annoyed with her. Why hadn't she told him? She can be whoever she wants to be. He knew he had no right to be angry, or even hurt, but he was. It gnawed away and he couldn't let it go. There was no reasoning with himself now.

'Who's Charlie?'

'What? Oh ... that's just a name I used in Kal ... in The Pump House. Sorry, I should have mentioned it before.'

'That's a skimpy bar, isn't it?'

'They're all skimpy bars.'

'You're a skimpy?'

'No, but yeah I was for a few weeks.' She could see disappointment register in his eyes. 'But that wasn't me. Charlie was only a character I invented. Do you have a problem with that?'

Jim hesitated again before answering, 'No.' OK leave it at that, you idiot, he berated himself. Leave it at that.

'No ... actually yes, yes, I do. You're a beautiful, intelligent woman, why demean yourself like that?' You stupid, stupid gobshite, you've gone and said it now!

'Stop! Stop right there.' She stood proud, arms akimbo, hands on her wonderful hips. 'How dare you!'

Jim pretended to be distracted by something in the trees. But Kelly was not letting him get away with it.

'Look at me!' she commanded. 'It's easy for you, from your cosy little middle-class background to go play at being Mick Dundee, knowing full well money was just a trip to the nearest Western Union if you needed it. I have nothing, nobody. No fucking safety net. I needed to eat and a place to live. I did what I had to. I didn't like it, but it paid the bills. We worked bloody hard for the money we got and put up with a lot of shit. I met a lot of great girls in The Pump House and believe me ...' Leading with her chin, she pointed directly at him to drive the point home, 'It wasn't the skimpies who demeaned themselves!'

'I'm sorry. It's just the whole skimpy culture in Kal bugs me. It's such a fuckin' juvenile, misogynist society here in the Goldfields and I can't help but be disappointed you were part of it. I know it's none of my business, but the thought of all those men leering at you, including everyone here in this camp!' He made a dismissive, waiving gesture with his hands. Jim's anger had got the better of him. He couldn't think of anything else to say.

'So that's it. That's your real problem. You're jealous. After all you said this morning about growing up, you're just jealous they got to see my tits and you haven't!'

'That's not fair!'

She refused to listen. 'Easily sorted.' Kelly unbuttoned her blouse. 'Here, if you have a dollar coin, I can show you some great tricks with my nipples—'

'Oh, Kelly, stop! I'm sorry. Listen. I know I'm being a prick. It was a clumsy choice of words.' He was taken aback at how upset they both were and tried to take her hand, but she brushed him away and continued to part her blouse.

'Come on, give me a coin. I always enjoyed performing for bald men!' She cried as the words came out.

'For what it's worth, I'm sorry ... again. Good night!' He pulled his swag off the back of the Hilux and walked off.

KELLY HEARD MUFFLED voices and saw the distant figures moving about the floodlit camp as everyone woke up, drank coffee, ate toast with Vegemite and prepared packed lunches. She watched a lone shadow stroll from behind the Hilux over to Andy's caravan. The engines revved and the headlights dazzled her when the trucks drove off in procession.

It was still dark, very dark. The magpies were not yet singing. She was warm and snug. Despite going to bed upset, the camp bed and swag gave her the most comfortable night's sleep she could remember. She wasn't finished. She wasn't going anywhere. Kelly rolled over and fell back asleep.

CHAPTER 13

AN EGG AND TWO SANDWICHES

D RESSED IN THEIR civvies, both officers stood in the centre of the
tiny, ramshackle, corrugated-iron amphitheatre. A circular strip
of patchwork roof sloped down from the wide central opening to the
rusty outer wall. The roof would only provide limited but temporary
shade to anyone lurking in the back and away from the action. But for
the two senior officers, the place was empty. Above the dusty arena,
the stars dimmed. Rods of light shot through the many holes in the arc
of the exterior wall that faced the rising sun. The light created dappled
patterns of bright and dark on the ground. Hidden back off a dirt
road, ten minutes north of Kalgoorlie, there was little chance anybody
would happen upon them at this hour. A thin crescent of sunlight fell
on the west side of the arena. As the minutes passed, the crescent grew,
inching its way east while the officers waited.

Detective Sergeant Stan Sidoli moved to one of the few wooden
benches. Leaning forward slightly, hands clasped together, elbows
resting on his separated knees, he couldn't help but wonder if someone

was going to be thrown to the lions today. Detective Superintendent Baz Harper stood looking anxiously through the opening and out along the track.

'Are you sure this place is safe?' he asked.

'Outside of Sundays, you won't see another sinner out here,' Sidoli assured his superior.

'No, mate. I meant is this dump going to collapse down on top of me?'

Sidoli laughed. 'Nah, it's looked this rough since the day they put it up. I suspect it's deliberate – to give the impression it's temporary. You know, so us boys in blue might just leave it alone. Same way as it is with Hay Street and the brothels.'

Harper folded his arms, turned a full circle on his feet and studied the dubious craftsmanship in front of him. 'Indeed.'

'Some serious money has changed hands here over the years. Legend has it high rollers from Vegas have sat on these ringside seats. Ever played Two-Up yourself, Baz? I mean outside of Anzac Day?'

It wasn't a loaded question. Two-Up was legal in Kalgoorlie for almost seven years now, although the arena dated back well before that. Similarly, at Broken Hill, another old mining centre over east. But for the rest of Australia, the game was allowed only on Anzac Day. It was just too quick and too easy to lose everything on the simultaneous toss of two coins.

Distracted by dust on the track, Harper didn't reply. 'Here's Collins now. That mongrel is never on time.'

THE TWO OFFICERS sat on opposite benches, both facing Max, who prowled the ring. Harper complimented Collins on how much better he looked since their chat at the hospital. A smaller, more discreet, dressing now covered the head wound and Collins had shaved. He wore a new off-the-peg suit and the shoes shone again. Harper felt Collins appeared to have his shit together and the Detective Superintendent knew that would go a long way towards resolving their little problem.

'Where do we stand? Any sign of them yet?' Max asked, done with the formalities.

'We had a no-show in Perth yesterday. That's not to say they won't turn up at the boyfriend's, but I suspect we've been sold a pup. Nothing along the pipeline either,' Sidoli said, while flicking through a notebook. 'We checked the phone records. Appears they made two calls from Yilgarn Station on Monday night. Not Kal, as was first assumed. The times tie in with it being shortly after you left there with Mitchell's wife.'

'Fuck!' Max said. He kept pacing and kicked at a stone, scuffing a shoe.

'Look, we're back out there this morning.' Harper stood to speak. 'Maybe they're still holed up in the vicinity,' he said, patting dust from the bench off the seat of his trousers.

'Christ, Baz! They could be anywhere by now, even Sydney.'

'No,' Sidoli cut in. 'Not on a bike and not without being seen. But yeah, they've had a head start.'

'What about the bikies, Baz?' Max asked, pointedly directing his question to the senior officer.

'Gone to ground, except for Clayton Marshall. He's been mouthing off about police brutality and corruption. Seems to have a different idea to the rest of us about what went down.'

'He burned my fucking pub down. What's he saying about that?'

'Says he was on the way to Kal with the victim and wasn't around for the fire. Can't remember who was there.'

'Scumbag! Right. Anyhow, that's immaterial. The court will say it was the backpacker who shot Marshall's mate and Marshall might just find himself back looking at four walls in Freo for arson. He's out on licence, after all.' Collins stopped pacing and shot Harper a knowing look. 'That's if we let it go to court.'

Sidoli bowed his head and, staring at the ground, wondered how he ever got in this deep. How did he let it come to this and why the fuck did he take that first kick-back? At the time, he convinced himself it was all just a perk of the job, by way of thanks for having to deal with the scum of the earth.

So what if he sexed up evidence to get drug dealers put away? The streets were safer without them. What was wrong with that? But, once he turned a blind eye to drug seizures going missing, he knew he was fucked. The price he paid now was so much more than the price he sold his soul for. It angered him that he let himself be so easily compromised and that he was such a cheap bastard.

He put everything at risk – his career, his pension, his reputation. He couldn't even attempt to justify his actions anymore. He had no integrity and, as much as he tried to convince himself it didn't matter, it sickened him because he knew it did. And now he was in hock to the likes of Harper and Collins. There was no getting out. He looked up at Max and continued to outline the state of play.

'We've leaked a few photos of explosions, pictures of ANFO barrels the backpacker had on a roll of film. There was a picture of an Irish revolutionary, or something, on the cover of a book he was reading. We're letting the media run with it and they've decided he was an IRA sympathiser and are painting him as some sort of fanatic, a looper, and the girl a sex-worker. Keeps the story on the front pages, which is good. It'll be impossible for them to go unnoticed. It's only a matter of time before they're seen.'

'Good,' Max said. 'Easier to get rid of a nutter. Fewer questions asked, when the tactical boys are brought in to finish things.'

'Much of that won't carry water in court,' Harper added. 'But, along with the more legitimate evidence, it might sow doubt in Marshall's mind and ease the bikie situation for a while. That would be a start.'

'What are you suggesting? It's all legitimate evidence! Do you think what happened is a fucking figment of my imagination? The backpacker did it. End of story. Go find him!' Max ordered.

'Max, calm down. We all want this sorted expeditiously, but the story, whatever it is, has to stand up.' Harper deferred, with a nod to the junior officer. Sidoli obliged.

'We can place the backpacker's thong prints at the battery, where we believe the fatal shot was taken from. Matching ballistics at the treehouse, the fight in your bottle shop, your robbery and assault. It all adds up. He was drinking for most of the day and mouthing off anti-Pommy sentiment. There was a small quantity of cannabis found at the treehouse. It paints a good picture.'

'I'll ensure we find something more significant taped inside the cistern of Porcini's dunny, too,' Harper added, without a hint of emotion. 'And you will have to make a formal statement sometime today, Max. We've delayed it too long already.'

'Sure, OK. I know.'

'Look, Max,' Harper tried to adopt a reassuring tone. 'I'd be lying if I said there weren't problems. For a start, why did you dispose of your clothes? That doesn't look good, mate.'

'Ah, Christ! I was in hospital. They were covered in the blood of a dead mate. I got a nurse to send them for incineration. Sure, if I was thinking straight, I might have asked her to hold off.'

'OK. Why approach the camp of a cold-blooded psychopath? Someone who just shot a bikie, then assaulted and robbed you. Were you even armed? A pistol, by the way, has been found on the road out of Aurora.'

'Baz, at the time I didn't know anyone was shot. My pub and home were burning down around me. Those two drugged-up losers attacked me and stole a significant amount of money. They left me for dead underneath the burning wreckage of my business. To say I was pissed, and not at my most lucid, would be an understatement. They must have taken my gun when they disabled my Land Cruiser. I put it in the glove compartment after the fight and only realised it was gone when I got to the camp. It's not the murder weapon, is it?'

'No, it hadn't been fired. But yeah, that works,' said Harper.

'What do you mean, that fucking works? That's what happened, OK?'

'Max, personally, I don't care what happened,' Harper's patience was being tested. He didn't like that Max treated them as fools, while maintaining the pretence he was the victim. 'I want this sorted, and in the best possible way for everyone. And I don't want a bloody biker war on my hands either. Like I said, there are problems. We need to fix them.'

With a cigarette in his mouth, Sidoli eased his heavy-set frame off the bench. He took a moment to tuck his shirt into the tight waist band of his trousers, before joining the other two in the centre of the arena. At no time in his years at the Department had he worked directly under Collins, but knew well the man's reputation and they both shared similar business interests.

Gripping the cigarette between his teeth, his words somewhat indistinct, Sidoli made his feelings known. 'Look, this is all bullshit,' he said eyeballing Collins. 'If I'm going to go out on a limb to cover your arse, I expect you to show some gratitude. You brought this shit on yourself. I'd be happy to let you hang for it, but it seems I can't, so you better stop acting the innocent, indignant hard man, and get your fucking story straight.'

He threw down the half-finished cigarette and ground it into the dusty concrete with a shoe. 'What you said about the gun in your glove compartment is bullshit. You weren't in your own vehicle. You took one from the mine! Your footprints are all over the camp. Yet you had a dying man in your cab. Was he happy to wait while you fucking sauntered around?'

Incensed, Max stepped into Sidoli's space. The two men faced each other. Sidoli refused to back away.

'Who the fuck do you think you are, tubbs, talking to me like that? Baz, who is this guy?' Collins demanded, pointing a finger almost into Sidoli's cheek. 'Maybe Baz hasn't told you, mate, so let me make it perfectly clear. It's not for me to get my story straight. That's your job. And you'd better fucking do it, right? If I go down for this, the two of you will be joining me on Main Block in Freo prison. Simple as!'

'Gentlemen, gentlemen! Come on. Calm down.' Harper put himself between the two antagonists. 'We have to work together on this. It won't be easy, and bloody impossible if we're at each other's throats. Max, Stan here is the best man to fix this, believe me. Look, you don't have to like each other. We just need to get it done. And, as we said, there are problems with your version of events. With calm heads, we can sort it. Tell him about the film, Stan.' He turned to Sidoli. 'Tell him, Stan!'

Max backed away and resumed his pacing.

Furious, Sidoli had considered nutting Collins. But Harper was right. They needed to work this through. 'Like I said. There were a few rolls of film found at the camp, but no camera recovered at the scene. Forensics seem to think two people were hiding near the carcass of that roo, when a third person, probably you, searched the camp. So it's possible they had a camera with them. Would that concern you?' Sidoli enjoyed putting the question to Collins.

Max didn't reply. He remembered the smell of the carcass. Even after inhaling the smoke and the stink off his dirty, sweaty clothes, the smell of the roo was overpowering. He had to walk away from it.

'Fuck! You need to find them, Baz, and before they can get anything developed.' Max bent down and, picking up a rock, hurled it against the corrugated wall. The sound reverberated, amplifying as it travelled around the curved interior of the building.

'Fuck!' he shouted again, his voice mixing with the clattering echo, before it bounced back into the centre of the ring. 'Fucking oath, Baz. If there is a film out there, I need it destroyed.'

Harper realised it was as definitive an admission they were ever likely to get from Collins. A plea for help.

Great acoustics in here, Sidoli thought, almost saying it aloud. He figured he'd better throw Max a bone, something positive to chew on. 'A relative of Helen Mitchell's out at Yilgarn was overheard on the HF suggesting a vehicle might have passed through their western boundary gate recently. There's no reason why anyone would. There's nothing out west. We're looking into it.'

'OK.' Realising he needed these people, Max adopted a more conciliatory tone. 'And for God's sake, get the correct photo out there.'

It was Sidoli's turn to be put back in his box. 'Yeah, don't know how that one got past us. We went with the press. Should have had it confirmed. We've been onto immigration for the right one. The girl is easy to recognise, though.'

After a few moments silence, and then to nobody in particular, Max spoke again. 'It was supposed to be Marshall. He's come out of Fremantle with payback on his mind and he needed dealing with. That scumbag could have us all put away.'

'Ah, shit! But Old Bill Mitchell, Max. For Christ's sake!' That, Harper felt was unforgiveable.

The three men spoke a while longer to refine Max's statement. Max then left for his hotel. The others were continuing north to Aurora and on to Yilgarn homestead.

'You asked me earlier if I played Two-Up,' Harper said, getting into the car, 'Stan, I never gamble unless I can't lose. I'm not going to start now.'

* * *

SPORTING THE MANDATORY hard hat, Jim sat sideways in the driver's seat and stared out the open door of Andy's Land Cruiser. He watched Jeff manoeuvre the rig over the site of the next drill hole. Once Andy was happy with the rig's position and orientation, he gave the drillers the go-ahead to start. Jeff flicked a lever and four enormous steel hydraulic jacks appeared from the side of the Bedford truck. They lifted the front wheels clear of the sloping ground, stabilising and bringing the rig into the horizontal.

Andy climbed into the passenger seat next to Jim and they both watched the mast rise to sixty degrees. The brothers scurried around dragging hoses and equipment into place. Jeff stood on the footplate, working his controls. Far too intrigued with what was going on, Jim had yet to open his sketchbook. He could see Andy was in no hurry to start his paperwork either.

'They're drilling an angled hole back into the hill. If we went straight down, it'd be forever before we hit the dipping mineralised zone.' Andy volunteered the information, without waiting to be asked.

The drill bit began to pound the unconsolidated surface material. A great cloud of dust rose from the ground below the mast and, for a moment, the powerful roar of air escaping drowned out the sound of the motors.

When the noise abated, Jim turned to his companion. 'Tell me about this banded iron formation,' he said, rather grandly.

'Pardon?'

'What is this BIF stuff and why is it in the hills?'

Delighted to oblige, there followed a long and detailed lecture from Andy on the law of superposition, sedimentation, plate tectonics, folds, faults and mineralisation. All explained beautifully and succinctly, using a hastily thrown together cheese sandwich.

The cool morning air had begun to warm, when Kelly stepped out of the Hilux, modelling a new short hairstyle. All heads turned. There was something a little wild about it now, Jim thought. It suited her, but then any haircut would. He noticed she was not wearing his denim jacket. She had hardly taken it off before now. Had he blown it, he wondered.

Jeff signalled for Kelly to meet him at the support truck, from where he conjured up a spare hard hat and a spanking new Ozdrill shirt from behind a seat.

'I always keep a few handy. I go through them pretty quick, as you might have guessed,' he said, pleased with himself. 'Put it on, just in case someone comes by. You won't be so conspicuous. Though let's be honest, that's just about impossible.'

Kelly gave Jeff a playful nudge and thanked him, before stepping behind the truck to change. Of course the shirt was far too big, but with the sleeves rolled up, it served a purpose. She considered tying the hem into a bow at the front. It might improve the shape, she thought, flatter the figure more, but that might not be appropriate. The idea after all was to blend in.

Andy stretched his legs, resting his large feet on the window frame of the passenger door. Both doors of the cab were open and a hot breeze blew through. Placing his notes across his lap, he endeavoured to write a drilling report, but struggled to find anything positive to say.

Jim watched Kelly appear out from behind the support truck. 'What's the story with Kelly and Jeff?' Jim asked, trying not to sound too interested.

'He's mad about her,' Andy said, looking up from his notes.

'Yeah? Were they, like, ever an item?' Jim couldn't help but sound anxious now.

'No, there's no need for you to be worrying yourself. Am I right in thinking the two of you had a barney last night?'

'Yeah, I suppose we did. Just a little misunderstanding.'

Jim wasn't so sure. He spent a restless night chastising himself. She was spot on. He had lived a cosseted middle-class existence, facilitated by a large network of family and friends. It afforded him the luxury of drifting through life ever since he left school, six wasteful years ago. What had he done with that time? When faced with dilemmas he would never have, what right did he have to take to his moral soapbox and judge anyone else's actions? Jim decided, and with good reason, he was a prat.

'She's a decent girl, is our Kelly. You know, everybody fell in love with her in Kalgoorlie. Nobody more than Jeff. He dragged me to The Pump House a few times just so he could sit at the bar and talk to … no … look at her for the night. I was his ticket in the door, that's all. Then I might as well have left.'

Andy went to write something on the pad. With pen in hand, he looked at it with intent for a few moments, then closed it over again. 'Don't tell him I told you, but he asked her out one time. She turned him down. Then out of the blue, she was gone and we came up here.'

Using the steering wheel, Jim pulled himself out of a lolled slouch and grabbed his sketch pad from the dash. 'Might as well make a start on something.'

'Oh, ho! Watch out, young man. She's coming our way.' Andy leaned across Jim and saluted Kelly, who approached the driver's door. 'Morning, Kelly. I like the hair. Shirt suits you, too.'

'Thanks. I'm a driller now, it seems.' She shoved a foil parcel into Jim's hand. 'Here. I made you lunch,' and before he could thank her, she was off again.

Jim became transfixed by the sight of the back of her neck for the first time and its gentle curve into her shoulders. She swayed her hips more than she needed to. It had the desired effect.

'Thanks!' he shouted after her, when he came to his senses. 'What's in it?'

'Pressed tongue,' she replied, not looking around, but gave him a subtle wave of her hand. Kelly then made a line for the drillers' coffee.

'There you go,' said Andy. 'Everything's back to normal.'

'She knows I hate tongue.'

'Mmmm. Possibly not, then.'

'It's just wrong,' Jim said, picturing what was in the sandwich. 'They squash it into a bowl for a few days hoping to make it look like a lump of proper meat. But it's still a rolled up cow's tongue, covered in these god-awful huge, white bovine, taste-bud things that feel like bloody sandpaper sliding down your throat. That's if you can even forget the fact it's a feckin giant tongue and actually be persuaded to try it in the first place. Jesus!'

Jim shivered at the thought of it. 'Old Bill and me Da loved the stuff. One of Bill's cherished tins of tongue made their way into our supplies by mistake and Kelly has been threatening me with it ever since we left.'

'Can't say I've ever had it myself.' Andy tried his best to be sympathetic.

'Here. This could be your lucky day.' Jim unfolded the neat, foil-wrapped package onto his knee and found the most magnificent ham, tomato and salad triple decker sandwich inside. Andy looked across enviously.

'Good Lord! She's even cut the crusts off!'

* * *

GOD, THAT'S A dreadful song, Helen thought. The tune faded out and the chirpy tones of the presenter took over.

'And there you have it. "If Tomorrow Never Comes", from the hot new American Country star, Garth Brooks, the second single from his debut album ...

'Right, we'll take a break from Country music for a while. Nobody could have missed the tragic news in recent days of that well-loved Goldfields character, William "Old Bill" Mitchell, who was killed at his Yilgarn Station this past Monday morning. Sitting in front of me now, and I have to say she's very brave to do this, is Bill's wife, Helen.

'Helen, I know this is a tremendously difficult time for you and your family, but you wanted to come in and say a few words about your husband.'

Helen sat quietly, rigid in the comfortable studio chair, her small, elegant figure dressed in her best dark-brown trouser suit, the one she kept for trips to see the bank manager. With help from her niece, she wore more makeup than usual. Despite being in shock and not having slept for three nights, Helen wanted to look strong and together for this. She was determined to do the interview. The time to grieve properly would be after she buried her husband and his murderer was caught. Helen spoke confidently into the microphone.

'Yes, thank you, Bob. It was important to me to come here today and I am extremely grateful for the opportunity you and your station has afforded me.' She cleared her throat. 'We are all part of a great community here in the Goldfields and wider rural WA, too. I am proud of who we are and what we represent. Hard-working, decent people, who look out for one another. It's a diverse and far-flung community, so much so, that much of the time we can only communicate, or even socialise, over the airways.

'I have come here to say, we are burying Bill at the weekend and it is to be a small family funeral. Bill had a lot of great friends around the state and farther afield. They are out there now toiling on the land, as Bill did all his life. To our dear friends, can I say, we don't expect you to travel to Kal on Saturday. Bill wouldn't have been comfortable with a fuss, and annoyed if you knocked off work on his account. I simply ask that you remember him, while you go about your business, and thank you everyone for all the great years of friendship.

'To those who have got in touch and offered your condolences, it has been of great comfort. If you are ever passing by Yilgarn on your travels, our gate will stay open. If you need somewhere to rest up, or just feel like dropping in for one of his dreadful home brews, you are more than welcome. He's left me with barrels of it. I intend to stay at Yilgarn and Bill will always be about the place.

'I also wish to extend my sympathies to the family of the young man shot at Aurora on Sunday. I will be thinking of you at the week-end, too.'

'Indeed, it's been a dark few days for the Goldfields. I know your family declined the opportunity of a public television appeal. Why was that?' Bob asked.

'I prefer to do it this way, Bob. It's easier. There is no media scrum, no cameras in my face. It's on my own terms. Radio is just the right way around here.'

'So, is there anything in particular you would like to say to the public, or even to your husband's killers, that might convince them to hand themselves in. They are, of course, still at large. Perhaps everyone should check their barns or water sources. I'm sure, if we rally the bush telegraph and our city cousins, we can bring these individuals to justice.'

'Yes, Bob. I'd like to make an appeal. To my husband's killer, this is important, and I choose my words carefully. I know who you are. You will be found out and you will be brought to justice. To the bush telegraph, somewhere out there is an innocent, frightened young couple, who need our help. They are in tremendous danger, from the environment and from a criminal element amongst us. I don't know where they are, but if anyone encounters them, I am asking all my friends, from the bottom of my broken heart, to look after them for me and Bill. Please help them in any way they require.'

Bob raised a quizzical eyebrow and shifted awkwardly in his seat. Behind Helen's head, his alarmed producer in the control booth caught his attention. She sliced her hand across in front of her neck. Her voice in his ear told Bob to wrap it up.

'I am sorry, Helen. I know this is a terrible time for you, but the police seem pretty certain they know who is responsible for these kill-ings. If you have read any of the papers, it's damning evidence. I don't think we can be seen to condone the obstruction of justice ... for what-ever reason. So my sympathies to you and thank you for coming in. We'll have to leave it there.'

'OK, Bob. I understand and thank you. I have said my piece, but just one more thing. Jim Macken is a fine young man. His family back home in Ireland, who are at their wits' end, can be very proud of him. And, if somehow you are listening, Jim, when all this is over, come by and say hello. We'll talk of Bill and feed the chooks. I'll serve you a golden egg. The paintings are enough.' Helen began to weep.

Bob was clearly embarrassed. 'As I said, we'll leave it there.'

* * *

ON THE RADIO, Bob played another whiney Country song.

'That took balls – respect!' Jeff said, throwing the butt of a cigarette to the ground. He snatched the last of Arthur's snags from the edge of the hot plate and called up to Kelly in the cab of the support truck. 'Thanks for cooking the snags, Kel.' Jeff then signalled to the brothers. 'Come on, you two. Back to work.'

Hendrik had beaten everyone to it and could already be heard tapping away over at his Land Cruiser parked on the opposite side of the rig. Andy patted Jim on the head, before moving off himself. Jim nodded in appreciation and stayed by the cab door, watching the drillers swing another six-metre drill rod into place.

High on the derrick, the rotary head spun, screwing the new rod down tight onto the top of the drill string just above ground level, forming an airtight seal at the join. The whole machine shuddered and the entire drill string turned again. Adding a new rod is an intricate operation, requiring a complicated sequence of small movements and perfect timing. Jim couldn't quite get his head around how it all worked.

Kelly lounged in the driver's seat, watching Jim. She could see the interview had upset him – particularly when Helen mentioned his parents. She noticed how he had bit his lip, hiding his emotion. She clicked off the radio.

Jim pretended to object. 'Hey! I was listening to that.'

'Are we OK?' she asked softly.

'Yeah, we're fine,' Jim replied, but avoided making eye contact. 'I was a feckin eejit last night. I'm sorry. I was just upset.' He continued to watch the drillers busy themselves around the rig. 'You know you can talk to me about anything.' Jim looked up and offered a half smile before running a nervous hand through his hair. 'The sandwich was delicious by the way.'

'Couldn't have you getting hungry.'

'Thanks ... I think I'll go try and make myself useful.'

As he walked away, Kelly noticed how his shoulders hung low. Just enough to convey all was not right.

'Hey!' she called down, 'I'm sorry, too.'

Jim turned and nodded graciously.

She grinned. 'By the way, what's a theocracy?'

Jim laughed and continued on his way. 'I'll tell you later.'

* * *

SHATTERED, BUT PLEASED with herself, Helen stepped out onto a quiet Brookman Street. It took a minute for her eyes to adjust to the brilliant sunshine. A cloud of blue tobacco smoke drifted into her face, catching in her nose. A man stood in front of her, cigarette in mouth, his expression devoid of emotion. Max Collins said nothing. He stared, refusing to give ground on the footpath. Helen stiffened. Her heart raced. She wanted to say so much to that man, but her voice failed her. Instead, she went to slap him hard on the face. But before Helen could raise a hand, Eloise took her arm.

'The manners of some people,' Eloise said, making sure the rude man heard her. She steered Helen by the elbow around Collins and over to their parked Land Cruiser. Opening the passenger door, she helped her aunt inside.

* * *

JIM APPROACHED THE young geologist who busily logged rock chips off the back of the Land Cruiser.

'How are yah, Hendrik?'

No acknowledgement came back. In fact, he could have sworn Hendrik deliberately turned away, when he spotted Jim on the way over to him. Stopping directly behind the geologist, Jim tried once more.

'Hi!' Again, no response.

Stooped over his samples, Hendrik kept his back to Jim and a small hand lens tight against an eye, while he scrutinised a fragment of green rock. Confident of his identification, he scribbled a brief note on his clipboard. Jim waited, hands in pockets, giving Hendrik every chance, before trying a different tack.

'Andy said you might want a hand collecting samples. Show me what needs doing and I'll do my best to help.'

'I don't need any help. I'm fine, thank you,' came the curt reply.

Hendrik refused to engage in conversation and continued to study his rock fragments. Suddenly, Jim saw the clipboard fly across the back of the Land Cruiser and Hendrik lash out with flaying arms at the flies swarming his head. For all his furious effort, Jim doubted Hendrik made contact with a single fly. It was always the way.

'You'll get used to them eventually,' Jim suggested.

'No, not sure I will, I've had just about enough of this place.'

'Ah, go on. Let me help. I'm feeling guilty sitting around. I've been annoying Andy with geology questions all morning. I think it must be your turn to answer a few.'

'Very well. If you insist, but try to keep out of my way.'

Hendrik gave Jim an abrupt demonstration on how to composite assay samples from the green bags and fill out the necessary paperwork for the lab in Kalgoorlie. He noticed how the Irishman picked things up quickly – unlike the previous fieldie he had to put up with.

'Just don't mess up my numbering,' were Hendrik's concluding words of gratitude, before returning to his geological logs.

Jim got stuck in and soon caught up with the sampling. While waiting for Garry to drop the next green bag into the row, he watched how Hendrik collected, sieved and washed the rock chips in five-metre runs, before examining them.

A little later, after a quick trip to the bushes, Hendrik returned to find Jim had placed five sieved and washed samples, ready for logging, on the tray of the Land Cruiser.

'There you go. I'll have more for you when you need them.'

'Metres twenty-six to thirty?'

'Yep.'

Hendrik grunted something inaudible, possibly a thank you. Jesus, he's an awful man for that, Jim thought, but continued to sieve and wash the rock chips, happy to be earning his keep. The two young men worked well together and fell naturally into a rhythm that allowed Hendrik time to clear his backlog from the previous day. Jim was pleased to see Hendrik relax in his company and tried for the first time to engage the taciturn South African in easy conversation.

'What's the purpose of hammering the rock fragments on that steel plate?' he asked. Andy had explained it to him earlier, but it was somewhere to start.

'It's a streak plate. The colour of the crushed rock powder shows the different minerals in the rock. Look, see the yellow? That's limonite, an iron mineral.'

Jim studied the vibrant yellow streak. 'Oh yeah, bet yah that's used as a pigment.'

'The ochres, used since antiquity.'

'Cool,' Jim said, a little surprised. 'Coming from South Africa, this Australian geology must be all new to you. Did it take long to get up to speed?'

'No, not at all. A large part of South African geology is similar to here,' Hendrik said, while continuing to tap away with his hammer on the plate.

'Yeah? Is that unusual?'

'Rocks of this age are not common. They represent primordial blocks of the Earth's crust that haven't been reworked for billions of years. That's what we have here in the Yilgarn craton and farther north in the Pilbara. You get a few similar ancient sequences of rocks around the world, like in the Kaapvaal back home.'

He sprinkled rock fragments from another sieve onto the plate and tapped again. More smears of vibrant yellow and some red appeared out from under Hendrik's hammer. 'The similarities are so great, it's believed many of these places were joined together as proto-continents billions of years ago!'

'Really? Isn't that something?' For a split second, Jim thought about asking Hendrik what primordial crust, cratons and proto-continents were. 'Hey, wasn't that brilliant news about Mandela's release?'

'Yes, I heard it on the radio. That terrorist should never have been set free.' Hendrik turned his attention back to his work. Jim couldn't leave it there.

'That's a little strong. The rest of the world seems pleased he's out. I don't claim to know much about the man, but blowing up a few train tracks hardly merits a life sentence. Particularly when he's fighting against ... well ... slavery!' Jim placed five full sieves down in front of Hendrik.

'You don't know what you're talking about. And believe me, it's not just him. I'd put de Klerk in the cell next to him. He's the most dangerous of the lot of them.'

Hendrik hammered his chips with more ardour than before.

'OK, hands up. I'm no expert on South African politics.' Jim paused on his way back over to the green bags to say his piece. 'But I did read Donald Woods's book on Steve Biko. I actually met Woods and he signed a copy for me. That's not important, but he's a genuine bloke, who was prepared to have his eyes opened.'

'Never heard of him.'

'You must have. How about *Cry Freedom*, Dickie Attenborough's movie about Biko?'

'Never heard of it.'

'Oscar nominated!'

'Nope.' Hendrik shook his head. It wasn't a lie.

'Don't you think that might perhaps suggest a whiff of censorship about the system in South Africa? You know, you could do worse than check out a few bookshops, when you're next in town. Educate yourself a bit.'

Although Hendrik did not agree with Jim and thought him impertinent, it was nice to have a conversation again. He only ever spoke to Andy about work and always brief and to the point. Hendrik was awkward in company, always had been, particularly so in groups. Often interpreted as rudeness on his part, and sometimes to be fair it was, but mostly Hendrik's social skills just let him down. From his first days in camp, Hendrik's dealings with his colleagues were tetchy. He dug himself into a hole and, as much as he would have liked to, he did not have the capacity to get himself out.

'Maybe I will. I might even buy a book on your Irish history, while I'm at it. That's an intractable mess you have going on over there. Isn't it?'

'Yeah, we have our own problems, that's for sure.'

'Jim, I didn't say it last night, but your paintings are excellent. I like art. I've studied it – you're good.'

'Ah thanks. Nice of you to say so.' Jim suspected a compliment from Hendrik did not come easy. He replayed it again in his head, just to be certain no underhanded slight had slipped past.

Jim looked up to see Andy striding towards them. The Englishman's eyes, wide and unblinking, demanded attention. Jim put down the sieves and alerted Hendrik. Something was up. Over Andy's shoulder, Jim noticed Jeff almost throw Kelly back into the cab of the support truck and close the door after her.

'There's someone coming. Stay calm. Get your face masks on. Hennie, go tell Jeff we have hit the mother of all veins of blue asbestos. He'll know what to do, and then you can start cleaning things down over here. Jim, get cable ties from the cab and tie all those green bags and, for Christ's sake, just look busy and like you know what you're doing. Hendrik, why are you still here? Go now, hurry!'

'Jeff, I'm not happy about—'

'Not now, mate! Just go tell the drillers. OK?'

Hendrik grabbed a pair of work gloves and marched off. Even over the drilling noise, he could be heard mumbling expletives. The elaborate way he put on the gloves, confirmed his disapproval.

'Jim, don't look. It's the Old Bill,' Andy said, once Hendrik was out of ear shot.

'What!' Jim couldn't believe what he heard.

'Oh Lord, sorry … I mean the police, the Garda! I've sent Kelly to hide in the support truck. Don't worry, I'll run them. Asbestos scares the shit out of people.'

Chapter 14

A pearl earring

After an unproductive night in Sandstone, Senior Constable Laurie Holt travelled back to Menzies along the same dirt road he came in on. By now, Holt had interviewed all but one of the station owners in the area, none of whom saw anything suspicious, let alone a couple on a motorcycle.

At Youanmi Gold Mine, he enjoyed a Milo with the mine manager, while they both listened to Helen's interview on the radio. Helen's remarks troubled Holt. He knew her to be an intelligent and measured woman, never given to idle gossip, but spoke her mind. Helen would not have said what she had without good reason. He undertook to call on her as soon as he could. In the meantime, Senior Constable Holt decided to detour and see where this new and seemingly well-used track he had passed on the way up would take him.

It took him first to an exploration camp where, after a quick stroll around he found no one home. But when the wind got up, the distant sound of drilling blew across the camp with the dust. Fresh tyre marks directed Holt out along the base of a long hill, where he soon spotted the rig's mast high on the ridge, shrouded in a cloud of yellow rock powder. As he got closer, the front of the great machine looked to be floating magically off the side of the hill. Holt turned and drove carefully over the rough ground, slaloming a line of surveyors' stakes up to the rig.

He was met by an individual shouting and gesturing for him to move back, which was unusual. For a police officer in uniform, it normally worked the other way around. However, despite a face hidden behind a dust mask and shades, the bloke hurrying towards him did not seem hostile. It had to be a safety issue, Holt presumed, and obliged. After reversing down the slope to what he considered a safe distance, Holt stopped again. The masked man hastily followed him down on foot.

BENT OVER, JIM pulled a cable tie tight around the crumpled green neck of a plastic sack and then waddled forward to tie the next one. To his left, Hendrik did the same, but had noticeably made little progress along his own green line. Terrified as Jim was, he could not help but be reminded of his first ever job.

Summer holidays were spent in a similar back-breaking position to how he found himself now, picking spuds for Duxie Grimes on Milverton Hill. Only then, the lines of plastic sacks were four-stone bags of potatoes, standing tall in freshly dug potato drills. For the princely sum of ten pence a bag, the potato pickers earned a wage dragging the empty bags between their legs and filling as many of them as they could in a day, with Queens or Golden Wonders. All these years later, he still bore the crescent tan line on his lower back where his T-shirt rode up. A badge of honour worn with pride among the young lads of Skerries. On sunny weekends, the distinctive mark told the girls sunbathing on the rocks by The Captains that these were men of means, good for an ice-cream and a few games of Space Invaders.

Jim doubted Hendrik would have lasted too long at the spuds. Duxie would have picked him off with a well-aimed potato to the back of the head and ordered him to get a move on or get lost! Why he thought of this now, Jim could not understand. It must be a defence mechanism, he guessed, a way of holding onto his sanity perhaps. But he needed to stay in the present, he needed to be alert. He pushed the memory aside.

'SORRY ABOUT THAT,' Andy said, through the open window. He pulled the dust mask slightly away from his mouth to speak. 'We've just hit a seam of blue asbestos. Here, put this on.' He handed the officer a used, dirty mask.

Holt studied it warily.

'Sorry, it's the best I can do for now,' Andy said, noting the officer's hesitancy. 'Asbestos! It's in the air. It's everywhere. Probably should shut off your air-conditioning for the moment. There's a chance it might get sucked into the cab. It's lethal.'

Andy laid it on good and thick. 'We've hit the same shit that turned Whittnoom into a dead zone. Would you believe there are calls for that town to be wiped from the map?'

Up the hill, except for the muffled thump, thump of a pump, the drill rig fell silent. Holt watched a man spray the ground around the derrick with a powerful jet of water. Another driller stripped to his trunks and hosed himself down. Off to their right, two people worked at sealing cuttings bags. A large burly man with a goatee, threw what appeared to be new plastic-wrapped shirts to the crew.

'Nearly killed Rolf Harris, asbestos. He mined up Whittnoom way as a lad!' The police officer said, before turning his attention back to Andy.

'Can't say I knew that. Anyway, it's a bloody nuisance. We have to shut this drill hole down now and lose a day to decontaminating the site.' Andy shook his head in despair. He let it all sink in, before pointing to the mask still in the officer's hand. 'Believe me, you really should put that on.'

Holt attended to the matter with no great enthusiasm, before turning the engine and air-conditioning off. 'That's unfortunate. I won't bother you too long,' he said through the mask, now keen to get away.

'Yes, forgive me. Andy Robinson, project geologist on this operation. You'll understand if I don't shake your hand. Can't be too cautious.'

Holt introduced himself and then ran through a few quick questions. But, as with everyone else he met on the journey, Andy and his crew had seen nothing unusual or anyone else pass through the area in weeks.

At first, Kelly hunkered down among the pedals and the discarded empty cigarette packets on the floor of the cab and waited for the door to open. Waited to be grabbed by the scruff of the neck and pulled out. Except now, Kelly rejected that scenario. She was finished with cowering. If they were coming for her, she would not make it easy for them. She got off the floor.

Keeping low, Kelly slid across the seat and peered out the driver's side window. The length of the drill rig opposite filled the view. Pressing a cheek up to the glass allowed her to see past the end of the rig to where Jeff did a good impression of looking busy. Garry and Dan pulled hoses around behind him. But where were the others and who had arrived?

Noticing her at the window, Jeff discreetly motioned for her to get down out of sight. Sitting back in the seat, Kelly cursed, frustrated, then cursed again. The large wing mirror on the truck offered a good view of the access track. Her worst fears were realised. A police vehicle had parked on the hill. She watched Andy rest an arm on top of the paddy wagon door, lean towards the window and talk casually to the officer. At least for now anyway, the officer remained inside.

'JESUS CHRIST!' JIM whispered through clenched teeth. Waves of cold pain shot up his arm. Fighting the reflex to shout and jump about, he grimaced and pulled his throbbing limb out from under a thicket of green plastic. Dozens of large, black and mahogany-tinted meat ants ran angrily up his forearm and over his elbow. These were not the dainty ants with whom he shared a bed in the treehouse. Neither did they tickle.

Careful not to draw attention to himself, Jim remained hunched over and shook his forearm violently in an attempt to dislodge the ants. A number had sunk their formidable mandibles into his skin and now dangled by their partially embedded heads. Continuing to curse, Jim frantically brushed away the remaining insects. A ball of inter-locking parts fell from his arm and immediately absorbed itself into the river of ants flowing at his feet.

Jim studied the streaming mass. An endless line of swarming ants, antennae waving madly, charged out from their low, stony mound of a nest. They poured over the bag planted next to the exit and over Jim's boots. An army now climbed his legs, legions of ants, collectively hell-bent on removing the giant trespasser, tiny piece by tiny piece, and feeding it to their larvae, safe in the cavernous nurseries deep underground.

Jim sidled away from the disturbed nest and the green bags, but it took what seemed like ages, and many more bites, before he freed himself of all his single-minded assailants. The pain subsided, once the ants released their hold or were plucked off, but the shivers lingered on. Jim stood up. It was then he realised he was alone. Hendrik had gone. Looking about, he spotted the South African walking past the rig.

A FIGURE APPEARED OUT from behind the rig and tramped down the hill towards the police vehicle.

'No, Hendrik, no!' Kelly called out, but her muted cries barely left the cab. Scratching for the door handle, her fingers pulled it back and the door clicked open an inch. A faint dissenting voice, in a head full of clamouring calls to run for the Hilux, told her to wait. But, where was Jim? What if he had already taken the Hilux and abandoned her? She persuaded herself he wouldn't do that. He had to be out there. With both hands pressed against the glass, Kelly watched Hendrik continue on his merry way. More angry than fearful, she readied herself for what would come.

'DO YOU HAVE females working on site?' Holt asked.

'Yes, we're an equal opportunity employer,' Andy replied glibly, but still nervous about the question. 'One of our field assistants, Jen ... she's away at the moment, down in Kal collecting assay results. Should be back in a few days. Why do you ask?'

'Just there are women's clothes on the line at your camp.'

'Christ! I thought you were going to give me bad news about Jen there for a second,' Andy laughed. 'Ah, fair cop. You got me, guv. They're mine.'

Holt didn't bat an eye.

'Apologies. That wasn't funny, officer. It's been a rough day, slow drilling and now asbestos,' Andy continued. 'Sometimes it's best just to laugh at these things. No ... they belong to Jen. She was in such a hurry to get away, she left her laundry up. And it can stay there till she returns. None of us are going to touch it,' he said, stepping backwards and holding his two hands up in defeat. 'She'd have our guts for garters!'

'That's fine. Just wondering. Anyway, I can see you're up to your eyeballs and I need to get a move on if I'm to make the main road before dark. Good luck with the clean-up.'

'No problem. Safe trip. I'd better go make sure the crew are following correct protocols. It'll be on my head if they don't.'

Andy tapped the roof of the paddy wagon to send Holt off. The officer reached to turn the key in the ignition. With a hand already primed for a goodbye salute, Andy waited for the reassuring sound of the engine. It didn't come. Instead, the officer's hand returned to rest on the steering wheel, where it raised an index finger and pointed to an approaching figure. Andy turned. His stomach heaved when he saw Hendrik.

Hendrik gave a cursory nod to the police officer, before stopping in front of Andy. His demeanour gave nothing away and his expression, well hidden behind his headgear and a dust mask, offered no comfort to his boss. Standing to his full height, Andy towered over the South African.

'Hendrik ... What the ... What can ...?'

Unable to get past an opening word, Andy abandoned trying to formulate a coherent sentence. He folded his arms across his chest briefly, before shoving them out of the way into the front pockets of his shorts. Although the heat had gone from the day, beads of sweat formed in the creases behind his ears and trickled down the side of his neck.

From his slender build and the few small, wrinkle-free patches of skin visible below the sunnies, Holt guessed the new arrival was young, possibly in his early twenties. He had young man's knees. Holt noticed him continuously make nervous fists with his gloved hands and avoid eye contact with Andy. If not for the few blonde curls peeking out under the hard hat and that he stood taller than Holt remembered of Jim Macken, he might have asked the young man to remove the sunnies and answer a few questions.

'Well, what is it then?' Andy asked tersely, when Hendrik was not forthcoming with any information. Andy closed his eyes and hoped.

'I'm sorry,' Hendrik said, shaking his head and looking into the empty space over Andy's shoulder. 'It's worse than I told you earlier!'

'What?'

'I've found asbestos in six bags. I should have spotted it sooner. I'm sorry ... thought you'd want to know.'

'A six-metre seam of asbestos! Ah Jesus, Hendrik. We've been drilling through that shit for half an hour, blowing carcinogenic dust everywhere!'

'I understand that. I can't offer any excuses.'

'Christ, I hope everyone is OK. Look, for now, just go back and get on with the clean-up.'

Hendrik nodded to the two men and abruptly left.

'South African?' Holt asked.

'Yeah, not here long.' Andy wondered what Hendrik was playing at and rested an arm on the roof of the vehicle, while he gathered his thoughts and let his heart recover. 'He's fresh out of university. Can't keep up with the drilling yet. To be fair, he has the makings of a good geo, but needs experience and needs to speed up.'

Andy stepped back from the window and blew out a cheek full of air. 'I suppose I should have kept a better eye on him ... Jesus, I hope everyone's OK. I do insist they wear the masks at all times. Anyway ...' He tapped the roof twice with the meaty part of his fist. 'Hope you find your killers soon. Terrible business that. Last the radio said, they were most likely in Perth.'

'Probably are. We're just checking all possibilities.' Holt turned the key in the ignition. He took off the mask and began to wind the window handle, when Andy placed a hand on top of the glass.

'Sorry, but if you're finished with that newspaper beside you, any chance I might have it?'

* * *

KELLY ALWAYS SET herself the challenge of removing the skin in one continuous long ribbon. She could not recall ever succeeding, but she must have many times. It was one of those things, like the exact score of a footy match, important, but soon forgotten after the final whistle. Her degree of success depended on the variety of tuber and how much starchy flesh from under the peel she was prepared to sacrifice to the knife. Even now, with a mind in turmoil, Kelly played her game. Garry, who sat next to her, scraped away with a potato peeler and worked his way through the basin of spuds a lot quicker than his glamorous assistant. He sprayed all around him with shrapnel.

What Kelly lacked in speed, she made up for in tidiness. None of her potatoes landed in the pot with a fragment of skin or an eye still on them. Two large legs of lamb, in truth more hogget than lamb, were roasting in separate camp ovens in front of where the potato peelers worked. Kelly concentrated quietly on the task in hand. It soothed her.

But again, along with everything else over the last few days, the stress of earlier events chipped away at her resolve. The immediate euphoria she felt watching the police wagon turn and drive away did not last long. She knew their situation remained perilous. Reading the nonsense printed about her in the newspaper did nothing to improve her state of mind. They lied. They twisted the facts. They made her out to be 'of questionable character', a 'known hard-drug user', a 'school dropout'. There was even a not so thinly veiled suggestion she might have been involved in prostitution. She fought back tears when reading the piece.

And then Andy mentioned the clothesline. Kelly still felt sick thinking about what the consequences of her foolishness might have been. Even though he insisted they not say a word to the others, she told them anyway. Nobody, including Hendrik, seemed bothered. Were they just being polite? What did they really think of her?

Another ribbon of peel broke off before she finished. She started again. She always started again. Jim popped out from behind the Hilux. He acknowledged her on his way to the shower. Since they arrived at camp, they had spent little time together. She missed their long meandering chats and being alone in his company. His own character being much maligned, Jim was similarly dismissive of the newspaper. Kelly knew what they wrote about him to be a complete fabrication, but what they said about her was closer to the bone – a masterful assassination of her character. She feared that, behind his sympathetic and understanding words, Jim might just believe at least some of what they wrote about her.

Having not been entirely open with him, she conceded she gave him grounds for suspicion. She could not be sure last night's argument was behind them either. Kelly knew she hurt him. It might have been her imagination, but he had not looked her in the eye since – not like he used to. That said, he had come straight over to check on her after Jeff helped her out of the truck, but disappeared again all too soon. Or was it possible Jeff's not-so-subtle advances had made Jim take a step back? Or worse, had Jim even noticed?

Kelly passed Garry her meagre contribution to the dinner preparations. Garry washed all the potatoes and divided them equally into both camp ovens to roast in the mutton fat. Before replacing the lids and raking the embers back over, she watched him add a few halved onions and a roughly chopped butternut squash to the mix. He topped it off with generous pourings of the cardinal sauces – sweet chilli and soy.

Jim passed by again. He had shaved. It suits him, she thought. He didn't have the capacity to grow a proper beard anyway. Kelly reminded herself that, despite the close call with the long arm of the law and the slanderous newspaper article, they were still at large, still breathing beautiful warm air and there were good people willing to help them.

'STONY SILENCE ... THE man's expression did not change, not one jot ... nothing!' Still giddy from the adrenaline rush, Andy stood by the campfire regaling his colleagues with an animated account of his conversation with the police officer. The geologist hurried a swig of beer, wiped his mouth and continued. 'Could you imagine me in that little pink number of yours, Kelly?' He shrugged. 'It seemed the nice constable could.' Andy swept an open palm across a stolid face, clipping his impressive nose on the way past. 'Nothing!'

After taking a seat and basking in the accolades conferred on him for his quick thinking, he added, 'I knew my time in the drama society at university would stand to me someday. If I'm to be honest, I must admit I came close to getting sick walking back to the rig, while the constable drove away.'

Nobody was naive enough to think the police officer's departure would be the end of it. The exploration crew knew their two guests were by no means out of the woods. Even so, there was a celebratory atmosphere in camp when they sat down to eat that evening.

When Jim arrived for the meal, he took a spot on the bench between Andy and Hendrik. Kelly sat opposite, between the two brothers. Jeff, who stood in front of a third bench when not eating, supervised the fire and agonised about the dwindling beer stocks. He debated going for his bottle of Jack Daniels, but held off for now.

Perched at the edge of the bench, hunched over, his back almost to the others, Hendrik picked at his food long after everyone else had finished. The food tasted fine, actually rather good. He just couldn't eat. His thoughts were chaotic, much like the great mass of furious ants that attacked Jim.

He had lied to a police officer. Not directly, but may as well have. Aiding and abetting, interfering with an investigation and harbouring criminals – for sure, he would do time in this fly-infested penal colony. And when they eventually let him out, he would of course be transported home in disgrace. What would he say to his father? More's the point, what will his father say to him?

Hendrik could not understand why he brought this on himself. Why could he not go through with it? What happened to him between starting down the hill and arriving at the police car? He tormented himself looking for answers and lamented how things were no longer black and white. Kelly hugged him when Andy told her what he did. He recoiled from her embrace, but to be honest, he liked it. Hendrik wasn't particularly adept at picking up on other people's emotions, but there was something about the way Andy thanked him too. Andy knew.

'IT'S ALL BOLLOCKS,' Jim remarked, pointing to the front-page lead story of *The West Australian*. He thumbed back the cover, following the jump line to the inside page.

'Yeah, we've all read it,' Andy said. 'So you're not a crack marksman, then? You didn't kill and butcher your own meat or have skins tanning at the treehouse?'

'Afraid not. Well, actually, I had one shrivelled fly-blown kangaroo pelt hanging in a tree, but that was the one the roo shooter gave me.'

'Don't tell me you're not even in the IRA, then? Or an ace bomb-maker?'

'Nope.'

Long past getting angry, the absurdity of what he read almost amused him. Jim knew he could put it right in time. He knew what they wrote about Kelly upset her more and, despite the various attempts from almost everyone in camp to console her, she had withdrawn into her own pensive thoughts.

Then he heard her laugh. It was something one of the brothers said. Looking up from the newspaper, Jim stole a glance across to the group opposite and it cheered him to see her smile. It had been a while. The fire and the fine meal must have helped. Still, he felt disappointed someone else made her laugh and not him.

The brothers grew up near Margaret River. Garry was sixteen months younger than Dan. When not surfing during the school holidays, they laboured in the vineyards. Kelly discovered this over the potato peeling and pressed them both for information on the business of growing and fermenting grapes. Apologetically, they confessed to knowing nothing about wine, other than hard days picking fruit for minimum wage. It didn't deter her.

Jeff too had been watching Kelly, joining in the conversation when it turned from wine to surfing. He enjoyed some good times along that coast, riding waves, especially at Mainbreak and Southsides off Surfer's Point. Despite Kelly's best efforts to put on a brave face, Jeff saw how scared she was. It bothered him. He wanted to take care of her, to get her away from here. If he could just bring her to his house on the beach. He would mind her there, until all this business with the Irishman sorted itself out.

'JESUS, YOU'VE BOTH been well stitched up,' Andy said, after a lengthy pause in conversation and a sip of beer. 'Hey, Kelly. Have to say, your photo is a lot easier on the eye than Jim's!'

'I don't know,' she replied, grinning. 'I think he looks handsome.'

'That's my mate, Chris. Last I heard, he was working a bar in Greece,' Jim interjected, then added, 'Good man, the Bubbles,' more so to himself.

Jim closed the paper and, out of habit, folded it neatly before putting it down. Andy took it and threw it in the fire. The gesture touched both Jim and Kelly. Jeff threw more wood on the fire. Sparks splashed high into the night air.

Dancing across her flawless olive skin, the warm glow of the resuscitated flames illuminated the delicate lines of Kelly's beautiful face. The show caught Jim's attention, causing him to break off his conversation with Andy and gaze at her.

He saw evidence of an exotic family tree in that face. He imagined how she was a wonderful mix of southern Italian and wider Mediterranean genes. There may even be, in the subtle shape of her beautiful chestnut brown eyes, a suggestion of the Roman trade along the Silk Road. And maybe, some early colonial convict in there too, if he was to take anything from her reticence to talk about her family. It all manifested itself in the form of the most exotic of creatures before him.

Sensing she was being stared at, Kelly looked over. Jim did not turn away as would be his normal reaction, when caught staring at beautiful women. Instead, he mouthed the words, 'Are you OK?' Her smiling eyes said she was and the gentle nod of her head confirmed it. Alluding to his recent shave, she rubbed her chin with both hands and mimed back her approval.

Then, for no obvious reason, the gesturing stopped. Their expressions became serious. The smiles disappeared, but the flames still flickered in her eyes. He noticed she hadn't blinked. They looked into each other's hearts.

'What did Helen mean by "golden egg"? Was it a coded message or is it an Irish delicacy or something?' Andy asked, forcing Jim to look away and bring the moment to an abrupt end.

'I left her a nugget, hidden in with her chickens,' he replied, while turning to take his drawing pad out from the ever-present bag at his side. 'It was part payment for borrowing the Hilux.'

'You found a nugget?' one of the brothers asked, his interest piqued.

'Yep, stumbled across three in the roots of a tree.'

Jim started to draw. Off to his left, he heard a mumbled 'Tirty tree and a turd' and saw Jeff chuckling to himself. Jeff then added a 'begorah!' for effect.

Jim contemplated letting it pass. He had other things on his mind. 'Yeah, the leprechauns put me onto it.'

'You should have seen the size of the one he gave Helen, fellas. It was bigger than my fist,' Kelly butted in and held up her clenched hand to illustrate.

Jim glanced over at her, opened his pad onto his knees and started to draw. Quickly, he decided on composition and sketched in all of Kelly's features. Checking the proportions of her face, he realised he needed to bring the nose down a tad, and fatten the lips. She noticed him sketching and knew from the way he kept looking up, he was drawing her. She liked that. She adjusted her posture, turned her shoulders slightly and straightened her back. Her face became less animated, but she continued to talk, all the while holding the pose.

'He reversed into the tree and knocked it over. Tell the truth now, Jim!'

'You sure it wasn't pyrite, fool's gold?' Hendrik pitched in, having perked up at the mention of the yellow metal.

'I hope not. Here … the big one was the same stuff as these two small lads.' Jim took the two cork-sized pieces of gold from his pocket and handed them to Andy.

The geologist was surprised. 'Wow, that's gold all right, and mate, they're not small!' he confirmed. 'In all my years working as a geo, I've only ever seen flakes in drill core,' he added, 'and you stumble across a giant nugget that has to be worth a small fortune.' Andy passed the gold along. The rest of the group around the fire were suitably impressed.

'Yeah, some guys have all the luck,' Jim said with a faux grimace, while continuing to concentrate on his drawing. He settled on her features, defining them with bolder lines. He began to work on tone and shading. The drawing acquired volume and weight, and a little drama. From time to time, Kelly broke her pose to catch Jim's eye again. The two would smile and she would return to her previous position. By now, neither spoke. The conversation went on without them. His throat went dry. Jim took a drink from his can of beer and noticed a slight shake to his hands. It began to spread.

Andy leaned across and studied the drawing. He dropped his eyebrows and squinted. He looked over at Kelly, back at the drawing, and then offered his opinion. 'Yep!'

Jim was pleased. He thought he had captured her too, particularly the eyes. They drew the viewer in. Sticking his pencil into the side of his mouth, he smiled over at his muse once more.

'The girl needs a pearl earring,' Hendrik suggested, angling his head sideways to get a better view.

'Ha! You're right. She does indeed.' Jim added the adornment and held the picture out at arm's length. 'That'll do,' he said, putting it down.

Kelly came over to have a look. She saw herself beautifully rendered in pencil, looking back demurely from over a shoulder.

Jim coughed and swallowed nervously. 'What d'you think?'

Stepping behind him, Kelly placed both her hands on his shoulders. She leaned forward, studied her portrait again, and then whispered into his ear.

'Come on, let's go.'

SHE TOOK HIM gently by the hand into the trees. Ribbons of papery bark hung down from high and caressed the shoulders of the couple walking below. They came to an opening, where earlier that morning she had dragged her bed to escape the lights and the dust of tomorrow's traffic. For the second time in recent days, but for a very different reason, he hoped his trembling legs were not conspicuous. She stopped by the bed and pulled him to her. She rested her head on his shoulder and whispered.

'You're staying here tonight.'

He said nothing. He wrapped his arms tight around her and closed his eyes. For the first time in a long while, Jim felt a heartbeat against his own. Christ, it felt good. He had not been entirely truthful before. He was lonely at the treehouse. He was lonely for a long time before that. He missed the physical contact of another person. She touched him in many ways, since they were thrown together. Now it was right to touch her. He listened to her soft breathing and felt her breasts rise and fall against him. He squeezed her tighter. The final piece of his long-broken heart fell back into place.

She kissed his neck, then his cheek and then his lips. Brief, tender kisses that asked questions and awaited a response. He took her face in his hands and answered by placing his lips on hers. Their softness surprised him, and their warmth, even in the balmy night air. Slowly she opened her mouth. He ran his hands through her hair and they kissed deeply and passionately.

Kelly was first to break off the embrace. She rested her forearms on Jim's chest, her head bowed. He kissed the top of her head.

'Listen, this is not easy to say,' she whispered, still looking down. 'I'm sorry, I don't want to ruin this, but it needs to be said.'

Jesus, what's coming now? Jim thought and waited to be disappointed.

'I've no idea who or what Troy was doing before we broke up … if you know what I mean.' She looked up at him. There was a sincerity, mixed with a tinge of sadness in her expression.

Jim's knees almost gave out from under him. He smiled. It could have been described as a schoolboy grin that almost split his face. He put two fingers on her lips.

'Wait here,' he said reversing backwards through the trees. 'Don't go anywhere!'

She watched the bark swallow him up.

Jim sheepishly approached the campfire to find Andy and the brothers finishing their beers and chatting. He greeted them with a subtle nod and a solemn poker face. The conversation stopped and he felt three pairs of eyes staring at him.

'Eh … forgot me bag.'

He grabbed the bag by the straps and showed it to them. Silently, the three men watched him beat a retreat and bid them a goodnight. He was sure he had gotten away.

'Ah, Jim, the very man. Wait up there a second!' Andy gestured him back. 'Listen, me and the boys here were just talking about Australia's place in the Commonwealth. As an Irishman, what would your considered opinion on that be?'

'Hmm. An interesting question indeed.' Jim raised a holding finger. 'Would you mind terribly if I gave it some thought and revert to you on that another time?'

'G'wan! Get outta here!' was Andy's gregarious response and, with that, the three men around the campfire showered Jim with a barrage of empty Emu Bitter and Swan Gold cans.

'BRILLIANT!' THERE THEY were. Predictably squashed and caked in layers of toothpaste and soap scum. But his only ever packet of Mates condoms still had the cellophane wrapper covering it and, remarkably, the seal was intact. Marvellous. They had survived untouched underneath the loose plastic card that defined the base of his tatty old toiletry bag for what must be three years now he guessed.

Had it been three years already, since the Bubbles and himself, two gormless, repressed callow youths, fresh off the boat from Dublin, found themselves in the Virgin Megastore on London's Oxford Street. Their pilgrimage happened to coincide with a Richard Branson promotion spectacular. Branson was flogging his new Mates condom enterprise. The boat had sailed from a Catholic Ireland, where it just became legal to buy prophylactics without a prescription and only in a pharmacy – many of which still chose not to stock those 'disgusting thingies'. From that, to having them thrust into your hand for free, by a glamorous woman at the foot of an escalator, in possibly the coolest shop in London. It only served to prove London was a different world and Branson a god. The Bubbles descended the escalator a few times trying to impress the lady in question with his bulk requirements. But Jim settled for the one packet and thanked her 'very much'. His mother would have been proud of his manners.

Months later, Ellen rejected the free Mates in favour of her own methods of contraception. She did not, and rightly so, trust Jim with matters of such importance. He smiled at the memory and wondered how the Bubbles was getting on with his 'stash'. It would all have been a relatively harmless time in their young lives, if it wasn't for the spectre of AIDS casting its long shadow.

Kelly was right to be cautious and need not have been apologetic. Christ, have they a use-by date? Jim wondered.

He retrieved the Mates from his pocket and, similar to how Hendrik had analysed the rock chips earlier, put the packet to his eye and scrutinised the small print in the darkness. Before he could decipher any encouraging information on the shelf-life of condoms, a point of red light moved in the shadows, grabbing his attention. Behind it, a dark silhouette stood by the driller's truck. The red spot moved again, stopping to burn brighter.

The short burst of light that accompanied the drag on the cigarette revealed Jeff's impassive face, staring at him. Neither man gave any acknowledgement. Jim picked up his swag and walked into the trees. Silently, Jeff watched him go.

THE TWO STOOD naked, facing each other, both bodies young and slim, both still showing the scars from Sunday night.

'You're not so skinny without your clothes, you know,' she said, with a smile and in a voice so soft, he barely heard it. 'How are your ribs?' He didn't answer. He didn't care how they were and gazed back at her.

She turned him by the shoulders and ran her feather light fingers over the bruises on his back.

'Thanks for saving me,' she said, before kissing his damaged shoulder. He put his head back and their cheeks touched.

She turned him again, this time by his slender hips, took one of his hands and placed it on a breast. She held it there. His eyes followed her hand down.

'You're beautiful,' he whispered.

THE PRESSURE ON Andy's bladder was enough to wake him. Cocooned in his cosy bed, he refused to give into the need to get up. All was quiet, except for the distant hum of the generator, exiled well out in the bush. After an uncomfortable few more minutes of internal debate, he looked at his watch to see if he could hold on until morning.

'Bugger!' Andy sat up, swung his long legs around and slipped his feet into the flip-flops beside the bed.

On his way back from the toilet block, he noticed a light on in the caravan. He climbed the steps to turn it off and spied Hendrik inside, sitting at the table, seemingly studying the most recent drilling sections. The illuminated green display on the HF radio at Hendrik's elbow caught Andy's eye. Alarm bells sounded in his head.

'Working late there, Hennie?'

'Can't sleep. All the excitement earlier, I suppose,' Hendrik replied, while continuing to flick through the charts spread out in front of him.

Andy folded his lanky, hairy form and slid sideways into the bench opposite Hendrik. With arms outstretched, he rested both his hands on the table and leaned forward.

'You weren't thinking of using that by any chance now ... were you?' he asked, nodding to the radio. 'Another change of mind, perhaps?'

The tone of Andy's voice surprised Hendrik, who quickly realised how things might appear.

'On my honour, no, I haven't. I wasn't. Besides, you never did get around to training me in on it. I haven't a clue how to turn it on!' He looked down and busied himself with the charts again.

'Ha! Yes. Sorry about that,' Andy replied, the edge gone from his voice. Whatever it was about Hendrik, except maybe for earlier, he never lied or even stretched the truth. That's part of the problem, Andy thought. There are no shades of grey with Hendrik.

'A close call today, Andy. Those two love birds need to get out of WA soon. Why don't we just pack it in tomorrow and go?' Hendrik pushed a chart across the table. 'I've been looking at your sections,' he added quickly, to explain himself further. 'Is there any point drilling this last line of holes?'

Then he looked directly at Andy. 'They're not going to add anything to the mineralised zone. It's already fizzled out. There is no big hematite ore body here.'

'Yeah, I know. We're on the edge of the geophysics, too. The only reason to continue would be to finish out the programme as designed. But, you're right. We could save the client money and drop those few holes altogether.'

Andy scratched under his arms and across his chest, then remembered he was dressed only in his underwear. 'All right, I can stand over that decision. I'll let Jeff and everyone know in the morning.' He pushed out sideways from the table and stood up. 'Sorry for doubting you, Hennie. And thanks for playing along earlier. I appreciate you're in a difficult position with the visa.'

'That's OK. I'm learning to change my mind about things,' he said, with the smallest suggestion of a smile. 'They're good people. I want to do the right thing.'

'OK. So, catch you in the morning.' Andy made to leave, but Hendrik had one more question.

'Hey, did you ever see the movie, *Cry Freedom*? Is it any good?'

EVEN WITH THE two swags laid out on the ground next to each other, it was not the most comfortable of arrangements. But the insects and reptiles left the couple alone. The night played out an extraordinary roller-coaster of emotions. Their lovemaking was slow, intense and quiet. No words passed between them. However, what followed was an almost manic release of pent-up anguish and fear, mixed with much good humour, laughter and tears from both lovers.

Eventually, after planning a future together beyond the Northern Territory border, and Kelly identifying the patterns of the southern night sky for Jim, she fell into the most blissful sleep. Jim lay beside her, daydreaming into the night. He fought his own sleep cravings to continue enjoying the sensation of her naked body against his.

Jim stared up at the Milky Way. It painted a mysterious ribbon of interstellar cloud, snaking across the sky. What was it Oscar Wilde said? It wasn't quite the gutter they were in, but Jim took great comfort knowing he only needed to reach out and would be among the stars. It's been an interesting start to the decade, he conceded.

A magpie carolled nearby. Jim heard the camp wake and the light break on Friday morning. Gone were the blue hues and silver greys of moonlight on her skin. Warm yellows and oranges took over. Gently, slowly, barely touching her, he traced a finger along her neck and around her shoulder. He counted the ribs as his fingers dipped down to her waist and up over her hips. Kelly turned and smiled at him.

'You still here?' she said, rubbing her eyes.

'Tell me about your life and growing up in Melbourne.'

'No, I'm sorry Jim. Not now.' Her smile faded. She sank onto her back and stared silently at the orange sky.

'That's OK. It's none of my business.' Jim saw how his question upset her. He took her hand in his and gently squeezed it. 'You know you have the most gorgeous dimples of Venus!'

'What?' She turned to him again. He wore that cheeky grin.

'You know, on the small of your back.'

'I'll take your word for it.'

'I've decided I'm finished with painting sheep. I'm a figurative painter now and you are to be my model.'

'That's fine, as long as I'm the only one,' she said, putting an arm around his neck and rolling over on top of him.

Jim beamed. 'Right, Branson, me old mate, you're up again.'

'Ah, Jesus. That's not the image I want in my head right now.'

'Sorry, won't mention him again, promise.'

Kelly lifted herself onto her knees and looked happily into Jim's eyes.

CHAPTER 15

THE PROPOSAL

L AURIE HOLT PULLED up alongside the fresh-faced officer, who sat eating lunch and reading the paper in the car parked out front of the Yilgarn station gate. Not recognising him, Holt assumed they had brought the young bloke in from Kalgoorlie for sentry duty.

'G'day, mate. Is Mrs Mitchell home?' Holt asked, through their open windows.

'Hope so,' came the reply, through a mouthful of beetroot and chicken salad. The officer put down his lunch and closed over the paper. 'She's supposed to be heading to Kal this arvo for the funeral tomorrow. I'm here to escort the family into town.'

'Very good. I see the Hawke's called an election for next month. Guess he'll make it four in a row now.'

'Can't see Aussie ever electing a Peacock.'

'True. Here, be a gentleman and get the gate for me, thanks. The old hip has been at me all morning.'

The officer was happy to oblige his older colleague and Holt went trundling down the long approach to the homestead. He passed the shearing shed and wondered when, if ever, it would see sheep shorn inside its corrugated walls again. He recalled dropping by one season and watching the shearers go about their work. Every few seconds, all clean and bald, a sheep would pop out from one of the six even-spaced hatches on the east wall of the shed. He remembered the bleating, their hooves tapping out a frantic rhythm on the metal chutes as the traumatised beasts scrambled and slid down to the pens below. Shearers earned their money. Back-breaking yakka if ever there was. His 'old hip' almost gave out at the thought of what they put their bodies through.

Holt pulled the squeaky, spring-loaded fly screen back with one hand and propped a shoulder against the frame to prevent the screen from slapping shut. The senior constable knocked on the heavy wooden front door. It opened immediately and an angry young woman glared up at him. She stepped forward, blocking his way.

'Haven't you people tormented my aunt enough already? She's told you everything she knows.' The young woman's hand went up, as if to push him back. Experience had taught Holt to let her vent and say her piece. 'For God's sake, she's leaving for Kalgoorlie shortly to bury her husband. Is it too much to expect a little compassion from the police?'

'I beg your pardon, Miss. I'm very sorry, but I'm here more in a personal capacity. If Helen is available, I'd like to have a quick word. It's important. Could you tell her Laurie—'

'Laurie Holt, is that you?' Helen stepped out from the shadow of the hallway. 'Please ...' She extended a welcoming hand.

Laurie took it warmly in both of his.

'Please come in, Laurie.'

Her niece moved aside, but kept a wary eye on the officer.

Laurie offered his heartfelt condolences and apologised for not calling on her sooner. Helen knew Laurie to be one of the good ones.

'Look, I'll get straight to the point, Helen. The story out there is that Macken, among other things, is a crack shot. The Aurora shooter would have had to be. To back it up, they're using evidence of a roo he's alleged to have killed.'

Laurie shook his head. 'Thing is, Ray the roo shot it. I passed this along to the detective leading the investigation into Bill's mur ... into the case. Yet, the official version is still that Macken did it and it's been allowed to find its way into the press. The mistake has not been corrected. That troubles me to be honest.'

'Detective Sidoli's a rude, angry man. He was here pestering me yesterday.' Helen's face hardened.

'Might that have had something to do with your interview? It was brave what you did. You made some controversial statements.'

'I did and I'll stand over them, too.' She pushed up each of her long sleeves, as if readying for the fight ahead. 'The police have been crawling all over the place for the last few days,' she continued. 'I'm practically under house arrest. You met my friend at the gate, no doubt!'

Laurie nodded and thought he best be honest with her regarding his old mate. 'Stan Sidoli and I go back a long way. He's always been partial to a bit of verballing.'

'Verballing?'

'Doctoring statements. Dammit, he'd fabricate any evidence, if he believed the ends justified the means – or furthered his career! I know there's something else going on here. You can trust me, Helen. What were you implying yesterday?'

'Ellie, I think you better put the kettle on.'

LAURIE FOLDED JIM's letter and pushed it back across the table before reaching for the nugget. Assessing its significant weight in his hand, he whistled and ran his fingers over the cold, polished surface, then set it down again. He felt almost privileged to have touched a thing of such beauty. Turning his attention to the two paintings Helen put in front of him, he gathered them up carefully, one in each hand, and held them out at arm's length.

'They're exceptional.'

'I don't think he had a prospecting licence, Laurie, or a driver's licence for that matter,' she said, taking back the nugget. 'Don't get me wrong. He's a great kid, honest as the day is long. Please, you must help him. All that rubbish in the paper, it's all lies.'

'Is he from southern Ireland or Belfast?' Laurie asked, not sure what difference it made.

'A small town near Dublin.'

'That's in the South.'

'Yes.'

'And no IRA connections?'

'No. Those pictures he took of the explosions were when we blew up some hard ground for a new dam. I'm the bomb-maker around here. He helped me mix the fertiliser and then enjoyed the spectacle. That's all. And the book they mention, *Reprisal*, I've read it. Jim loaned it to me. It's a beautiful, historical novel set in Ireland after the Great War. It doesn't bang any drum.'

Laurie carefully considered everything Helen said. 'It's Collins, isn't it?'

'Yes,' Helen replied, relieved. At last she could talk to someone she trusted and who might actually be able to help. She told Laurie of Max's plan to torch the Aurora and claim the insurance. 'But I have no proof. Would you believe he was outside the radio station when I left there yesterday? He just stood, staring.'

'I would. He's a dangerous bastard. Macken is right. Don't confront him.'

'I refuse to be intimidated by that man.'

Laurie reached over and tapped the letter. 'He says he has proof. We need to get to him before they do. Have you any idea where he might have gone when he left here?'

'Yes, I think I do. God, I hope they made it and are not stranded somewhere out there in this heat.'

ON ARRIVING AT the Mitchell homestead, it surprised Detective Sergeant Sidoli to see Laurie Holt coming out the garden gate. 'Shouldn't you be on checkpoint duty somewhere, Laurie?'

'Just paying my respects, Stan. All part of the community police officer's job. Yilgarn is on my patch, after all.' Laurie held the gate open. 'Mrs Mitchell mentioned you were in yesterday. Any progress?'

'We're on to them. Won't be long now. Looks like they headed west from here. We're flying a grid over the hills at the moment and the trackers are following up. Did she tell you they were skint and her husband only recently leased a new Toyota Hilux?'

He waved a bundle of photocopied documents under Laurie's nose. 'Thing is, none of my men have been able to find it! I wonder why she forgot to mention it. Any idea why Mrs Mitchell might try to protect her husband's killer? Somewhat peculiar I'd say. Did you know she lost a child?'

'What are you implying, Stan?'

'Stranger things have happened.'

'Like evidence being lost or ignored.'

'Word of friendly advice, mate. Don't play with the big boys. You'll find you're way out of your depth.'

'For once in your life, Stan, be a man and do the right thing. Do your job. You know, the one we both signed on for together.'

* * *

RON SLIPPED A fresh bottle of Victoria Bitter into his stubby holder. Another hot Friday afternoon, but this one followed a strange week, disrupted by newspaper interviews and the police. Only proper they knock off early to mull over all that had happened and enjoy a few cold ones.

With the Aurora no more, the two old diggers were forced to return cap in hand to the Broad Arrow Tavern, where Ron displayed his considerable diplomatic skills in mediating between Pete and Swanny. The barman took great pleasure in watching the old-timer squirm and mumble an apology. Pete wasn't too happy about having to give it, but these were extraordinary times. Swanny's insistence that pie was all he had left after the lunchtime rush, did not help matters. Pete saw no evidence of any such rush. By the second beer, the edge had gone from Pete's rancour, but not his appetite.

'What's in the pies, Swanny?' he asked courteously.

'Meat.'

'Yes, indeed, but perhaps some supplementary information on the species might be helpful.'

'Look, I think it's mince ... Do you want one or not?'

'Don't mind him, Swanny, two pies when you're ready ... When were you ever fussy about what you ate?' Ron said, chastising his companion. He twisted on the stool to observe his surroundings. 'I see nothing has changed around here in the last few weeks.'

Apart from the ever-increasing amount of graffiti on the walls, nothing ever changed at the Broad Arrow, not since the galvanised steel building appeared overnight in 1896. Again, once part of a bustling gold town, it now stood against all the odds, defiant, a curious time capsule in a dusty, bleak wasteland – but it had one big claim to fame. The Broad Arrow Tavern starred in *The Nickel Queen*, the first feature-length movie ever made in Western Australia. If one were to study the opening scene closely, two wide-eyed young miners working as extras for the day might just be recognisable enjoying a drink, pretty much where they now sat.

Along with a fork each and two chipped plates, Swanny dropped the pies complete in their charred cellophane wrappers onto the bar.

'Enjoy!'

Pete scrutinised the wrapper and was none the wiser about the filling. Ron, who had already started into his, was having difficulty breaking through the rubber crust with his fork. He decided to eat it the proper way and picked the pie up in his hands. Distracted by their food, the men failed to notice the police officer stroll into the bar.

'Well, if it isn't my two favourite diggers,' the officer said, slapping a hand on each back.

'Officer, arrest that man for crimes against gastronomy ... immediately!' Pete demanded, directing a threatening fork and an evil eye over at Swanny.

'Thin ice, mate ... thin ice!' muttered the barman, who did not bother looking up and continued to wipe the counter around the pie plates with a cloth.

'G'day Laurie. How's it going?'

'Not bad, Ron. Listen, you two. I've just been over at Yilgarn talking to Helen Mitchell and I need your help. When Captain Flint there has finished his pie, bring your beers outside and I'll explain everything.'

* * *

KELLY SAT HIGH up behind the wheel of the old Bedford. She sported a green and yellow Ozdrill mesh-back trucker's cap, pulled low over her hair and angled to push her ears out perpendicular to her head. Andy's borrowed Ray-Ban Aviators covered most of her face and the oversized collar of the company shirt hid her slender neck. From a distance she looked every bit the big-rig driver. Except, of course, she was a woman.

Much to the alarm of the novice driller, the rig's lowered mast, extending out beyond the front of the cab, creaked and groaned to the pitch and roll of the truck. Every jarring shudder caused by the wheels slipping over rock, or falling into a dip in the rough trail, passed up the steering column and pulled violently on Kelly's arms. Random bangs and thumps reverberated through the cab from the organs of the machine shifting around in the back. She fought hard to keep the rig on the straight and narrow. Jeff, not bothered at all, sat poker-faced in the passenger seat. He agreed, it was a heavy old bird to handle.

'Jeez, this'll do wonders for the guns!' Kelly hoisted an arm briefly to display a feeble bicep.

Her comment failed to raise a smile from her companion, who had barely said a word since they started out. In fact, he had scarcely said anything since breakfast, when Andy broke the news they were finished drilling. Moreover, Kelly got the impression Jeff avoided her while they packed the camp. Only when all were ready to hit the road did he approach and suggest she drive the rig.

'You'd never see a sheila doing that out here now, would you?' His idea met with universal approval, except for Kelly, who thought it a little foolhardy. Jeff insisted. 'No true blue Aussie bloke on the look-out for a runaway skimpy would look twice at the driver of a drill rig.'

A damning and broad generalisation, he admitted, but one in which Jeff included himself. Reluctantly, Kelly agreed to give it a go. He made a valid point and, because Jeff trusted her with his pride and joy, she felt obliged to try.

Another loud bang shook the truck, startling Kelly.

'Jesus Christ!' she said, gripping the wheel tighter. 'If anything happens, remember it's your fault. You came up with this bloody idea.'

Finally, Jeff smiled and assured her he could probably fix just about any damage she might inflict. Ha! A smile at last, that's better, she thought.

Kelly was both apprehensive and pleased to be on the move again, albeit slowly. All the vehicles pulled elements of the camp behind them, or were weighed down with gear piled high on the back. The Hilux acquired itself a caravan. A ruse they hoped would draw any curious eyes away from the homemade paintjob.

Garry, far more experienced at towing than Jim who had none, drove the Hilux. Jim sat in with Andy. This all meant that, should it become necessary, any quick getaway or car chase through the bush might prove problematic. Kelly decided it would not come to that, at least not before Sandstone. She and Jim were, for now, part of a herd. That brought safety in numbers and comfort.

'As soon as we get off this track, it'll be easier on the arms. I'll leave you to it there. Then it's straight, flat, graded dirt for two hundred kilometres all the way to Sandstone. Trust me, you'll be fine,' Jeff said, staring impassively out the window.

Another ten long minutes passed. In that time, Kelly missed gears, tested the clutch on several occasions and apologised every time. At most, she drew a weak acknowledging nod from her silent passenger, his arms folded, his distant stare steadfast. His demeanour concerned her. She expected he might be a little miffed now that she and Jim were a couple, but it seemed he took it harder than she anticipated. Or maybe something else bothered him. Kelly braced herself to address the delicate subject, when Jeff unfolded his arms, cleared his throat and turned to her.

'Ahem … Look, Kelly, I have to ask and don't humour me.' He drew a slow breath in preparation. The big man sounded nervous. 'I understand you're with Jim now, but I need to know … did I ever have a chance? Not here, but back in Kal?' Another pensive breath followed. 'You broke my heart, when you left town without so much as a goodbye.' He looked over at her for a reaction, a little tell to show he might have mattered some small bit.

'I'm sorry, I didn't …' Taken aback by his words, the emotion in his voice, and unable to hide the surprise written broad across her face, Kelly glanced over at the driller. She saw the sincerity and hurt in his eyes. Hand on heart, she believed she never led him on.

'You knew I wanted out of The Pump House. I didn't plan on leaving that quickly. It's just … you know, I was offered the job and a lift was going pretty much immediately. I couldn't pass it up.' She turned briefly to him again and shook her head. 'Listen, I'm sorry. I didn't know. I assumed that, to you and all the boys there, I was just another skimpy.'

'No, no, you weren't. You were more than that ... to me, anyway.'

He was a good man. She liked him – so she lied.

'If things were different ... absolutely. Yes, you had a chance. You knew I'd only just come out of a bad relationship. Otherwise, of course. Yes. It was like ... just too soon for me. That's all.' She smiled in an effort to lighten the mood. 'I always thought you were a spunky guy and could easily have overlooked our age difference.' Kelly reached across and squeezed his hand.

But Jeff never had a chance. Well, maybe once. That first night he came into The Pump House and she watched him stroll towards her ... for those brief few seconds. Then he flipped her for two dollar coins and expected a performance. From that point on, her friendship with him became an act, part of the job. In fairness, in the weeks that followed, when he stopped treating her as a skimpy and more as a person, she warmed to him, to the point where she became fond of him. But it could never have developed beyond that.

Kelly hated her life at The Pump House and all who frequented the place. She wanted out of there, even before she started. Pure and simple, she needed the money. Skimpying is not regular bar work. Regular bar work she enjoyed, having grafted in plenty. Work was sanctuary from the brutal reality of what passed for a home life and, when old enough, it offered her independence and security.

She thrived in the atmosphere of the bar, or the ambience of the plusher Melbourne hostelries, where she occasionally plied her trade. It was never a career, just a job. Not without its own challenges of course, but the positive experiences from her years in the industry moulded much of her character and occupied room in her head that might otherwise have been filled with the darker episodes of her young life. The same could not be said of her brief time working in the subculture of the skimpy bar.

When the skimpies were in town, and they were always in town in Kalgoorlie, most of the blokes became vulgar idiots, even the nice ones. Arseholes, if she were to be less polite about it. Skimpy bars were places, where respect for the fairer sex was left at the door, where grown men behaved like teenagers and teenagers behaved like dirty old men. Everyone leering at the girls, drooling at tits, shouting obscenities and flashing money around. After which, the punters went meekly home, many back to their wives and children.

The skimpy culture tried to justify itself under the pretence of being an integral part of the Goldfields story, a place where real blokes could be men and unwind after a hard day down the mine. There was good money to be made for sure. Some girls were bloody brilliant at it. They could work the room into a frenzy and squeeze every last dollar from the wankers, and more power to them. It just wasn't for her.

Jeff returned to his silent contemplation, maybe a little embarrassed. But they had cleared the air at least and she no longer felt quite so uncomfortable. Besides, they must be near the junction with the main graded road, where he said he would get out. She noticed him twist the wiry hairs of his goatee between forefinger and thumb. Perhaps he wasn't finished yet.

'What happens after Sandstone? You realise the two of you have Buckley's chance of making it on your own from there. To be honest, I don't think you'd get across the Warburton without being recognised.' Jeff watched the beautiful shape of her lips below the Aviators subtly change and her expression turn to one of dejection. He turned the screw on her recent optimism. 'You will need to refuel at some point.'

'Even with all our jerry cans?' She already knew his answer.

'Yeah,' Jeff said, with a nod. 'But, suppose you make it to Alice, what then? The Territory cops'll only hand you over to Collins' mates!'

'But we have proof. We're innocent, they'll see that!'

'What is this proof? It'd want to be good.'

'I can't say, but it is … Well, it should be. We'll have to see.'

'Ah, look. OK, maybe it is, but you still need to get there. Travelling together, that's just asking for trouble.' He paused again before putting his proposal to her. One that had knocked around in his head since the afternoon she turned up at his rig.

'Come with me. I'll look after you. I'll take you to Perth.' He wanted to add that he would love her and protect her ... more than the Irishman possibly could. But he didn't. There would be time enough for that, if she agreed to go with him.

'Stay at my place on the beach. You won't be seen there. Jim can continue east on his own. The cops are looking for a couple. You're more recognisable. He'll have a better chance without you. It's very unlikely I'd be mistaken for a skinny Irishman.' Jeff leaned over, almost pleading with her. 'Once he's delivered his evidence, sorted the mess out, you're both in the clear. It's a no brainer, really!' He raised his hands to show he had nothing to hide. 'I'm away most of the time. You'll have the place to yourself.'

It upset her to admit it, but Jeff was right. Her face was splashed across the papers. Jim's wasn't. Sure, Jeff may have an ulterior motive. She could handle that. But she and Jim were in this mess together and she wanted to get out of it with Jim, not without him. It would kill her not knowing how or where he was. What if they caught him? She must do what was best for him. She loved Jim. It surprised her how emphatically she told herself that. Jeff's idea set off a chain reaction of turmoil in her head.

'Thanks. That's very generous. 'Let me think about it and talk to Jim,' she said, hiding her emotions.

'Of course. We have all day. I know Jim will agree with me.'

BEFORE THE CONVOY reached the junction with the main road, a small wooden stake punctured the side wall of a tyre on the rear of the support truck. While the drillers worked to change it, Kelly brewed some tea and discussed Jeff's proposal with Jim. Aware something significant was up, the others gave the two of them space to work it out alone. Jim hated the idea. It took Kelly away from him. Yet, despite her protests, he agreed she must go with Jeff.

Throughout his time at the camp, an unspoken but mutual coolness had developed between Jim and the driller, to the point where he now felt uncomfortable around Jeff. Their conversations were brief and stilted. He believed Jeff looked over at him with some contempt from across the flames of the campfire. It was not paranoia, especially after catching Jeff last night watching from the shadows. There were other little things too, stereotypical remarks about the Irish or, when in front of Kelly, Jeff would belittle Jim's efforts at tying down the gear on the Hilux. Jim pretended not to be bothered or even to notice. He could ill afford to make more enemies and he knew what lay behind it. It was not as if they were two rutting stags locking antlers. But, then again … it was.

'Oi, Jeff! Listen, that's a great idea,' Jim said, approaching the driller with no hint of reservation. He would not give Jeff the satisfaction. 'Yeah, I think Kelly needs to go with you. She's on for it.'

Jeff closed the lid on the toolbox triumphantly and took out a cigarette.

'Look, mate, it's for the best. We'll leave in the morning and I'll have her safe by the beach tomorrow arvo.' He put the cigarette in his mouth and lit the end with an extravagant flick of a zippo.

'That soon?'

'Ah, yeah. From Paynes Find, it's bitumen all the way down the Great Northern.'

'OK, that would be brill. Thanks. Just make sure you look after her. She means a lot to me.'

'Mate, you won't have to worry about her. Trust me.'

Jim trusted Jeff had Kelly's best interests at heart. He wasn't so sure they both agreed on what her best interests were.

The noise of air brakes being applied travelled along the line of stationary vehicles. The two men turned to see a low loader pulled in beside Hendrik's Land Cruiser. Andy strolled over to chat with the driver. Kelly snuck behind the rig to Jim and held his hand. The others jockeyed the vehicles around to make room for the low loader to squeeze past on the narrow track.

'SPLENDID!' ANDY SAID, getting back into the cab. 'That's the toilet block sorted. I'll have a few fieldies up next week to do a final tidy and rehab the campsite. Another drill programme confined to history, apart from the bit of core logging I've been avoiding, that is.'

'Good. You wouldn't want to be leaving rubbish behind and upsetting Arthur again,' Jim said, having tuned out after the first part of Andy's sentence.

Jim took Ellen's old jumper from his bag and shoved it between his head and the door frame. Again, he barely remembered the girl who knitted it for him. He thought only of a different girl now and how to make sure he got back to her. He folded his arms and stared quietly out the passenger window at the passing margin of the boring, endless road. Andy knew something was up and left Jim alone.

Driving the least-burdened vehicle, Hendrik rode point in the convoy and fell into the role of gateman, responsible for closing the few gates they encountered leaving Dismals Station. Once onto the main but often badly corrugated dirt road, the group made better time on its steady journey north under the sun. A persistent, stiff westerly blew the dust across the road and away from the trailing vehicles, allowing them to travel close together. Kelly handled the rig well. Jeff left her to it and her heavy heart.

The infrequent rattle of a cattle grid broke the monotony of the journey when they crossed onto and out of pastoral lands. One ute passed in the opposite direction. All drivers and passengers saluted, but thankfully the occupants of the ute were not in a sociable mood and nobody stopped for a chat.

For a few kilometres, a marked change in vegetation and the occasional salt pan hinted at their proximity to Lake Barlee directly to the east. Jim did not appear to notice the changing scenery or he chose to ignore it. After a while, the course of the road veered back inland and away from the shore.

'Right, Jim. I've given you enough time, even let you sleep on it. What's wrong, mate?'

'Kelly is going to Perth with Jeff.'

'What?'

Jim explained the reasoning behind their decision to split and Andy saw the sense of it.

'Listen, I've been wanting to ask. What's this evidence you've got?'

'Photos of Max Collins shooting Bill. At least I think we do. I can't be sure until the film is developed.'

'Jesus! That should get you off the hook, all right.'

'Sorry I didn't tell you before.'

'I understand. I presumed you had your reasons.'

'If word got around before I had prints made, we'd be sunk. It's the first thing Collins would have his people destroy. Until it's developed, it's nothing.'

'Make sure you print multiple copies. Don't dare give the film or the negs to the Territory police either, just the prints. It only needs one person in the long chain of command to lose it. Develop it first.'

'Yeah. I'm kinda hoping the tourist village at Ayers Rock do a one-hour photo service.'

'I doubt it.'

'I know. I need to get to Alice, develop the film there and then hand myself in.'

'That won't be an easy one to pull off. But I'd wager the photo lab would ring the Old Bill. Save you the hassle of turning yourself in!'

Andy looked over at his passenger. Jim's eyes had closed again, but worry still troubled his face. Andy liked the young man and enjoyed his company. His enthusiasm and endless questioning on matters of geology and mining were amusing and commendable. A good-natured lad, despite the terrible situation in which he found himself. Understandably, he must be scared, but at no time did he show it. Only the thought of being separated from Kelly, and not knowing what might be happening to her, finally seemed to have broken Jim's spirit. It was little wonder those two had become so close, after all they had been through together.

Andy noticed the pair steal glances across the fire last night. He watched intrigued as Jim drew her portrait. The young fellow captured so much emotion in that simple pencil sketch. It was all Kelly and no Charlie. Clearly, there was something special between them. They made a handsome couple he thought. He hoped they would get a fair go.

'There is another way!' Andy announced, breaking the long silence. Jim opened his eyes and turned his head to the driver. Andy continued, 'What if I take the film?' Jim sat straight up. 'I know a chap in Perth who's into photography. He has his own darkroom. You two can hide out in the Ozdrill yard and I'll get the photos printed. I'll do a mail shot, faxes, the lot.'

'You'd do that for us?' In Jim's mind, the film promised everything, their only way out of this mess and the only way of getting their lives back, their salvation. He could never have imagined handing it over. If anyone else offered, straight off, he would have politely said no. That he did not, was a measure of his trust in Andy and his appreciation for all he had already done for them.

'You wouldn't mind posting a copy of the prints to the Puppet Masters, while you're at it?' Jim said, half-joking.

'Yeah, no worries. I'll need to swing by Kalgoorlie first or I might lose my job, and then I can continue on to Perth. It would mean an extra day holed up with Kelly in our caravan, but you'd manage OK, I suspect!'

'Can't have you losing your job.' The smile had returned. 'Feckin hell! I'm not a great man for hugs, but if you weren't driving, I'd chance giving you one now. Feckin hell!' Jim sat back in his seat and looked straight ahead. 'Feckin hell! That's a huge relief, mate. You can't possibly know how indebted I am to you. Jesus!' With a smile that touched his ears, Jim shook his head in disbelief.

'Ah, I know you'd do the same for me, as would Kelly I'm sure.'

'Hey, look! There's the salt now,' Jim said, excited, and pointed ahead to where the road swung west for a short distance along a narrow east–west trending arm of the great lake.

The dazzling white panorama of a salt landscape filled their view. The road would soon turn north again and ford at the narrowest point close to Lake Barlee homestead.

'It'll most likely be dark when we get there, but wait till you see Youanmi Gold Mine. It's rather impressive, and we drive right through it.'

CHAPTER 16

THE SKIMPY

K ELLY YELPED WITH excitement, when Jim told her of Andy's offer. Unlike Jim, she had no qualms about grabbing Andy and squeezing him tight. Standing on her tiptoes, she planted a large kiss on the base of the tall Englishman's chin.

'OK, right then,' Jeff mumbled his acknowledgement of the changed plans. He went to turn his back on the excited group and briefly his eyes met Kelly's.

'Thank you,' she mouthed and smiled. She appreciated his offer and hoped he was OK with the new arrangement.

Jeff declined to respond and skulked away to help the brothers manoeuvre the rig into its position in the yard.

The sun had long set by the time the convoy pulled into the Ozdrill depot. When the powerful floodlights came on, a spacious rectangular expanse of yellow dirt greeted the weary travellers. Set back from the northern edge of the high steel boundary fence, a small brick shed opened onto a shaded work area. A block and steel rack, stacked with drill rods, ran along the fence opposite the work area. A borehole kept a large elevated water tank full and a heavily secured, but depleted, fuel depot hid tucked away in the farthest dark corner of the yard. A beat-up Holden Commodore belonging to Garry or Dan and the white Land Cruiser Jeff used to ferry himself up and down to Perth gathered dust next to each other to the right of the gate. Much to Kelly's relief, she spied a corrugated lean-to of a dunny against the shed – but feared the worst.

When finished unloading their equipment, the drillers retired to the National Hotel, where they took rooms for the night. The National was a fine brick building and, these days, the only bar operating in the small mining town of Sandstone. It served the local population and the traveller well. While hooking the caravan to a power supply, Jim overheard one of the brothers mention something about skimpy night at the National. None of the drillers hung about too long after that.

Kelly called Hendrik over. She noticed him mulling around, unsure what to do with himself. Pressing a wad of notes into his hand, she ordered him to make certain everyone got a decent meal and beers out of the cash. Jim had suggested Hendrik would be the best man for the job. Giving it to him would guarantee the money got divvied out equally and spent wisely. She hoped the errand would encourage Hendrik to mingle and not retreat straight to his room, which he might otherwise have done. Hendrik seemed happy to oblige, but then it was hard to refuse Kelly.

'Thanks, and I'll see what I can do about some breakfast for you two in the morning.'

Hendrik was pleased to have survived his first job in the outback. The flies were dreadful and the days bloody hot, but he found the work interesting. He got better at it, the more he did. After four years of university he thought he knew it all. A big mistake, he appreciated now. He had lots to learn and was already looking forward to the next exploration project farther north in the Weld Range. This time, he promised himself, he would relax more and make a bigger effort to be sociable from the get go. He accepted he would always be awkward in company, but if nothing else, he could work harder on his manners. Time now to rehydrate after the day's drive.

'Sorry you can't join us,' Hendrik added, and he meant it.

ANDY LOADED THE last drilling samples for assay onto the back of his Land Cruiser and checked he had all the paperwork necessary for the Kalgoorlie office. Satisfied it was in order, he approached the caravan. 'Ahoy, bushrangers!'

Inside, Kelly and Jim were clearing enough space to move about and unroll a swag on the floor. Andy stepped up and stood at the door. 'I'm off to grab a bite to eat and then I thought I'd continue on.'

'You're leaving that soon?' Kelly had assumed he would wait until morning.

'I'll pull in for a few hours sleep near Leinster and head for Kal at daybreak. No point hanging around. The sooner we have all this sorted, the better. Anyhow, I think Jen is back up on Sunday. I'll try to catch her before she makes a wasted journey.'

He did not mention that, unknown to anyone else in the company, Jen allowed Andy to call on her whenever they were both in Kalgoorlie. 'Hennie will be away tomorrow after tidying up. I'll make sure he stocks the fridge for you before he goes. There's no point starving while you're here. So all that's left is the film.'

Jim took an insignificant plastic carton from his bag and shook it. A roll of film rattled inside. He popped the lid, tipped it out onto his hand and squeezed it briefly to send it on its journey with his blessing, before dropping it back in the carton.

'Just to be sure, to be sure,' he said, pressing the lid on and handing the film to Andy.

'It's not a hammer, so don't lose it!' Kelly added with a grin.

'Trust me, folks. I'll guard it with my life.' Andy put the film in the breast pocket of his shirt and fastened the single button over it. 'Here's hoping you're a good photographer, Jim.'

'No, I'm shite. But the pictures should be clear enough … I think … I hope.'

Kelly hugged Andy again. 'Thank you so much. Let me give you some money for fuel,' she said, stepping back and delving into a pocket.

Andy wouldn't hear of it. 'It's paid for by the company. I'd be making the journey anyway.'

'OK, then. Take this.' Jim held out one of his pieces of gold.

'Good Lord! I can't take that.'

'You will. Won't he, Kelly?'

'Take it for luck,' she said. 'The luck of the Irish.'

Jim passed it over and shook Andy's hand firmly. 'There may well be more where that came from. I might be needing the services of a geo to work a claim with me sometime.'

'Right. That's a deal … and the best of luck to you both! I'll be off, then. Keep an ear close to the radio. It'll tell you when the job's done.'

He climbed into his Land Cruiser and drove away. Jim pulled the heavy metal gates closed behind him and turned the yard lights off. Kelly sat on the step of the caravan, her gentle curves silhouetted in the light from inside.

'Is there anything to eat?' she asked.

Jim shrugged.

'How about a cold shower under that water tank?' she suggested.

'I don't see why not!'

* * *

THE CHALKBOARD ON the wall outside the main door heralded an arrival, 'Tonite, Skimpy Chantel'. Inside, the two brothers were cleaning up on a pool table. Hendrik sat over another beer at the bar and, farther along the counter, Jeff chatted to the somewhat mature-looking skimpy. Andy had been and gone. Luckily, they had made it in before the kitchen closed and all five had dined well.

It may have been skimpy night, but the place was quiet. Dressed only in cheap lingerie, Chantel single-handedly tended the bar. It bothered Hendrik that her bra and knickers did not match. Pulling a scrunched ball of notes from his pocket, he checked the kitty before ordering another round of drinks. The curious, creaseless-plastic ten-dollar bills sprang to life and lay perfectly flat on the counter in front of him. Hendrik crumpled the notes again and chortled when, like a time-lapse recording of a flower blooming, they magically opened a second time.

There were ample funds to go a couple more rounds. Technically, she stole it, Hendrik reminded himself. But from a murderer! The longer the night went on, the less his conscience nagged at him about benefiting from the proceeds of crime. Kelly left him in no doubt they were to enjoy it ... and besides, she's so beautiful! How could I refuse? What would a magistrate make of that defence, he wondered, and signalled an order to Chantel.

'Quiet night tonight,' he said to the skimpy, when she approached with his fresh stubby. Why are you wearing mismatching underwear? As much as he wanted an answer, he managed to cut the question off at the mouth. He hoped, after a few more drinks, he could still contain it. And your suspenders are just ridiculous ... Now stop it! He checked himself again.

'Mining is a bit thin on the ground around here at the moment,' Chantel replied. She took payment out of the notes on the counter and went off to distribute the rest of Hendrik's order to the others.

Hendrik had frequented a skimpy bar once before, in Kalgoorlie. A more raucous experience entirely. Here, apart from ordering drinks, the customers ignored Chantel. As far as he could recollect, nobody had flipped money the skimpy's way all night. That's not nice, he thought. He felt sorry for her and contemplated obliging her with a few dollars – just to help kick things off. But he wasn't sure how to go about it. Maybe, when he finished the next beer.

Maybe, if she wore matching underwear, business would be brisker. At one time, he suspected she must have been a good-looking woman, not that she was ugly or anything now, just long in the tooth for her current occupation. Bet you did a roaring trade twenty years ago! The thought almost slipped out, but again Hendrik stifled it in time and reminded himself about inappropriate comments, even if true. He took another sip from his beer and quietly recited a mantra he often used to silence his mind. 'I'll release the things out of my control.' Nobody noticed his lips move.

Hendrik need not have fretted. A sound similar to one a child might make pretending to drive a car grabbed his attention. There it was again. He looked around and saw Jeff had stepped in to oblige the skimpy. She had removed her mismatching bra and was slapping her flaccid breasts against Jeff's ears – while he buried his head into her chest. Jeff trumpeted his lips and out came the noise again. Ah, that should kick things off, Hendrik thought, happier for her now. Almost immediately, his concern turned to the possibility of the driller's beard scratching the poor woman and causing a nasty rash.

Chantel left the bra off to whip up more customers. It helped some. There was a slow stream of takers and no longer mismatching underwear to bother Hendrik. Jeff seemed to enjoy himself and went in a few more times.

'How's me old Saffa mate, eh?' Jeff enquired, when Chantel stopped to serve a drink. 'Hey, Chantel! Say hello to my friend here from South Africa. He's a geo, I'll have you know.'

'That's all right, love. We've already met.'

Jeff, who had been augmenting his beer with Jack Daniels for some time, wasn't having any of it. He wagged a drunken finger at Chantel.

'Nah! He's a very, very quiet bloke. You probably didn't even know he was there.'

'Now look here, darling! He's been sitting there all night. I've served him beer and he's been paying for yours.'

'Nobody buys me a drink without me getting them one back. What'll it be Hendo ... Hendie ... Hen?'

'Ah, sure. I'll have another Emu, if you're buying.'

Jeff slid his elbows along the bar and slumped into a stool beside Hendrik. He pointed in the general direction of Chantel. His aim wasn't great.

'She's a skimpy, mate. Bet you don't have skimpies in Africa!' He stared quizzically at Hendrik for a moment. 'You don't look African.' He then returned to his original point. 'As I was saying, she's a skimpy. She's all right, but she's old.' His final observation was conveyed from behind the back of his hand, but too loud to qualify as a whisper.

'Oi! I heard that. Watch it, you.'

'No! No! Sorry, Chantel. I mean no disrespect, but you are!' More waving of the finger ensued. 'Now, if you want to see a real skimpy, I'll show you a real skimpy. Charlie's a real skimpy. I mean Kelly. Proper hot she is. She worked The Pump House in Kal, Chantel. I'll introduce you if you like.'

Dan, bringing a few empties over to the bar, caught Jeff's last few comments. He signalled to his brother to get over here quickly. 'Hey, think we'll call it a night. Waddya say, boss? We've that rig to clean down tomorrow.'

Chantel turned to Hendrik. With her curiosity now heightened, she was prepared to overlook Jeff's rudeness. 'Is he talking about that girl from the Aurora fire? The one the coppers are looking for?'

'Yes,' said Jeff, interrupting. 'Yes, as a matter of fact, I am. She's one beautiful tart, is Kelly.'

'Come on, boss, we'll go!' The two brothers tried to shepherd Jeff out of the bar, before anyone else showed an interest in what he said.

'Yeah, I'll leave. But first, I want to introduce you all to a real skimpy. She's staying in my yard. It's just round the corner.' He followed that with a broad sweep of his arm, encouraging everyone in the bar towards the door. 'Her and that scrawny little Irish backpacker friend of hers.'

Jeff had Chantel's complete attention now. Dan stood to his full height. He had considerable presence for a young man.

'Jeff, let's go!'

Never had so few words put the fear of God into Hendrik before. He dreaded what might happen next. But somewhere deep inside Jeff's dusty, drunken brain, an alarm went off. It wasn't loud, but loud enough to warn he'd better shut up and go lie down.

'Right, Dan. Show me the way.' He stumbled towards the door assisted by his two offsiders.

'Did he say what I think he said?' Chantel enquired. The slow night just got more interesting.

Hendrik looked around the bar and then back to the still topless skimpy. Nobody else appeared to be paying them the slightest bit of attention. The beer had dulled both his thinking and his sense of caution. Unable to come up with a suitable response, he simply shrugged.

'He did, didn't he?' Chantel leaned across the bar. Hendrik moved his beer out of the way of a nipple. 'She's hiding in the Ozdrill yard, isn't she?'

'Shhhh! Please keep it to yourself. She's not at all like what they're saying in the paper.'

'Ha!' Chantel followed her exclamation with a gravelly cackle and a wink. 'Don't worry, son. She's a skimpy. She's one of us.' Chantel then put a finger to her lips and whispered, 'I don't think anyone else heard your friend and I'm not going to dob her in.' She pulled back from the counter, standing tall. Hendrik thought she looked rather elegant in her nakedness. 'Besides, I heard that woman on the radio, who's burying her husband tomorrow. It would break your heart.'

'Thank you! Thank you so much.' Greatly relieved, Hendrik figured it a perfect time to work on his manners. 'Listen, I'm new to this. I've a pocket full of coins rattling around. Please, will you show me what to do with them … But first, what was with the mismatching underwear?'

* * *

THE SIDE OF the caravan shook. Bang! Bang! Bang! Someone pounded on the door. It didn't stop. Jim heard his name called repeatedly, then Kelly's.

'Oh, Christ! Something's happened,' Kelly said, turning to where Jim lay.

Already into his shorts and up, Jim opened the door. Garry stood below the step, alone. Beads of sweat on his face glinted in the dim light.

'It's Jeff. He's drunk and been mouthing off in the bar about you two staying here.' Garry forced the words out, while trying to catch his breath.

'Ah, shit! That's not good.' Jim began to frantically pick the rest of his clothes off the floor. 'How far is the nearest cop shop to here?'

'Couple of hours' drive. Mount Magnet maybe. But there's an airstrip here. Sandstone's only a short flight from Kal.'

'Christ, Kelly. We'll have to leave! If word gets out, the whole fuckin' army could be here in no time.'

She didn't have to be told and, almost fully dressed, hopped on one foot while tying a lace on her trainer.

'We need fuel,' she said, putting her arms through the sleeves of Jim's denim jacket.

'There should be enough diesel here to fill your tank and a few jerry cans. I can siphon it out of the trucks if I have to,' Garry said calmly from the door. 'I'll have a scrounge around. Here Jim, you'd better take my Ozdrill shirt. I'll swap ya.'

An air of controlled panic reigned for the next ten minutes, before Garry pulled back the gates and the refuelled Hilux passed through. Water containers were full again. However, food supplies were meagre. One tin of Spam, one of pressed tongue, a packet of dry biscuits and two tins of Coke were all they cobbled together for the long journey ahead.

'It'll only be for a short while,' Kelly said. 'Andy'll come through for us.'

THEY DEBATED WHETHER or not to go bush and hide out until the photos landed in mailboxes. In the end, they went with their original plan to travel east and get out of Western Australia. An Ozdrill Hilux going about its business on an outback road had to be far less suspicious than a Hilux seen from the air parked alone in the middle of nowhere. If the wrong people got to them first, who knew what might transpire? It's always easier to disappear a problem, when there are no witnesses.

Demonic eyes shone up ahead. Kangaroos, dazzled by the oncoming headlights, stood their ground and stared death in the face. Others on the margins, startled by the sudden arrival of the Hilux, bounced onto the road in some crazy kamikaze ritual. Fearful of the damage a large male kangaroo crashing through the windscreen might do, Jim took it painfully slow. The destruction a stray cow or camel could wreak, he dared not contemplate. The Hilux made steady progress towards Leinster, but a rapid escape it was not.

The kangaroos were not the only creatures to be mesmerised in the headlights. Soon, the Hilux had gained a layer of decapitated heads, bits of legs and wings, all suspended in a putrid, olive-coloured matrix. Clouds of giant moths, grasshopper-type things and a myriad of different beetles regularly exploded onto the windscreen. The wipers struggled to clean the entrails off and left smeared arcs of opaque insect guts obscuring the driver's view. Stopping the vehicle from time to time and vigorously applying a damp cloth was the only way to restore visibility. The dimming light from the headlights took on a disturbing greenish tint.

Dawn had yet to break when the Hilux approached Leinster and the glorious bitumen of the Goldfields Highway. They met no other vehicles on their way across. No flashing blue lights, nothing in the sky but stars and insects. Some hours previously, on the same stretch of road, a vehicle pulled off and its lanky occupant enjoyed an uncomfortable few hours of broken sleep. While answering a call of nature before continuing on his own journey south to Kalgoorlie, the Hilux passed in the dark.

CHAPTER 17

ALICE SPRINGS 1587

A BEAUTIFUL SATURDAY morning sun rose over a busy Goldfields Highway on the day Old Bill Mitchell was to be laid to rest. After an anxious night's drive on dirt, the smooth sealed road and increased speed felt like freedom to the young couple. Spirits were high, despite the next leg of their journey speeding them south to Leonora and almost back to the scene of the crime. At Leonora, they would leave the highway and the Goldfields behind and turn east for Laverton and into the great deserts of the interior.

The Hilux hid itself well among the mining and pastoral traffic on the road. The new patina, now partially obscuring the painted Ozdrill logos, only added to the illusion of legitimacy. Road trains of two and three immense trailers hitched together rumbled along, freighting nickel ore from the mines at Leinster to the railhead at Leonora. Overtaking these goliaths proved quite a drama for the inexperienced driver. Kelly handled it better than Jim. At some point, a police car passed at speed in the opposite direction. Jim lifted a casual index finger from the wheel to acknowledge the occupants, before watching the vehicle disappear in his wing mirror.

Spirits were even higher after that, so much so, Jim began to sing along to the old Country favourites playing on Goldfields radio. Much to Kelly's infuriation, knowledge of lyrics or any God-given ability to modulate a note were not something that concerned Jim when duetting with a radio. Long after most reasonable people would have taken matters into their own hands, Kelly decided she had suffered enough and turned the radio off. Undeterred, Jim continued a cappella, his deep subconscious digging out some words to one of the great Irish classics, which he sang with gusto.

> They don't sow potatoes, nor barley nor wheat
> But there's gangs of them digging for gold in the street.
> At least when I asked them that's what I was told
> So I just took a hand at this digging for gold.

'That's beautiful!' Kelly interrupted. 'You know, you do have a bit of a voice. Ever think of having it trained?'

'Do you think so?'

'No! Please stop! You're wrecking my head!'

Impervious to her objection, Jim finished off what he could remember, but lowered the volume considerably.

> But for all that I found there I might as well be
> Where the Mountains o' Mourne sweep down to the sea.

Did you know, that was written by a chap called Percy French, while on a visit to Skerries. I know the view well.'

'Hope it sounded better coming out of him.'

The tune had burrowed its way into Jim's giddy brain and become something of an 'ear worm'. Kelly endured numerous spontaneous outbursts and various interpretations, in and out of tune, until they reached Leonora.

Unlike at Leinster, Leonora had no obvious ring road. The sun was well up and the town awake, when they drove down the main street. Having sworn she would never cower again, Kelly lay across the back seat under luggage and an open geological map. Jim sang in a whisper now.

Oh, Kelly, this London's a wonderful sight …

Leonora gave the impression of a tidy, picturesque town of ornate facades and wide streets organised in the grid pattern common to the Goldfields. It reminded Jim of Kalgoorlie, but significantly smaller. To be honest, much of it passed him by, while he concentrated on the road ahead and not missing their left turn for Laverton, the last outpost of the Goldfields and end of the bitumen. Once out of town and off the highway, Jim lifted the volume again, only to acquire a clip around the ear from the back seat for his troubles. It put paid to the worm. The singing stopped.

* * *

THE LONG HOT summer that emptied the dams at Yilgarn and decimated stock numbers took a similar toll on the other species roaming the paddocks. A dwindling food and water supply splintered the station's larger mobs of kangaroos into smaller family units.

One such group of six greys foraged for small shoots growing on the margins of Callion airstrip. In anticipation of the mid-morning sun reaching its zenith, the dominant male led the group to his preferred shady spot, where they would spend the afternoon on the opposite side of the dirt runway. The mob, crawl-walked after the patriarch – a slow, lolloping movement, where the long hind feet are swung forward, while supported by the tail and front limbs. They had no good reason to hurry in the heat.

Bouncing out from the scrub, Pete's noisy Series III Land Rover hit the small ridge of earth along the edge of the airstrip left by the grader blade, and took to the air. Testing its own suspension and the constitution of the three occupants, the station wagon landed heavily on the runway. Startled, the kangaroos bounced off at speed. With each leap, a small puff of dust thrown up by their long feet caught the light and left a punctuated trail, reminiscent of how a cartoonist might suggest speed with deft, cloudy squiggles of the pen.

With three in the front of the cab, space was at a premium. For much of the journey, the two passengers braced themselves against being thrown into each other's lap. Until Pete hit the berm, they had succeeded. After coming to land, Pete saw his own hat had left a fresh red mark on the cab ceiling and all three hats were scattered to the floor.

Laurie extracted himself from the window and squeezed back into the middle seat. 'Jesus, Pete! When this is over, I'm impounding her until you have the seatbelts fixed.'

Pete rattled down Callion airstrip blasting the horn. In the back, they carried a small electric cooler, two swags, enough food and water for a week, three well-secured sixty-litre drums of aviation fuel, a hand pump, ropes, chains, a winch, two shovels, mining helmets and various other bits and pieces the two old diggers thought might be useful. On the roof were some metal pipes and two ladders.

The Land Rover turned at the end of the airstrip and stopped. Facing down the runway, it waited.

Late yesterday afternoon, the three men had travelled together to Kalgoorlie airport. Laurie paid a visit to the Royal Flying Doctor hangar, while Pete and Ron acquired the avgas. Their business at the airport complete, Laurie then spent an enjoyable, albeit uncomfortable, night with the two diggers at their camp. The foam mattress in his swag knew better days.

History had passed between the three men and occasionally Laurie had reason to feel both their collars. Their habit of flouting the West Australian drink-driving laws did not go down well with Laurie. In their defence, Pete and Ron always claimed to make the return journey home from a night's revelry along their own private bush tracks, swearing only ever to use the public roads for the outward leg. Laurie wanted to believe them too, and they usually got away with a stern warning or their keys borrowed for the night. It mystified Laurie how the two old mates and the Land Rover never ended up some moonless night upside down in the bottom of a pit.

They heard the drone of the approaching aircraft, before Pete spotted it coming in above the tree line.

'Raise some dust for him there, Pete. Show him the breeze,' Ron suggested.

'Piece o' piss.' Pete revved the engine and spun the Land Rover around in a tight circle. He was having fun. A column of red dust lifted and drifted off to the east. The twin-seater Cessna buzzed the ground to clear any animals that might have strayed back onto the runway. It climbed again before banking tightly above the waiting vehicle and landed into the wind. Pete followed the aircraft down to where it came to a stop.

AFTER A FINAL visual check of the undercarriage, Merv, the pilot approached the waiting group of three.

'OK, Laurie. I've got two barrels into the tanks and decanted the last one into jerry cans in the baggage. I'll be honest with you. Carrying the extra fuel this way isn't strictly kosher, but as long as you don't report me to CASA, she'll be fine and we're good to go.'

'OK. With you in a sec, Merv,' Laurie said, before issuing his final instructions to Pete and Ron.

'Remember, you can disregard about a kilometre around the Irishman's camp. The Major Crime Squad blokes have been all over that ground. If Collins ditched the rifle, most likely he did it somewhere between the treehouse and this airstrip. The obvious place is an old mine shaft. I've checked the time from when he made the emergency call to when he met the Flying Doctor here. He didn't have enough to drive off the beaten track. Work on the presumption he could see it from the road. It's a long shot ... still, you never know. But Jesus Christ, be careful. Please, fellas, don't take any risks.'

Laurie climbed into the Cessna. He worried about the two old boys. In fairness, they were spritely men for their age and knew more about the old workings in the area than anyone else. Reprocessing old mine waste was their business after all and they were keen to help. If they found a rifle belonging to Collins out there somewhere, and if ballistics link it to both shootings, it would go some way to getting justice for Old Bill and the bikie.

Laurie saluted the two men through the window. The pilot taxied the aircraft back down the runway and took off again into the wind.

* * *

THE CESSNA BEGAN its climb from Callion airstrip at about the same time Kelly and Jim were saying goodbye to two hundred and sixty kilometres of smooth, sealed road. Ahead of them lay the almost endless red dirt of the Warburton track. A large green and white aluminium road sign raised high between two metal posts read, 'Warburton 559', 'Alice Springs 1587'.

Parked in front of the sign, a motorbike buried under a mountain of camping gear and far too many panniers, teetered on its kickstand. The rider, a young Asian man, hung his helmet from the handlebars and walked backwards to get all the sign and bike in-frame. The photo would either record the distance travelled or what he faced into. He turned and gave the passing Hilux a cheerful wave.

By their crude back-of-the-envelope calculations, they figured they had enough fuel to make it to the roadhouse at Warburton. Whatever transpired there, the two felt Warburton was far enough away from Kalgoorlie or Perth that they would have at least bought themselves some time. Hopefully, it was enough time for Andy to get to Perth, release their photos and pull the ground from under the case against them. About a kilometre past the sign, the thin strip of bitumen narrowed until it faded away. If everything went well, they hoped to next see a proper road in about two days, at Ayers Rock.

* * *

FORTY-EIGHT HOURS AFTER Laurie first passed through the area and discussed the horrors of asbestos with the geologist, he found himself back at the site of the exploration camp. This time, he enjoyed the company of Arthur, the station-owner, and Merv, the bush pilot.

'Appears they decontaminated the site all right,' Laurie muttered drily.

Gone were the benches around the fire, but a ring of blackened earth and silver-grey ash still marked what had been the social centre of camp life. A large barren arc of yellow bulldust ploughed into deep, powdery rills told of where the crew parked every evening. Polygonal desiccation cracks, curling at the corners formed on the surface of a muddy, natural depression where the shower drained. A small pile of timber, some old tyres, a barrel filled with conical concrete drill hole caps and a second barrel of rubbish were stacked neatly together waiting collection. The clothes line that ran between the trees, where the women's clothing had hung, was gone. Laurie smiled recalling the expression the geologist used, 'guts for garters'.

'Merv, you OK with Sandstone?' Laurie asked, having decided on their next stop.

'No worries, but we'd better not hang about. I don't like how the wind has changed direction. There's weather coming our way.'

With Old Bill's death, Merv lost both a client and a good friend. When Helen rang asking for help, he dropped everything and made the long flight across from Perth. Happy to go wherever necessary, all he needed was access to enough fuel to get there and enough to get home. Something that wasn't always easy to source deep in the interior.

RARELY DID THE opportunity present itself these days, but bouncing around in the back of a truck still brought out the child in Laurie. If only the FJ40's tray opened to the elements, he could enjoy the freshening breeze and watch the scenery roll away, while mocking the flies for failing to keep up. The pile of empty sacks he sat on provided little in the way of cushioning and every bump was acknowledged with a mild expletive. He wondered if the absence of jump seats in the back said something about the Tojo's owner. Discomfort aside, Laurie enjoyed the return drive to the bumpy airstrip at Dismals.

Bracing himself as best he could against the passenger seat, he listened to Arthur and Merv upfront reminisce about happier times mustering sheep for Old Bill. Jim Macken got a mention too, a good, honest worker, they agreed. Could not tell his north from south until Old Bill, copping the Irishman took his bearings from the position of the sun in a northern hemisphere sky, chased him down on the bike and steered him right.

Laurie watched a windmill disappear into the tail of dust coming off the FJ40. There was something contemplative too about looking back at where you came from, not knowing what lay ahead. For a city boy, he now felt he belonged in the outback. Had his career taken its expected path, the one he planned for himself when signing up, he might never have left Perth. It had not been easy in the beginning. A period of resentment and soul searching followed his banishment to the back country, but the stark beauty around him and the pace of life won him over. Laurie now wouldn't have it any other way. See what you'd be missing, he told himself, staring out at the purple and orange ironstone ridges and a big blue sky.

He had few regrets these days. One would be that he should have spoken to Helen sooner. A couple of hours earlier and they would have caught up with the young couple. Still, he was mighty relieved they had found help and were not lying dead beside a clapped out old motorbike in the middle of nowhere. How they evaded capture for this long impressed him. However, their luck has to run out. The Department was investing considerable resources in this case. Now that his colleagues understood they were travelling in a Hilux and where they set off from, he knew Sidoli and most probably Collins were not far behind.

Whatever happened, they would never contemplate suicide in custody. Those were the chilling words attributed to Macken. Having seen first-hand what one senior, albeit retired, police officer was capable of, Laurie knew Macken and Porcini had every reason to be scared. Laurie could picture the headline already, 'Star Crossed Murderers' Suicide Pact.' It would sell papers and few would question its veracity.

What did it say about their perception of the Department that they feared suicide could casually be used to cover up an untimely death in detention? Laurie wondered if Macken heard talk of the Royal Commission into Aboriginal Deaths in Custody. The report was expected shortly. There were disturbing rumours out there. Laurie knew them all, but refused to believe any. He categorically never saw a fellow officer set out to injure a detainee. Neither did he ever come across anything that might indirectly lend weight to such stories.

He conceded there were at times serious deficiencies in the standard of care afforded to prisoners of all ethnic backgrounds. The Department was under-funded. It needed money and greater numbers in the ranks. Hopefully, the Royal Commission would make recommendations to rectify this. Some horrific things happened way back in the state's early history. But his was a modern police force now, in everything but name, with better checks and balances. Society has progressed since those dark days.

Or was he being naive? Laurie knew the Department had its delinquents. But, until recently, he hoped even they conducted their sleazy affairs within the boundaries of some poorly calibrated moral compass.

He remembered an incident many years ago, when as a young officer, not long out of Maylands Police Academy and working alongside Stan Sidoli, their superior tried to slip them fifty bucks. Fifty measly bucks. Nothing really. Dirty money they recovered at a chaotic crime scene. It would have been the easiest thing to take it and avoid the unwelcome attention he brought on himself. He refused, but Sidoli took the fifty bucks. From that moment, their careers diverged. Thinking of it again angered Laurie. How many inexperienced young officers were similarly compromised? It probably still went on, maybe always would. A self-perpetuating culture of corruption.

Laurie had witnessed at close quarters the damage wreaked by the arrival of hard drugs in the 1970s. One did not have to scratch too deep below the veneer of civilised society in WA to find a sordid subculture of criminality. The trade in narcotics and prostitution fared rather well among a young, cash-rich and often dislocated population of miners in the Goldfields. For some in the Department, illicit drugs presented their own dirty little gold rush.

Again, there were rumours. For the most part, these rumours Laurie believed. The volume of drug seizures spoken about between colleagues did not always match the official records in the evidence book. He even heard talk of individuals cutting out the dealers and avoiding the hassle of having to make arrests to acquire product. Instead, they went straight to the source. In WA, that typically meant dealing with the bikie gangs.

Laurie hoped the number of officers who engaged in such activities were very much in the minority. No doubt, they justified their corrupt involvement as some sort of warped containment policy, with fringe benefits to compensate for the extra risk. But framing innocent people for murder ... that suggested a line in the sand had been crossed. The

Royal Commissions, he believed, and the winds of political change sweeping through Western Australia, may just rid the Department of the likes of Collins and Sidoli.

Laurie Holt was still a proud WA police officer. He knew many good officers too, some of whom he might well need to call on for help. As ever, Holt would do his job and help an old mate, a mate who was to be buried today. That was important. That was Australian.

* * *

THE GIANT BROWN bird stepped inquisitively around the carcass, searching. She picked her spot. Powerful talons clamped down onto the ragged flesh near an exposed rib. The wedge-tailed eagle pulled hard with her great hooked beak. A sliver of meat tore from the bone. She swallowed it whole. A sinew hung from the side of her beak, like a doomed worm.

Jim slowed the Hilux to a stop close enough to see the beautiful copper highlights in the bird's feathers. Alert to the new arrival, the eagle stood defiantly on her thick, full-feathered legs. Her piercing brown eyes, darker than Kelly's, looked back from a noble face and stared the Hilux down. She beat an eight-foot wingspan to flaunt her potent majesty, to let it be known she would fight for this rotting kangaroo. She had no quarrel, it seemed, with the hundreds of flies who claimed their share. As hungry as Kelly and Jim were, they were happy to concede this one to the wedgie and drive on.

No more than the occasional roadhouse or miles and miles of straight road epitomised driving in the outback, so did the sight of roadkill. It must take quite a toll on the native fauna, Jim thought, as he drove in silence across the desert track. At least it provided a conveyor belt of easy food for the scavengers.

The farther they drove into the desert, the more industrial the roadkill became. The ghostly shells of decomposing vehicles began to dominate the littered margins. Dumped, broken-down, crashed or rolled, abandoned to decay and cheaper to leave there, like bodies on Everest, they served as a stark warning to anyone who passed this way.

Kelly dozed in the passenger seat. Her gentle snoring amused Jim. He made a mental note to slag her about it when she woke. More out of boredom, he decided to rid himself of a bothersome fly buzzing inside the windscreen. With one hand holding the wheel, he swatted at the fly with the other. In its bid for survival, it dropped low on the glass and, head-butting the windscreen, worked its way over to the opposite side. Jim's hand followed it across.

The Hilux veered from a straight line and careered off the road. It pitched sideways down a small bank of sand. Panicking, he over-corrected and pitched the vehicle the opposite way. It wobbled a few more times and then back to the vertical. Jim pressed the brake. The Hilux stopped, hidden among a screen of tall spinifex.

He took a minute to compose himself. He had just learned how easy it was to lose concentration on a dead-straight track and add to the roadkill. Kelly woke to the sound of foliage slapping at her window and the sight of an oblique horizon out front. She took charge of the driving. Jim never mentioned her snoring.

* * *

'Look mate, people here in Perth are nervous, important people. Collins has been talking to them and I'm coming under a shitload of pressure from all quarters,' said the exasperated, metallic voice on the line. 'Stan, you need to give me something to go back to them with.'

Detective Sergeant Stan Sidoli sat behind the desk of the small office he commandeered for himself at the back of Kalgoorlie police station. He stared over at a large but crooked road map of Western Australia on the wall, while only half listening to his Superintendent bang on about 'the importance of resolving this delicate matter expediently'. Wedging the telephone to his ear with a shoulder, Sidoli lit his last cigarette. That's no good, he thought, not even lunchtime and I'm already through a twenty pack of Camels!

On the map, coloured drawing pins marked the location of the crime scenes at Aurora and the Irishman's treehouse. A third pin picked out Yilgarn homestead, from where a red line drawn with texta traced the suspected route of the Hilux west, out into a large expanse of emptiness and across to east of the Manning Ranges. A fourth pin emphasised the end of the line, where the trail was lost. Sidoli knew in his waters, they were gone from that area, but what direction did they go?

'We've tracked them to near the Manning Ranges. That's about one hundred and thirty kilometres, as the crow flies, northwest of Yilgarn.' Sidoli took a drag on the cigarette and braced himself for the anticipated response. 'From there the trail gets ambiguous—'

'Ambiguous! Sweet Jesus, Stan. What the hell do you mean by ambiguous?' Harper bellowed. 'Come on. I need better than that.'

Sidoli remained calm and imagined the tiny moustache twitching at the other end of the phone line. He did not appreciate Harper's tone, but knew he had to suck it up.

'There are other tracks in the area, Baz, all similar. The ranges are a popular spot with four-wheel enthusiasts from the city. Exploration companies have blokes out mapping the rocks around there, too. It's proving difficult to tell the tracks apart. And nobody has seen a damn thing … Ah look, on the plus side, we have a vehicle and a rego to look for. They can't hide much longer. If they need film developed, it's only a matter of time before they show themselves.'

Sidoli heard Harper sigh. 'Bloody oath, Stan. We can't just wait. We don't have time. The way Collins is acting, I'm not sure he won't lose it again and decide to fuck us all over anyway.'

'I appreciate that. You know he crashed the funeral? That's sick. He's not well in the head.'

Stan Sidoli knew his future in the Department, the comfortable life he made for himself in Perth – everything, it all hung on appeasing Max Collins. Given the man's current state of mind, that might just prove impossible.

A plain-clothes detective entered the room, shaking his head. Sidoli lifted a finger, directing him to hold on a minute.

'And Stan,' Harper began to finish up, 'need I remind you about common law precedent here … with respect to suspects attempting to avoid arrest by flight. We're not talking burglary, if you know what I mean. I trust you know what needs to be done!'

Sidoli knew only too well. His superior's chilling words disturbed him. He took another long, thoughtful drag from the cigarette. Ash from the tip fell onto his shirt. He brushed it off. Again, Sidoli felt sick and disgusted for allowing himself to get suckered in this deep. He wasn't sure he had the stomach for it. 'Look, if there's nothing by tomorrow, I'll bring Helen Mitchell in quietly and push her again to tell me everything she knows. I'm sure she's holding out. I thought it best to wait until after the funeral.'

Sidoli knew there must be more to that radio broadcast than the mad ramblings of a distraught widow. The conversation ended. Sidoli put down the phone and beckoned the detective over.

'What you got for me, Nugus?'

'His colleague in Menzies hasn't heard from him, Sarge. Not since he came back from Sandstone on Wednesday.'

'OK, I want to know what business he had with the Flying Doctor, and be discreet about it. It's probably nothing, understand?' Sidoli stubbed out the unfinished cigarette into an overflowing ashtray. 'Christ, it's hot in here,' he added, spinning in his chair to adjust the decrepit air conditioner bodged into a window frame behind the desk.

'Oh, and one other thing, boss. A light aircraft was seen overflying the search area. Some bush pilot up from Perth, it transpires. Musters for the Mitchells.'

Sidoli swung back around to face Nugus.

'The flight plan specifies he was to land at Yilgarn, but never did. I thought he might head for the funeral, but there is no record of him landing here in Kal.'

'Find me that plane and pilot. It'll need fuel and it has to be at an airstrip somewhere in the Goldfields.'

Nugus left the room, leaving Sidoli to his thoughts. The aircraft sighting might just be the break the search needed. Had it anything to do with Holt being spotted at Kalgoorlie airport? Sidoli wondered. What the hell is that prick playing at? From their first meeting as young recruits, Sidoli knew Laurie Holt was not a team player. Holt never fully understood what's required to police the largest single police jurisdiction in the world. That's why we cast him out into the wilderness to ply his trade. And what did Helen Mitchell say to seemingly set him off on a one-man crusade? Sidoli chastised himself for not bringing Holt in for a chat after he challenged him at Mitchell's gate. Holt better be careful or his already blighted career in the Department would be well and truly over.

Sidoli got up from the desk and approached the map. How there had not been a single sighting of the fugitives puzzled him. With both hands spread wide, he picked at the tape that held the top corners of the map to the wall. Eyeing in the horizontal, he released the corners along with some flakes of magnolia paint and pulled the map level. The four coloured marker pins didn't budge. Four parallel tears appeared in the search area.

'Shit!' Sidoli gave up, reattached the corners and stepped back. 'Where have you gone?' he whispered.

Whatever the motivations of his superiors, or the impossible situation he found himself in, even the innocence of the suspects – that two kids somehow evaded him for almost a week, he could not accept. It was an affront to his ego and his many years' service as a decorated officer.

Sidoli ran a frustrated hand over his stubbly double chin and decided to attempt another shave whenever he got back to his hotel. He tired of that room, its crappy washbasin, the noisy taps with the scalding water and the lethal disposable razors he had to make do with. He craved his home in Perth and the pool with the cooling Fremantle Doctor blowing in off the Indian Ocean. If it wasn't for that bastard, Collins, he would be there now.

Sidoli looked again at the map and pondered possible routes out of the Manning Ranges. They would not have been far from the main Bullfinch track. That would take them quickly to Southern Cross and easy access to the Wheatbelt region with its endless network of small roads, small towns and thousands upon thousands of isolated farm buildings. All Wheatbelt roads eventually lead to the city, so they may very well have made for Perth. Just not along the water pipeline and not to that idiot former boyfriend's place.

What if they went east, he asked himself, back into the Goldfields and kept going for the Nullarbor? But, the Goldfields had been shut down tightly, well before the second shooting. It would have been a risky gamble. Sidoli put his money on them going northwest to the Northern Highway and trying for the larger fishing and tourist towns on the coast, their best bet if they had film to develop. Without pictures, they would need to get out of the country or, at the very least, the state. The big iron ore ports might offer an opportunity to stow away. In reality, he couldn't see it. They were as good as done for. Like he said to Harper, only a matter of time.

North of where his team lost the trail, Sidoli's eye landed on the convoluted outline of Lake Barlee. In particular, a small black dot on its southern shore, above which it read, 'Mount Elvire'. It marked possibly the most isolated homestead in the state. Some months previously, Sidoli worked on Operation Cerberus, a series of police raids that foiled a plan by the L'Onorata crime syndicate to farm cannabis at Mount Elvire station and at two other remote Western

Australia pastoral leases. Operation Cerberus represented a great victory for the Police Department of Western Australia and for some of course, its success preserved a sordid status quo. It brought home to Sidoli just what they were up against. Not a job for the faint-hearted and not one that could be done successfully, hamstrung by a rulebook, or by someone overly imbued with morals.

That might be OK for Senior Constable Laurie Holt and his ilk, who spend their time picking drunks off the street or cats out of trees. Nevertheless, what Max Collins did went too far. In no way could it be justified. Unfortunately, that no longer mattered. Sidoli was left with no choice but to go along with what they demanded of him. There wasn't even money in it.

Mount Elvire homestead lay vacant now, while the authorities decide what to do with it. In decent order, it could be a good place to lie low for a time. Might be worth having a look, he thought. Sidoli went out to buy twenty Camels. Behind him, the top-right corner of the map curled off the wall.

Chapter 18

Penguins, crocodiles and snakes

Some way along the Warburton track, a caravan of eight dromedaries crossed in front of the Hilux. Perfectly at home in the Great Victoria Desert, the camels were direct descendants of the Afghan camel trains that brought vital supplies to the early prospectors and opened up the interior to the colonists. In no hurry, the ungainly, scruffy beasts were happy to keep Kelly waiting, while they sauntered across the dirt road. Despite their illustrious history in the bush, wild camels were still incongruous, an absurdity that amused Jim in a country full of absurdities.

'Have you ever been to Phillip Island?' he asked, enjoying the spectacle.

'Penguins or motorbike races?'

'Penguins.'

In a roundabout way, the sight of the camels reminded Jim of the few days he spent in Melbourne with the Bubbles on their circuitous trip from Sydney to Perth. The two friends took a tour out along the coast to see the fairy penguins of Phillip Island, who every night comically scampered en masse from the surf across the moonlit sand to their nests inland.

'This really is a crazy country, Kelly. Name another that can boast penguins and crocodiles. And now herds of wild camels!'

'Chile!' she replied without hesitation.

'Do you think? Nah.' Jim shook his head. 'That's not a real country. It's just a long mountain chain. Real countries have to have length and breadth.'

'Nonsense. Isn't the llama a sort of camel? And they're indigenous, too.'

'No, not having it.'

'South Africa!'

'Shuddup!' Jim stuck his bottom lip out, pretending to sulk, his grand theory of the great red land's absolute uniqueness torn apart.

'Shit, Jim! Here's a bike. Be casual.' She put on Andy's aviators and made sure all her hair was tucked under her cap.

The motorcyclist they had passed back at the road sign pulled alongside.

'Konnichiwa,' he said, through the open driver's window. Although hampered by a large rucksack and being astride the overloaded small Kawasaki, he still managed a bow of sorts.

Kelly, more experienced in matters of etiquette than Jim, returned the bow and smiled.

Jim uttered a Dublin 'Howaryah!' He threw in an upward nod for good measure.

The young Asian man spoke little English, but using pidgin and gesture, they deduced he was a Japanese tourist, undertaking an epic road trip from Perth through the Red Centre all the way to Cairns in tropical North Queensland. If their understanding was correct, he needed to get to Cairns before his flight to Osaka took off in a fortnight. Nothing about his demeanour or reaction on seeing them, gave any indication he knew who Jim and Kelly were. Even if he did, without a radio, there was little the young man could do to hamper their progress – at least until Warburton. The camels disappeared into the scrub.

'Probably best if we get to Warburton first, Jim ... just in case.'

But the motorbike fired up first and chugged off. Over the next few hours, and as much as they would have preferred to get ahead, the Hilux and the Kawasaki leapfrogged each other along the track. Every pass met with a cheerful salute and a thumbs up. No other travellers were on the road that morning or into the afternoon.

* * *

Except for the knocking, the machine stood silent. Cleaner than he remembered, it dominated the drillers' yard.

'Hello up there,' Laurie called out.

Surprised to be disturbed, Dan looked around, spanner in hand. When he saw the uniform, he acknowledged the police officer and climbed down.

'Don't suppose I'll be needing the dust mask this time, will I?' the officer remarked.

Dan held up his oily black hands. 'Here, you hold it out and I'll read,' he said.

Laurie unfolded the letter of introduction Helen wrote for him and positioned it in front of Dan's face. Dan scanned the page while wiping his hands on a rag.

'I'm sorry, mate. All I know is that once they heard about Jeff mouthing off in the bar, they fled. I couldn't tell you where they went.'

'What about the rest of your crew?'

'No idea where Jeff is. He drove off into the bush this morning and we haven't seen him since.'

'And the geo?'

'Went to Kal last night.'

'He left in the night as well? Must have been important if he didn't catch a few hours' sleep first.'

'Urgent business, apparently. Listen, talk to the South African. He's at the National. He might have more info.'

ON THE SHORT walk over to the National Hotel, a sudden cooling gust of wind swept a snaking arc of dust up in front of Laurie. His eyes followed it up and he saw the sky. Angry clouds were building to the north. Below the clouds, an eerie bank of ochre-coloured air came in ahead of the weather. The light changed. Laurie had to hand it to Merv. He was spot on with his forecasting and right to tie down the Cessna.

Laurie arrived to find Merv already occupying a prime position at the bar, his teeth buried deep into a juicy steak sandwich 'with the lot'. A second ice-cold tinnie of Victoria's finest bitter still fizzed with freshness on the counter next to him. Merv spotted Laurie over the toasted crust and swallowed what he had in his mouth.

'May as well pull up a stool, Laurie. This storm will shut down the Goldfields for a while. We won't be flying outta here today.'

Laurie did as Merv suggested.

'I can recommend the sangers,' Merv added, reaching for the second half of his. A fried egg squirted out from between the two stuffed triangles of toast and belly-flopped onto the plate.

A fully dressed Chantel, moonlighting as a humble barmaid for the afternoon, returned from the kitchen with a basket of hot chips. She paused at the bar door when she copped Merv's new companion. Muttering a swear word under her breath, she thought about turning around and going to warn Hendrik. But Merv had spotted her and his keenly anticipated second helping of chips. Chantel stepped in behind the bar and placed the basket on the counter in front of him.

'Thanks, Chantel. With the storm coming, my friend and I will be looking for rooms here tonight.'

'That shouldn't be a problem. Can I get you anything to eat, Constable?'

'Bloody oath, I'm hungry now you mention it, but first, I've been told you have a South African guest staying. I'd like to have a chat with him.'

'Back again already, Laurie?' the manager warmly greeted the policeman, while passing behind Chantel and taking a couple of stubbies from a fridge. 'That was you two in the Cessna, then? Caught out by the storm, eh!'

Merv, not appreciating the suggestion he might be caught out by weather, bit his tongue.

'Still looking for those murderers, eh, Laurie? We haven't seen them, Chantel, have we?'

Chantel shook her head. Laurie wasn't convinced. He thought she looked nervous.

'Two of your mates were in yesterday morning asking about them too,' the manager continued. 'Do you think they could be around here?'

'No, long gone. Perth or Sydney, I'd say. Like you said, it's the storm has us here. We're hoping to get to Meekatharra.'

The manager turned his attention to Chantel.

'I've let them know at Mount Magnet you're not travelling on account of the storm coming. You OK for another night here?'

Chantel shrugged. 'No worries. Sure, why not?'

'Ripper. I'll update the board so. Might drum up some business on a stormy Saturday. Enjoy your night in town, gentlemen,' he said, disappearing down the bar with his stubbies.

When the manager left, Laurie asked Chantel again about Hendrik. 'It's important I talk to your South African guest. If you could direct me to his room, I'd be much obliged.'

Chantel remained silent and, sensing her reticence to dob anyone in, Merv piped up.

'Look, darling. He's a good bloke, this copper. Don't be alarmed. Trust me, Laurie's here to help,' Merv said casually, while squeezing a large dollop of ketchup over his chips.

'The young man is in no trouble with me, I promise you,' Laurie added. 'I need to have a chat with him about two mutual friends of ours ... and before anyone else does.'

CHANTEL TOLD HIM a police constable waited outside. Hendrik's blood pressure dropped to the floor and he almost followed it down. His eyes spun a little in their sockets and his legs oscillated briefly. She offered her elbow for structural and moral support. Then, guiding him over to the bed, she called to the constable for help.

At that moment, the sky fell in. The sound of rain hammering the corrugated roof drowned out Laurie's first calming words. Convinced his arrest was imminent and that a period of detention and deportation would follow, Hendrik teetered on the edge of a full-blown panic attack. It took much reassurance from Laurie and soothing from Chantel, before he relaxed enough to provide any useful information to the constable.

Hendrik believed they went east, travelling the Warburton track and were hoping to get to Alice Springs. They would need to stop for fuel along the way. He understood they had evidence that proved their innocence, but he did not know what it was. He thought Andy's sudden trip to Kalgoorlie might be related, but he could not be sure. Laurie put a gentle hand on Hendrik's shoulder and thanked him for his help.

Laurie knew about the film. Arthur told him on the airstrip at Dismals. 'The geo must have it and be looking to get it developed. A shrewd move on their part, Laurie thought, but kept his deductions to himself. 'Listen, I reckon I'll have some tucker now, Miss, whenever you're ready.' He got up to leave.

Chantel put her arm around the much-relieved young geologist. 'I'll be with you in a minute, Constable.'

A TROPICAL DEPRESSION formed in the warm waters off the Pilbara and crossed the coast tracking south southeast through the Mid West and Goldfields regions. It brought moderate winds and heavy summer rains. It gave life to rivers and filled the smaller salt lakes, billabongs and dams in its path. After months entombed in the near lithified saline mud, long-necked turtles came alive again and sought each other out along the watercourses. The rains grounded flights. Roads and mines were closed. Tracks washed away. Nothing moved off the bitumen in the Goldfields. For a short while, water ran through the streets of Sandstone.

* * *

FIVE HUNDRED KILOMETRES northeast of the sodden Goldfields, the sun still shone on the small Aboriginal community of Warburton. The township sat comfortably in a broad valley between the Warburton and Brown Ranges. It knew floods in its past, but not today. A kilometre west of the township, the Warburton Roadhouse – a drab, single-storey, unrendered block building, with a low-pitched corrugated roof – stood back from the main dirt road. By the time the Hilux stopped next to one of the four well-spaced fuel pumps out front, the jerry cans of diesel were empty and the fuel warning light on the dashboard glowed red.

Again, Kelly hid while Jim stepped out from the air-conditioned cab into the blistering heat. He pulled the peak of the Ozdrill hat down until it met the top of his shades. Ambling around the padlocked metal cage that enclosed the bowser, he wondered how the bloody hell was he supposed to get at the fuel? The other pumps were similarly caged off. A prominent notice cable-tied to the cage warned in bold red and black lettering that photography in the area was strictly prohibited. Jim remembered now – they were on Aboriginal land, where things were often done differently. Paying for fuel in advance must be one of those things.

Strolling nervously over to the main building, his thoughts turned to his empty stomach and food. Might even chance a couple of Chico rolls, you never know! The possibility almost excited him. Jim reached the door and stopped. A security grill blocked the way. 'CLOSED' read the sign in blunt capitals.

'You're kidding me!' Incredulous, he pulled the grill. It didn't budge. Undeterred, Jim pressed his face to the steel and peered through the gaps, looking to attract the attention of anyone inside. The opening hours were painted on the glass door behind the grill – 'Closed 3pm Sat. Open 9am Sun.' Beyond the glass, everything was dark. Baffled why anyone would close an essential service early on a Saturday, he banged the grill, hoping someone somewhere might hear and come to his assistance. Nobody came.

'This is fuckin' ridiculous!' Jim yelled, not quite at the top of his voice, while stepping back to line up a possible kick. 'NO AFTER HOURS FUEL', boldly stencilled to the wall next to the door, like some roadhouse manifesto, suggested he would probably be fighting a losing battle if he made a scene. Of course, considering his current circumstance, that would be unwise. Reason prevailed and, although Jim continued to fume, he reigned in his temper and his boot. There was nothing else for it, they would have to camp out hungry and come back in the morning.

* * *

As it happened, Merv flew for a time in South Africa and quickly struck up something of a monologue with Hendrik at the bar. Merv, it seemed, had a terrible habit of getting into and out of life-threatening scrapes, not uncommon among bush pilots. Well, the good ones anyway, he was at pains to point out. Oblivious to Hendrik's reticence for conversation, Merv persisted in regaling him with stories of the Great Karoo and the temperament of your typical African sheep versus their antipodean cousins. Interesting as that comparison might have been, the vision of Chantel back behind the bar and undressed for business occupied Hendrik's thoughts. The storm granted him another night in her company.

The presence of a uniformed police officer was proving difficult for Chantel. The upshot being she reined her antics in slightly. Then, to her surprise, Laurie waved a ten-dollar note her way.

'Some dollar coins when you're ready, Chantel.'

A little taken aback, and somewhat nervous at the prospect of performing for a uniformed officer of the law, Chantel thought she'd better say something. 'But you're in uniform! You sure it's OK? People will talk!'

'Chantel, it's for the phone!' he said, raising one eyebrow above its partner. Then making a clicking sound with his tongue, Laurie winked at her.

For the first time in many years, somewhere under her thick make-up, Chantel blushed. Cackling, she sashayed off to the till with Laurie's note.

'There you go,' she said, placing two neat stacks of dollar coins on the bar. 'Listen. Answer me this. Why are you going out of your way to help a couple of complete strangers? I mean, it might cost you your job. And if, as you say, they've evidence to prove their innocence, it'll all work out fine for them anyway.'

'I'm not certain it would. Look, those two frightened youngsters are innocent. But it suits some powerful and dangerous people, if that

were never known. Accidents can happen. Evidence can disappear.'
He pushed the coins off the edge of the bar, letting them drop into his
waiting palm. 'I intend to bring them in safely and make sure they get
a fair hearing before a judge. If it means going against some of my
colleagues, so be it. It's my job. Like you say, maybe not for much
longer.' Laurie laughed, but Chantel could see his eyes weren't smiling.

* * *

THE LATE AFTERNOON sun beat down on an arid desert. Beyond the
narrow strip of trees that shadowed the dry riverbed, sand and rock
reluctantly gave way to parched spinifex and saltbush. Three kilometres west of Warburton, the Hilux turned off the dirt road at the place
where, in wetter times, the Elder Creek flowed across the track.

Jim navigated the sandy bed the short distance to a stretch of the
riverbank, where the fringing trees provided the best cover. While
closer to the road than they would have liked, a near-empty fuel tank
gave them little choice but to make camp there for the night. Without
fuel to idle the engine and power the air conditioner, the couple
decamped to a shady spot under a tree to bide their time and wait for
the sun to set.

Jim sat hunched over on an upturned bucket, a sketch pad across
his knees, his watercolour paints at hand. Stretched out on a swag
next to him, Kelly rolled through the channels of a pocket short-wave
radio with her thumb, listening to the transient sounds of the world.
The regular splash and rattle of a brush on the sides of a saucepan of
water was the only other sound to be heard. Not unlike two well-fed
amorous snakes, a pair of intertwined wet socks hung from a branch
above their heads.

Demanding to be painted, a single ghost gum stood apart from the
other trees lining the dry river bank. In contrast to all the saturated
primary and secondary colours of the scene, the ghost gum's eerie bark

glowed a brilliant white. Painting it would help kill time, Jim figured, and take his mind off food. Straightaway, the hoary problem of paint drying too quickly, as well as the bloody flies, tested his already tried patience. He cursed under his breath. Kelly let it pass without comment.

Somewhere in the world, a voice spoke of the new two-stage plan to reunite the Germanys and, eight years after the Falklands War, the BBC heralded the restoration of diplomatic relations with Argentina. At the top of the hour, Radio Australia did not mention Andy or their photos.

'Maybe we're just not a big enough story,' Kelly declared. 'I wonder where he is now? Everything better be OK,' she said, sitting up. 'Hey, come on. They must be ready.' She swatted at a fly determined to explore an ear. 'Aghhh! I need sugar, or I'm going to get as cranky as you, Irishman.'

A Russian voice interrupted the static before being passed over and fading out.

'All right!' Jim said, reaching to untie the socks from the tree. Thanks to his frequent watering, they were still wet. Like an excited child on Christmas morning, he put a tentative hand into one sock and pulled out a can of Coke. He held it to Kelly's forehead. He then touched it to her cheek. She presented him with the back of her neck.

'Jesus, that Ron fella is a bloody genius,' she said, enjoying the cold against her skin.

Jim handed the can to her and opened the second. He took a sip. 'Ah yes, that's all right, that is!' He offered it up in celebration of a small victory. 'I have created cold!' he exclaimed dramatically, before sitting down to continue painting. 'Awful pity it's not beer though.'

'You'd want to be careful opening a beer around here. Warburton's a dry community. Alcohol is banned.'

'True, very true.' He paused remembering his few brief encounters with Australia's first people. 'What is it with Aborigines and alcohol?

Is it genetic? Have they a different physiology or something to us Europeans?'

'Jesus, no! That's a myth,' Kelly said, so adamantly that Jim took a moment out from his painting and looked at her. 'I've seen alcoholism up close in the white population. Christ, it's just as tragic and messy,' she continued.

'Yeah, but to affect entire communities?'

'Makes no difference what the colour of your skin is. Addiction strikes people who are already hurting.' She took a cooling sip from her Coke. 'There's usually something else going on, some social problem or trauma in the background, even something from childhood. Addiction then heaps prejudice and rejection on what's already there. That can pass down the generations or spread through communities. It's a vicious circle.'

Kelly had obviously given the matter careful thought, and not just now. Her sombre tone, even how she held the Coke can, told Jim she might have more experience of alcoholism and addiction than something she encountered working behind a bar. Finishing her drink, Kelly produced a loud, rasping belch to convey her appreciation.

'There can't be many communities, who have been traumatised and hurt more than Aboriginal people,' she said, getting to her feet.

Taking the empty can with her, Kelly jumped down the low bank into the loose sand of the creek bed and walked the short distance over to the opposite side. She placed the can on top of a rocky outcrop. With elbows swinging and her hands pushed into the tight front pockets of her shorts, she sauntered back over to Jim. Hearing her step onto the bank, he paused again, left his brush in the water and continued their conversation.

'That's one thing that struck me on my couple of days in Kal. Family groups aimlessly sitting on street corners or verges. Many of them drunk. Or at least they appeared drunk. Maybe they weren't, but that's how it looked. It was a shock, to be honest.'

'Yeah and add petrol sniffing on top of that. It's just harrowing.'

'That explains the caged fuel pumps. Why the fuck would anyone want to sniff petrol? I don't get it. It kills yah! Then again, I can't understand the attraction of heroin, either. That shit is fuckin' up entire communities back home in Dublin.'

'Bet you no one is claiming a heroin gene, are they?'

'No, fair point.'

'Look, it's petrol because the kids can't afford ecstasy or cocaine or heroin! Us whitefellas have the luxury of being fussier about our drugs of choice. It's pretty simple.'

'Christ, it's not what we saw on *Skippy*. Boomerangs and Ernie Dingo – that's what I expected to find out here.'

Bending over, Kelly picked a polished green pebble. Holding it in place with her thumb, she positioned the oval-shaped stone in the crook of her right hand and wrapped her index finger around its smooth edge. With the fingers of her other hand, she rotated the pebble until it felt right.

'You ever heard of Maralinga?' she asked.

Her eyes narrowed, focusing on the target. Leading with her elbow and twisting at the hip, she withdrew her throwing arm back behind her shoulder. She cocked her wrist. Pointing to the Coke can with her free hand, Kelly took a rapid single step forward. Her centre of gravity shifted. A wave of motion passed beautifully up her body. Her drawn-out arm whipped around in front of her. The fluid movement finished with a final flick of the wrist. The pebble rolled out along the midline of her index finger. The tip of her finger imparted a stabilising backspin on the pebble leaving her hand. It flew across the dry creek bed in a low, parabolic arc. Bending at the hips, Kelly leaned, Greg Normanesque, encouraging the projectile to come right. Ping! The can hopped and fell from its perch.

'Shit! Now what am I going to do? I'd planned on that taking longer and killing time!'

Wow! What a shot, Jim thought. He didn't know what to say. He never saw a girl throw a stone like that before. A girl who did not bring a hand anywhere near an ear during the entire movement. Impressed as he was, he knew if he complimented her on not throwing 'like a girl', he would land himself in a world of trouble.

'Nice shot!' he said nonchalantly and dipped his brush into the saucepan of water.

'You ever heard of Maralinga?' she asked again, sitting back down beside him.

'Nope.'

'It was a nuclear test site, not far from here, across the border in South Australia. Before that, a traditional homeland. Suppose it still is. I don't know the details. It's not something they taught us at school. But I think the British exploded seven nuclear bombs there in the fifties. Many of the refugees from Maralinga ended up here at Warburton.'

Her use of the word 'refugee' surprised Jim, a term he normally associated with a war zone or a famine, not the Land Down Under, where beer flows and shrimps get barbied. 'No, I thought they did that on some uninhabited coral island in the middle of the Pacific.'

'It's not just the Japanese who have lived in the shadow of fallout from a mushroom cloud or two.'

'Jesus! It's little wonder Aborigines are hurting. How do you raise kids when your whole way of life vanishes in an instant?' A fly attached itself to the painting resting on Jim's knees, its wings trapped by the surface tension in a drop of water. Jim flicked it away with the bristles of a brush. 'I'd love to teach you your culture, son, but our government just dropped a fuckin' nuclear bomb on it. What does that do to a person's self-respect? It's a wonder they aren't more militant.'

Kelly rested her chin on Jim's shoulder and looked over it to the painting.

'That's nice,' she said, intrigued by how he painted the white bark.

There were tones of purple, blue, brown and orange, everything but pure white. Yet combined, they created the impression of a beautiful white tree. She kissed him on the cheek.

'Old Bill didn't teach you where to find bush tucker by any chance? I'd kill for a juicy witchetty grub or honey ant right now.'

'Afraid not,' Jim shook his head.

'How about a stone-throwing competition, then?'

'You're on, but I don't fancy my chances!'

* * *

To LIE IN a proper bed and enjoy the luxury of clean sheets, clean ironed sheets at that, was something to savour. So too, the shower. It may have been the only one in the hotel, but the water pressure almost knocked him over. The tingle from the powerful jet on his skin lingered well after the hot water blasted the sand from his crevices and he scurried immodestly back to his room. The last week of long miles and rough sleeping had set his hip against him, but this was nice. Laurie anticipated his first decent night's kip in a while.

He lay on the bed watching the ceiling fan spin. A wet but clean pair of navy-blue uniform trousers and a sky-blue shirt tied to the fan's blades flapped and fired off more than the occasional drop of water against the wall. The change in weather brought a significant dip in temperature and Laurie worried his trousers might not be dry by morning. His well-wrung underpants and socks still dripped on a towel rail by the room's small hand basin.

A single man of advancing middle age, Laurie developed certain housekeeping practices that any potential spouse might find hard to live with. Changing bed sheets was never top of his 'to do' list. But he appreciated clean underwear. His mother constantly warned, 'What if you were knocked down and needed to go to hospital?' In his line of work, an unscheduled trip to hospital was always a possibility and, many years after his mother's practical advice, Laurie still fastidiously kept his underwear spotless.

Outside his room, the storm abated. With any luck, they could fly out sometime tomorrow. The earlier the better, but that depended on how long the airstrip took to dry out or if the flowing waters damaged the surface. A new gully across the middle of the runway would not be good. Merv seemed confident everything would be 'sweet as'. His pilot's casualness unnerved Laurie.

Laurie planned to ring the roadhouse at Warburton again in the morning and, with any luck, speak to someone this time. He knew he could trust two old colleagues at Laverton police station, but the phone kept ringing out there too. It must have had something to do with the storm. He needed to get word to the young couple, let them know that they had an ally in him. Laurie hoped to convince his mate at Warburton to stop them and give them refuge until he arrived. Then everything might indeed be 'sweet as'.

* * *

SOMEWHERE BETWEEN CUNDERDIN and Kellerberrin, on a dark empty stretch of the Great Eastern Highway, flooding blocked the road ahead. Among the line of stranded traffic at the lay-by, inside a Greyhound bus, Andy Robinson sat contorted on a seat not made for the likes of him. Tensions in the bus were rising, along with the flood waters. For hours, nothing had moved west on the highway.

Andy's knees screamed, 'straighten your bloody legs like a good chap' and with every restless movement, he knocked his shins on a metal bar under the seat in front. If the lady next to him, an inconsiderate round thing, whose own feet hung inches above the ground, had an ounce of humanity, she would have offered him her aisle seat. He did ask but, annoyed at being disturbed, she dismissed his request with a superior shake of her head.

The air in the coach already hummed from the pressure on the toilet down the back and damp passengers getting in and out of the bus. A baby two rows behind cried constantly. Andy found the child's long, silent inhalation and the anticipation of what would follow more distressing than the roar itself.

For the second time since setting out, a grainy VHS of *Dirty Dancing* played on the small television set bolted to the roof above the driver. Occasionally, the picture onscreen would fall sideways and roll up. Earlier, the driver had adjusted the tracking, to little effect. They all had to live with it. As much as Andy tried to silence 'that song' from the matinée showing, it kept going around in his head, mocking him. Nobody on the bus was having the time of their lives.

Too tired to drive, Andy took the bus, intending to sleep on the journey to Perth. But sleep, he now accepted, would not be possible. Turning away from the television, he looked out the window into the dark night. The strength of the gusts lashing rain against the side of the bus appeared to have weakened and their frequency decreased. Maybe the weather had improved. He closed his eyes and hoped.

Baby was about to mention her watermelon to Johnny, when the muffled knocking sound of the microphone being switched on silenced the soundtrack and all the adult passengers.

'Folks. I've got the OK from the blue heelers,' the driver announced. 'We can return to the Shell roadhouse at Kellerberrin. It's about forty K back. Hopefully it won't be long, before you can get a coffee and stretch your legs inside, out of the rain. We'll wait and see what develops from there.'

The driver's announcement met with grumbles, sighs and applause in equal measure. Andy's neighbour, who woke to hear the news, thought it 'ridiculous and a disgrace'. She intended writing a 'strongly worded letter'.

'Madam, unless Moses happens to be travelling with us tonight, this bus is going nowhere near Perth until the floods subside, and who knows when that will be!' Andy felt all the better for calling her out, but could not deny the sense of panic that began to rise inside him. 'And would you be so good as to let me out to stretch my legs?'

As soon as he stood, the pain in his knees vanished. Andy walked the aisle between the rows of seats. He checked the roll of 35mm Kodak colour film was in his shirt pocket and thought about what might be on it. The images, no doubt, will be tough viewing, but he looked forward to seeing the fallout. At this rate though, he would be lucky to make it to Perth tomorrow, Sunday.

Passing by his seat, Andy peered down at his neighbour. Still awake, he noted. Best wait until she snoozed again before disturbing her. Childish and petty, he admitted, but with the long night ahead, he had to alleviate the boredom in any small way. Besides, nobody puts Andy in a corner. He doesn't fit.

CHAPTER 19

'HEID DOON ARSE UP'

A HUNGRY SUNDAY morning dragged on, waiting for Donald's hands to approach nine o'clock. Jim became withdrawn. Kelly left him to his thoughts and his fussing around on the back of the Hilux. She returned to listening to the radio, but the poor reception offered little distraction. After a night of broken sleep and nervous dreams, when all the sounds of the bush threatened and prudence cautioned against setting a fire, Kelly knew if they pulled this off, they could be watching the next sunrise over Ayers Rock.

Jim tugged hard on the rope and tied the end. That was the last one. Nothing would fall off now. He checked his watch again. They should go. He tried to ignore the butterflies that now beat their gossamer wings in his stomach. Their ripples spread and began to wreak chaos on his confidence.

Of course, the prints will be out of focus and dark, the figures too far away. Jim wasn't sure anymore if he even loaded the film correctly in the first place. Now that he thought of it, it hadn't sounded right winding on. Andy's mate might make a balls of the developing, assuming Andy didn't misplace the film. When rooting out the empty jerry cans earlier, Jim came across Andy's prized geological hammer. Andy had form.

'You're not leaving me here!' Kelly said and cleared a space for herself on the back seat.

'I thought you'd had enough of hiding on the floor. I won't be long, promise.'

'There's no way you're leaving me here on my own. I made that clear at the treehouse. It's not up for discussion.'

'OK, if that's how you want to do this. Fine.'

Jim didn't mind either way. It bothered him that Kelly had to conceal herself any time they encountered civilisation. If it weren't for the fact that a female driller travelling the outback on her own would raise eyebrows, he would happily swap places.

'Just make sure it's you who fills us up. Don't let whoever opens the cage do it. Anyhow, with the tinted windows, nobody will see me. Right?'

'Right you are. Let's be going, then.'

The Hilux rounded a bank of boulders and started for the gentle sandy rise out of the channel up to the road. Jim turned the wheel to the left to come at it from a better angle and minimise the slope. He kept steady pressure on the accelerator. The Hilux slowed, sank and then eased itself to a graceful stop. The wheels started to spin. Straightaway, he killed the engine. To floor the accelerator would only bury them deeper.

'Shit! Spot of bother. Don't worry, we'll be going in a jiffy,' he said, talking over his shoulder to what appeared to be luggage behind on the seat. 'Don't move.'

'What's wrong?'

Already out the door, Jim didn't reply. She heard the hiss of air coming from a tyre and then the sound of him scurrying around lowering the pressure in all four.

'This is becoming a habit,' he muttered, before poking his head inside the window. 'Nearly ready,' he said cheerfully to the mound in the back. 'Stay where you are.' And off he went again, this time gathering fallen branches to pack in front of each wheel. Finished, Jim climbed into the driver's seat and shifted into the low-gear ratios. Kelly heard the ignition turn over.

'Right, fingers crossed,' he said.

She thought he sounded chirpy. It couldn't be that bad. If she were sitting next to him, she might have seen how he crossed two fingers on each hand and gripped the steering wheel with the remaining digits almost as tightly as he squeezed his eyes shut. With some trepidation, Jim released the clutch. Reminiscent of a sinking ocean liner's last gasp for life, the branches tipped up before being sucked down into the sand under the spinning wheels. Behind the tyres, splinters of wood bobbed to the surface. The Hilux inched forward. The break in slope came and then they were on the road.

'Laughin!' Jim said, before reaching over the back and tickling a side of exposed flesh. Kelly jumped. She cursed him to high heaven.

Two trucks had passed in the night and parked outside the roadhouse, waiting for it to open. Jim knew their presence complicated matters. At least two more pairs of eyes could be watching. He did not mention the trucks to Kelly and steered into the sandy forecourt, stopping in front of the same fuel pump he had tried yesterday, and applied the handbrake.

Resting his forearms on the top of the steering wheel, he stared across to the roadhouse door.

'This accent of mine, it's a bit of a giveaway. I was thinking I might try Cockney.'

'What?' Kelly whispered back.

'All wyte darlin, wot's gawing orn?'

'Er, no. I don't think so.'

'It doesn't have to be perfect out here, just a bit of a smokescreen is all that's needed.'

'OK then, give us some more.'

Jim thought for a moment, 'Emmm … nah. Three years living in London and that's all I got. I could try Scottish?'

'No. Just talk natural,' came the sensible advice from behind.

'Fair enough.'

He rolled down his window to let the morning air circulate inside the cab. Swallowing hard, he pulled the Ozdrill hat lower on his head, like before.

'Here goes nothing,' Jim opened the door and stepped out. Then, just for devilment and before moving off, he added an emphatic 'See you, Jimmy!'

The familiar sound of an overloaded Kawasaki approaching drowned out his words. Ah, the fecker must have known the road-house closed early and camped out of town, too. But this is good, Jim convinced himself. An exotic traveller on a bike would be a handy distraction. A scruffy driller, even an Irish one, heading for a job in the Territory might hardly merit a second glance now.

Jim walked over to the biker, who had stopped at another pump and dismounted. Watching him remove his helmet, Jim guessed they were both of similar age and, based on their previous encounter and the language barrier, he figured the lad might not be up to speed on West Australian current affairs.

Smiling, Jim bowed, because Kelly told him it was polite. 'We're early. Not open yet,' he said and extended a warm hand, which the young man cheerfully accepted.

'Ohayo! Good morning.'

'Good morning to you.'

They exchanged names. The traveller called himself 'Kaito'. Jim used the name, 'Paddy', a moniker he became well used to since arriving in Australia and answered to it automatically. Jim now understood the Japanese translation to be Paddy-san. Kaito appeared to have no idea Paddy-san was on the run.

'Nice bike.' Paddy-san pointed to the pillion, where a camp stove, sleeping bag, bed roll, mug, water bottle and what looked like a tool kit, along with various other camping essentials, were all tightly jig-sawed and folded together. They were secured to the bike by a multitude of bright-coloured occy straps. There was so much gear billowing out from the back, it gave the impression of folded wings and, with a little imagination, the front of the bike appeared to have the head of a swan … well, more duck, Jim thought.

'Origami,' he suggested, with an approving nod. 'Nicely packed.'

'Yes. Yes.' Kaito nodded back, amused by the observation.

The two young men strolled over to the roadhouse together and the hand gesturing started in earnest, like a walking game of charades. En route, Kaito asked Paddy-san about 'your amigo?' Jim put his hands together in prayer and mimed sleep, before rubbing his stomach to imply Kelly was sick.

'Sorry. Yes. Yes.'

Jim got the impression Kaito might have been a little disappointed.

'After you.' Jim held the door.

Although officially still closed, nobody turned them away. Stepping in, Jim inhaled the cool air, infused with the fabulous aroma of deep-fried grease and coffee. He lifted his sunglasses onto the peak of his cap, but the interior of the roadhouse remained dark. He half expected to be greeted by a 'wanted dead or alive' poster of him and Kelly, but if there was one somewhere, it was not obvious.

Striking Aboriginal dot art hung on the walls and, even in the dim light, it grabbed his attention. More canvases stacked high in shadowy corners invited customers to browse. Jim would have loved to take a closer look, but thought he best not.

Glad-wrapped kangaroo tails poked out of a chest freezer in the centre of the room. There may have been ice-creams in a different compartment, but the contents had frozen into one solid block of ice and snow.

Fresh food seemed in short supply, but another large, albeit sparsely stocked, wall freezer of perishables offered hope. He could see the outline of frozen milk cartons and a fish-finger box through the glass doors.

Australian souvenirs and trinkets hung on stands beside the till and a stack of loose cassette tapes was displayed on a low table. Dolly Parton's big hair and smiling teeth gleamed back at him from one of the covers. And, much to Jim's amazement, stacked right there next to Dolly, the blue-sweatered figure of a wistful Daniel O'Donnell stood in front of some Irish lake, longing for his Donegal home. Now, there's an interesting match-up, Jim mused, wondering if he should buy wee Daniel's tape for Kelly. Just the thing for a bit of wooing.

A neat, spectacled man looked over the top of a hot-food display cabinet, while continuing to load it with paper and foil-wrapped goodies.

'Hoo's it gaun?' the man said, greeting his first customers of the day.

'Good morning. Howaryah?' Jim replied in his normal Irish accent.

'Nae baud. Yersel?'

'Ah, good. I'd be better for a fill of diesel and my friend Kaito here is looking for some petrol.'

'Jist haud on. A'll be wi' ye now in a wee moment.'

'No problem, I might just dig out some supplies while we're waiting.'

Jim collected a basket full of tinned Spam, tinned fruit, frozen bread and milk, pot noodles, biscuits and a bunch of almost black bananas. He piled them on the checkout counter. The storekeeper carried on loading the cabinet and Kaito rummaged through the tapes. Reaching over, Jim extracted the Daniel O'Donnell cassette from the pile.

'Very good. You would like.' He handed it to Kaito, with a wink.

'Yes. Yes, Daniel O'Donnell. Ireland.' Kaito studied the track list on the back of the cassette.

'Serious? You like?' It seemed they knew of Daniel in Osaka.

'U2, Sinead O'Connor. Irish good.'

'Whaur dae ye come frae, boys?' The spectacled man asked, sliding the glass panel shut on the cabinet – more to keep the flies out than the heat in.

'I'm from Ireland. You're Scottish yourself?'

'Aye. A'm frae Aberdeenshire, th' land o' th' sheep. 'N' yer pal?' He gestured over to Kaito.

'Ah … Oh, Japan. Would you believe he's riding across from Perth on his Kawasaki, heading for Queensland?'

Jim bit his lip. There was every possibility he could start to giggle. It was mostly a reaction to being nervous, but the situation he found himself didn't help. Three men went into a shop in the Australian desert – an Irishman, a Scotsman and a Japanese … Oh, cut it out, Jim!

'Whoo,' the storekeeper whistled. 'Och, that's a fair wee journey, ma mukker.'

Jim turned his back to compose himself. A discreet but audible snort escaped into the world. He coughed twice in a woeful attempt to disguise it.

The manager stepped out from behind the till and lifted a bunch of keys off his belt. 'Will ye come wi' me, boys, 'n' we'll git ye sorted.'

The three filed out the door as one of the truck drivers entered.

'G'day, Malcolm,' said the truckie, holding the door open for everyone to pass. 'I have the papers.'

'A'll be wi' ye in a wee minute. Th' coffee is fresh,' Malcolm replied and marched on.

In the time Jim was inside, a truck had moved over to the pumps and now its cab overlooked the Hilux. Jim's stomach tightened. Walking across, shoulders hunched and hands in his pockets, not wanting to catch anyone's eye, he hung his head and stared at the ground.

'Straighten up, shoulders back!' he heard his mother nag.

His heart ached for those happy winter nights at home, the fire blazing, the family gathered in front of the television. There was something very cosy about the seventies back in his little corner of Ireland. But his mother just didn't appreciate cool. A guarded smile formed on his face. David Starsky had much to answer for. Jim long since gave up on his dream of fighting crime in Bay City, or getting that perm, but he could still do the walk.

Before standing guard by the fuel cap, Jim took four jerry cans out from under the tarpaulin on the back and placed them at his feet.

'Whaur's ye headed yersel', laddie?' Malcom asked, when unlocking the pump.

'Ah ... I'm on my way to a drilling job in the Tanami.'

'That's a fair wee drive tae.'

'Aye!' Jim found it hard not to answer in Scottish. The very thing that annoyed him – his own accent mimicked back to him in conversation. 'I'll break it up and take a day at Ayers Rock. Enjoy the sights. Have never been over that way before.'

'Dinna ye mean Uluru?'

'Oh, yeah. Nice name. What's it mean?'

'A dinna ken!'

Jim hadn't the faintest idea what Malcom just said, so he soldiered on. 'Really looking forward to seeing it. I'm meeting a colleague in Alice after and we'll head up the Tanami track from there.'

'Noo ye tak' this, laddie, 'n' a'll see tae yer pal.' Malcom handed the nozzle to Jim and went over to unlock the petrol for Kaito.

While the tank filled, Jim opened the back door with his free hand and pretended to fiddle with something inside. 'So far, so good!' he whispered. 'Would you believe he's Scottish? I haven't a feckin clue what he's saying.'

'Hurry, my arse is numb,' came an equally whispered response.

'HEID DOON ARSE up,' were Malcom's parting words of wisdom to Kaito, when the young man paid for the petrol and stepped back.

'Very good,' Kaito replied, bewildered. But added a hearty 'Cheers, mate', bowed and left.

Not to be outdone, Malcom responded with a 'Sayonara', showing off his Japanese, before turning to tot up Jim's shopping.

'Not sure he got that,' Jim suggested. 'Sound advice, though.'

'Here ye goo, four sausage rolls 'n' two Chico.'

'Thanks, take for two coffees. I'll grab them on the way out.'

'Twa coffees?' Malcom said, looking out over his spectacle frames.

'Yep.'

'Ye sure, twa?'

'Ah ... yeah! One's never enough. Wouldn't want to be falling asleep at the wheel.'

'Yon wis a tairible business in Kalgoorlie lest wikk,' Malcom said, gesturing to the lead story on the small pile of newspapers that had appeared on the counter.

Jim looked down and the headline grabbed him by the throat.

'PUBLICAN VOWS TO REBUILD INN'

A defiant Max Collins stared out at him from the paper. If Jim had not been reading, Malcom might have seen how a more disturbing sub-heading bled what was left of the colour from Jim's face.

'ANONYMOUS BUSINESSMAN PUTS UP $20,000 REWARD FOR INFORMATION LEADING TO THE CAPTURE OF THE GOLDFIELDS KILLERS.'

And there below it was a photo of himself. Thankfully, an old one and the print quality not great, but it was still him. It came as a hell of a shock. He pulled the top paper closer and folded it over to indicate he would buy it. The fold hid the front page, while still concealing the incriminating parts of the paper below. Without looking, he replied to Malcom and began filling plastic bags with his purchases.

'Aye, it was tragic all right. That idiot didn't do his fellow Irish in Oz any favours either. He'll give us all a bad name for sure.'

'A dinna ken. Ye're a guid lot maist o' th' time.'

Jim mustered a smile and glanced up, 'Yeah, most of the time … Here, I'll take a *West* too.'

After paying, Jim finished loading the food, picking up the folded newspaper at the last minute and only after Malcom had moved off. On his way out the door, he hurriedly filled two polystyrene cups of coffee and pressed a plastic lid over both.

By now, Malcolm had gone outside to join the two truckies for a smoke. Jim reversed backwards out the fly-screen door, before turning with his coffees in hand and the plastic bags dangling from his fingers. As the door slammed shut behind, Jim overheard Malcolm say something along the lines of, 'Yer bum's oot the windae. Yer talking nonsense, man,' to an irate-looking trucker.

'All the best!' Jim acknowledged the three men, while pretending to focus on not spilling the coffee.

'Guid luck 'n' hae a guid journey.'

The phone rang inside the roadhouse.

'Kin a man nae be alloo't' enjoy a quiet smoke. If it's important thay kin ring me back.'

Jim thought again of Skerries and wished, more than anything, he could have called home.

When he reached the Hilux, Jim heard the phone ring again. Malcolm did not budge, he appeared to be enjoying his chat, whatever the hell it was about.

'Stay still. We're being watched,' Jim said, barely moving his lips, and climbed in behind the wheel. Before he started the engine, he stuck an arm out the window and saluted his audience. Suddenly, the two truckies gestured to him to stay put, not to move.

'Ah, Christ! What is it now?'

Jim braced himself for a quick getaway and revved the engine.

Malcom pointed to the roof of the cab and then appeared to mime drinking from a cup. He included a saucer for effect.

'Ah, shit! The coffees.'

Much to the amusement of the onlookers, Jim jumped out and retrieved the cups from the cab roof. Back in his seat he took a sip, saluted the three men again and drove off. A long day's drive lay ahead, but now they had food and enough diesel to take them well over the border into the Northern Territory and, with any luck, a romantic sunrise by Uluru.

***

'OK, HENDY, HAND her over,' Merv said, halfway up a stepladder he borrowed from the drillers' yard. Hendrik passed up the last of the jerry cans of avgas stored in the Cessna's luggage compartment. Supporting the can underneath with one arm, Merv took it by the handle and, bracing the weighty object against his shoulder, began emptying the fuel into the tank on the wing.

A rather damp, crinkled, but scrupulously clean police officer approached.

'Everything OK with the bird, Merv? She got through the night in one piece?'

'Yeah, Laurie. The tie downs did their job. No water inside or in the fuel. She's fine. We're ready to go once the strip dries out a tad more.'

'It looks as if the tide has gone out around here,' Laurie said, alluding to the ripples left by flowing water in the sand. 'Any damage to the runway?'

'No washouts or gullies. It's just soft in spots. I wouldn't be happy landing on it, but I'd nearly chance taking off.' Merv tipped a shoulder higher to adjust the angle of the jerry can and improve flow.

'Great! That bloke, the works manager from the shire office, called in again. He's adamant the airstrip is staying closed until tomorrow. Waddya think?'

'Give me an hour in this heat and then we'll do a barrel roll over his desk!'

'There's another complication, I'm afraid. Sidoli is onto us. I got through to a colleague in Laverton to arrange a fuel pickup on the quiet. He said Sidoli's people are checking all the airstrips for your Cessna. They must have rung here by now. Wouldn't be surprised if it had something to do with why we're grounded.'

'That's not good, not good at all. Any luck with your mate at Warburton? Here, take this, Hendy.' Merv handed the empty jerry can down and stepped off the ladder.

'Would you believe, they bought fuel earlier. Malcom is getting in touch with Docker River for me. Hopefully, your two friends, Hendrik, can be persuaded to stop running and wait there.'

'Hope so officer,' replied Hendrik, putting the empty jerry can back in the luggage.

'I suppose we better get out of here,' said Merv. 'I'll finish my checks and she'll be ready to roll.'

'Merv, I can't ask you to take any chances,' said Laurie. 'If the airstrip is not one hundred percent safe, we should wait.'

'What does that bloke behind a desk in town know about flying?'

Laurie smiled. 'Waddya think, Hendrik? Who would you trust, Merv here, or the works manager?'

'Ah, I'd have to go with the one who has taken off into a charging rhino, I suppose.'

'Jeez, Hendrik,' said Merv. 'I didn't think you were even listening to me old yarns last night!'

'I heard you, Merv. Even if I was a bit distracted.'

'Ah look, Laurie,' Merv continued. 'It's no worries. I'll have us airborne in half an hour. It's a big sky. We'll go into stealth mode up there,' he added with a grin.

＊

JIM TOSSED THE newspaper back, while he repeated the Scotsman's words.

'Yer bum's oot the windae. Yer talking nonsense man.' It was all too much for him. Tears of laughter ran down his face. He giggled and drove along, 'Yer bum's oot the windae.'

From the back seat, Kelly couldn't help but chuckle as she watched his shoulders tremble. It was contagious. Now they were on the move again and there was nothing like a full tank of fuel and an open road to lift the spirits.

'Jesus, Jim. Twenty thousand dollars? I'd nearly turn you in myself! Max must really have something on whoever stumped up that.'

Despite her 'threat', Jim's giggling continued until they stopped to inflate the tyres and eat. Predictably, the Chico rolls disappointed. The two trucks from the roadhouse honked when they passed.

Eventually, Jim settled into reading about Max's bogus recovery plans to rebuild the Aurora. They set off again, but Jim would not let the paper spoil his mood. 'Yer bum's oot—'

'Hey! What's that?' She cut him off mid-impersonation, pointing to a distant object shimmering in the heat haze.

Jim squinted, but couldn't quite make it out until they got closer. 'It's just another old wreck.'

'It's not, you know.'

As they neared, the frame of a mustard green Land Cruiser, similar to Arthur's FJ40, revealed itself. It lay on its side, metres from the road and at the end of a diffuse debris trail. A shredded blue tarpaulin hung down from the mangled roof rack and flapped in the breeze.

'Jesus! That's just happened,' Jim said, stretching across for a better look out the driver's side window, almost blocking Kelly's view of the road.

The Hilux slowed to a crawl, while they both rubbernecked the scene.

'Oh, Christ, Jim. There's someone in it.'

Kelly braked so hard, it threw Jim against his seatbelt, jarring his shoulder. The Hilux stopped at the spot where the overturned Land Cruiser appeared to have left the road. Silently, they both jumped out and ran to check on the occupant, sidestepping the disgorged contents of the Land Cruiser on their way. Although fearful of what gruesome sight might await, being hardened by the events of the previous week, neither held back to let the other take the lead.

The Land Cruiser rested on the driver's side door, its roof facing the road. The rear doors were thrown open. A whiff of fuel lingered in the air. Still restrained by the lap strap of the seatbelt, a figure slumped against the driver's door, the head and arms draped awkwardly over the steering wheel. The body didn't move. Jim climbed onto the side and tried to prize the passenger door open. The roof pillars, bent in the accident, wedged it shut.

Jim called in through the partly open side window and heard a muted groan.

'He's still alive, but the door won't open.'

Kelly took matters in hand and kicked in what remained of the narrow windscreen. Jim jumped down and helped her clear the rim of broken glass. The head lifted off the steering wheel and the battered face of a middle-aged man with red puffy eyes looked back at them. Some superficial scratches marked his face and a trickle of blood dripped from a crooked nose. Thankfully, nothing more gruesome greeted them, nothing to make the rescuers recoil in horror.

'Anyone else in there with you?' Kelly shouted.

It appeared to cause him some discomfort, but the man shook his head to confirm he was alone.

'Are you OK? Can you move your arms and legs?'

The man took another few seconds to compose himself, before

grasping the wheel with both hands. With a grimace, he tried to pick himself off the side door. It hurt. A good sign, all things considered. Jim reached in over the wheel and unclipped the seatbelt.

'Can you feel your legs?' Kelly asked again, praying he could.

'Yes,' the driver confirmed, his voice weak. 'I think I'm in one piece and I can move my legs.'

'What's your name?'

'Morris.'

'OK, Morris. Are you sure you haven't hurt your back or neck?'

'I've hurt everything, but my legs and arms are OK.'

'Then we better get you out of there.'

* * *

'SANDSTONE! I WANT feet on the ground in Sandstone. I don't care if the runway is still closed, or if the roads are impassable. Interview everyone in the town. Get started over the phone if you have to. I want to know who exactly left on that plane and where the bloody hell it went. Will someone find out what the range is on a Cessna 150 and plot it on my map?'

Sidoli became animated. He waved a folded bundle of papers around and used them to point out individual members of the team, while issuing them specific instructions. 'I want every airstrip checked. I don't care if there are hundreds and you've already checked them. Do them again. Start with the sealed runways where fuel is available. Put it out on the radio that a Cessna is believed to have gone missing in the storm. Someone will find it for us.'

Having finished with the room of plain clothes and uniformed officers, Sidoli retreated to his office. At last, something was happening. After the embarrassment of the wrong photo and a frustrating week of dead ends in Perth and in the Manning Ranges, he believed this might be significant. While he sat quietly and smoked, his mind ticked over. Had Holt rendezvoused with the backpacker near Sandstone and flown them out and to where? Is it even possible to squeeze more than two people into a two-seater? Perhaps Holt stayed on in Sandstone, while the others flew off. But why draw attention to yourself? He knew the runway was closed. Holt was not stupid, naive maybe, but not stupid. They could have sat tight for another day. Maybe he was chasing an urgent lead. Was he tipped off that we were onto him?

Whatever Holt was up to, Sidoli knew he would find out soon enough. In Holt's misguided efforts to assist the fugitives, he might just help end this sorry mess.

In the other good news of the day, the boss, Detective Superintendent Baz Harper, rang to postpone a planned trip back to Kalgoorlie, citing family reasons and the recent bad weather. This pleased Sidoli, he did not appreciate Harper looking over his shoulder constantly and banging on about the concerns of 'the people in Perth'. He much preferred dealing with the man over the phone – if he bothered to take the call at all.

* * *

MORRIS SAT QUIETLY on a camp chair Jim retrieved from the roadside. He looked down at his high-laced boots, his arms folded across his stomach. There was a strong possibility he could faint or throw up – or both.

Morris had said little since they lifted him out through the window, his only words to confirm that, apart from a broken nose, everything else seemed OK. Slowly, Morris assessed his situation and came to terms with what happened. To walk away from that crash without serious injury, he knew was a bloody miracle. A miracle that did nothing to lessen the shock. His beloved mustard green FJ40, now lying smashed on its side, had not been so lucky. He couldn't bring himself to look at it anymore.

'There you go,' Kelly said, handing him a cup of sweet billy tea. 'Feeling any better?'

Morris shrugged. 'Mustard green has seen better days.' The newly acquired nose fracture enhanced an already strong nasal twang.

'What happened?'

'No idea. All I remember is waking and the two of you looking in at me.'

Jim set about collecting Morris's belongings from the road. He stacked them neatly next to the Land Cruiser. It was impossible not to be nosey. The man's life lay open on the road in front of him. Much of what Jim found so far pointed to Morris being an experienced and well-prepared off-road driver. A large trunk of what looked like spare parts, and another packed with tools, had cracked open, spraying their contents everywhere. Finding a set of four traction mats made Jim smile. He could have done with those earlier. Lucky for him, the sticks did their job and he didn't have to dig the Hilux out of the creek.

Jim noticed a dusty canvas satchel in the sand. Poking out were what he knew to be butcher's knives and a bone saw. He recognised them immediately from a similar assortment Old Bill kept in the abattoir shed at Yilgarn. Nearby, Jim found a short, hard-plastic rod, about a half-metre long with a moulded handle and barbs. He saw one of these at Yilgarn too, although Old Bill claimed never to have used it and wasn't sure how it found its way into his ghoulish collection. Old Bill called it a 'game dressing tool', designed to remove a deer's anal alimentary canal. A more horrendous indictment of the 'sport' of hunting Jim couldn't come up with. What a way to spend a free Sunday afternoon. It appeared Morris was partial to a spot of hunting.

From the length of the debris trail, Jim reckoned Morris must have been travelling at a decent speed when the accident happened. It looked like he drifted several times off the track before, on his last transgression, he went farther down the slope, turned abruptly in sand, hit a small bank and rolled quite some way back up to the road. He wondered if Morris lost concentration or just fell asleep at the wheel. The many empty yellow XXXX Bitter Ale cans littering the cab might suggest the latter. He may be doing Morris a disservice, so Jim kept his thoughts to himself.

Taking a break from gathering, Jim poured a brew and sat on the ground next to Kelly. 'Where did you come across from?' he asked Morris.

'Came down from Darwin. My off-road club was on safari up there.'

'Sounds like fun.'

'Yeah it was good, mate. Bagged me a few nice trophies. Wild boar and a water buffalo.'

'A hunting safari, then?' Kelly did not sound too impressed.

'Ah, look, not everyone's cup of tea, I know, but they're feral. The water buffalo and boar need eradicating. It's big business.'

'Can't deny the boar make great sausages, eh, Charlie?' Jim said, remembering Arthur's fine snags.

'Not too interested in the meat,' Morris said. 'Yeah, I'll take some, but it's the tusks and horns to hang in the shed I'm after. Expecting a big delivery from Darwin shipped to the door next month and I have a nice spot on the wall all ready for them.'

'Whatever you're into. The rest of the group must be following close behind, then?' Jim asked.

'Nah, I left early to get back to Perth. I'm already going to be a day late for work as it is.'

'That's a pity. I'm sure the animals were sorry to see you go,' said Kelly.

First Morris laughed, then smiled. He was well used to being challenged about his hobby and was not bothered about what others thought of it, or him.

'Suppose you can add a few more days onto that now. You're not your own boss, by any chance?' Jim asked.

'Na, mate. I'm in assurance.'

Dressed in a bloodstained camouflage T-shirt, camouflage trousers, boots and a US Navy Seal cap rescued from the debris, not to mention the two blackening eyes and prominent crooked nose, Morris looked nothing like your typical pen pusher.

'Yeah! Car insurance?'

'No, life.'

'Pity. This won't be cheap to fix.'

'Do you think you'll be able to help with your Hilux – get us back onto four wheels?'

'I can try,' Jim said, not entirely sure how you go about righting a Land Cruiser.

'Shit! I loaned my winch to a mate in Darwin. Didn't think I'd need it for the run home,' Morris said, while trying to work things out in his throbbing head. 'I have snatch straps in there somewhere.' He scanned the scene from his chair. 'Pity it's not facing the other way. Running a line to your Hilux through the thick bush will be difficult. Going to be hard just getting your vehicle in there, mate.'

'Have you checked out the damage yet?' asked Jim. 'I know nothing about mechanics, but even if we get it upright, I don't think it's going anywhere soon. Two wheels are hanging off and the front axle thing looks smashed up.'

Morris threw the last drops of sweet black tea to the ground. He eased himself to his feet and hobbled over to the crippled Land Cruiser. Working his way around, he assessed the damage to the frame and examined the chassis and wheels. He reached into the cab and tried the HF radio. Some vital piece of circuitry had broken loose in the crash and now prevented the faintest hiss of static from coming through the speaker. Morris flung the microphone back in through the broken windscreen. The others watched on.

'I think you're right, mate. She's fucked!' Shaking his head, Morris pointed to the Hilux. 'Don't see an aerial. You haven't got a radio have you?'

Jim shook his head.

'Ah, someone'll be along in a while. They'll have one. Thank God for insurance, eh?' Morris appeared to be coming to terms with his predicament.

'How about you jump in with us and we'll drop you off at Docker River. You can organise a tow truck there.' Confident by now they had not been recognised, Kelly was eager to get going, but reluctant to abandon Morris.

'Na, love. That's kind of you, but that's some long ways back across the border. I'll take my chances flagging someone with a radio here. I'm not leaving my pride and joy and my tools unattended – the fuckin' coons would have it stripped in no time!'

Kelly shifted on her seat. 'You can't stay here. You need to get checked out by a doctor,' she said, concerned about a possible delayed reaction from the blow to the head.

'Me, nah! I'm right as.'

'OK then.' Jim jumped up, clapped and rubbed his hands together. 'Right, we'll finish getting your stuff off the road. You sit there and rest. Once everything is in and you've made yourself comfortable, we'll mosey on.'

Suddenly, the thought occurred to Jim that 'someone' might just have the appalling idea of volunteering him to babysit Morris' mangled portable abattoir, while she took the injured man to seek medical attention. Jim wasn't having that. They were getting back on the road, before such a brilliant idea might occur to anybody. If it had been his mother with him, Jim knew he'd already be sitting on his own by the roadside, while his mum took Morris to Warburton. On the journey over, she would naturally discover they shared a common convict ancestor or some other tenuous connection. She was like that, always picking up strays. Sorry, Mum. It's not happening here. Jim was having none of it.

**

LAURIE LOOKED DOWN on the barren, sodden, pockmarked land-scape. Generations of miners had left their marks. Yesterday's water still ponded in rocky depressions and creeks. It was a different country after the rains. The paired flight controls in front of him moved in tandem with the pilot. It took everything in his power not to reach out and fly the plane himself. He considered asking Merv for a go. Maybe, when all this is over, he would take a lesson.

Soon the vibration coming off the engine calmed his restless mind. The flicker from the propeller imposed a subtle filter, reminiscent of old Pathé news footage, over the images his sleepy eyes took in. He drifted off, letting his imagination take flight.

Laurie found himself behind the controls of a Sopwith Camel, above a muddy, bombed-out Somme. Out of the sun appeared a marauding Manfred von Richthofen and the all-red Fokker. Laurie's synchronised twin machine guns fired magically through the propeller, strafing the Baron's tail. Laurie's mother often spoke of her eldest brother's claim to have witnessed von Richthofen's last dog fight. In his uncle's more lucid moments, the old man claimed to have fired the famous bullet from the ground that downed the legend. Laurie harried the Fokker towards the ANZAC lines and his waiting uncle.

'Have you thought about what you'll do after all this is sorted?' Merv's voice cut in through the headset. 'Look mate, I admire you for it, but if I were in your shoes, I wouldn't fancy going into work the next day.'

'Might as well finish my career with a bang, Merv. You know, I'm thinking of asking Helen for a job. Help her hold onto Yilgarn.'

Even with the headsets on, the noise in the cabin almost drowned out their conversation. The sound reminded Laurie of a tractor motor, particularly when Merv turned the key and the propeller first stuttered to life. But there was nothing heavy about the Cessna. It danced and bobbed freely in the pockets of disturbed air, taking Laurie back to his dogfight. Confident now he was in the hands of an artist, his stomach went eagerly into every turbulent drop and bank with the aircraft, the same way it used to on the rides at the Perth Royal Shows of his childhood.

At the start of their journey together, Laurie had been a little wary of his pilot. Many of Merv's stories were genuinely hair-raising, but Laurie took solace in that the majority of the man's most magnificent adventures in a flying machine were from the distant past. Merv had won him over. The fact that Merv stopped drinking beer after the two he had with his dinner yesterday helped.

Before take-off, in his pre-flight routine, Merv would caress every inch of his aircraft, feeling for the slightest imperfection in the fuselage, the smallest rivet out of place. He tested all external moving parts, guiding them by hand through their ranges of motion. He may have appeared casual at times, like when stashing jerry cans of fuel behind seats or taking off on a closed runway. Switching off the transponder and radio might not have been best practice either. But Merv knew what he was at.

Here, Laurie now appreciated, was someone who, every time he took to the air, even after all these years, fell in love with the mechanics and beauty of flying. Possibly the slowest, smallest, cheapest light air-craft out there, the pilots of Cessna 150s don't swagger through exotic flight lounges in snazzy uniforms. That didn't bother Merv. His days of swaggering were well behind him. He simply loved flying his plane, or any plane. Whether for work or pleasure, it made no difference.

Stopping to refuel at Laverton Airport, again there were no plush lounge to swagger through. Used once or twice a week, when the mines changed shifts, the airport boasted nothing more than a fine bitumen runway, a fortress of a caged-off fuel depot and a wind sock. They approached from the north, to avoid being seen from the town.

A single paddy wagon waited on the apron for the aircraft to taxi over. There were a few anxious moments, when the two occupants of the Cessna wondered if it was a welcoming party from Sidoli or Laurie's mate with fuel. Merv's trepidation evaporated in the blistering heat of the apron, when he spotted the plastic bags of food in the hands of the young policewoman standing by the vehicle.

MERV WOLFED INTO his share of the sandwiches. Not a drip of mayonnaise landed on his charts. Neither did he let the aircraft deviate from its course even one degree while they ate their lunch. He navigated from a chart on his lap and meticulously checked off geographical features along the flight path he plotted for Warburton. If anything new, a mine or dam, did not already appear on his map, he inked it in. If he identified a suitable landing spot, he marked it on the map too.

'You should always have a few backdoors up your sleeve, in case of emergencies,' he explained.

From his detailed timings between the features on the ground, Merv could deduce if they were flying into a headwind and he adjusted their ETA accordingly. He was certain they would land well before sunset this fine Sunday afternoon.

Laurie felt bad asking Merv to continue on to Warburton, a small community deep in the Gibson Desert. It was a long way into the interior and would be a long way back. A big call on Merv's time. But he knew Merv was in his element and pleased to be adding a new adventure to his catalogue of escapades.

* * *

'FUCK HIM!' JIM said through gritted teeth, 'We'll head off when this is done! Worst-case scenario, his mates will be along in a day or two. I'm not wasting any more time on that redneck prick.'

'Look, we can't just leave him. He's had a head injury. What happens if he collapses later? We have to hang around and make sure he's OK. We don't have to like him or anything.'

'What if he cops who we are? Jesus, Kelly. There's a price on our heads!'

'So, what's he going to do? He can't alert anyone, and if he recognises us, we just go. Anyway, he's been bush-bashing for a week and probably hasn't seen the news in days. If he hasn't copped us by now, he's not going to!'

'Fine,' Jim caved. 'We'll give him a few hours. Then we're gone!' He wasn't taken with Morris, largely because Morris never thanked Kelly for the tea. Granted, it's hardly grounds for leaving an injured man stranded, even if he was a racist prick.

Jim picked a camouflage-patterned backpack from the road and went to sling it over his shoulder, when he noticed the familiar sight of dust rising in the distance.

He nudged Kelly. 'Looks like more company on the way.'

THE TRUCK DRIVER jumped down and took in the scene. In his general unkempt burliness, he had the cut of a biker about him, but the flip flops and lack of forearm tattoos put Jim's mind a little at ease.

'Jesus, you made shit of that. What happened?'

'Camel ran out in front of me. Had to swerve, mate,' Morris said, his memory apparently restored.

Jim saw no evidence of camels having been on the road.

'The radio is there. Feel free to use it … Strewth, mate! Hope you've some good insurance,' the truckie added, once it was established nobody was coming to recover the damaged vehicle. The man then disappeared around the back of his trailer, before returning with an armful of beautifully chilled cans of Lemon Solo and passed them out. Morris took his with him and climbed into the cab to call for help on the truck's HF.

'Hope you don't mind lemon. It's alls I get. You know ... for the citric acid.'

'Jesus, not at all. Nectar of the gods,' Jim said, opening his. 'What's with the citric acid?'

'Keeps them bastard mossies away. Dengue fever, mate.'

Jim took a sip of the lemon drink. He had heard of Dengue fever. A nasty contagion that can knacker a person for years. But drinking fizzy lemon to ward off mosquitoes was news to him.

'Are you sure you're not thinking of citronella?' he said, after the cold bubbles bit and stung his throat. Jim noticed Kelly throwing daggers his way. The truckie too gave him a quizzical look. Jim thought it best not to pursue the line of questioning and mumbled, 'Delicious,' before putting the can back to his lips.

'Colder than your sock. Eh, Paddy?' Kelly said, moving tactfully along.

'Ha! You tried the old bush-sock cooler trick? Works pretty well, doesn't it?'

'Not bad,' she agreed. 'But this sure hits the spot, thanks.'

'He's a very lucky bloke to walk away from that. Probably has a long wait ahead of him, though. Where're you two off to yourselves?' the truckie asked, addressing his question to the young Irish driller.

'Drilling project in the Tanami.'

After a while, Morris rejoined the group.

'Thanks, mate. Word is out now. It's just a matter of waiting. Someone will be along this arvo to bring her to Warburton.' Morris sounded upbeat.

From there, he needed to arrange for everything to be freighted to Perth and 'that could take weeks', but at least the process was in train. Soon after finishing his drink, the truckie wished them luck and left. Kelly helped Morris rig up a shade out of his tattered tarpaulin, while Jim made one last pass along the road for anything he missed earlier.

Happy he got it all, Jim strolled back to the vehicles. The skin on his forehead and scalp felt tight and hot. It occurred to him he had not worn a hat since the fuel stop earlier. Neither could he remember when he last applied sunscreen. He looked forward to getting out of the sun, into the air-conditioning, and on the road again. Morris was fine. He'll be bored out of his mind and out of pocket in a big way. But that wasn't his or Kelly's problem.

Coming round the side of the Hilux, Jim saw Kelly standing, head bowed, her hands behind her back. She would not acknowledge him and seemed to be alone.

That's odd, he thought. Something's up.

Chapter 20

Moments in the sun

S talking his next trophy, Morris crept around the smashed-up truck. Kelly stayed silent, her head stayed down. Morris snuck up behind Jim unheard and pressed the muzzle of his rifle hard into the back of Jim's neck.

'Ah, Jim! You've returned. Be a good bloke and kneel for me.'

Jim stood still. 'For fuck sake, Morris. What are you doing?'

'Shut up! Take off your boots and kneel.' Morris shoved Jim again with the rifle. 'And then you can put your hands behind your back.'

'Jesus, OK. Just be careful with that thing.' Jim did as he was ordered, taking a little more care removing his boots than might have been necessary.

With his quarry helpless on the ground, Morris bound Jim's hands together with a long white cable tie. He pulled it tight, hurting Jim's wrists and aggravating the injured shoulder.

'Now, when this tow truck arrives, the three of us are taking your Hilux on a little journey and I'm going to hand you over to the authorities.' Morris grabbed Kelly by the arm and threw her against Jim. 'The two of you can kneel there and not a fuckin' word.' Morris moved his chair under the newly erected shade and sat in relative comfort. He put the gun across his lap and grinned. A self-satisfied, excitable grin.

'Don't bother pleading your innocence with me, Paddy. Your girlfriend here has already tried. That's for the courts to worry about. Frankly, I couldn't give a fuck if you were as innocent as that coon, Mandela.'

'We came to your aid and this is how you repay us!'

'Ah look, Paddy. Waddya want? A fuckin' medal? Stopping in the bush to check on a fellow traveller – that's Australian, mate. It's hardly an exceptional act of kindness. Shit, I've done it myself.'

Ignoring their captor, Jim turned to Kelly. 'Are you OK?'

Kelly shuffled closer, closing the few centimetres between them. She leaned into Jim and, behind their backs, she hooked one of her fingers into one of his.

'Ah, isn't that lovely,' came the sneering remark from under the shade. 'Hey! If you want to put on a show of affection, feel free. You better make the most of your last moments together. You'll be spending a lot of time apart soon. Hope you don't mind if I watch!'

'I presume you called the police over the radio. Is there even a tow truck coming?'

'Ah, yes and no, Paddy. I didn't call the coppers. I'm bringing you two bastards in myself. Going to get my picture on TV. I'll be a bloody hero and get to salvage something from the unfortunate situation I find myself in.'

'Why all the venom, man?'

'Ah, look. Wouldn't want you trying anything stupid. Just letting you know how it is. And remember, I'm a pretty decent shot!'

'You've obviously seen the papers. So am I, didn't you read? And I'm a merciless son of a bitch, too! You can't win, Morris. If I'm who the media say I am, you don't want to piss me off. If we're innocent, like Kelly has said, people want us dead. We know too much and you'll become a loose end. The best thing you can do for yourself is let us go!'

'Bollocks!'

But Jim had planted a seed in Morris' volatile mind. To tip the odds a little more in his favour, Morris bound Jim's feet with a cable tie. He then ran his hand along Kelly's leg before zipping a tie around her ankles too. She kicked out at him, so he kicked Jim and returned to the camp chair.

Hours passed and there was no sign of the tow truck, or any other traffic on the road. All the time, Morris forced Kelly and Jim to kneel out in the sun. The heat and the swarms of inquisitive flies crawling over their faces brought Kelly close to tears and even closer to passing out. She took some comfort from leaning into Jim and it helped her stay upright. Jim, far more used to the flies and heat from his hours painting on the back of the old Ford, managed better and for the most part saved his anger for Morris. Only when an individual fly ventured too far up a nostril did Jim react and blow it out. But he never let Morris see his discomfort. Staring, Jim's eyes followed the man's every restless move.

'Jesus, Morris. We're burning up here. Just get us the hats,' Kelly asked for the third or fourth time. 'Come on, for God's sake! They're in the cab.'

'All right, all right, for fuck sake! Stop nagging me.'

Morris got out of his seat and made his way slowly over to the Hilux. Passing the bound couple, he lifted his hat and poured water over his head. Kelly watched furious when he picked her bag off the back seat and looked to be about to open it. Something else caught his eye and he threw the bag down.

'Well, waddya know?' Morris held up the front page of the news-paper and shouted over. 'Appears I'm going to be twenty grand richer for my troubles. This day just keeps getting better.'

After the excitement of spending the reward in his head faded, the long wait for the tow truck began to irritate again. To kill time, and for his own amusement, he teased his captives again with the offer of water and food, only to devour it himself. The afternoon dragged on.

Having had enough of the Irishman's constant challenging stare, Morris shoved the hat down over Jim's eyes and kicked him again for spite. But Morris, too, grew weary in the heat. He would doze off for a few seconds in the chair, suddenly wake, jump up and pace for a few minutes to revive himself, before sitting again.

'I need to pee,' Kelly demanded.

'Can't help you there,' Morris said, with a grin.

'Please!'

'No! Just do it here. Don't be modest. Paddy can't see a thing.'

'For Christ sake! Just let her go. What's she done to you that you treat her like this?'

'Nothing, but she still ain't going nowhere.'

'You're a sick creep,' Kelly said and gave Morris a defiant look that brought another smile to his face.

'Listen, darling. I'm not untying you.' He stood up. 'Ha! All this talk and now I need to go myself. Hey, Kelly, don't do your business until I come back. Wouldn't want to miss it! And Paddy, don't fuckin' move. Ha! Oh, that's right. You can't,' he chuckled, while disappearing around his Land Cruiser.

Behind her back, Kelly wriggled her hands and stretched her fingers to get some feeling into their tips. The cable tie cut into her skin and the pressure on the bones in her wrist became so severe, she thought they would snap. Slipping one finger under Jim's watchstrap she held their wrists tightly together. Then she manipulated her hands into a position where she could feel the loose end of Jim's cable tie. Her fingers touched the strip of tiny plastic teeth and followed it back to where it entered the square head of its opposite end.

'Quick, squeeze your arms together as much as you can,' she whispered. 'I need you to take some pressure off the cable tie.'

Jim forced his elbows together, so that his forearms didn't pull quite so hard against the plastic strip. He held it for a few seconds before having to stop, rest and try again.

'Jesus, Jim, hold still!'

The constant movement, the searching with her fingers for the best angle to work from, pulled and tore at Kelly's wrists. The pain was almost unbearable, but she persevered. With the palm of one hand, she bent the loose, tapered end of Jim's cable tie out of the way. Her thumb picked at the inside of the head.

'Shit!' Her fingers slipped. She went searching again.

Much like her potato peeling, Kelly had another quirky habit. She endeavoured to recycle every cable tie she was ever required to open. To cut was always the last resort and an irritating admission of defeat. From experience, she knew her thumbnail was strongest at the point where the inside curve of her nail straightened and curled into the bed. A stiff corner of nail formed there, just enough to wedge into the pawl of the cable-tie head and lift it away from the teeth on the strip. After two more unsuccessful attempts, and tearing some nail from the bed, the pawl yielded. She knew she had the ratchet open.

'Pull your wrists apart. Quick, now!'

Jim obliged and the plastic strip slipped loose. Morris returned, still adjusting his belt.

'Did I miss anything, Kelly?'

He got no response. They hadn't moved. They couldn't. He knew he had broken them in the heat. Like an exhausted, wounded animal, they had given up. They were stuffed. The tow truck would be along soon. Compliant and easier to handle now, he would make the Paddy drive and keep the girl in the back with him. Morris retook his seat, delighted with himself. Soon the urge to sleep returned.

Discreetly, using Kelly's shoulder for leverage, Jim nudged the hat up enough to look out under the brim. He saw Morris sitting with the rifle across his lap. The man appeared tired. He watched Morris' head drop, then spring back up, then drop again. It stayed down. Morris' breathing grew louder. Jim waited, then took a deep breath and held it.

Moving quickly, he reached for his boots. To Kelly's astonishment, he produced a knife from inside the left boot. With one swift up-cut, Jim severed the tie around his ankles. It took four explosive strides before he crashed into his dozing captor, toppling Morris and the chair backwards to the ground.

Before Morris could open his eyes, Jim landed with his knee on Morris' chest and had the knife to the man's throat. Next, Jim tossed the rifle beyond Morris' scrabbling hands. Smiling, Jim smashed the tip of his forehead down hard on the disfigured bridge of Morris' nose. He felt the already broken bone turn to pulp in the contact. Blood sprayed amid roars of agony. Jim stood and pulled the screaming, snivelling man to his feet by the hair.

'I told you I was a merciless son of a bitch, didn't I?'

Blood streamed from Morris' nose. Dripping off his chin, it left a line of drops in the sand as Jim dragged him over to Kelly.

'On your fuckin' knees. Down!' Jim pushed Morris' face hard into the dirt and held the knife to a bloodied cheek, while forcing a knee into Morris' back.

'Apologise to the lady!'

Through the dirt and spit and blood, Jim heard a faint 'Sorry'.

'Not good enough, Morris. Say it again. This time, louder and mean it!'

'Sorry. I'm sorry!'

'Still not good enough.' Jim punched Morris hard between the shoulders. 'Louder ... and say her name.'

'Jim, stop!' Kelly screamed. 'That's enough.'

Jim stared back at Kelly, his face speckled with blood.

'No! He'll apologise to you. Properly!' He threw another punch and connected hard with the man's head.

'Kelly, I'm sorry. I'm sorry!' Morris shouted.

'That's enough. Let it go. Come on. Let's just get out of here.' She had not seen Jim like this before. Not in the bottle shop, not even when Max lay buried under the burning timbers. Right now, there was a viciousness about him that disturbed her.

Jim pushed Morris' face hard into the dirt one last time, before he relented and went off to collect the rifle.

'Right, you! Over there into the middle of the road, where I can see you!' Jim yelled, while aiming the barrel at the prostrate figure. 'Now!'

Wiping the blood from his face with the front of an already blood-stained T-shirt, Morris shuffled across to the spot Jim pointed to and sat down. Unable to breathe through the congealing mess in his nose, Morris wheezed loudly, sucking in the hot dry air through his open mouth. It was the only sound to be heard, while Jim fetched Kelly a bottle of water and knelt to cut her loose. Noticing her bruised wrists, he reached out to touch them. Kelly pulled away.

'YOU'RE A FUCKIN' mess, Morris. Clean yourself when we're gone,' Jim shouted, before taking his water canteen and the rifle and climbing into the back of the Hilux. He made himself comfortable among the camping gear and the displaced geological equipment.

'Hope that truck comes for you soon,' Kelly said and closed the driver's door behind her.

Jim sat proud in the back, with the rifle visible in his arms. He watched the assurance clerk shrink into the distance. Long after he could see him no more, Jim kept staring, his cheeks red from the sun and the dry smears of Morris' blood.

Kelly drove on. She waited for a tap on the roof to signal her to stop and for Jim to climb back in out of the heat. She wanted to talk about what happened. But no knock came. She decided it was for the best. They both needed to calm down.

***

'THE MANAGER AT the National Hotel says they mentioned heading North to Meekathara, and that appeared to be the direction they took off in,' said Nugus.

'Just Holt and the pilot?' asked Sidoli.

'Yeah.'

'And nobody there has seen the girl or the Irishman?'

'Afraid not, Sarge.'

'Just as a matter of interest ... find out if you can get film developed in Meekathara. That's the second time in a week Holt has been in Sandstone. They must have been holed up somewhere near there. Anything or anybody else, apart from tumbleweed, pass through that godforsaken town in recent days?'

'An Ozdrill crew came in on Friday night ... skimpy night at the National, coincidentally. They'd just finished a drilling project on Dismals Station.'

'Dismals Station!' Sidoli turned to look at his map. 'Dismals Station is not that far from where we lost the trail. And it's on the way to Sandstone. Fuck! That's where they've been all along. I'd put money on them having been shacked up with the drill crew. Have we interviewed them?'

'They all appear to have gone off on break.'

'And the station owner?'

'Yeah, this morning. He's a crotchety old bloke, who's been at war with the exploration companies. Says he hasn't seen a thing. Keeps pretty much to himself apparently. It's a big area, so I'm inclined to believe him.'

'Look, find every one of those drillers and bring them in. I don't care where you take them, just find out what they know. They have to know something. Make them tell us.'

'Boss, why do you think Laurie Holt is helping them?'

'Look, I don't know, mate. Maybe he's cracked a fruity, gone fucking mad or finally spat the dummy over not getting promoted. Maybe he's trying to apprehend them and wants the glory for himself. You wouldn't know with Holt.'

* * *

EVENTUALLY, THE KNOCK on the roof came and Kelly brought the Hilux to a stop. He opened the driver's door from the outside. Ned Kelly stood before her.

'Jesus Christ! Jesus, Jim. What the … what are you doing?'

'If it comes to it,' he said, his voice echoing through a bucket. 'I've decided I'm doing a Ned Kelly. I don't fancy going down like Butch and Sundance. Waddya think?'

'You're mad!'

In the hurry to pack up camp, two of the cast-iron streak plates the geologists used for mineral analysis found their way onto the back of the Hilux. By wiring them together and hanging them over his shoulders in the manner of a sandwich board, Jim had created a bullet-proof vest of sorts. He punched an eye slit through an aluminium bucket with the sharp end of Andy's geological hammer and now wore the bucket over his head.

Standing in front of Kelly, with the rifle held across his chest, she couldn't decide if he looked sinister or just daft.

'Come on, waddya think?'

Kelly got out of the cab for a better look.

'You're crazy,' she said in disbelief.

'Such is life.'

'Oh please! You're not serious, are you?'

'Of course not. I can hardly move with the weight of it and can't see a bloody thing.' He removed the bucket from his head, then lifting the body armour off, jarred his shoulder and winced.

Serves him right, she thought. 'Christ. This is no time for messing. And since when did you carry a knife?'

'I don't. It's one of Morris' bone knives. I found it on the road and reckoned it might be handy for making the shade.'

'Where is it now?'

'I'm not having anything else go wrong.'

'Where's the knife?'

'Did you see the way he looked at you?'

'I did, and I saw the way you humiliated him. That wasn't necessary. You went too far. Where's the knife?'

'In my boot.'

'And why have we still got the gun? Why haven't you chucked it? Remember what you said at Aurora? What's changed?'

'I was wrong at Aurora and wrong at Yilgarn. Bill might be alive if we'd kept the pistol, so I'm keeping—'

'Keeping the gun won't bring Old Bill back. It can only put us in more danger. It's not going to happen again. We've won. The photographs will vindicate us. We're so close to putting ourselves beyond the reach of Collins.'

'Just until we cross the border, then.'

'Please ... for me. Get rid of the gun. It's over Jim. We've won.'

'For God sake! It's only a gun. Everyone has one out here, it seems. It might save our lives yet.'

'Get us killed, more like.'

'No more rednecks are going to try and stop me getting to the Territory. Anyway, I can't be sure if I even got a photo of anything anymore. And where's Andy? Something's happened. Maybe he wants the reward! Who knows?'

'Don't say that. You know it's not true.'

'And what about the bikers? There could be an Alice Springs chapter of the Puppet Masters coming this way, for all we know. I'm keeping the gun.'

'There's no need for this bravado. You're a nice guy. You paint beautiful pictures. You make me smile at the darkest times. This is not you. You can't even use it.'

'Yeah, of course I can fuckin' use it and where the fuck has being nice ever gotten me?'

Something moved in the bush, a small animal or a gust of wind. Jim lifted the rifle and fired. Morris had it loaded and, much to Jim's horror, a shot rang out. The noise resonated in their ears, long after the puff of dust from the bullet hitting the ground had settled. Then silence. Kelly no longer appeared angry. Her expression had changed to one of disappointment and sadness.

'Being nice got you me! You got me, Jim Macken. I thought, for once in my life, I found someone nice, someone to love and to be loved back.'

His shame and remorse were apparent, if only she would bring herself to look at him. He held out the rifle for her to take.

CHAPTER 21

SUNSET

T HE FRONT WHEEL deformed the steel tubing. The rear wheel tore the wooden stock from the mangled barrel. Confident the rifle was well beyond use and repair, Kelly stopped and waited.

'For God's sake, get over it and get in!' she shouted after a long minute and he had shown no signs of moving.

Her demand failed to provoke a response. Jim stayed where he was, standing with both hands on top of his stooped head. For Christ's sake, what's he playing at now? She sounded the horn and again, Jim put one hand in the air indicating for her to hold on.

'This is childish,' Kelly muttered. He's making me drive ten metres back to score a point. That's just silly. 'OK, so be it!' Angrily, she shoved the gear lever hard to the right and back. I'm the bigger person here, she told herself. Still, he'll be getting another large piece of my mind.

Zipping backwards, the engine sounded a high-pitched whine. The

Hilux stopped with a skid and Kelly flung open the passenger door. Immediately, she began dishing out various home truths. Oblivious to her arrival, Jim continued to stare at his feet and made no effort to get into the cab. That incensed Kelly more. She paused to take a breath.

Jim looked up, his nostrils flared on his now pallid face. Unblinking, he stared at her. The full orbits of his irises were visible. Indifferent to the brilliant sunlight, his pupils dilated. A look of rage or terror, she could not tell. What did he have to be terrified about? It must be rage, she thought, and Kelly's heart broke a little more. She blinked hard to catch the meniscus of water rising in the corner of her eyes, before it could escape as tears. Why had she not seen this side of him before today? Her feelings for Jim were changing.

'Look, I don't need more anger in my life,' she said, before Jim could start whatever he had in mind. 'It crushed me before. I thought you were different!'

'I've been bitten by a snake!' he said calmly, no hint of anger at all in his voice.

'That's just juvenile and pathetic. You're a fantasist, Jim Macken. Why can't you simply apologise?' Now confused, she wiped her eyes and sniffed. Had she read him wrong? Had something happened to him or was he being a jerk?

'OK, I'm sorry,' he continued. 'I'm truly sorry for everything, for my behaviour. You're right, that's not who I am. I was tired, I was angry and the sun may have gotten to me. I was always only thinking of you, of protecting you, because I love you. But I've been bitten by a fuckin' snake! Here look, just above my ankle.'

He grabbed hold of the open door and planted his boot on the floor inside the cab. Above his sock, she saw two small red marks. Could he possibly be telling the truth? No, that would be crazy. He wouldn't lie about something like this, would he? Obviously, he's mistaken, she decided.

'Ah, shit! That could be anything, spinifex spikes can do that. Get in. Let's go.' Yeah, a scratch. That's all he had. He'll be embarrassed about this later. She felt stupid and relieved at the same time. Jim could never be angry or violent to her, not in the way she knew before, not in any way at all. Kelly smiled nervously. 'I'm sorry, too. Come on. Get in. You'll be fine. It's probably just two ant bites. Let's go, if we want to make Ayers Rock by sunrise.'

'Kelly, I saw it. It's crazy, I know, but I saw the fecker attack me. The speed was something else. I must have stood on its tail. It sank its teeth right there into my leg.' He ran a finger slowly around the marks. 'I got a good look at it after, I'm telling you. It was definitely one of those legless, slithery bastard things with fangs!'

She stared into his wide eyes. Behind the humour, she saw fear, a fear she too began to feel. Jim pulled himself into the passenger seat.

'I bet it's still in that patch of spinifex over there, if you want to check for yourself,' he said, pointing the way.

'I believe you. What do we do now? You're going to be OK, aren't you?'

'Ah, yeah. I'm young, fit and healthy. Even went for a jog last week. You'll see, I'll be grand.'

'Is it sore? What kind of snake was it?'

'It's a little numb, but it's early days.'

She took his hand. 'Shit! What'll we do, Jim?'

'We both need to stay calm. I'm trying not to panic. But my heart is about to explode out of my chest,' he said, forcing a smile. An ugly vein on his temple beat a visible pulse. 'I'm sorry, but I think I'll need medical attention soon.' Tears collected on the bottom of his eyes. 'I'm so sorry, Kelly. I've messed everything up.'

'Don't talk like that. No, you haven't. Look, as far as I can remember, we need to wrap the area tight and then we'll go find help. Warburton has a nursing post. They'll have what you need.'

'So you're not going to suck the poison out. Damn, I was looking forward to that,' Jim said, trying to make light of the situation again.

'No, I'm pretty sure that's not recommended these days. Besides, would you believe, we don't have any whiskey.' She wiped away tears of her own, but managed a smile.

In the few minutes since the snakebite, the area around the puncture marks had already become swollen and small broken veins now tracked under the skin. Kelly tied the sleeves of a shirt over the bite and tightened the makeshift bandage by twisting a stick into the material. By pushing one end of the stick down inside Jim's boot, she prevented it spinning loose. Before starting the journey, she gave Jim a bottle of water and put her hand on his cheek to reassure him. His beautiful, lively, ever-inquisitive green eyes had already dulled. His eyelids drooped. What she saw shocked her, but she did her best to hide it.

'Don't worry, my love, I'll make sure you're OK.' Kelly reached over and fastened his seatbelt. This is so unfair, she thought, starting the engine. She wanted to hammer the steering wheel and scream. Instead, she pulled off and they began their long, lonely journey back to Warburton.

'What about Morris? What if he's still there?' Jim asked.

'I'll offer him a lift or maybe I'll run him over. Either way is fine by me.'

'Now, now.'

The glare from the setting sun was blinding. Ordinarily, she might have pulled in, but Kelly pressed on. Jim began to experience difficulty breathing. He concentrated on every breath and hoped she did not hear him wheeze.

'Listen, I'm telling you this now only because it might be important later ...' He paused to catch two quick breaths. '... And I may not be able to say it myself. The snake that bit me was short and fat with reddish-brown bands. It had a triangular head and a small, worm-like tail. I'd be quite sure it was ...' He coughed and struggled for a moment to clear the phlegm from his throat. '... a death adder. Don't forget that ... It may affect treatment.' Not wanting to alarm Kelly more, he had held off naming the snake until now. But things were progressing more quickly than he expected.

Kelly pointed out an interesting rock formation. She talked incessantly, to keep herself alert and Jim's mind occupied. He joined in, but as time passed his contributions became fewer, his voice weaker.

'Hey, I think we should have passed Morris by now. I didn't see him, did you? The tow truck must have come and gone. I can imagine he's now on a radio or phone in Warburton dobbing us in. He'll be in for a surprise.'

She saw Jim try to smile. He lifted a crooked thumb on a shaky hand and tried to speak. After a few gulps of air, some weak, slurred words came out, 'Remember our argument ... at the camp?'

Kelly had to lean in and concentrate hard to make out what he said. 'Yeah?'

'Something about bald men ... Why?'

'Ah, look. I'm afraid, brace yourself for this, but you've started to lose your hair!'

'Noooh!' he chuckled, then coughed again. 'That can't be ... I've more hair now than ever.'

'Afraid not,' she shook her head. 'Growing a ponytail and scruffy beard doesn't change the fact there's a little bald spot on the top of your head.'

'Seriously?'

'Yep!'

'That explains the sunburn ... and you still fancied me?'

'Yep, sure did. Aren't bald men way sexier?'

'Good, that's good ... Kelly ... I didn't mean what I said about Andy. He'll come good for you.' Jim's voice trailed off.

NOBODY DIES FROM snakebites in Australia anymore. Old Bill told him that. Antivenom is never too far away. But Old Bill spoke in generalities. Jim couldn't recall him mentioning a specific time window, or how far was too far. But by Old Bill's reckoning, sure, they had enough time to get to Warburton. Antivenom is never too far away, after all. But now a great weight pressed on his chest. Getting air into his lungs became a struggle. Jim tried to move his arm, but it barely responded to the messages from his brain. With great effort, he got his hand into his pocket.

The sun sank below the horizon. Kelly described a wonderful array of rainbow colours playing across the sky. Jim saw only grey, a grey that turned darker with every kilometre. Out of the grey flashed a picture of St Patrick and his goat. The saint was kicking the shit out of some snakes. Kelly thought she heard Jim chuckle. But he did not answer when she asked. His last words were to 'slow down, for your own safety'. She ignored the instruction and hammered along into the dark.

All voluntary muscle control went. The occasional word from Kelly still snuck through, offering some hint of a beautiful world beyond the darkness. He couldn't tell if he was even frightened anymore. Outside of a dimming consciousness, he had no sense of being part of a physical person. Jim had no religion and, apart from the fleeting image of the patron saint, there was no last-minute road to Damascus conversion. He tried to think of home, but his mind would not allow it. The venom shut his thoughts down. There were no more emotions, just resignation. The vibration from the wheels hitting the corrugations on the road, passed right through his rigid body. The grey went black.

Kelly heard the water bottle fall. Jim sat slouched in the seat, his face blank.

'Don't abandon me now, Jim Macken, not after all we've been through. It's not fair. I've told you before, don't leave me in the bush on my own. You're damn well going to stay with me, Irishman. We've made plans. You're taking me to Margaret River and that's that.

Please, Jim, there are lights ahead. We're almost there. Please, for me ... I want to tell you someday about my childhood ... please ...'

The few lights of Warburton grew large through her tears. She reached across and took his clenched hand in hers to hold it in celebration. We're here. Look we've made it. His lifeless hand still warm, she burrowed her fingers into his fist to hold it tighter. His last gold nugget slipped into her palm.

* * *

LEADING THE WAY, the beam from the headlights on the Ford Falcon ute swung into the parking bay. The light bounced back off the white garage roller door, illuminating the Falcon's interior. The ute stopped. The driver grabbed a large canvas duffel bag from the seat next to him and got out. He walked around the side of his grand period, turn-of-the-century home to the verandah at the back. The cicadas clicked in the bushes beyond. A hint of salt seasoned the humid night air. He dropped the bag on a wicker chair and wandered over to the dark shadow of a prostrate figure crashed out on his lawn. A gentle tip with a boot to the thigh of the sleeper, produced a loud snore and some random movements. The tall man rolled over and eyed his assailant.

'Ah! Murray. Good man, you're back. When are you ever going to get a decent lounger for that verandah?' he said, picking grass from the side of his mouth. 'I'll be all itchy now, I'd wager.'

'G'day, Andrew. What's up, mate?'

'I was getting worried about you. Called into Clancy's. They said you were probably gone fishing. So I had a few drinks and a feed, then strolled back here to wait. I expected you home sooner, even considered alerting the coast guard. But then I fell asleep!'

Murray reached out a hand and pulled Andy to his feet. 'I'm touched by your concern. Anyhow, it's good to see you.'

Andy explained the predicament he found himself in. 'These are nasty people, dangerous individuals, Murray. There is no way I can risk a regular photo shop. The images would set alarm bells off and their film might never see the light of day.'

'Strewth! I wish you hadn't told me that. If you'd just said you needed it for work, I wouldn't be so nervous about it now.'

'Possibly a matter of life and death, I'm afraid, but I trust you not to balls it up.'

'Right. No pressure!'

'So you'll do it, then?' Andy went through his pockets as he spoke, but was getting visibly agitated.

'Absolutely!' Murray scratched his chin. 'I haven't used the dark room for a few weeks, but I'm sure I have enough chemicals and paper … I think. What's wrong?'

'Oh, Lord! I can't find it … It was here in my pocket. The button's come off!'

'Don't tell me you've lost it?'

'Jesus, what have I done!' Andy tore at the pockets of his shirt and trousers, then with his hands to his mouth, sank to one knee in despair. Panting through his fingers, the sound of his breath drowned out the cicadas.

Murray bent down and picked up a small canister from the patch of flattened grass, where Andy had lain.

'Right,' he said, deadpan, and rattled the canister. 'Better get on to it.' He walked off.

Andy's recent meal and the few drinks he enjoyed in Clancy's abandoned their long journey up his oesophagus and settled back into his stomach.

'Whoah!' He sprang to his feet, flapped his long arms and briefly shook like a wet dog, before following after Murray. 'I told you, you needed a lounger. Anyway, where were we?'

'What I'll do is develop the roll of negatives and print only the more incriminating images,' Murray replied. 'I have some eight by tens,' he continued, fingering the roll of film in his hand. 'It's colour. Thing is … the prints will have to be black and white. It might look odd, but you'll get the picture.' Murray stopped and looked to the sky. Only his head moved, nodding from side to side.

Andy suspected his friend might be undertaking some mental arithmetic.

The nodding stopped. 'Look, mate. There's a good few hours in this, between setting up, mixing the chemicals and all that.' Murray strode off again, 'I'll get onto it shortly, but I need you to do something for me first.'

He brought Andy around to his ute and unhooked the stretched canvas cover from the back. Underneath lay a fish box, brimming with large, lustrous pink snapper. Their still-clear jelly eyes gaped up at the two heads peering down.

'Nice snapper there, Murray. Where d'you catch them?'

'Yeah, all good pinkies. Got them off Garden Island, Cockburn Sound. The storm brings them in.'

They carried the box between them into Murray's kitchen and lifted it onto the table.

'Wait there a second!' Murray said and disappeared into another room.

He came back with an expensive-looking Nikon camera and a flash. Murray then moved furniture around in the kitchen to free one wall of clutter. He positioned Andy in front of the wall, took readings with his camera, focused on Andy and tested the flash. He thought about digging out a bounce and studio lights, but it was already late and they had a busy night ahead.

'OK. We're going to swap positions and all you have to do is stand there … well, hunker down to my height … hold the flash out like so and push the big button on the camera.'

He handed the equipment over to Andy, before lifting one of his prized snapper from the box, held it out front and beamed like a proud parent. Click! Andy took the photo and Murray put the fish back. Andy went to put the camera down.

'Hold on! There's more, mate.'

Murray picked up another snapper, held it out in front and beamed again. Andy took the photo. And another. After the fourth snapper, Andy just couldn't help himself.

'Wait! That's backwards. It's facing the wrong way. Is there not a convention that stipulates fish should face to the viewer's right?'

'Don't be ridiculous. They're exactly the same, no matter what side you photograph from. What does a Pommy know about snapper, anyway?'

'I know the fish in that box are all the bloody same!'

'Come on now, a couple more to do and then I'll develop your film. Actually, while I shower and set up, how about you sauté up one of these beauties and we'll have some tucker, before I turn the darkroom lights out. I'll gut the rest in the morning. Unless you fancy doing it?'

Chapter 22

The Rainbow Serpent

T HE NAKED FIGURE stood alone, shivering in the dark. The place where he found himself was barren and uniform, unbroken by hills or valleys. There was no water, no fire, no rocks, no silhouettes of trees or tall grasses. There were no animals. Nothing, except for the occasional trail of man's footprints in the dust criss-crossing the land. There was no sound, not even the sound of air entering his nostrils.

Had his breathing stopped? Jim wasn't sure. He looked to the stars. A giant serpentine body, composed of endless pins of light, bisected the sky and cast a dim glow over his face. A faint shadow fell on the near-black dust at his feet. He took solace in recognising some of the patterns in the night sky. But the galaxy of stars seemed much closer than he remembered.

A low, scratching noise broke the silence. Jim felt a tapping against his ankle. He looked down. In the gloom, a small black and white bird looked up at him with piercing gold-brown eyes. It had a neat pile of sticks at its feet.

'It's time to go, Jim.'

'Where are we going, Magpie?'

'Away from here. This is not your place. Wagyl has awoken and we need to move on.'

The bird spoke in a guttural tone that contrasted with its familiar morning lilt.

'I can't move. The venom has taken hold. It won't let me.'

'That will soon pass.'

The bird gathered the sticks in its beak and walked ahead. It beckoned Jim to follow. Jim struggled at first, but the magpie was right. It became easier in time. They walked in silence for miles in the dark, the way lit by the stars, Jim always a little behind. Eventually, it spoke again and called back to the wretched figure.

'I see you got yourself a gun now!'

Unable to raise his voice, Jim said nothing until he reached the waiting bird. 'No, she took it off me.'

'Ah, she's a bonnie lass!' the magpie said, hamming the accent. 'Whatever does she see in a gormless git like—'

'Steady on, Magpie. You're no wedgie yourself.'

'You were blessed to meet her, you know.'

'Aye, I was.'

'She could have chosen anyone at the bar or at camp. That driller has a house on the beach … and money. You've nothing to—'

'I get it, OK!' Jim interrupted again, then mumbled something about 'a crow in a monkey suit' under his breath.

The magpie reared up and puffed out its chest feathers. 'I'll have you know, I am a passerine, a songbird, and not a corvid, like your common or garden European magpie. I am most certainly no relative of the crow.'

'Isn't the European magpie said to be one of the cleverest of birds?'

'Perhaps, but have you ever discussed that with one?'

'Touché, Magpie.'

They walked on.

'She was right to get rid of the gun. What the hell were you thinking? It might have got you bloody killed.'

'Moot point now, Magpie, but yeah, she was right. I was angry. I
wanted insurance. We were so close to making it.'

'Mmmm.' The bird pondered Jim's reply a while.

'Are you judging me, Magpie?'

'You were a bit of an ass, weren't you? You wouldn't touch a gun
a few days ago and now you're blasting one off at anything that moves
in the bush.'

'That's something of an exaggeration, to be fair!'

'It appears you have angered Wagyl now.' The magpie pointed a
wingtip to Jim's ankle and the two puncture wounds. 'Pity. He took
quite the shine to you after you did the drawings for the children in
Davyhurst cemetery. And let me tell you, you're bloody lucky your
name isn't Patrick. That would not have gone down well around here.
Anyway, you don't need a gun where you're going.'

'I suppose not. Where am I going?'

Without answering, the bird gathered its sticks again and skipped
ahead. The ground rose under their feet. They kept moving and they
kept climbing. The magpie needed to stop and wait for Jim more and
more now.

'Wagyl has come this way,' it explained, during one of their rests.
'He's been busy about his work and left this mountain in his trail. Are
you thirsty? He may have cut a stream or a waterhole nearby.'

Jim shook his head. Despite his exertions, he was neither hungry
nor thirsty.

'Who is Wagyl, Magpie?'

'The Noongar people call him Wagyl. The Talainji people call her
Wanamangura, the Gunwinggu, Ngalyod. All the different mobs have
their own name for it. You white fellas know it as the Rainbow Serpent.
It's the ultimate creator of everything in the universe.'

They pushed on up the mountain, the magpie still with the sticks in its beak, Jim labouring at times on his hands and knees, slipping often in the dark.

The higher they went, the more relentless and testing the climb.

'Stop!' Jim called out. 'Stop. I'm done for. I can't go on anymore.'

'Not far now. Come on, Irishman. Where's that fighting spirit? Don't have me count you out. You don't want to be counted out, believe me. You know Douglas was down for ten. The ref started the count late. Bloody lucky for Douglas he did too. But what a comeback, eh?'

Jim could have sworn the magpie did an Ali shuffle before moving off again.

And then there was nowhere else to go. They were at the summit.

'What is it you Irish say? "May the road rise to meet you." I never understood that expression.'

'Neither do I, Magpie. A rising road does not make it any easier, does it?'

'What it makes is a bloody mountain.'

'Shouldn't bother you. Can't you just fly over it?'

'Not with all these bloody sticks in my beak.'

Jim began to laugh. 'No, I suppose not.'

The magpie dropped the sticks. 'Sit down here and tell me what you see.'

Jim sat, pulled his knees into his chest and shivered. 'Nothing. The abyss, blackness!'

'Keep looking. You can't see it yet, but a lot has changed below since we started this climb. Wagyl has finished his work, at least for now.'

The bird took a single stick and flew off to the east, where the stars met the black of the land. Positioning the stick with one foot at the exact point of the contact, he wedged it under the sky with his beak. A vein of gold shot through the crack, spilling deep into the rocks. A narrow golden horizon broke into the night. Shadows and form began to emerge below. Campfires glowed as faint dots in the valleys and plains.

The magpie returned for another stick and repeated its task. More light slipped through with every new piece of wood stacked precariously on a preceding one. Jim soon saw flecks of golden light reflect off dark water in the cold blue–grey landscape.

After more work from the bird, the scene brightened into a wonderful, rich, colourful panorama stretching out below him. Meandering rivers flowed from mountains through lush forests and deserts, before disappearing into the sea. The skies were full of birds. The unique wildlife of the great land was in abundance.

People walked among it and left their mark. Rock faces were adorned with art. Great canvases stretched out like a patchwork of fields, some blank, yet to have their stories told. Those that were complete depicted scenes painted in earthy-coloured dots and visceral images of life. All their layered histories and instruction for future generations were chronicled in paint – none of which could Jim understand.

The magpie stood next to him again, the last stick at its feet. The bird joined Jim in looking down at the social groups gathered around their canvases, painting.

'Lost in their work,' the magpie whispered, almost to itself.

'Lost in their own land. Our world, unfortunately, Magpie.'

'But they have found themselves again in their art.' The bird tipped its head sideways and eyeballed Jim with one perceptive eye.

The young man nodded in agreement.

'One more stick, Irishman, and it's a new day. Listen, don't be throwing shapes, that's not you. You're no hard man. Be true to yourself. Keep smiling. And promise me, Jim. Keep painting those beautiful pictures of yours.'

'I'll do that, Magpie. I promise.'

'Oi! And thanks for the spiders and moths back at the treehouse!' With that, it flew away.

Jim lay back on the warm, soft grass that now covered the rock.

He looked high into the azure sky and watched the bird fly towards the risen sun. Relieved of its burden, with the last stick in place, the magpie sang its familiar song, the same song that woke Jim every morning at Yilgarn. The light now hurt Jim's eyes. Fighting the urge to shut them, he went to block the sunlight with an outstretched hand.

A shadow fell over him. A beautiful, brown, smiling face looked down.

'Ah, look who's back! You gave us a bit of a scare, you did.'

Seeing him try to answer, the nurse removed the resuscitation mask from Jim's face.

'I was a little troubled myself,' he said, his voice weak and his throat dry.

* * *

A HIGH CYCLONE-WIRE fence enclosed the seven-building compound of the nursing post at Warburton. Three strands of barbed wire, slung along the top, hinted that life in the small community of about three hundred and fifty, was not without its troubles. A covered walkway joined the small four-bed ward to the main wing and the verandah outside the front entrance.

Not happy being incarcerated behind the imposing fence when she stepped outside the ward, Kelly followed the walkway to the main building. Taking a plastic chair with her from one of the dark offices, she made her way out to the verandah. Exhausted and cold, she sat down.

After a long night at Jim's bedside, Kelly craved fresh air and the sun's early rays to warm her. She ran her hands over her face. The dry salt from her tears rubbed off on her fingers. The skin around her eyes felt tight. Her hands came together under her chin. Resting her nose on the tips of her fingers, her chin on her thumbs, she inhaled the crisp desert air, held it, and released. All she could do now was wait.

Children began to gather for school across on the opposite side of the unsealed main street. Two barefoot girls of about ten years of age, came over and giggled when Kelly waved to them. She watched them play and draw pictures in the sand with wires they kept hooked around their necks when not in use. Nearby a group of youths started an impromptu three-on-three basketball game before class. The match seemed evenly poised, when a teacher summoned the protesting players to lessons. The game would have to be finished later.

After all she had heard of substance abuse out here, to see kids being kids, healthy and having fun, lifted her spirits. Coming from Melbourne, she knew the benefits and pride sport brought to a community. One of the few positive stories she heard about this place was the passion they had for their footie and the VFL ... AFL, she corrected herself. It would all change next month. The Victorian Football League would become the Australian Football League. That will take getting used to.

The Hilux, with Jim's Ozdrill logos holding up well on the side, trundled down the main street and parked in front of the nursing post. Laurie Holt got out, jogged around the front and collected two covered Styrofoam trays from the passenger seat. Trays in hand, he bounced up the steps of the verandah. He stopped when he saw Kelly.

'How is he?'

'Still out, but supposedly getting better. His vitals are stable.'

'That's good. Here, Malcolm sent these over from the roadhouse.' Laurie handed her a tray. 'You have to eat.'

Kelly took the tray and placed it on her lap. The heat was nice against her skin. 'Tell me. How is it that in 1990, a place like this can still exist in Australia? I mean, it could be a South African township. Nelson Mandela has just walked out of prison into this.'

'You know, it's improved a lot since I used to do the Laverton patrols out this way. There were far more nomads and wiltjas in my day.' Laurie stood and took in the scene before them.

'Wiltjas?'

'Temporary shelters made from branches. Still used when family members visit, or if there is tribal business to be conducted in the bush. The nomads are those aluminium shacks.' He pointed to some examples in the distance. 'Most of them have been replaced by brick homes. Would you believe there's a brick factory here now?' Laurie lowered himself onto the verandah and hung his legs over the edge. 'It's just a pity they build all the houses the same and they never look properly finished. But then again, most living around here is done outdoors.'

Kelly removed the lid from her tray and uncovered a tasty-looking fry-up.

'I forgot how hungry I was. This looks great. Thanks.' She rescued a plastic knife and fork from a puddle of beans and began to eat.

'See the swimming pool over there?' Laurie said, pointing with a nod to a large sail-like canvas shade that rose above a colourful painted wall in the near distance. 'That pool is brand spanking new. Cost about three hundred thousand dollars. Built and paid for entirely by the community. Things are happening here. There's no shortage of community spirit.'

'How do you feel? Can you move your arms for me? How's your breathing?'

Jim obliged the nurse and gave her a wave. The nurse smiled.

'And your breathing?'

He took deep, deliberate breaths, all with no discomfort. He wondered if she had seen enough. 'OK?'

'Fantastic. Try wiggling your toes.'

'Easy.' Everything seemed to work fine, except he felt tired and weak. 'Can I have a drink of water, please?'

Jim watched the nurse fill a plastic beaker from a jug on the bedside locker.

'You know, I used to fancy you something rotten, when you were on the telly.'

'I beg your pardon!' The nurse wasn't sure she heard him correctly. Maybe it was his accent.

'My big brother fancied you, too!'

'I'm flattered,' the nurse said and put two pillows behind Jim's back to prop her patient up in the bed. 'But I think you might be confusing me with someone else.' She held the beaker to his lips.

'Thanks,' he said, after a few welcome sips. 'Ah, you were great. What's it like meeting the Queen?'

'Can't say I know.'

'Apologies. Must have been the Duchess of Kent who presented you with your trophy then. What's Ginny Wade like? She always struck me as austere. Do you still play?'

'No, and I've never won Wimbledon.'

'Ah, dear. I was sure of it. Didn't train hard enough then?'

'I'm not a tennis player, but I do paint,' the nurse said, trying to conceal her amusement.

'Hey! So do I. Fancy that!'

'I know Jim. Kelly showed me your paintings. They're really beautiful.'

'Thank you. That's nice of you to say. Have you any of yours with you?'

'No, I don't normally bring them to work ... but actually, that painting there on the wall is one of mine.' She pointed to an unframed canvas over his bed.

Jim struggled to turn his head. The nurse unhooked her painting from the wall and held it out in front of him. The painting showed a magpie standing before a magnificent bold and radiant sun. A mesh of black silhouetted sticks propped up the last of the night sky. Executed in a striking mixture of western and aboriginal styles, Jim thought it marvellous.

She noticed a single tear slide down his cheek as he stared silently at the image. 'You don't like it?' she asked.

'It's wonderful. What does it mean? Did you give it a name?'

'Coolbardie. My people are from the southwest. Coolbardie is the Noongar word for "magpie". Every day, the magpie brings us the sunrise.'

'You know, if I were a rich man, I'd offer to buy that from you.'

'How about a swap, for one of yours?'

'Deal!'

They shook on it. The nurse tidied away some of the evidence of a difficult night and Jim took in his surroundings. A tube ran from his arm to a near-empty bag of clear fluid hanging from an IV stand. He was the only patient in a small dreary, rundown ward of four beds. A film of red dust seemed to coat almost everything in the room.

'Painting is part of the reason I came out here to work,' she said, taking his wrist in her hand and measuring his pulse. 'All good ... There's an art movement happening here now, you know, something very special. It could change a lot of things for the Ngaanyatjarra people and how they see themselves and how the world sees Australia – show them we existed before the First Fleet.'

She picked her painting off the bed and placed it against the wall next to Jim's bag.

'Sorry, Nurse. I ought to ask ... am I in Warburton?'

'You are, indeed. The Flying Doctor is coming in to transfer you to Kalgoorlie Hospital this morning,' she replied, returning to the bedside and folding her arms as she spoke. 'You know, you're a very lucky man.'

'I do. I don't know what she sees in me. I nearly blew it.'

'I know, Kelly told me, but what I actually meant was, we tried to fly you out last night. But they couldn't get a plane up here. Your vital signs weren't good when you came in and, to be honest, you should have been intubated. We're not set up here for emergencies like yours.

We don't even officially keep antivenom, because of the potential for an adverse reaction.'

'Glad I didn't know that!'

'Yeah, there just happened to be a vial of polyvalent antivenom in store. Been here since before my time and almost out of date.'

'As soon as the heur got me, I knew I was in big trouble.'

'You're actually lucky it was a death adder. Their venom's a neurotoxin.

'Does that attack the nervous system?'

'Yes. It shuts it down. If not treated, it can be fatal. But antivenom works well against a death adder bite – assuming there is no negative reaction to the serum. That's always a risk.' She adjusted his blankets, more out of habit than necessity. 'Had it been a different snake with the kind of venom that attacks the blood and destroys tissue, your recovery would be much more problematic and long term.'

'Phew! I suppose I am lucky then. And I feel grand. But, Nurse, I can't go to Kalgoorlie. And sure, there's no need for me to go now anyway, is there?'

It suddenly dawned on Jim that Kelly was not in the room. He looked around in alarm. 'Where's Kelly?'

'She's outside. She's safe and she's fine. I ordered her out to get some fresh air. You know that girl sat there all night with tears in her eyes, talking to you, holding your hand, while we waited to see if the antivenom would work. For the life of me, I can't believe she made that journey back here in the dark, with you dying beside her and didn't crash.'

'She's been great. I owe her everything, and you too it seems. Thanks … Thanks very much.'

'No worries. I'll go and get her for you now.'

'Listen, I can't call you "Nurse" or "Sister", especially now we are to undertake a business transaction. You'd better tell me your proper name.'

'Evonne.'

'I knew it!'

EVONNE WAS STILL laughing when she found Laurie and Kelly sitting together on the verandah. On hearing the nurse approach, Kelly jumped to her feet.

'He's awake, Kelly.'

Kelly waited before reacting to the news, her eyes asking the question she could not bring herself to voice.

'He's fine. He thinks I'm Evonne Goolagong, but he's coming round. He's asking for you.'

Kelly ran at Evonne. She wrapped the diminutive nurse in a bear hug and kissed her on the cheek.

'Thanks, Evonne. Thanks for being here.'

Kelly released the nurse and ran inside, through the front building, under the covered walkway and into the ward.

'Here, Sister. Malcolm sent you over a brekkie.' Laurie handed Evonne her own Styrofoam tray. After thanking him, she sat down, opened the lid, picked out a snag and took a bite. 'God, I'm shattered. What a night! What did you do with that angry bloke, who came in earlier with the broken nose? I thought you might have to lock him up.'

'He's over at the roadhouse nagging Malcom and Merv. They're not letting him near the phone. He claims we're cheating him out of his reward money. The Scotsman is losing his patience. I reckon I'll have to intervene again. Might just ask the Laverton blokes, when they arrive, to take him back with them and put him on a truck to Kal.'

He paused a few moments, as Evonne continued with her breakfast. 'What are we going to do now about Jim? Does he still have to go to Kal?'

'Jim needs to be checked by a doctor and properly monitored for a while,' Evonne replied. 'Maybe the doc can look him over when they land and might deem him well enough to stay. Who knows? Too early to make that call.'

'I won't ask you to. But I would like to keep the two of them away from Kal, until I find out what's happening with their photos.'

'He seems remarkably well, considering. You never know. Christ, he was lucky. Wow! This is delicious. I normally avoid Malcom's food, but this is just the thing right now.'

'What! Malcom's takeaways were legendary back in his Laverton days. He does a mean haggis on Burns Night too. Mind you, God only knows what goes into it out here. Still, worth a try if you ever get the chance.'

'He's very kind to think of me, Constable, but I'm a health professional!'

'You were great here last night, Evonne. I appreciate the conditions you have to operate under and still you pulled off a near miracle. Bloody good going, if I may say so.'

'Thanks ... Come on inside and say hello. You know you're scaring off all our clients for the morning clinic. We wouldn't want you making it too easy for the day shift.'

'Listen, finish your brekkie first. We'll give the youngsters a few more minutes alone.'

CHAPTER 23

A GREAT AUSSIE ADVENTURE

B LURRED SHADOWS CURLED down across his field of view, annoying him. Passing a damp finger along his eyebrows, Max Collins pressed the unruly hairs back into place. Were they ever this dishevelled before he wondered? The face staring back from Herbert Hoover's magnificent carved mirror looked older than it did last week. He still had presence though. He still believed he looked good, but there was no denying his age. Times may be tough, the situation may be fraught, but standards need not slip. He would see what could be done about the eyebrows when next in Perth.

Why their clandestine meeting needed to be quite so early in the morning escaped him. Max readied himself for the irritating encounter ahead. 'Remember, you're the man Bondy brought into his inner sanctum for a private viewing of Van Gogh's *Irises*,' he told his reflection. 'You stood next to him, when all Australia stood behind him at the America's Cup.'

Max had an appointment with his old mate, Detective Superintendent Baz Harper, who apparently was back in town. If Harper could not show significant progress in the case, he would remind the natty moustache just what was at stake. The lack of a satisfactory resolution one week on was not acceptable. Max assured himself that if he had been orchestrating affairs, this shit would already be done and buried.

As was his way, Max ran late, but made no effort to hurry. Keeping people waiting was a ploy he utilised in his professional life that seeped into his every day. His elegant shoes sank into the fine foyer carpet of the Palace Hotel as he ambled across to the main door and stepped out into a cool, still morning. Taking his cigarettes from his inside jacket pocket, he put one in his mouth and crossed the road at the wide junction formed by the intersection of Hannan and Maritana Streets. Cupping the match to protect the flame, he lowered his head to light his smoke and noticed a scuffmark on one of his shoes. Max stopped walking, lifted his foot and rubbed the scuff out on the back of his trouser leg.

The unyielding, cold, rolled-steel roo bar hit him side on. He died instantly.

A white Toyota Land Cruiser had broken the red light on Hannan Street and accelerated into the retired policeman. Sometime later at Kanowna, a ghost town twenty kilometres northeast of Kalgoorlie, a Land Cruiser burned on the once busy, but now empty, bush track of the main street. The number plates were removed and all other identification marks filed off. A single dirt bike left the scene in the direction of the Goldfields Highway.

* * *

NOT CARING WHAT anyone might think, Kelly climbed onto Jim's bed. She kissed him and, taking his arm, brought it over her shoulder to wrap herself in him. They spoke a lot of last night and what now. She told Jim to stop apologising and just hold her. Then she fell asleep.

The young couple were intertwined when Evonne returned to the ward with Laurie in tow. Jim's immediate reaction was to untangle himself from the sleeping girl, but he stopped and squeezed her closer. A week ago, he would have been embarrassed by such a public display of affection and, before anyone came in, might have engineered a discreet decoupling. But it would be impolite not to greet his visitor properly. Jim lifted Kelly's arm off him and eased over to the edge of the bed. Sitting upright, he acknowledged the police officer. Kelly continued to sleep peacefully.

'I believe, Officer, you're here to help us.' Jim extended a hand to Laurie. 'Thanks.'

'No problem young man.' They shook hands. 'Helen Mitchell asked myself and Merv to go find the two of you. Make sure you came to no harm. If Malcolm only bothered to answer the phone yesterday morning, we might have saved you from the snake. Don't tell Helen that of course or I'll be in trouble.'

Jim smiled. The police officer appeared genuine, like Kelly said.

'To be fair, apart from almost killing you, that snake has saved us an early flight to Docker River. But we're not home and dry yet.'

'We've met before, haven't we?' Jim thought he looked familiar. 'And I don't mean at the rig.'

'We have, at Menzies. Wasn't I going to pull you for driving that wreck of a Ford?'

Laurie grinned.

'Ha! You really should have.'

'Nah, once you mentioned Old Bill, I knew it'd be OK, and I didn't want to disturb your sketching. How'd it finish?'

'Ah, not bad, yeah.' Jim decided he would give the officer the picture later. 'I did a good few around Menzies in the end. It's an interesting spot. But take a look at that little beauty there,' he said pointing to Evonne's painting leaning against the wall. 'Evonne here did that. And it's now mine! If it wasn't for the snake, I wouldn't own that beautiful piece of fine art!'

'You can't take that.' Kelly had woken and got the end of the conversation. 'Sorry, Evonne. He must still be a bit muddled.'

'It's OK, Kelly. We've done a deal. I'm getting one of Jim's as a trade.'

'They want to fly me back to Kalgoorlie, Officer.'

'We'll see. You can't risk your health. We have to do what the doc recommends. But whatever that is, you have my word. I'll see no harm comes to either of you.'

'Any word on our photos, yet?' Jim asked, while he put his arm around Kelly.

'I'm afraid not. But having spoken with your mate, Andy, I know he'll do the right thing. And as soon as he does, Max Collins will be someone else's problem. You'll be free to go ... However, there are two old diggers back in the Goldfields, who are pretty annoyed with you for not showing them that nugget. They'll be having words!'

Jim laughed. 'Someday, I'll make it up to them. And you're right. Andy will come through. It's more my photography skills I'm worried about.'

* * *

DETECTIVE SERGEANT STAN Sidoli placed the brown paper bag on his desk. The folded copy of *The Kalgoorlie Miner* inside tipped over, pulling the side of the bag down. A Glad-wrapped ham and egg salad roll with the lot rolled out. On the short walk from the deli, mayonnaise had bled out under the cellophane and now coated the outside of the bread, rendering the roll's appearance rather unappetising. Sidoli debated going out for lunch instead. The few glasses of wine with dinner last night left him with a delicate stomach. He ferreted in the bag for the Brownes Chocolate Milk in the hope it might settle things down. Squeezing the front of the carton until the spout popped, Sodili necked the cold, sweet-flavoured milk and immediately it went about its work. He sat down and took the weight off his legs.

Detective Nugus came hurrying in. 'Hey boss, you'll want to hear this! I'm just off a call from Leonora. A truckie up there happened upon an overturned Tojo east of Warburton yesterday. He mentioned it in the pub last night and talked about a hot-chick Ozdrill offsider, who also came across the incident.'

'A hot-chick driller? Don't see many of those, do you? Wouldn't have thought they even existed.'

'Yeah, but wait. Seems her colleague was Irish. They were in a Hilux. His mates in the bar copped who she might be and told him to get in touch with us.'

'Why didn't someone inform me of this last night?'

'Ah, you know, the usual. Too much grog. He fell asleep and only came forward this morning. Leonora put him straight through to me.'

'Christ, it has to be them. Fuck! They could almost be in Darwin by now!'

'No, here's the thing. A twenty-three-year-old, non-local Caucasian male, was treated for a snake bite at Warburton nursing post last night! Stan, Jim Macken is twenty-three!'

Sidoli leaned back in his chair and put his hands behind his head. 'Shhitt!'

'Yep, and it gets better. They intend transferring him here this morning.'

'Do we know if he's Irish. Is the girl with him?'

'We're onto it, but nobody's answering.'

'Right, if it hasn't left, get me on the Doc's flight up. If it's airborne, divert it … until we know what we're dealing with. It may be a trick. Contact the Tactical Unit in Perth. Bring them back in. They can collect me at the airport if need be.'

'The weekly Laverton patrol are on their way over to Warburton at the moment. We're trying to make contact with them discreetly.'

'Jesus! Don't worry about being discreet. But tell them to keep their distance, while making damn sure Macken doesn't walk.'

'Not sure he can.'

'Ever the optimist, Nugus, but we can't take that chance. Remember, as far as we know, they're armed and dangerous and might be planning to hijack the fucking Flying Doctor aeroplane!'

Sidoli didn't believe it for a second. If anything, Laurie Holt and the doctors had arranged some sort of mercy flight out of WA under the pretence of a snake bite. Nah, unlikely, he thought. 'We have them! Any sightings of the Cessna yet?'

'Not a thing.'

'That bastard Holt can wait.' Or with any luck, his plane crashed, Stan hoped. Wouldn't be the first time a Holt went missing, hopefully never to be found. Sidoli kept the last two sentiments to himself. 'By the way, what happened on Hannan Street? An ambulance flew past on my way in.'

'Road traffic accident, I hear. Probably hoons racing on the quiet street.'

'Have someone bring me a coffee to celebrate the good news. Better go now and make those calls. Start with the doctors. And Nugus, don't forget the coffee.'

Sidoli sat forward, pleased matters appeared to be coming to a head. With one long gulp, he finished his chocolate milk, while at the same time wondering if his stomach could tolerate a flight. Ideally, he needed to get up to Warburton, create a bit of a situation, call in the tactical unit, and move on. He unfolded *The Miner* to skim through the headlines. Nothing hooked him in – more bloody politics. He turned his attention to the large photo on the cover.

Caked in mud, stubbies raised in salute, two old diggers were pictured in front of the skimpy bar of the Exchange Hotel. Looking at the state of them, they appeared to be celebrating that they made it to town in time for a beer – having dug their way through the mud left over from Saturday's rain. That one cover photo reminded Sidoli why he avoided the Goldfields. He detested the dirt, the noisy skimpy bars and the middle-of-the-road media, who were always slow to acknowledge the town's dark underbelly. He also added dodgy wine to his list.

Along with a stubby, one of the men shouldered a decent rifle. Wait a minute! The caption under the photo read, 'Prospectors claim to have unearthed Aurora murder weapon.' Then he remembered. Shit! They're the old boys who were drinking with Macken!

While Sidoli tried to figure out why the fuck he was only reading about this in the paper, a coffee arrived on his desk.

'Excuse me, Sir,' the uniformed female officer said, interrupting his growing fury. 'There are two gentlemen at the front desk wanting to speak to someone about a sniper rifle they've found. They claim it might have something to do with Aurora.'

'They didn't carry it in, did they?'

'It's outside in their vehicle, apparently.'

'OK ... I'll see to them in a minute.'

But first, Sidoli needed a hit of caffeine and he needed to calm down. Not mutually compatible, he appreciated. While reaching for his coffee, he flipped the cover page of the newspaper over with his free hand. Jim Macken smiled out at him from the top of the inside page. Farther down, Kelly Porcini appeared alongside her own dedicated paragraph of newsprint.

'Finally!' Sidoli muttered.

At the door, the officer glanced back. Sidoli waved her on.

He studied the two images. The girl looked serious, posing for her driving licence mugshot. She reminded him of his own daughter, now living overseas and having the time of her life. He remembered the drama of his daughter's driving test, and the tension in the house before it. Macken appeared excited, perhaps about to embark on his great Aussie adventure.

Sidoli should have been pleased to see the local press correct their mistake and run an accurate picture of the backpacker. Instead, to his surprise, it saddened the detective sergeant. They're only kids, Stan, he told himself. Innocent kids, who gave it a bloody good try. I'm sorry. It's over now. He stared a while longer at the two young faces before closing the paper and leaving the office.

Approaching the front desk, Sidoli saw the two old boys waiting patiently. At least they've cleaned themselves up, he thought. Right, I'd better get a statement. But before he could reacquaint himself with Ron and Pete, Crime Squad Detective Nugus cut across in front of him.

'Look, Nugus, I've been thinking. We'll call off the tactical unit. No need to inflame the situation. I'll travel alone to Warburton with the Docs. And say nothing to Harper if he rings. Fuck it, we're doing this my way.'

'Stan! You're not going to believe this, but Max Collins was knocked down on Hannan Street and died this morning.'

'What? You're shitting me!'

'Bloody oath, hit and run.'

'Fucking hell!' said Sidoli, visibly shocked. 'Have we got anyone for it?'

'Apparently not, no.'

'Jesus!'

Sidoli sent Nugus to take a statement from the two diggers and recover the rifle. Meanwhile, he made his way outside to the car park for a quiet smoke and to put some order on his thoughts before all shit broke loose.

What were the chances? He debated a number of scenarios with himself. It's an accident! No, no way. Has the situation just escalated or come to a brutal end? Sidoli slumped against a wall, before easing himself onto the bare ground. What about Collins' files? What about Harper? What a bloody mess. He lit a cigarette. Too agitated to smoke, it slowly burned away between his yellow-stained fingers. He watched the thin stream of smoke rise, somersault and dissipate. Whatever happens now, Sidoli knew he was still trapped by his years of lies and corruption.

Inside, behind the front desk, a fax machine received an incoming call. The automatic answer clicked in. Above the static hiss, a series of seemingly arbitrary, high-pitched tones sounded. The noises went unheard above the loud murmur of the news about Collins spreading through the station. Silently, sheets of grainy but perfectly resolved images began to emerge from the fax machine.

CHAPTER 24

ALL THAT GLITTERS IS NOT GOLD

ANDY ROBINSON WALKED out of Mineral House on Plain Street with a backpack strapped tightly over his shoulders. He mounted the rusty, Raleigh Scorpio five-speed he left beside the main entrance and wobbled onto the road. Liberated from a pile of junk in Murray's garage, Andy prayed the bicycle would hold together long enough for him to deliver photocopies of Jim's photos to the various government agencies and media outlets around Perth.

Inside Mineral House, in the office of the cartography section of the Western Australia Geological Survey, Murray fed the fax machine with graphic black and white prints of a murder. The images proved that a former senior West Australian police officer killed Old Bill Mitchell.

ANDY'S FINAL STOP before returning the bike to Murray was in East Perth, not far from Mineral House, where he set off from earlier that morning. Nervous, he pulled the brakes and stopped outside a grim fortress of a house. Intimidating graffiti covered a high corrugated steel fence out front of a small bare, concrete yard. The heavy, double-locked metal gate appeared reinforced. Inside the fence, steel shutters protected the narrow windows of a two-storey building. Even on the brightest day, with all the shutters open, Andy imagined the clubhouse of the infamous Puppet Masters outlaw motorcycle gang to be a dark place.

Observing the morning's comings and goings from a parked car up the road, an undercover police officer watched the odd-looking bicycle courier leave a bundle of papers on the ground in front of the gate. After pressing a buzzer and not waiting for an answer, the courier sped off again on his undersized bike. Pedalling furiously, all legs and knees at right angles, the view from behind reminded the amused officer of an egg whisk.

Freewheeling down Plain Street, his brakes squealing like a tomcat with nocturnal ambitions, Andy spotted an ABC van, complete with a satellite dish on its roof, parked across the road from Mineral House. The media were gathering. Things were kicking off.

* * *

THE GREAT RED monolith rose majestically from the surrounding land, its surface scarred and pitted from millennia of frosty desert nights, rain, baking heat and the more recent unremitting clamber of tourists making their way to the top. Snubbing the darkening blue sky, the last rays of sun concentrated their efforts on illuminating the rock. A continuous stream of sightseers, green fly nets over their heads, champagne flutes in hand, paraded in to take the obligatory photo of themselves in front of an Ayers Rock sunset.

A Laverton police-liveried troopie occupied a parking space in one of the official sunset viewing areas. Two figures sat on the bonnet watching the colours change and the shadows track across Uluru. The man took out a small notebook to do a quick watercolour sketch of the scene in front of them. He considered incorporating dots into his picture, but thought it might be improper. The woman, enjoying the view and looking forward to when the flies called it a day, scooched in closer to her artist companion.

'That red is something else. It's like a piece of Mars just dropped from the heavens.' Kelly paused for a moment. 'Wonder what type of rock it is.'

'Ha! You've read my mind,' Jim said, before it occurred to him. 'You're taking the mickey out of me, Porcini, aren't yah?'

She nudged him with an elbow. Jim's brush jumped on the page.

'Oops! Sorry.'

Jim flicked a drop of water at her. Kelly chuckled, rested her arm on his shoulder and caressed his cheek.

'So Jim, Ellen's getting married.'

'That's what the letter said.'

'How do you feel?'

'If I'm honest ... last week it would have floored me. Not now. I only hope she's doing the right thing. I want her to be happy.'

'Helen didn't mind reading it to you?'

'No, I thought it might distract her for a minute. Then she got upset, because she expected I'd be upset.'

'Your parents sounded nice ... very relieved. They've been through hell, too.'

'Yeah, in many ways these last few days must have been worse for them.'

'I had to laugh when they didn't believe it was over until you put Laurie on.'

Jim painted away, happy to listen to her talk. The worry had gone from her eyes. Now that he had spoken to his family and Helen, Jim relaxed too. He looked forward to relaxing more at the resort, with a hot shower, a soft bed and her. They would begin the journey back to the Goldfields in the morning and after a full Irish Australian breakfast, he hoped.

'Are you ever going to tell them about the snake?'

'Nah, probably not.'

'They'll find out.'

'What makes you so sure?'

'The first time you go out for a few drinks with your mates, there's no way you won't tell them of the time you were bitten by a deadly snake. It'll get back.'

'True, probably will. Which reminds me. I must ring the Bubbles and tell him about the snake bite before we leave … and about you, of course.' He gave her a playful squeeze.

'I envy you your friends, and especially your big family. I never had one.' Her tone changed, she became serious.

Jim put down his brush and took her hand. 'You have a family now, if you want.'

'I never told you, but I sold a drawing once. A unicorn – got fifty bucks for it.

'Yeah! Really? That's more than I ever got for a painting. Actually, I've never sold one.'

'I painted it in school … It even had glitter and a rainbow … I was only nine.' Kelly tried to hold back nascent tears with her fingertips while struggling to get her words out.

Jim put his arm tight around her waist. 'Come on now, it's all behind us.'

'I couldn't wait to show it to Mum. I just had to stop and take it out on our way home. That annoyed her. She was always in a hurry. Of course, just like every time before, she rubbished it. The poor woman was not well. She kept shouting at me, blaming me for her miserable life.'

Kelly's focus never left the Rock while she spoke and the beautiful light reflecting off Australia's exposed heart touched her soul. The words came easier now.

'That was a regular thing with Mum. And, do you know, no one ever stopped and asked were we OK – no one! I learnt to switch off when she was like that. I'd always skip a little ahead, dancing, thinking if I acted happy she'd cheer up.

'I still hear the screams. They said she ran under the tram. I don't know. She may have been drunk and stumbled. She always ... *always* drank.

'Apparently, I was still holding the unicorn picture when they took me to a police station, while they got in touch with the rellies. From there, I got bounced between extended family for a while – then I ended up in care.'

Jim studied her face and felt her pain. He had it so easy, and yet he wasted so much opportunity over the last few years. All that wallowing in self-pity, the giving out about London that he'd bothered her with. It embarrassed him now.

'Ah, Kelly. I'm so sorry.'

'Why? It's not your fault.'

'I'm still sorry.' Jim wiped his eyes on the back of his hands. 'I can't begin to imagine what you've been through.'

'It was dark. There was some light, not much, to be honest. But, to this day, I distinctly remember how kind the police were to me that time. They bought my picture. Ironic, eh?'

'What about your dad?'

'Never knew him. Not sure Mum did either. Do you know what hurt me most about all this? The papers said I was a school dropout. But I worked so hard in school – all the different schools they sent me to. It would have been so easy to give up. It's what I am most proud of. They just never gave me the chance to finish.'

* * *

Outside Kalgoorlie police station, Detective Sergeant Sidoli answered questions from the assembled reporters.

'Yes, I can confirm that, thanks to the sterling work of one of our own, they are both safe and well. You can appreciate that the doctor advised rest and recuperation for Mr Macken, before undertaking the drive back to Kalgoorlie.'

The scrum of people, microphones and cameras in front of Sidoli jockeyed for position. The detective pointed to a woman from the ABC near the front, inviting her to speak.

'Have all charges against Macken and Porcini been dropped?'

'Yes. It's unfortunate that those two innocent young people found themselves, through no fault of their own, caught up in a personal feud between a local publican and an outlaw bikie gang. Again, I must reiterate that, thanks to good old-fashioned police work from one of the Department's finest officers, Senior Constable Laurie Holt, no harm ... snake bite excepted ... no lasting harm has come to two innocent people.'

'What about the drugs allegations?' continued the ABC reporter. 'There was a sizeable quantity of Class A narcotics attributed to Miss Porcini after all.'

'We suspect someone who had access to the Aurora corrupted the crime scene to deliberately mislead the investigation. It's all under consideration at the moment, so I won't comment further, except to say Miss Porcini and Mr Macken are innocent and blameless in the tragic events that have occurred in the Goldfields this past week.'

'Why would someone do that?' shouted a man from the back of the group. 'And are you looking for anybody else – specifically in relation to the Aurora shooting?'

'Look, you've probably seen the harrowing photographs. Indeed I believe all you media people received copies of them!'

'And the publican, as you referred to him earlier, retired Police

Chief Collins,' piped up another voice. 'There is talk his death may not have been an accident.'

Sidoli wiped his forehead with a handkerchief and regretted not choosing a shadier spot to hold the press briefing. 'Look, I will not comment on speculation, except to repeat everything is under investigation.'

* * *

SENIOR CONSTABLE LAURIE Holt switched off the radio. He had heard enough nonsense from his old mate, Stan Sidoli. Laurie promised himself he would not let it lie, but all in good time. He eased himself from the driver's seat and walked around to the back of the troopie.

'Wake me when you want to go!' he called to the young couple up front.

Opening the rear doors, Laurie climbed in and stretched out on one of the padded benches that ran the length of the sides. Within minutes, he was dreaming.

THE FLIES WENT and Uluru enchanted the gathered crowds once more. With three seemingly random dabs of black, a small bird magically appeared in the foreground of Jim's watercolour. He put the finished sketch down, when Kelly climbed back up and handed him a folded sheet of yellowed card.

'My most precious possession.'

Jim opened it to reveal a faded child's drawing of a unicorn and a rainbow. Most of the glitter had long gone, but the rainbow still shone.

'They snuck it back into my school bag. Read the other side.'

He turned it over and read aloud the short handwritten note, 'We think you should keep this. Let the unicorn take care of you and maybe someday you'll find gold at the end of a rainbow.'

'Kelly, I'm kinda lost for words.'

Smiling, she opened her hand and showed him the gold nugget he had slipped her on the drive back to Warburton.

'You're not getting this back. Hey! I love the little magpie,' she said, spotting his finished picture. 'It wasn't there earlier.'

'No. But you know what? It will be there in the morning.'

* * *

IT SOUNDED ROUGH and probably wasn't worth the money he'd just paid for it. But it was the correct model. He knew he could get it running smoothly. Leaving the West Coast Highway, the rusty Land Cruiser turned its back on the ocean and drove up the side entrance of a slightly dilapidated private residence. It parked behind the house, beside a stripped-down bus swaddled in tarpaulins to protect against the ravages of salt.

As he pulled the heavy chain through the security bars on the workshop door, the rasping noise rattled Jeff. The dark, windowless interior assumed the appearance of a prison cell. He pushed past the dismembered parts of his dirt bike and quickly retrieved a set of number plates from their hideaway in the rafters, then left.

Outside, a stiff offshore breeze blew across the yard. Jeff stopped and watched flurries of sand peel off the new Scarborough Beach dunes on the other side of the highway. He knew that, buttressed by the headwind, the waves break later and the surfing would be good today. After swapping the plates over, he would go down. There, he could make sense of his actions. He was happiest on the water, the only place to truly cleanse himself of the desert.

Printed in Great Britain
by Amazon